Rebellious Scots To Crush

Dark Money and Darker Deeds

Ron Culley

Inspired by a true story.

Grosvenor House
Publishing Limited

This book is published by
Grosvenor House Publishing Ltd
Link House
140 The Broadway, Tolworth, Surrey, KT6 7HT.
www.grosvenorhousepublishing.co.uk

This book is inspired by true events. However, certain scenes, characters,
locations, names, businesses, organisations, incidents and events have been
fictionalised for dramatic and narrative purposes because elements of the
Establishment might litigate and attempt to silence and dismiss these
words if they could prove that I stated as fact something which they
felt might be uncomfortably close to the truth.

A CIP record for this book
is available from the British Library

ISBN 978-1-83975-341-1

Previous books by Ron Culley

The Kaibab Resolution. Kennedy & Boyd 2010.

I Belong To Glasgow (foreword by Sir Alex Ferguson) The Grimsay Press, 2011

A Confusion of Mandarins. Grosvenor House. 2011.

Glasgow Belongs To Me. Grosvenor House (electronic media only) 2012

The Patriot Game. Grosvenor House 2013

Shoeshine Man. A one-act play. SCDA. 2014.

One Year. Grosvenor House 2015

Alba: Who Shot Willie McRae? Grosvenor House 2016

The Last Colony Grosvenor House 2017

Odyssey. Grosvenor House. 2018

The Never Ending Story (Editor) Downie Allison Downie 2018

The Bootlace Saga (Editor) Downie Allison Downie 2019

Web address
www.ronculley.com

Rebellious Scots To Crush

Dark Money and Darker Deeds

Third in a trilogy of books dealing with Scottish independence

'Alba: Who Shot Willie McRae?'

'A brilliant book. You won't be able to stop reading.'
Donaidh Foirbeis

'A great read.'
Annette Davidson

'A controversial story brilliantly told.'
John Alder

'Fast moving, gripping and a must, must read.'
Iain Allan

'One of the best books I have read.'
Graham Baker

'The Last Colony'

'A superb piece of work.'
Craig MacInnes

'Just finished 'The Last Colony'. Recommended.'
Catherine Campbell

'A very important read for those interested in the independence of Scotland.'
John Alder

'An exciting tale of a the battle for a small country's freedom.'
Roddy Martin

'Excellent plot line, well written. A good read!'
Deirdre Boyd

'Brilliant! When is your next book published? I'll be sure to order it'
Jordan Lindsay

'Rebellious Scots To Crush.'

'Completely believable and partly based on a true story.'
J. McManus

'This is a scary premise. Brilliantly written.'
Allan Thomson

'This story requires to be told. A great read.'
George Cuthbert

'A real page-turner. Ron Culley is a gifted storyteller.' Duncan Spence

'A marvellous Scots story of political intrigue. Donald John
Morrison follows dark money to its corrupt destination -
undermining a nation.'
Grousebeater

ACKNOWLEDGEMENTS

In 2016, I wrote a book entitled, '*Alba: Who Shot Willie McRae?*'. It has been very well received and remains popular even unto this day. One of the delightful spin-offs of the reaction to the book was meeting up with the real Donald John Morrison, a retired Glesca polis from Benbecula who witnessed first-hand the pursuit by the security services of McRae from Glasgow city centre, hours before he was found on the point of death in a remote Highland glen. He had been shot in the nape of the neck and the Procurator Fiscal decided (rather too quickly for any measured analysis) that it was suicide. Now my friend, Donald has attempted to see the truth of McRae's murder prevail prior to and subsequent to his retirement and has been a stalwart supporter of my writing. In consequence, I have named the lead (male) character after the man himself. Mind you, in my mind's eye *my* fictitious character, *my* Donald John Morrison, is much younger and considerably better looking.

As ever, I'd like to acknowledge the support of my wife Jean, my two dugs, my four sons, Ron, Campbell, Conor and Ciaran, and my four grandchildren, Arran, Eilidh, Olive and Emily even if it was merely them overlooking the amount of time I spent in my home office or in pubs (I enjoy writing in quiet pubs). Many of my friends - both independence-minded and Unionist - helped me think through some of the issues involved by arguing the toss with me in pubs (I enjoy arguing the toss in quiet pubs) and for that I'm grateful.

The forensic eye of Duncan Spence and my dear friend John McManus helped considerably to ensure that plot holes, typos and grammatical mince were all remedied before publication; I can't thank them enough. I'd also like to thank the formidable polemicist, Grousebeater (Gareth Wardell; writer, essayist and filmmaker) who took the time to read and comment on the book. His assessments mean a lot to me and I'm very grateful to the man. Also, I'd like to thank those in the Independence for Scotland movement; SNP members,

All Under One Banner and the YES Movement for their continued encouragement and indeed their suggestion that I might consider writing a book on dark money. Many of these conversations took place in quiet pubs. (I enjoy conversations that take place in quiet pubs). Finally, I'd like to thank all of those who've read one or more of my books and who've taken the time and trouble to write to me thanking me for my efforts and encouraging me to continue writing.

So I have.
Alba gu Bràth.
Ron

" **R**on Culley is that unique thing, a writer of hybrid novels; he weaves fact with plausible fiction so expertly you could swear he had been a fly on the wall. In this marvellous Scots story of political intrigue, his protagonist Donald John Morrison follows dark money to its corrupt destination - undermining a nation. It's time television took note of Culley's factual-fiction political novels; they are the very stuff of film noir."*

Gareth Wardell (Grousebeater) writer, essayist, filmmaker.

Ron Culley, a best-selling Scottish author whose books are read internationally, hails from Glasgow in the west of Scotland where he lives with his wife and family of four sons, four grandchildren and two dogs. His *'Who's Who'* entry lists his hobbies *inter alia* as making music, convivial temulence, contumacious irreverence and laughing out loud.

INTRODUCTION

In what passes for a Scottish summer in 2020 as this book is being written, all polling shows that Scottish electors favour an independent nation, separate from English dominion. If and when this were to come to fruition, England would lose the tax and export base of Scotland, its water, oil, gas and renewable energies, its fish stocks and timber. It may easily lose its seat as one of the five permanent members of the United Nations Security Council. It'd lose its base for nuclear submarines and what's left of its international prestige. It'd also inevitably boost demands for an independent Wales (and possibly Cornwall) and a reunified Ireland.

Given these realities, perhaps it is little wonder that the Establishment down south would seek to work assiduously to hold on to its grouse moors. But might they do this at any price? In recent years their tactic has been to announce loudly through the media outlets that they control that Scotland is 'too wee, too poor and too stupid' to be a confident, self-governing nation. This message is now falling largely upon deaf ears. So what might be their next steps?

Regrettably within the United Kingdom, the battle of ideas, of policy proposals or even the comparison of personalities, the ethical behaviours of politicians, are these days overshadowed by the extent to which money finances the dissemination - even the precise *destination* - of the message, as mainstream and social media target the fears and aspirations of electors.

In order to protect the electorate from a political entity 'buying' an election by massive spending that other parties cannot afford, the Electoral Commission has laid down rules that govern the amount each party and each candidate can invest in their campaign.

Each party must record every item of advertising they make from You-Tube videos to banners, leaflets, press conferences, rallies, even transport to party events. The rules are pretty tight. In the 2017 General Election, some sixty-two receipts for eating at a McDonald's

Restaurant were submitted. At the time of writing, each party is allocated a spending cap of £30,000. In addition, each candidate can spend up to a fixed amount of £8,700 plus nine pence per registered elector in their constituency. In order to finance this, parties may accept donations and can raise funds. At a national level they have to report any donation of more than £7,500 and any constituency office has to report and donation above £1,500. If this cap is exceeded or if there are other infractions of the rules, the Electoral Commission has the capacity to fine the offending candidate or party up to £20,000 per offence. These offences can include the submission of late returns. However - either in testimony to the inherent probity of candidates in the 2017 election or to the essential toothlessness (or neglectful disregard) of the Electoral Commission - the largest fine imposed was against the Conservative Party in the sum of £6,250. In that election, the Conservatives spent £18.6 million.

There is also a raft of eligible permissible sources of funding within these rules. UK registered companies, trades unions, building societies, businesses, individuals registered as electors either within the UK or overseas, unincorporated organisations (a group of people who have decided to work together to accomplish a common agreed purpose - other than to make a profit - more of which later) and many others are permitted to loan or donate money towards a political campaign. However, political parties must record that information, check that it derives from a permissible source and report it to the Electoral Commission.

However, in Northern Ireland, while legislation these days ostensibly controls spend on political parties as it does in the UK, examples abound of monies being spent on influencing political campaigns in the UK. Due to the earlier problems associated with the 'Troubles' which permitted such as 'McGuire The Butchers' to donate to *Sinn Fein* without their shop becoming the target of firebombers, anonymity was permissible. The 'Troubles' are usually deemed to have ended with the Good Friday Agreement of 1998. However, in 2016, some eighteen *years* later, the Democratic Unionist Party, a Conservative, Unionist and pro-Brexit party, bought four pages of advertisements in the Metro newspaper, promoting Brexit and the Leave campaign costing £282,000 without disclosing its source. Self-evidently, it was not 'McGuire The Butchers' that donated that sum to the DUP.

It might be arguable that this was perfectly fine but for the fact that the Metro doesn't publish in Northern Ireland. So why did the DUP buy the wrap-around advert in the first place? It clearly had no benefit to the DUP, as no one who could vote for the DUP could read the adverts. The answer is simple; through the DUP, unknown, anonymous donors could funnel vast sums of money, dark money, to push for a Leave result without fear of being publicly disclosed. However, it is *known* where the £282,000 came from for the Brexit advert as a DUP MP admitted it was funded by a £425,000 donation from a group known as the Constitutional Research Council, headed by former vice-chairman of the Scottish Conservative and Unionist party, Richard Cook who lives in the Eastwood Constituency where he was once a Conservative candidate.

But where the CRC got its money from is *not* public knowledge. The CRC is an unincorporated association but as the Irish Times reported, in August 2020, 'Cook has a history of involvement with a very senior and powerful member of the Saudi royal family, who also happens to have been a former director of the Saudi intelligence agency. In April 2013, Cook jointly founded a company called Five Star Investments (Five Star never filed accounts) with the now-deceased Prince Nawwaf bin Abdul Aziz al Saud who had been Saudi minister for finance, government spokesman and diplomatic fixer before becoming head of intelligence'. His son, Mohammed bin Nawwaf, has been the Saudi ambassador to both the UK and Ireland since 2005. The prince, whose address is given as a royal palace in Jeddah, is listed on the company's initial registration as the holder of seventy-five per cent of the shares. Cook had five per cent. The other twenty per cent of the shares belonged to a man called Peter Haestrup, a Danish national accused by the Indian Government of gun-running. The CRC has also funded the European Research Group a Conservative organisation whose *single* purpose is Britain's withdrawal from the European Union. The CRC has no website, publishes no accounts and does not reveal the names of its donors. The only office-holder to be made public is its chairman, Richard Cook.

So, as is evident, elections aren't just won by political parties. Who gets to appear on television, on news items, Question Time and the like, what the papers use as a headline, how radio biases its news reporting, all influence voters. And the main mouthpiece of the UK, the BBC, routinely interviews seemingly expert 'Think Tanks', apparently neutral 'Commissions' or 'Institutes' without any attempt to put before the viewer the source of funding that pays for their views to be expounded. While many organisations such as these are entirely reputable, others are merely biased political lobbyists who are interviewed as if they were neutral observers while they are in fact paid agents of a political entity. The Institute for Economic Affairs, for example, a right-wing organisation that seeks the privatisation of the NHS, is interviewed as if its representatives were completely disinterested researchers seeking only the best policy option for the UK. Following a report the IEA issued on Brexit, the Charity Commission issued an official warning saying that its report amounted to 'misconduct and mismanagement' and was 'insufficiently balanced and neutral'. The Institute was also criticised by the Commission for offering Ministerial access to potential US donors. Hardly neutral - but treated so by the media. Also, there is evidence that these right-wing lobby groups coordinate their work so that they can present the issue as being generally agreed by different organisations independently of one another. Presently, several of them work from the same offices at 55-57 Tufton Street, Westminster, London.

And their backers are seldom disclosed. Those with wealth can intervene surreptitiously in British politics merely by funding these organisations and having them quoted in newspapers or interviewed on television. At least most people know that the major on-line providers and mainstream newspapers in the UK are owned and funded by right-wing Australians, Americans and Russians, where the news content and emphasis are not directed by the right-wing views of the UK's own Jonathan Harold Esmond Vere Harmsworth, 4th Viscount Rothermere, Richard Desmond or the Barclay Brothers. Just three companies (News UK, Daily Mail Group and Reach) dominate 83% of the national newspaper market.

The wealthy who own the press, set the agenda and whoever owns the media shapes what stories are featured in morning TV and radio broadcasts. All of which is also influenced by corporate advertising revenue, which always censors content. The media relies heavily on corporate investment from large multinationals and would not recklessly offend them by featuring copy which dissatisfies them. Essentially, our free press in the UK equates to those of the proprietor's prejudices that the advertisers don't mind. Also, privately educated white men dominate the media. The Oxbridge and Eton boys are frequently to the fore in all elements of the mainstream media and make comprehensive use of their political contacts list in utilising supposedly neutral sources.

The BBC itself is hardly beyond criticism for its lack of neutrality. Its 2020 Chairman, Lord Tony Hall, said in August 2020, "The BBC's role as a provider (of news) is crucial", adding: "It's right at the heart of this duty to help bring the nation together". By 'the nation', he means the UK. Scottish Independence is a threat to the charter of the BBC and that is evident in its output. As Open Democracy, an independent global media organisation reported, 'A team of academics led by Professor John Robertson of the University of The West of Scotland studied the coverage of the Scottish independence referendum between September 2012 and September 2013, looking at seven hundred and thirty hours of evening TV news output broadcast by BBC1, Reporting Scotland, ITV and Scottish TV (STV), and found them *all* to be biased against Scottish independence.

The research also showed a clear tendency to use anti-independence over pro-independence 'expert' sources, including from organisations presented as independent or impartial despite their linkages to UK government departments with a vested interest in maintaining the union. After Robertson's research was published it was stonewalled and was mostly unreported by the BBC. The BBC then went above Robertson's head to his Principal to try (unsuccessfully) to discredit the research.

However, if dark money is hidden money and not disclosed to anyone, there is absolutely no impediment to its use for *any* purpose - and using *any* means - which achieve the political objectives set by its source. Dark money is a crime that makes other crimes possible. It undermines democracy and destabilises the electoral process. Its effectiveness is all the more potent because most people are completely unaware of its presence in financing and enabling the biased and often false information they are receiving.

In Scotland, the three main opposition political parties, all registered in, financed and controlled from England, the Conservative and Unionist media including the BBC, and the shadowy world of the security services all work collaboratively to subvert the democratic right of the people of Scotland to determine their future.

RON CULLEY

While this book, *'Rebellious Scots To Crush'* attempts to reveal and unpick a dystopian future which will face Scots if the tactics financed by dark money are not challenged and addressed effectively, it is nevertheless an entertainment. It aims to illustrate through a narrative vehicle designed to allow the issues to be more easily accessed, the boundless range of dark deeds that can accompany dark money.

Britannia waives the rules!

Chapter One

The inhabitants of the island of Benbecula in the Western Isles of Scotland prepared themselves for a storm. Formed from *Lewisian Gneiss*, the oldest rocks in Britain, the island is characterised by its flat land mass, pock-marked by small lochans. That evening, its sky was slate-coloured reminding local inhabitants of its nickname, 'The Dark Island'.

Old Archie Dempster had been a road sweeper and general handyman on the island for over twenty years. He sniffed the still air, noticing as he did that the smooth pebbles on the beach near the island's small airport were hardly troubled by the gentle swell. Renowned as someone who was ever ready to help those in need, he'd popped in to Mrs. McCrae's somewhat run-down cottage to ask after her health, fix her tap and to give her a filleted trout he'd caught the evening before.

"Here, Effie, the radio says they're naming the storm. That means it'll blaw about fifty miles an hour. The radio says it," he repeated, underlining the significance he attributed to the weather forecasts of Isles FM, the community radio that served the Outer Hebrides."

Effie McCrae tugged gingerly at the curtain of her front room window and looked out.

"Seems okay at the minute, Archie."

"Aye, well the radio says it's an Irish storm called Ciaran. It'll no' be long till it's here. Five o'clock they're sayin'."

"How's it an Irish storm, Archie?"

"It's no' Irish as such, Effie. They just get to *name* this one. The next one's named by the English. They'll call it Marmaduke or Rupert or somethin' 'cause they're English names. Ciaran's an Irish name."

"Have we no Scottish storms, Archie? God alone knows I've experienced a few of these over the years."

"Aye, we've plenty of these but Scottish storms all belong to the English these days. Anyway, will you be okay? Have you plenty in?"

Effie nodded. "I'll be fine so long as we don't lose the telly wi' the storm. Tonight's a good night on the telly."

Archie signalled his agreement. "Aye, well, your auld tap's no' drippin' any more and you've a wee bit of fish for your supper so I'm walkin' away before I'm blown away."

"You're a saint, Archie. I was just tellin' Constable Campbell that when he stopped for a wee chat this afternoon."

"I'll look in the morn to see if you've still a roof."

"Fingers crossed, Archie."

* * *

As had been predicted, Storm *Ciaran* hit the island just as dusk fell. A high wind found no hindrance; the island, like most in the Hebrides, being bereft of tree cover. The rain lashed down like descending hyphens. More used to these conditions that the average person, locals merely turned up their collective collar and went about their business as usual.

* * *

As rain lashed Benbecula's Dark Island Hotel on the outskirts of the village of Balivanich, inside the warm confines of its bar, Donald John Morrison considered the sizeable glass of Macallan whisky before him and confided in his friend.

"It's to my eternal shame, Hamish that despite growing up in the Western Isles, despite my love of Benbecula, despite every nook and cranny of every bar, cottage and village hall being awash with whisky from these islands, I cannot abide the taste of our most famous product. Whether *Bunnahabhain*, *Laphroaig*, *Lagavulin* or bloody *Bruichladdich*, I can't stand the stuff...but give me a glass of a wee malt whisky from Speyside and I'm as happy as a sand boy. "This here," he continued, examining the glass, "is the work of the Almighty altogether. Pure nectar!"

"It's that London that's makin' you soft, Donald John. You're just getting a taste for the finer things in life so's when you come back up here to God's own country you've forgotten what a good whisky tastes like."

2

Morrison grinned and placed his hand on his friend's shoulder, squeezing it affectionately.

"Aye, there's some truth in what you say, Hamish. But then again, when I'm back home here I can eat fresh scallops, langoustine that comes from crystal clear waters, lamb from an organic farm round the corner or porridge made from unadulterated oats sold to me by big Jimmy MacPherson over in North Uist. Down by in the big smoke I survive on fish and chips that our seagulls here would turn their beaks up at."

"Right enough," confessed his friend, "Thon time I visited you for a weekend, they jellied eels near gave me the dry boak!"

Morrison laughed. "Only got you them for some sport, Hamish. I've never tried them myself. If I did, I suspect my boak wouldn't be dry."

The bar in the Dark Island Hotel was busy, as Saturday nights always were. Friendships were sustained, new familiarities engendered and a general bonhomie washed over those present. Despite the hour being late - well past closing time - no effort was made to invite topers to desist. A ceilidh band played cover songs of local island groups such as *Runrig, Face The West* and *Skipinnish* to the delight of many who sang along boisterously. Hamish Bain had offered a short interlude, his Hebridean honeyed tones quieting the otherwise noisy room as he sang three slow airs before business as usual was restored with gusto. Angus Campbell, the local police constable, rather than hiding in a police vehicle behind a hedge, sat instead with a soft drink near the door gently ensuring that no one incapable of driving home attempted so to do. Often he'd invite them to leave their keys behind the bar and would drive them home himself if Torquil the Taxi had ventured off to the far end of the island, a distance of about seven miles.

Sipping a final glass of orange juice, old Andy Anderson brought his car keys from his pocket and placed them on the table as a signal that he was about to depart. Thirty years without alcohol, the previous twenty having had been spent in something of a drunken haze, he brought his rusty minibus down to the Dark Island most evenings for the music and the *craic* and offered a free lift home to anyone who needed one and who was prepared during the journey to listen to Andy fulminate, albeit gently, about the perils of over-indulgence. Such was the conviviality of life in Balivanich, on Benbecula.

3

Morrison felt a light tapping on his shoulder. "Look who's home! If it isn't Mister Agriculture and Fisheries himself!"

"*Iona*! I wondered if you'd turn up tonight," he smiled. He shouldered himself off the wall against which he'd been leaning and raised his glass. "You're as beautiful as ever."

She smiled bashfully. "And you're still the same handsome hunk that pulled my pigtails all through my school years." She raised her own glass, a full pint of Guinness stout. "How long are you back for, Donald John?"

"Ah'm here too, Iona," grumbled Hamish.

Giggling, Iona Forbes stood on her toes and reaching up, gave him a peck on the cheek

"Aye, but you're here every week, Hamish Bain...every *night* of every week, so I hear tell. You sang beautifully earlier and it's lovely to see you too but the big fellah here, it must be the best part of a year since he's been back home in civilisation."

Mollified, Bain ceded ground to Morrison who dripped his almost empty glass of whisky into his unfinished Guinness before answering Iona.

"Near enough. And I'm away back down soon. I travel to Glasgow on Saturday to catch the overnight train to London. That way I can spend more time with my mother up here in the croft."

Hamish became excited. "We're off to Glasgow on Saturday early. You could join us on our bus." He swallowed a substantial proportion of his lager as another insight came to him. "There'll be cans available from the off! You could be pissed by the time we reach Mallaig!"

"Great idea," echoed Iona. "You'd be very welcome."

Morrison's brow furrowed. "Why are you running a bus to Glasgow?"

"There's a big 'Yes' march on", answered Hamish. He awaited recognition from Morrison. None came. "For Scottish Independence. Organisers expect about two hundred thousand people there. It'll be a great laugh with millions of like-minded people. And there's *bevy*!"

Morrison's forehead continued to reveal his uncertainty. "Doesn't get much coverage in metropolitan London. Anyway, I'm expected to be neutral politically. I can't be seen to be mixed up in a march for Scottish Independence."

"S'pose now you're a sophisticated Anglo you'll have seen the advantages in Conservatism and Unionism," teased Iona. "I remember you being Tartan Army Scottish through and through. And a bit of a lefty," she continued.

Morrison smiled. "I couldn't possibly comment." He sipped at his Macallan. "Maybe I could cadge a lift...but I'd imagine it'd be better if I ducked the march, enjoyed a couple of beers then went straight to Central Station for my train."

"Thought it was an overnight journey?"

"Maybe quite a *few* beers then while I wait for my train." He hesitated. "Are you guys coming straight back up after the march?"

Iona's eyes wrinkled. "Well, it's our bus...it's a mini-bus. We'd need to check with the others but we've arranged to stay at a B&B in Crianlarich on Saturday night to split the journey back home so I suppose we can decide what time we arrive. We could keep you company for a bit so you don't get lonely in the big city."

"C'mon," urged Bain. "Join us. Keep your politics to yourself and I'll get you a postal vote so you can help free your country from within the midst of the enemy encampment."

Morrison shrugged resignedly. "I'll give it some thought."

* * *

As the evening eased into the wee sma' hours and the crowded bar began to witness some departures, Morrison found himself in a lightly drunken haze watching Iona Forbes chatting to the band's accordion player who was now relaxing after an evening's work. *God, she's beautiful,* he thought. Her impossibly pretty face lit up in a dimpled smile as she placed her hand affectionately on the accordionist's arm and held him in giggling conversation. Some stray strands of her sleek, shoulder-length hair fell across her eye and she tucked it behind an ear, still focussed on her conversation with the accordionist. *How the hell does she keep her body in such good shape when she drinks Guinness? How the hell is she still single?* He remembered school dances when even then she'd open a can of beer and drink as much as he did. *She's a genetic freak,* he decided. As his gaze remained fixed on her beauty, she turned her head, made eye contact just a little longer than might have been socially acceptable and her smile broadened. Embarrassed, Morrison grimaced an acknowledgement as Iona made her apologies, stepped away from the band member and made her way towards him.

"You look like you've had an enjoyable evening, Donald John. I'd know that vacant look anywhere."

Emboldened by his intake of whisky, Morrison found himself saying out loud the words he'd been asking himself.

"How the hell do you do it, Iona?"

She raised her eyebrows.

Morrison knew he was drunk but ploughed onwards, slurring his words somewhat.

"You have the figure of an Olympian but you drink Guinness like a rugby player."

She covered her mouth with her hand, stifling a giggle.

"Am I supposed to take that as a compliment?"

"Just sayin'."

"I still run most days. It keeps me trim."

Morrison ran out of road. Muddled, he changed the topic.

"Still working in our new hospital?"

"Yeah, still working in the theatre as a nurse anaesthetist. Still knocking people out for the count."

I bet you do, thought Morrison trying to muster up a sobriety he didn't feel.

"The new hospital looks great. Big difference, eh?"

"Absolutely. *Ospadal Uibhist agus Bharraigh,*" she said lapsing into her native Gaelic tongue. "It's only a community hospital. Twenty-nine beds. But it's a huge improvement in health care on the island and it's allowed me to remain here in Benbecula and do the job I love. When I was training I just assumed I'd end up in Glasgow or Edinburgh...or in London like you."

"You've been fortunate."

"Very. And what about you? Agriculture and Fisheries?"

Even intoxicated, Morrison was practised in his response. "Very boring. Quotas and more quotas. All desk work. If it wasn't for evenings spent in the gym I'd have an arse the size of Hamish's."

"Here! You metropolitan London types are very pass-remarkable. I happen to think that Hamish has rather a fine arse."

"No you don't. You're just being kind." The alcohol overtook him once more. "Actually you're also one of the kin'est people I know."

Iona's face dimpled again. "Donald John! You're too drunk to flirt." She took his arm. "C'mon. I'll ask Constable Angus to drive you back to your mum's. I'm going to help Barman Tam clear up."

Unsteadily Morrison allowed himself to be ushered towards the door where Constable Angus Campbell shook his hand as Iona made her request.

"Not seen you for a while, Donald John."

Morrison didn't hear his words. He spoke over his shoulder as he was escorted unsteadily to the police car.

"See you on the bus, Iona, eh?"

"We'll convert you yet, Donald John!"

Chapter Two

The ten-seat capacity booth in Belfast's Royal Bar resounded to five men singing stridently, if discordantly, their arms around each other's shoulders. Having offered a rendering of the usual first verse of the British National Anthem, they moved as one man on to its earlier-rehearsed fifth verse, arms raised in celebration, their grinning faces contorted in song.

"Lord, grant that Marshal Wade
May by thy mighty aid
Victory bring...
May he sedition hush...and like a torrent rush,
Rebellious Scots to crush,
Goaaaaad saaaave...the...Queen."

Laughing raucously, they raised their glasses in an unspecified toast, brushing the Union Flag and St. George Cross bunting that looped down from the low ceiling. Other groups broke into songs in praise of Rangers Football Club.

"Fuck 'em!" Shouted a heavily built carouser whose fifth pint of lager that session was raised unsteadily in the air. "Fuck 'em!" he repeated... "Fuckin' nationalists," he clarified, lest others in the booth presumed his comment had been directed at his favourite football team.

Emil Rotermundt, seated against the wall of the booth, raised his glass in silent testimony and nodded his endorsement. Beckoning the man nearest with a small gesture of his fingers, he reached into his inside pocket and produced an envelope which he passed to him below the table.

"There's seven thousand of your English pounds in that, Ian. Use it to keep the boys entertained when they're on the ferry to Cairnryan on Saturday. If there's change over, just you keep it but I don't want to see a man jack of them sober when they hit Glasgow. If everything goes well there'll be another envelope to see you all right on the way back."

"Appreciated, Emil."

"And you reckon there'll be about a hundred making the trip?"

"Eighty to a hundred. All playing flutes and whistles. No drummers like you said."

"Aye, it'll be easier that way. Less damage. And I'll provide transport and protection."

"No need, Emil. We've about seven burly guys we take with us who know the score."

Rotermundt shook his head. "We use my men, Ian. I need this march for Scottish Independence to end in a riot and my people have been training for it. All I want you boys to do is provide the soundtrack. There'll be other locals joining us but I need to make sure that the media can report that the Irish troubles are going to take root in Scotland if the Nationalists persist in trying to break up the United Kingdom."

"Your money, your rules, Emil."

"The Nats are telling the media there'll be two hundred thousand people on the march. Maybe more. Can't see it myself but if the weather's good they'll certainly be there in number. They walk from Glasgow University through George Square to Glasgow Green. Our people might only be a few dozen but when your contingent arrive, we've enough flags, flares and fighting men to cause the police problems when they reach the square. The news story has to be about the prospect of future sectarian trouble, not their somewhat optimistic message of independence and hope."

"Sounds like fun."

* * *

Emil Rotermundt had a permanently furrowed brow and narrowed eyes giving the impression of constant hostile and immutable disapproval. Affected by alopecia when aged twenty, he suffered some years of torment before changing trends in hairstyles made completely bald heads in males somewhat trendy. Rotermundt however, did not appear trendy; his dress sense always characterised by well-tailored, expensive suits, crisp white shirts and club ties. He had been a

Conservative Party councillor for nine years, looking after his ward in the wealthy, leafy suburb of Newton Mearns near Glasgow in Scotland where he lived. His uneventful political career had seen him spend much of his time as a lowly member of the Planning Committee and the East Renfrewshire Health and Social Care Partnership Integration Joint Board.

Very few were aware of his role as a member of a little-known organisation which he chaired called 'The Council for the Union', a Unionist funding organisation. Over a period of several years it had helped to fund the anti-independence campaign during the 2014 Scottish Independence Referendum, as well as the in 2016 Campaign that saw the United Kingdom leave the European Union. Registered in the small coastal town of Portrush in Northern Ireland, the organisation published no accounts, had no web site and had never revealed the names of its donors due to Northern Ireland being exempted from the controls on donations to registered political parties which applied in the rest of the United Kingdom. Freed from these obligations, some seven million pounds had successfully been invested in the Council's political ambitions. Donations of several hundred thousand pounds had ensured wrap-around covers of newspapers advocating the Union and supporting Brexit, just as seven thousand pounds had that day bought alcohol, transport and sustenance to one hundred or so Loyalists soon to descend upon Glasgow. A further three million pounds lay available to frustrate any future moves to bring an end to two Acts of Parliament: the Union with Scotland Act 1706 passed by the Parliament of England and the Union with England Act passed in 1707 by the Parliament of Scotland.

Emil Rotermundt was also an enthusiastic member of Trades House in Glasgow, a long-standing member of the Loyal Orange Institution, a regular attendee at football matches featuring Rangers Football Club and was a committed Freemason. His devotion to the United Kingdom was absolute.

* * *

His business completed, Rotermundt left behind the Royal's crowded, noisy atmosphere, stepped outside onto Shankill Road and hailed a black cab.

"Crown Liquor Saloon," he instructed gruffly. "Great Victoria Street," somewhat unnecessarily given the bar's world renown as a gem of Victorian gothic extravagance.

Down Shankill Road and along Great Victoria Street, the ancient black taxi's diesel engine coughing and protesting all the way, it took ten minutes to deposit Rotermundt at the front door. Stepping over the ornate crown embedded in its doorway entrance floor, he recollected the tale told him of how the bar was popular with the local Protestant community due to the prominence of the British crown and, somewhat paradoxically, equally popular with the Roman Catholic community in Belfast, due to the establishment having been built by an influx of Italian craftsmen brought over to work on new Catholic churches and by being able to 'wipe their feet, then walk all over the feckin' English crown' as they entered. Always impressed by the sheer beauty of the Victorian gin palace, Rotermundt took in the rather salubrious decor and the refined atmosphere of the establishment before finding himself at the third of ten oak-panelled, stained-glass snugs complete with match-striking-plates and bells to summon further refreshments. He looked over the top of the booth wherein sat the man he'd come to meet.

Neither man smiled. Rotermundt sat opposite the man he knew only as Grantham. An Irish whiskey had been placed on a beer mat on the table to direct him to his seat.

Grantham lifted his own glass of Bushmills in a half-toasted welcome. "Mister Rotermundt! You look well."

Rotermundt didn't respond to the toast. His neck muscles strained as he spat his dismay.

"These snugs have only five foot walls that permit us to be overheard and overlooked," he remonstrated in a stage whisper.

"Ah, relax why don't you. There's no one in here gives a toss who we are or what we discuss."

"Maybe. But you're an anonymous suit from London. No one knows you here. If you don't mind I'd rather our association was somewhat more discrete." He gestured with his arm. "The fucking Crown Bar?"

"Hiding in plain sight, dear boy. Simply lower your voice and drink your Bushmills. All will be well." He sipped his Irish whiskey, acknowledging it as such to the Scotsman. "When in Rome, eh?"

He grimaced as he tasted it. "Much prefer your Scottish whisky. Thought this purchase might prove less noticeable."

Rotermundt shook his head and lifted his own glass. "You bring me to one of the most high profile pubs in the fucking *world* but think you can disguise your presence here by ordering Irish *whiskey*?"

Grantham sighed. "Tsk tsk, Emil. Such paranoia." He shifted upright in his seat, suddenly all business. "Very well. Let's deal with the matters at hand and we can go our separate ways." He held Rotermundt's gaze. "Have you financed the Glasgow trip on Saturday?"

"I have."

"At a cost of ?"

"Seven thousand...plus a few quid for the return journey."

"I anticipated five...but I acknowledge that it's your decision how to spend it. Once money passes from me to you, my suggestions are merely that... suggestions. I need a measure of deniability, although I would hope you'd take them into consideration to ensure that any further tranche isn't jeopardised."

Rotermundt ignored the implied threat. "I've allowed some scope for a fee for Ian Gibson. I know him. If I hadn't, it'd have been taken anyway and would have reduced the monies available to allow the boys to celebrate appropriately."

Grantham measured the wisdom of the arrangement and nodded his agreement.

"Let's await the proof of the pudding, eh dear boy?" Another sip. Another grimace. "We have another task for you. Somewhat more serious than creating a nuisance in George Square. But what I'm about to tell you is so sensitive that I regret it may cost you your life should it be revealed...not my decision, you understand...but of those who finance and strategise these things." He hesitated, allowing the import of his statement to be understood. "It's important to the good functioning of the United Kingdom but I'm afraid you have to agree '*blind*' as it were."

Rotermundt tapped the edge of a beer mat on the table as he considered the proposition. The task asked of him sounded as if it would be significant, he reasoned. And he'd pledged his life to the continuation of the Union. Part of him was gratified at the level of gravity accorded his next operational duty, part of him disliked Grantham intensely and sought to disagree any offer that came from his toffee-nosed mouth. He bristled.

"Look! My name gives away my antecedents. I'm Dutch...at least my parents were. My lineage goes way back to Prince William of Orange. I am a committed Orangeman and enthusiastic Unionist. I am a naturalised Scotsman but have committed my life to the cause of a United Kingdom, the Queen and the defence of Protestant civil and religious liberties. So I accept. I *will* carry out the task you give me and will not convey this information to anyone. I will do my best...but will wish to offer constructive comment should I believe it to be unachievable."

"My sponsors will require to be the final arbiters but I suppose that is an acceptable agreement." He held his hand out to solemnify the agreement. Rotermundt shook it in dismissive fashion, somewhat repelled by Grantham's theatrics.

"Okay, go! Tell me what you'd have me do."

"We have a contact in Belfast who has access to two pistols previously owned and used by the IRA in the commission of a couple of atrocities in Ballymena. He's prepared to see them 'lost' for a consideration. Your first task is to make over this consideration at reasonable cost, secure those pistols..." He took a final sip of his whiskey, made a face intimating his distaste and ended his sentence. "...and shoot your friend, Alan Colquhoun the Conservative Secretary of State for Scotland, leaving the pistol you use to be found and identified by the forces of law and order."

Rotermundt's eyebrows raised despite his determination to retain his poker face.

"Shoot and *kill*?"

Grantham equivocated. "Not necessarily. Our objective is to paint the Scottish Independence movement as allies of the IRA, thereby permitting our political masters to make hay with notions of proscribing various suspected Scottish organisations and to sow unrest in the undecided Conservative middle classes. The second weapon will be used against a second target, as yet unidentified, once we assess the impact of the first event. You will deliver the second weapon to me prior to the discharge of the first and I will determine how, when and where it might be used. You may or may not be involved."

"And I am able to determine the when and where of all of this first shooting?"

"Up to a point. He'll be a soft target. Internal polling figures show a distinct movement towards support for independence. As the prospect of a second referendum looms, we'd like to take the wind out of their sails somewhat. So perhaps within the next month."

Rotermundt allowed a silence. "As you say, the Secretary of State is a friend of mine...although not close. He's a good man. But I may use an intermediary. I'm an enabler not a gunman. So I'll see him wounded. Maybe a leg shot." He thought further. "Give me the contact details, the money and stay out of my way until I phone you to tell you the job's done."

Grantham lifted a small bag from the seat next to him and placed it upon the table.

"No intermediary. This is to be accomplished at your hand." He patted the satchel. "This should be sufficient cash to see you achieve what has been asked. It's untraceable. There are contact details inside. Burn them once you use them. But before you do, further clearance is required for a job this sensitive, so no activity until I contact you."

Rotermundt pulled the bag towards him and unzipped it revealing cylindrical wads of sterling tied tightly in rubber bands. A sealed envelope lay beneath. He made to leave.

"Just remember. *You're* not my superior. I do this for the cause." He placed his hand on the door of the snug. "I won't bank this cash. I'll use it as it is unless I have to subsidise it from our own resources. Phone me when you have something to tell me."

Chapter Three

Jack Kemp tugged at the lanyard holding his ID card to his belt and proffered it to the reader on the door leading to his boss's office suite in Thames House, the imperial neoclassical building that hosted Britain's security service, MI5. Holding his hand up in familiar recognition to the elderly secretary to the Director General of Britain's domestic security service, he passed her desk unacknowledged, knocked on the door of Sir Humphrey Ashton and entered without invitation.

Ashton, a man whose face even in repose looked stern, was consulting one of three computer screens that fringed his desk and without raising his head, invited Kemp to take a seat. Some moments later he punched a *send* key and swivelled his dark leather chair so it faced his Deputy Director General.

"Morning, Jack. Sounded urgent on the phone!"

"Judge for yourself. I took a call from Sir Thomas Melford, the Chief Executive and Keeper of the National Archives. What Tom told me I suspect deserves a few minutes of your time."

Ashton's secretary appeared silently at the desk and laid two coffees before the men and then retired.

Kemp nodded at the now deserted doorway. "She doesn't like me," he volunteered. "I don't think she's said more than two words to me since I joined the service."

Ashton smiled. "She's taciturn, I'll give you that."

"I've a garden gate that's more communicative, boss...and at least it squeaks when I pass it now and again."

Ashton clicked two sweeteners into his coffee ending the banter.

"S'pose! Anyway, what's so urgent?

"Well, our right-wing friends might seek to take advantage of Melford's discovery." He paused before continuing. "The National Archives' collection comprises more than eleven million documents spanning nearly one thousand years of the history of our nation, and the number grows every year."

"And?"

"The Archive has been providing public access since the eighteen fifties, but every so often an item is misfiled. Of course they attempt to uncover these, usually by some researcher drawing the mistake to their attention and other than mild embarrassment, they seldom raise the eyebrows of Tom Melford. However on this occasion, a misfile served to have him lift the phone to MI5 and speak to me seeking advice."

"More spurious allegations about Edward Heath?"

"Nah, these are more than the usual paedophile allegations. Melford made the point that while they make concerted efforts to ensure that everything is filed in its correct place, there are inevitably a few documents that are misfiled from the roughly two million document moves that they undertake each year."

Ashton's famous irascibility surfaced. "Cut to the chase for God's sake, Jack. What did he unearth?"

"Well, boss, it appears that Adolph Hitler may have had a love-child who walks among us to this very day and is presently somewhere unknown, possibly somewhere in Oxfordshire, possibly John O'Groats. We simply don't know."

Ashton appreciated the significance of Kemp's revelation immediately.

"Well, that'd allow a fox into the hen-house!"

"Indeed, boss. In anticipation I've asked one of our number to join us. Speciality right-wing politics. In an earlier life he taught modern history at Cambridge and is well-versed on the background to this saga. He's outside. Name's Henry Joseph. Shall I ask him in?"

Ashton nodded thoughtfully. "I know him. Good man. He helped me with some work I needed done on the neo-Nazi organisation, National Action which we proscribed back in 2016 around the time they celebrated the death of Jo Cox, and the England First Party which we understand hopefully no longer exists. Bring him in."

Kemp rose and stepped outside where a small, bearded man in his fifties sat, his arms folded. He beckoned him into Ashton's office.

Kemp offered a summary. "Thanks for coming upstairs, Henry. Your insight here would be invaluable. It seems we've stumbled across a misfiled document that suggests that when Unity Mitford returned from Nazi Germany just before the war, she carried Hitler's child."

Joseph nodded. "Indeed, that story did the rounds immediately following her arrival but there was no corroboration." He shuffled in his seat. "May I offer some context?"

Before consenting, Ashton searched his memory.

"I know of the six Mitford sisters. Communists and Fascists within the same upper-class brood?"

Joseph needed no encouragement to speak of his life's work.

"All born to David Freeman-Mitford the second Baron Redesdale and his wife Sydney Bowles, the daughter of Thomas Bowles, a journalist and Conservative MP who founded the magazine *Vanity Fair* back in 1863. Six daughters and one son. All very controversial socialites. The one we're concerned about is Unity who was known for her relationship with Adolph Hitler. She was a prominent supporter of Nazism and anti-Semitism. Indeed, she proudly wrote articles for English newspapers prior to the commencement of World War Two celebrating Hitler and denouncing the Jews. She travelled to Germany before the war and appears almost to have stalked the man until she was introduced to him formally. They became firm friends to the extent that she summered unchaperoned at Hitler's *Berghof* where she continued to discuss a possible German-British alliance with him, going so far as to supply lists of potential supporters and enemies in England who would rally to his cause. She not only attended the Nuremberg Rallies as his guest but actually spoke at some of his other rallies. She was a confirmed anti-Semitic and proclaimed proudly that she was so. That she belonged to Hitler's inner circle of friends is beyond dispute, and when considering the number of favours provided her personally by Hitler; a flat in Berlin, a car, an escort, it seems entirely reasonable to believe that she and he were intimate. Eva Braun certainly thought so and recorded her accusatory sentiments on the matter. After Hitler declared war against England..."

"Britain", corrected Kemp."

"Britain," accepted Joseph. "She attempted suicide in Munich and was then officially allowed safe passage back to England in an apparently invalid condition, and according to official reports, she never recovered."

"You say, 'apparently'. Do you accept the official reports?" asked Kemp.

Joseph's jaw rose in indignation. "I most certainly do not. That she shot herself in the head is certain and that the bullet that lodged in her brain caused her a lifetime of incontinence is a matter of medical record. However, newsreel footage of the era shows her arriving back in England as a composed and sentient young woman. She was taken to 'recuperate'," he gestured two downward fingers in each hand to emphasise the quoted notion that he was conveying the opinions of others before repeating himself. "She was taken to 'recuperate'", he repeated the gesture, "in Hill View Cottage, a private maternity hospital in Oxford."

"Really?" quizzed Ashton. "And why is this not known throughout the land?"

"In a sense it is, Sir Humphrey. But much has been discounted as rumour and tittle-tattle."

"Your own view?"

"Completely feasible...I mean, for completeness, Hitler *inter alia,* had a half-nephew, one William Patrick Hitler. He changed his surname to Stuart-Houston after the war. Why not sooner, remains a mystery. He was born to Adolf Hitler's half-brother, Alois and his Irish wife Brigit Dowling who were in Liverpool at the time. He relocated to Germany but immigrated to the United States, where he served in their navy during World War Two. He eventually received American citizenship...but if new evidence emerges, then..."

Kemp interrupted. "New evidence *has* emerged, Henry." He opened a file and placed it before Ashton. "This shows that a boy child was born to one Unity Valkyrie Freeman-Mitford whose date of birth was 8 August 1914...clearly that of our person of interest. She named him Karl."

Ashton harrumphed. "*Valkyrie?*"

Joseph returned excitedly to his narrative.

"Valkyrie is accurate, Sir Humphrey. Not only that...and this is scarcely believable but I assure you it's true. When her parents were younger they travelled to Canada where they invested in a gold mine. Unity was conceived there. The town in which she was conceived was called 'Swastika'. It still exists."

"Fuck *off,*" spat Ashton, incredulously.

" I know," responded, Joseph. "But it's all a matter of public record. In consequence you can see why Hitler, who was notoriously superstitious, believed her to be some kind of messenger from the heavens."

Ashton fashioned a disbelieving look which prompted Joseph to underline his assertion.

"Sir Humphrey, I can quite understand any cynicism and disbelief regarding this story but I insist that all I have told you currently exists in our files. These facts are simply not contentious. Indeed our records show that far from being a drooling husk of a woman, after she had been discharged from Hill View Cottage and having been delivered of young Karl according to your report, she was consorting with airmen around Oxfordshire and interrogating them, then had a fling with a married RAF test pilot...John Andrews, if memory serves...throwing some considerable doubt on her invalidity. So...if new information has come to light, it may support the theory that Hitler's love child is indeed in possession of an English passport."

"British," corrected Kemp once again.

"Have we DNA evidence?" asked Ashton.

"Hitler's body was burned twice then removed by the Russians who messed everyone around for decades but what is incontrovertible is that access was eventually given to a set of dentures which proved beyond peradventure that they belonged to Hitler. It's well-documented that he had notoriously bad teeth and gum disease and at the end of his life he had only a few of his original teeth left which left him with a complicated set of bridges and dentures. That, according to the forensic team, made identifying his jawbone relatively simple. The teeth matched X-rays taken of Hitler in 1944 and descriptions that were provided to the Soviets by Hitler's dentist. However, we have no DNA from them so we're still somewhat in the dark."

"So it's not proof positive?"

"It's still a very good bet. And in addition, The investigators did not find any remains of meat in the teeth, which is consistent with Hitler's vegetarianism. Bluish stains on some of the false teeth indicate that he may have taken cyanide to precipitate his end." He hesitated. "If I were a betting man, which I'm not, I'd put a large fortune on Hitler being long dead, a small fortune on Unity Mitford having carried his child and quite a few quid on his son and heir being a house painter somewhere in Oxford." He gave further thought. "It was generally reckoned that the last of Hitler's bloodline...the last of his surviving immediate family was his sister Paula who died in 1960 at the age of 64. It was a generally recognised truth that those of Hitler's family still alive after the war settled on a pact whereby they'd have no further children in an attempt to end the bloodline. If there is truth in this document we've uncovered, it changes things historically and politically."

Kemp read from the file. "Well, this file advances our knowledge about what we know about the son of Unity Mitford. He was born with a weight of seven pounds, one ounce. His mother was Unity Mitford, the father column is blank...which troubles me. I'd have imagined that Unity would have wanted to shout the birth from the rooftops."

Joseph intervened. "Perhaps, but in those days, single-parenthood was frowned upon, our colleagues back in the day might just have refused the entry, she might have calculated that her son would have been 'disappeared' by the state...and we don't know that she *didn't* acknowledge it! She was carefully shepherded by her family and ended her days aged only thirty-three, only three years after the war, on Inch Kenneth Island...a remote and otherwise uninhabited island just off the coast of Scotland's island of Mull at Oban. For all we know she may have taken to the battlements of the family home there and proclaimed it loud and long each morning at daybreak."

Kemp studied the document. "Says here that immediately the boy child was born he was sent for adoption."

Ashton's eyebrows rose. "Details?"

"'Fraid not in this file but it does seem that this merits further research. If we have the son of Adolph Hitler in our midst, the right-wing here and throughout the world would raise their stiff right arms in salute."

"Indeed." He pursed his lips in contemplation. "Let's keep this tight. Have you someone on staff you could put on this? Working alone and reporting only to you?"

"I'll find someone and get back to you."

Ashton turned to his expert on Far Right Politics, Henry Joseph.

"Much appreciated, Henry. Keep this stuff to yourself, old chap, eh? I dare say Jack here'll have his colleague knocking your door before very long. Your help has been invaluable."

Chapter Four

The early morning, the red and black liveried Caledonian MacBrayne Clyde & Hebridean ferry deposited the mini-bus and its nine marchers on the dockside at Mallaig bang on time at eight-fifty allowing the three hour drive to Glasgow for the march at 1.00pm to be completed comfortably.

True to his word, Hamish Bain had brought on board a case of Tennent's Lager which he had begun to distribute before the driver had turned the key in the ignition. Most ignored the offer. Some didn't.

Morrison had accepted the lift and had sat next to Iona Forbes both on the journey from Benbecula to Lochboisdale and again when they boarded the ferry. As the minibus began to manoeuvre its way from the Mallaig pier down through the Highlands towards Glasgow two large Saltire flags affixed to the rear of the vehicle were roused from their torpor and blew strongly in its slipstream. Morrison and Iona sat side by side once again.

* * *

Having arrived in Glasgow, the group emerged into milky sunshine and stretched their tired limbs. The mini bus was parked safely and legally in Hillhead's Great George Street and in high spirits they walked the short distance towards Kelvin Way where the march was scheduled to commence.

"Honestly, Donald John," said, Iona. "You don't need to carry a flag, just mingle with the crowd. No one'll see you. You won't get in trouble."

"I know enough about our intelligence services to know that in the army of photographers that will be taking shots of the march, there'll be a few guys who will be capturing the images of as many people as possible and subjecting them all to facial recognition. These boys don't miss a trick and while you all smile for the camera you need to know that on some occasions you'll be smiling for Her Majesty's Security Services. If my fizzog showed up, questions would be asked. I'd rather avoid that." He smiled, hoping he hadn't revealed too much insight. "Nah, I'll spend some time at the Art Galleries then go to the Gallery of Modern Art next to George Square. Their cafe downstairs is excellent. I'll maybe do some reading there and meet you guys after the march for a few beers before I catch my train."

Iona considered his intentions and sighed, defeated. "S'pose you're right about the cameras. We always moan about surveillance on marches. The BBC's never there to film us so we never get publicity but we all know that some of the photographers are a bit suspect. I suppose we take the view that they can't arrest half of Scotland." She brightened. "Tell you what, why don't I join you in visiting the Art Galleries? Never been there. Then we'll catch a taxi and we'll join up with everyone at George Square while you go to GOMA. I'll then join the rest for the final leg of the march." She consulted her watch. "I figure we've a couple of hours to get some culture."

Morrison knew when he'd been outmanoeuvred.

"Okay. You tell the troops. I'll square it with Hamish."

* * *

Morrison and Iona walked along Kelvin Way to the nearby Art Galleries, Glasgow's popular Spanish Baroque museum built using Locharbriggs Red Sandstone, a sedimentary Scottish rock so attractive and popular it was transported and used to form the steps of the Statue of Liberty in New York.

"Life must be very exciting down in London to keep you away from the island."

Morrison demurred. "Don't like the place. It's noisy, dirty, unfriendly and just too big and impersonal. But it allows me to do a job I'm enjoying..."

Iona interrupted. "You can't do Agriculture and Fisheries stuff where there's *actual* agriculture and fisheries, like on the islands?"

"S'pose there's some tasks, but the stuff I do needs a central base, I guess. We'll see. I'd love to find a way of returning home but at the moment my life is down south."

He chewed his lower lip thoughtfully calculating the prospect of rejection.

"You should visit London sometime. I could put you up and show you round."

"Thought the place was noisy, dirty, unfriendly and just too big?"

"Well, it has its attractions. It's maybe just that I never take advantage of them beyond going to an occasional Millwall match in Bermondsey just along the road."

"Watching Millwall's the height of your cultural adventures? I thought you'd be drinking Champagne in the Ritz or dancing with the stars every evening."

Morrison grinned at Iona's teasing. "Not my cup of tea."

"Sounds awful," she frowned ignoring his earlier offer.

"And what about you, Iona? Why aren't you settled down with two kids and a mortgage?"

"Just never happened. Most males my age up and left the island, just as you did. Then I became consumed first by my training and then by my work in the hospital and discovered that I'd no time for much of a social life." She held his gaze awkwardly as they walked. "I'm happy though. I'm an island person. I'm doing something that helps other island people." She laughed. "We'll see what the future holds. Some of the girls and I went to see old Mrs. McSween, the *seer*. She read the tea-leaves, then my palm and told me that I'd end up together with one of my patients and that I would have a long and happy life with children who'd become world beaters." Her grin broadened. "Every time I pull back the curtains on a cubicle to deal with a new patient I wonder if this is the day I meet Mister Right."

Morrison digested this information awkwardly as they climbed the steps and entered the museum. "Christ, would you look at the size of that dinosaur!"

* * *

Over an hour later they exited the Subway station at Buchanan Street and walked down towards George Square where the rest of the group had agreed to wait for Iona. Moving from the escalator onto Buchanan Street, the noise of the marchers was immediately apparent. Horns, whistles, marchers chanting and the now-ubiquitous prams fitted with a battery-driven speaker that blasted out songs at a decibel count that'd make ears bleed, filled the street. The ever-popular Proclaimers' song *Five Hundred Miles* was prominent as they eased their way through the crowd. Just ahead, blocking Iona's passage to her waiting friends, a group of Unionist supporters stood behind a phalanx of policemen. Shouting their opposition to the march, they were somewhat drowned out by a pram operator wearing a kilt who, arms folded and standing expressionless and still, played loudly on a loop the chase theme tune used by Benny Hill in his comedy shows.

"Let's cross," suggested Morrison. Together they walked to the other side of the West George Street where Anchor Lane led to St Vincent Street and on to Morrison's destination, the Gallery of Modern Art. Empty, apart from a few marchers who'd decided to break away and head for a pub, the lane was joined at right angles half way along by Citizen Lane, a cul-de-sac. As they proceeded, the sounds of flutes and whistles became evident. It became obvious that trouble was brewing. Some ten or so police officers had contained a noisy band of Unionists and, as the notes of 'Derry's Walls' rang out commemorating the siege of Derry back in 1689, they struggled to keep the musicians kettled.

Morrison took in the scene whilst moving Iona protectively to the left, positioning himself between her and the Unionists. Slowing, he observed the fervour displayed by the protestors who, noticing the Saltire flag draped around Iona's neck focussed their ire on her.

"No surrender!" bellowed one of the crowd, his face twisted in rage. At once the police barrier was overcome and the crowd surged forward. Morrison was punched in the face as Iona's neckwear was torn from her and trampled on the ground. Both were pushed to the cobbles. Morrison rose quickly and expertly disarmed a man who seemed intent upon using a bottle to injure him. In one smooth manoeuvre he swept the man's feet from him and delivered a chop to his throat which incapacitated him instantly. A second man, pulling at Iona's jacket was felled by Morrison's looping right fist and a third who, bent head-first and charging them, was thrown using his own forward momentum against the wall of the lane. He slumped to the ground. Seeing no further threat, Morrison picked Iona from the ground and holding each of her shoulders, asked earnestly if she was alright. As she answered he let out a roar and fell forward. Iona looked over his falling body to see a man, his face in a rictus grin, raise a now-discharged flare launcher to his lips and theatrically blow the smoke emission from the barrel. Laughing he turned and hurriedly followed his friends out of the lane, the police in hot pursuit.

Iona struggled to hold the weight of Morrison and screamed as she saw flames where the flare had penetrated his bedenimed rear. Instinctively she kicked the still-alight cartridge away and used her Saltire flag to muffle and extinguish the remaining flames on Morrison's backside. Grimacing in pain, Morrison struggled to his knees, noticing as he did so, a bald, be-suited man in a camel coat observing the scene before walking slowly from the lane now emptied of both police and protestors.

"We need to have that wound looked at," shouted Iona over the still loud but now receding din. "Lie flat," she instructed.

"I need to get up," countered Morrison.

"Do as I say, Donald John. I need to look at that wound."

With Morrison still on his knees, she looked at the site of the wound. Morrison's denims were blackened, torn and bloody where the cartridge had penetrated.

"Change of plan," she directed. "Unbuckle your belt!"

Despite the pain, Morrison shook his head.

"I'll do *no* such thing!"

Iona moved round and bent forward so her face was level with Morrison's.

"Remove your fucking belt." She looked directly into his eyes, "Now!" she insisted.

With no assistance forthcoming, she grabbed at his belt, opened it and unzipped his fly. The denim trousers fell unaided to his knees, his boxer shorts then surrendering to Iona's tugs. She lowered him forwards so she could inspect the wound. Quickly she removed her backpack and unzipped it, taking from its innards a box and from the box, two sanitary towels which she unwrapped and placed on Morrison's left buttock, compressing the wound much to Morrison's discomfort.

"It's only a flesh wound, Donald John." She reassured him. "Burn treatment and a couple of stitches. Painful, but unless that flare had chemicals that infects the wound you should be fine in a wee while." She looked over her shoulder at a now empty lane where the flare lay, still producing flame and dense red smoke. "What a bloody idiot!"

* * *

The police constable in the Royal Infirmary noted Morrison's description of events as they awaited the all-clear from the Registrar who'd been attending him.

"So, you didn't see the face of the assailant?"

"No but my friend did. She's sitting outside." He reflected further. "We did see someone who looked very suspicious though?"

"Oh?"

"Yeah, a guy in his late forties, early fifties, I'd guess. Tall, light-brown overcoat. Collar and tie. Completely bald. He'd been standing behind the group in the lane and after they barged their way through the police cordon he just walked out behind them. No suggestion that he was up to anything illegal but I just thought it unusual. He certainly took no compassionate interest in me lying on the cobbles with my arse on fire."

"I'll make a note, but I'm not sure it's anything significant."

"As you say."

The curtain was pulled back its full measure and Dr. Ali Randhawa interrupted the conversation.

"You're good to go Mr. Morrison. Flesh wound but you're patched up. You might find sitting uncomfortable for a while but other than that you'll be fine." He gave him a prescription for some cream. "I researched the projectile you brought with you to check the ingredients." He held the now expended cartridge before him. "This thing burns for over five seconds at a minimum of 10,000 candela. If it had had the velocity of a regular gun and had penetrated your skin more than it did, you'd be in very serious trouble just now. Your backside would have been a real mess. However, the flames were extinguished very quickly so we're really just dealing with a minor injury." He handed the projectile to the police officer. "You might want this - although several people have their prints on it."

Morrison stood stiffly and walked out to the waiting room where Iona stood as he entered, a concerned look on her face.

"What did the doctor say? You okay?"

"Nothing a left buttock amputation won't fix," he smiled, then reassured her. "I'm grand."

Busy scribbling some notes as he followed Morrison out, the policeman interjected.

"Excuse me, Miss. Can I have a chat about the person who shot the flare charger at your boyfriend?"

"He...he's not my...he's...not...never mind."

She looked embarrassed and changed the subject.

"The thug who shot Donald John was about six feet tall, heavily built...no, make that fat...podgy...aye, more podgy! He was wearing a red, white and blue scarf, a denim jacket, a Union Jack T-shirt saying Rangers or something and had long unkempt hair. Unwashed. Black hair."

The policeman wrote down the description saying, "That describes about five hundred people in Glasgow today.

"Still," he took a moment and finished writing before pocketing his notebook. "Thanks."

* * *

That evening, the Steps Bar still thronged with marchers who'd returned to the city centre after listening to the independence speeches in Glasgow Green. Morrison stood stiffly at the bar protecting another pint of Guinness, his hand surrounding the glass and holding it to his chest. Now mildly intoxicated, he'd told his story several times and had sated the demands of his friends for all aspects of the incident. Eventually, having denounced the behaviour of his assailants, and joked about his holed trousers revealing a bandaged backside, it became a source of great ribald amusement that his injury had caused Iona forcibly to remove his pants and treat his left buttock. He was teased remorselessly.

Unusually, the small, Art Deco bar, its dark wood gantry displaying an impressive array of whiskies, resounded to frequent outbreaks of songs. Normally a watering hole for senior drinkers who enjoyed a quiet pint, a newspaper and an always-available seat, this night was given over to a coterie of now-drunken supporters of Scottish Independence. Morrison surveyed the room woozily and leaned forward towards Iona to make himself heard.

"Quite a turn out today." He hiccoughed, "Pleased?"

She stretched upwards to shout in his ear. "Aye! By and large! Ruined by the Unionists looking for trouble. That'll be the news headlines tomorrow. Not the usual happy march for grannies, children, dogs and the rest. Truthfully, also ruined by having to spend the afternoon in hospital waiting while you had your backside dealt with."

Morrison shrugged phlegmatically and sipped at his Guinness.

"And another thing", she continued. Where on earth did you learn to handle yourself like that?" She frowned. "Three guys attack you and you lay them all low, like in a James Bond movie? Bim, bam, boom!"

Morrison smiled. "Remember old Andy McLean?"

Iona's eyes narrowed in thought. "Wee guy over in Gramsdale. White croft with a rusty, dilapidated caravan outside?"

"The very same. Well, when Hamish and me were teenagers...maybe eighteen or so...we used to go over to his place every Tuesday night. An old barn behind his croft. My mum drove us over. He taught a group of about ten of us mixed martial arts. He used to be a PT instructor in the Gordon Highlanders. *Sergeant* Andy McLean. Great guy. He was five foot nothin' but he was unconquerable. I swear he'd have given Mohammed Ali a run for his money. What he taught kinda buried itself in my soul, so what I did this afternoon was completely instinctive. Completely! I didn't have to think about anything. It all just flowed... just like Andy said it would."

"Well, it was very frightening but most impressive." She looked at her watch. "Nearly time for your train south."

Morrison peered at the clock above the bar. "Still ages before my train. Ten minutes to the station. There's time yet."

Discussion ended for a moment as they each took in the atmosphere in the bar. Morrison spoke first, hesitantly.

"You know, I've really enjoyed today. Chatting with you all the way down from the island. I don't think we've spoken like that since we left school."

"Me too. I was worried when that guy shot you with the bloody flare gun. These things are murderous. You could have been really badly injured."

Morrison smiled. "Your quick action saved me going up in flames." The Guinness took control. "Does that make me one of your patients?"

Iona felt her face burn. "Now you're just being impish." She attempted to disguise her embarrassment by lifting her pint glass to her lips. "I'm sure the *seer* also said that whoever I got in tow with, he wouldn't be a boring civil servant with a violent streak who'd rather spend his life in London despite thinking the place is noisy, dirty and unfriendly."

Morrison's grin widened. "Just teasing."

Iona couldn't help herself. "Well just bloody *don't*." She finished the last third of her pint in one visit. "We should be going. We've to get to Crianlarich and you need to stop drinking or you'll miss your train." She turned on her heel and began to gather up the other islanders as a precursor to leaving.

Morrison, you're an eejit, he remonstrated with himself.

Some ten minutes were spent outside listening to a completely intoxicated Hamish promise his undying man-love for his pal and saying farewell to the rest. Iona was hurrying them up.

"Crianlarich isn't just around the corner you know."

Morrison placed his hand on her shoulder. "Hey...it's been fun. I'll see you when I'm back up."

Iona still felt complicated.

"I'll be in *Ospadal Uibhist agus Bharraigh*. Look after your arse!"

Chapter Five

The Boeing 777 banked to starboard as it approached Riyadh.

Liam Scott M.P., newly appointed Secretary of State for International Trade yawned loudly as he fastened his seatbelt. He looked down at the gradually emerging King Khalid International Airport and turned to his Permanent Secretary, Lucas Bennett.

"So, anything more I need to know about this Dr. Mansour Almazroui?" He hesitated. "Have I pronounced it properly?"

"Perfectly, Minister. Although in later conversation, you'll get away with addressing him as 'Doctor'."

"I confess I'm a bit anxious about all this corruption stuff you've been telling me about, given that this is my first foray into a trade deal."

"It's the price of doing business in the Middle East, Minister. The lines between state assets and the personal wealth of senior princes are blurred. Many commentators take the view that corruption is pretty systemic and endemic but you needn't worry. They price in any take that will swell their coffers. Any sum agreed between our governments will be beyond reproach. How they divide up the spoils after we settle is up to them."

"But the deal is agreed? I'm just rubber stamping your earlier negotiations?"

"Indeed minister. My counterpart is Oxford-educated Sheik Zayed bin Khalifa. One hundred and seventy million pounds comes our way for a desalination plant and we buy fertiliser at a cost to us of eighty-seven millions." He snapped his own seatbelt shut before continuing. "I should say, Minister that the Crown Prince is very pleased with this. He's grateful to you for coming out here to seal the deal and may well make his pleasure known by some means. You just need to be careful not to accept a gift that might offend propriety back home."

"Indeed."

"He's no mug, the good doctor. A bachelor's degree in civil engineering from Yale, a master's degree in civil engineering from Albany University in New York and a PhD in engineering management from Harvard. He's as American as apple pie in many ways - at least his accent is. His spoken English is excellent and he's held in high regard by King Salman. He's thought of as something of an operator. The Americans rate him highly. King Salman allows him a lot of scope for diplomatic initiatives."

"Well, he'll be held in high regard by me as well if he greets us with a tray of strong drink for immediate consumption."

"Unlikely, Minister. In Saudi Arabia they are quite down on that sort of thing...although perhaps later in private with the Prince he'll surprise you. All these years in America may well have given him a taste for western refreshments."

"Bloody hope so."

* * *

Ushered into a large room, three walls of which had been distinguished by a skirting of wide, identical armchairs, upon which sat a coterie of men all dressed in Arabian garb, Scott and Bennet were directed to the two vacant seats to the right of a man who stood as they arrived, smiling and offering his right hand in friendship.

"Minister, you can't understand what an honour it is to receive you here in Riyadh." His American accent gave way to American colloquialism. "You must be very tired from your flight. Come sit."

Shaking his hand and attempting to present a confidence he didn't feel, Scott took his seat, grateful that his Permanent Secretary had been seated next to him. The next forty minutes or so passed in a trance as tea was taken and some warm words exchanged prior to the Prince announcing that there was a deal to be signed and that the Minister and his advisor should accompany him to an ante-room where the documents had been prepared for inscription. Doing as they were bid, the British twosome sat at a signing table where documents, forensically examined previously in both London and Riyadh were duly signed.

Almazroui clapped his hands as the Minister neatly blotted his signature and folded the cover of the second document, thereby sealing the agreement between the two nations. The Crown Prince leaned closer to Scott, further emboldened by the event having gone so smoothly.

"Minister! You are aware that alcohol is absolutely not permitted in Saudi Arabia...but I developed a taste for your Scotch Whisky while in America and I have managed to smuggle a bottle of twenty-five year old Glenkinchie Distillers' Edition into my private quarters next door. Why don't we permit our two advisors to deal with the boring implementation details of our trade deal while you and I pour ourselves a large one?"

Scott, now persuaded that he was an international negotiator *par excellence*, agreed instantly, explaining with a wink to Bennet that he should engage with Sheik Zayed bin Khalifa while he and the Crown Prince dealt with 'more sociable matters' next door.

A sumptuous room equally as large as the main room in which he'd first entered accommodated two large armchairs and a small table behind which stood a man in Arab dress holding a bottle of whisky. An upward lift of Almazroui's hand as he entered was all that was necessary for two large whiskies to be poured. The bottle was left on the table as the pourer left the room.

"Minister...or can I call you Liam?"

"Most certainly...Doctor..." he trailed off.

"Then you must call me Manny. Short for Mansour," he explained. "When I was in America I learned many things. One of these was the fact that no one is permitted to use their given name. Robert becomes Bobby, Mansour becomes Manny. You are fortunate. Liam is not a name that invites a diminutive."

"Quite!" Replied Scott, quite giddy with his first foray into international diplomacy as he saw it.

Mansour held the Glenkinchie up to the light and inspected its amber glow.

"D'y'know, Liam, this whisky could see a man in the street here hanged from a lamppost...but seniority has its rewards. It is a simply magnificent whisky, don't you agree?"

At last a subject matter had emerged in which Scott felt more than comfortable. He poured a small dilution of water and sipped greedily at the whisky, savouring it.

"Manny, this just might be the finest whisky I've ever tasted, although once while on holiday in Inverness in Scotland, I was privileged to enjoy an eighteen year old Bowmore Single Malt which I swear was simply magnificent."

"Then when you return...indeed when you return as my *friend*...we will together enjoy your eighteen year old Bowmore Single Malt and we will have a competition to see which we enjoy most."

Further whisky conversation continued for some time until Mansour placed his glass on the table and adopted a more serious demeanour. He sat forward, clasping his hands and adopting a more formal posture.

"Minister, I want you to know how grateful I am to you and to your government for your assistance in sealing this deal. It matters a lot to my country. I very much hope it signals many more such agreements that we negotiate to our mutual benefit in the future."

"As do I, Crown Prince Doctor," replied Scott as the whisky began to affect both his inhibitory neurotransmitters, generating feelings of well-being while dulling his cerebral cortex. "As do I!"

"Might I turn to a political matter that concerns my nation...and I suspect your own?"

"Be m' guesss," slurred Scott.

"Saudi Arabia needs stability in the oil market...as does the United Kingdom."

Scott nodded sagely.

"But as I look at the political situation as it affects the United Kingdom at present, it appears that Scotland is determined to detach itself from perhaps the most successful Union that has ever existed."

Scott nodded knowingly.

"My friend, would it not be in both our interests to nip this nationalist threat in the bud?"

Scott nodded wisely.

Sipping his whisky, he attempted to project a demeanour that he imagined befitted an international politician.

"Couldn' agree more, Manny."

Mansour emptied his glass in one swallow.

"Then I have a proposal that must stay between you and me, Liam."

Ah, thought Scott drunkenly, *here comes the gift of a luxury holiday in the Seychelles.*

"Might ten million pounds sterling assist you?"

Scott almost swooned, still imagining the bribe he'd been warned to resist.

"Ten mill...?"

"If we could find a way to gift your government a sum of money quietly...a significant sum of money that you could use..."

Ah, the government... He recovered his composure and began slowly to organise his thoughts.

"I'm afraid my civil service looks dimly upon contributions of this nature, Manny." He pondered further, conflicted. "Ten million, you say? And this might be done quietly?"

"*Very* quietly. I wouldn't trouble your Permanent Secretary with information about the offer. Indeed, perhaps only your Prime Minister need know of our arrangement."

More whisky was poured as Mansour continued.

"We keep a close eye on political matters within the United Kingdom, Liam, and are not unaware of recent moves to make the types of political donations we've been in the habit of making in the past more transparent. Under your last PM's marvellous leadership, we managed to support the Conservative Party fairly substantially but the drawbridge is being raised. We feel that an early and substantial measure of support might permit us to get round this little awkwardness for a while."

Scott's ability to focus, limited at best, was now severely hindered.

"Much appreciated, Manny. My own Conservative Association routinely accepts small amounts from dining clubs and business forums donating as unincorporated associations as they do not have to provide names of members. It is entirely legal for anonymous groups to donate to political parties without disclosing individuals' names if it's done properly...within the rules as it were."

"Well, as I've stated, I have in mind a sum that rather dwarfs these contributions, Liam. Our problem is that in the UK, parties must report all donations but the names and addresses of donors to Northern Ireland's political parties and campaigns are not made public, ostensibly because of 'special circumstances'. This has allowed much mischief in the past but public opinion and improving security matters in Northern Ireland are about to make this more difficult. This transaction might be the last occasion in which we can help you influence policies dear to your heart."

Scott had difficulty forming his words.

"And what might you seek in return for this...gift?"

"Absolutely nothing but your continued friendship, Liam. We both see advantage in maintaining the status quo. We'd rather not deal with Scotland. As an assertive small nation, they'd instantly become major players once independent. Scotland is the largest producer of oil in the European Union. We imagine that Scotland would become a favoured and powerful state within Europe due to their fishing rights, their oil, gas and green energy production." He hesitated before continuing. "I've also been speaking with our friends in the United States. They're also very nervous about Scotland's geo-political position which permits unparalleled overview of the Soviet sea lanes around Cape Wrath. Politically, Scotland is very much against having nuclear weapons on their territory and if and when they joined NATO, would doubtless join with those members that seek nuclear disarmament. Both the States and ourselves would expect that Scotland might well become very wealthy but they'd be very unlikely to invest in arms manufacture and sales as does the UK at present. Inevitably, what remains of the United Kingdom would become somewhat poorer resulting in less arms manufacturing, a reduction in both quantity and quality that would concern us." He changed tone, entreating Scott's investment in his proposition. "But Liam, basically we're *used* to dealing with the UK. We understand each other and would rather not have to deal with a new European nation that is evidently more left-wing than your own government."

"Well...quite!"

"And while you're still the *United* Kingdom we can still smuggle in some of their rare and luxury contraband whisky, eh?"

Scott was intrigued. "How might this contribution...it might be used for *any* particular political purpose do you say?"

"We see Scottish Independence as a threat as do you. We'd like to help you deal with it. Ten million pounds appropriately applied in public consultation, promotional materials and advertising might edge the attitude of that nation towards the status quo don't you think?"

"Perhaps one of our think-tanks?"

"We were thinking more of a *particular* think-tank." He took Scott's glass from his grasp and poured him a further generous measure before topping up his own glass. "Legislation is now imminent and if we're to assist you in your fight against Scottish independence, we must act now. Our proposal would be that we make a contribution to an organisation of our choice in Northern Ireland which might then fund your ambitions in maintaining the Union."

Scott swallowed more whisky than he'd intended as he struggled to make sense of the proposal.

"The Prime Minister has a Special Advisor...a Spad...who normally deals with campaign strategy. I'm sure he'd find this a most acceptable and generous offer...and there are no strings?"

"None, Liam. Just to assist us both in maintaining the status quo... although there is a person in your government to whom we've channelled funds such as this before now and he might usefully accept a proportion of the funds...say, half. It might be unwise for me to mention his name but I assure you that he is a well-regarded individual in your very own and highly respected security services. He would allow monies to be used to supplement the sums allocated by your government to gather intelligence and act in your interests. You should know nothing of this, lest questions are asked but this Spad you mention could certainly arrange for a proportion of the money to be placed at the disposal of your think-tanks in Northern Ireland."

Scott absently chewed the inside of his cheek as he wrestled to find the confidence to accept the proposal. Mansour proffered his hand and forced an agreement.

"Let's shake on this."

Scott relented. *What could go wrong?* he asked himself. He grasped the hand of his new political friend and shook it warmly.

Chapter Six

Brixton, in London's Lambeth district woke early. It was market day. *Every* day was market day... and stalls were being erected on the street below as Morrison eased back the curtain to greet the morning. Canopies were being pulled and tightened to protect prospective customers and stall holders from the rain that had begun to fall on Electric Avenue. He sighed at the realisation that as ever, he'd have to navigate large white vans, each disgorging copious amounts of fruit, vegetables, curios and *bric a brac* on his way to work and that upon returning in the evening he'd have to negotiate huge piles of discarded cardboard boxes containing the detritus of the day then cope with the noise of the following early morning collection by cleansing operatives who weren't too concerned about their dawn chorus.

"London!" he muttered disparagingly under his breath.

Showering and dressing, he ignored a box of cereal in his small kitchen and determined to make do with a coffee upon his arrival at Millbank. Normally he'd walk the forty-five minutes it took, but the rain encouraged a rethink. Bus, rail, taxi or underground were all available and would get him to his office in about fifteen minutes door to door if everything went smoothly.

He walked into his office at eight-thirty, hung his overcoat on one of a set of communal pegs, entered his small cubicle, sat at his desk and placed his thumbprint over the button that opened his computer.

* * *

The Director General of MI5 buzzed his secretary, the elderly and somewhat prim Miss Leyton-Willis.

"Elizabeth, would you contact the Deputy and also a Mr. Donald John Morrison down in the Joint Terrorist Analysis Centre on the third floor and ask them to meet me here in one hour, at nine thirty?"

Morrison was called from his desk and sat in the Director General's ante-room, the Deputy having gone in some five minutes earlier, presumably to brief his boss prior to the meeting. *Christ knows what's on the agenda here.* He reflected first on his annoyance that he'd not taken the opportunity to fetch a cup of coffee before walking upstairs and second on his recent tasks, but could find nothing that would merit a disciplinary meeting. *In any case,* he told himself, *that would involve HR and my own boss, Commander Edwards. Unlikely I'll be getting a row for something.* His musings came to an end when the door was opened by Jack Kemp and he was ushered in to sit in one of four armchairs, the closest of which was occupied by Sir Humphrey Ashton who was reading a file. No handshake was offered by either man. Without raising his gaze from the file, Ashton asked, "You joined us from Agriculture and Fisheries?" He placed his spectacles at the end of his nose and looked over the rims. "Unusual point of entry to the security services."

Morrison, still irritable, responded with a confidence born of testiness and corrected the Director General.

"Agriculture, Fisheries *and Food...*" He continued. "I suppose so. Haven't met anyone else in the service who has such deep knowledge of the convention for the conservation of salmon in the North Atlantic Ocean."

Ashton shared a glance with Kemp before continuing.

"And you're now an analyst and an intelligence officer in the Joint Terrorist Analysis Centre? Care to explain?"

"Bored at Fisheries. Saw an advert for MI5. Applied. Got accepted."

Kemp developed Morrison's terse response. "Mr. Morrison came to the attention of this floor following a highly competent piece of work on blockages to the resumption of power-sharing in Northern Ireland. Before that he did sterling work on the England National Socialist Party, a proscribed, far-right neo-Nazi organisation. His work led to them being found to be continuing to meet in secret despite their proscription. Their leaders were convicted and sent away for a while."

Ashton again consulted the file. "Quite!" He continued reading. "Commander Edwards thinks very highly of you...as does my Deputy, Mr. Kemp here. Normally, you major on in-depth reports on trends, terrorist networks and capabilities and advise on where the Government should place its threat level?"

"Indeed. I confess I was very pleased with my annual appraisal last year." He told himself to tone down anything that might suggest boastfulness. "I found the task of not only understanding the law, the political impediments to agreement but also the personalities of senior players in Northern Ireland and how they might be persuaded to adjust their positions very satisfying. I was just glad that it appeared to have been found useful and that there are the beginnings of a new co-operation over there. The neo-Nazi thing was actually a pretty straightforward job but I was glad it was resolved quickly and without loss of life or any disruption."

"You worked alone on these tasks?"

"On both of these tasks, yes."

Ashton closed the file. "You're a native of the Outer Hebrides."

"Benbecula."

Ashton smiled for the first time. "I can hear it in your accent. My wife's from Dalmore, on Lewis. We keep a croft there and visit it whenever we can. I've always found islanders to be amongst the finest human beings I've ever encountered."

"I can't disagree with your assessment, Director General. There's not a day goes by when I don't miss the islands. Especially when navigating the Underground here in London."

Ashton ignored the comment. "Well, Mr. Kemp here thinks you might be the very man we can trust to work on your own, reporting directly to him on a matter of some delicacy...some sensitivity. No one must know of your work. At present, only Jack here, myself, the Keeper of the National Archives and Professor Henry Joseph over at Far Right Politics on the fifth floor are aware of what Jack's about to brief you on. Jack's about to share a mystery with you." He turned to Kemp. "I presume there's some other member of staff at the Archives who drew it to Tom's attention?" Kemp pursed his lips in agreement as Ashton continued. "An early visit to ensure it's not being discussed down their pub tonight, eh?"

He engaged Morrison again. "I want you to follow it up and report to me on your findings. Desk work, field work, go where you must...do what you must, but get to the bottom of this. Jack will see that you've a budget commensurate with your task. You won't want for resources and you won't want for support if you seek it." He leaned forward, suddenly more affable, and shook Morrison's hand. "I've been pleased to meet you."

* * *

Along the corridor, Morrison was seated in Kemp's office as the coffee denied him by Ashton and his own forgetfulness was laid before him by a smiling young lady who appeared to be Kemp's Pretorian guard.

Kemp spooned an extravagant amount of sugar into his cup and stirred.

"He's a good sort, the boss. Can be a bit gruff but he has a mind like a steel trap and you can count on his support. He looks after his people." He threw the file that Ashton had been reading on a side table next to his own coffee and sat. "So...the file I'll leave with you is pretty self-explanatory. It tells the story of one of Britain's young female aristocrats who befriended Hitler prior to World War Two, returned to this country just before hostilities commenced and was alleged to be carrying his baby. If this is true we might find that the extreme right have a rallying point we could do without. You can consult with Professor Joseph down at Far Right Politics and with Sir Thomas Melford, the Chief Executive and Keeper of the National Archives. Each knows of the contents of this file. It goes without saying that this information is a state secret of the highest magnitude. Go where you need to on this. Interview anyone you feel might shed light on the case but don't reveal the nature of your mission. I don't micro-manage so just keep me briefed as you deem appropriate."

"I'll keep it tight and get right on it. Can I assume this has all been cleared with Commander Edwards?"

"Not yet had confirmation, but Sir Humphrey will have been on the phone as soon as we left his office. Take it as read."

Chapter Seven

With some minor difficulty, Morrison stepped from his small, hired car in Swinbrook, a village on the River Windrush, about two miles east of Burford in Oxfordshire, and made his way to the St Mary Churchyard. He began to walk between the rows of nondescript gravestones which circled the old church. After a short time, he came across one whose legend reported *'Nancy Mitford, Authoress'*. Instantly he halted and noticed that at the next lair, a similarly sized gravestone stated, *'Say not the struggle naught availeth'* and above it the words, *'Unity Valkyrie Mitford, Born, 8th August 1914, Died 29 May 1948.'*

So this is the woman who may have carried the child of Herr Schicklgruber? thought Morrison, referencing the British World War Two nickname of its adversary whose mother, Maria Anna Schicklgruber was the mother of Alois Hitler, the paternal grandmother of Adolf Hitler. *We'd have defeated someone called Schicklgruber in the first week of the war,* he decided.

The patter of a few heavy raindrops had him lift his gaze to the sky for confirmation, turn up his collar and head back to the car, the last several steps taken at a run to escape what now threatened to be a deluge. Turning the engine on, he wiped his sleeve across his brow and swept back his wet hair before consulting his notes and setting off, calculating that the nineteen miles to the Oxfordshire Registry Office would take him some thirty minutes, dangerously close to closing time.

Pulling into Tidmarch Lane in Oxford, he stopped the car and thumped the steering wheel in frustration as an office worker turned the *'Open'* sign on the front door to *'Closed'* before locking it from the inside. Denied access to the certificates of births, deaths and marriages available within, he reversed slightly and drove forwards from outside the sturdy, blond brick building towards his plan 'B'.

Morrison's earlier desktop research had referenced the arrival at the port of Folkestone, of one Unity Valkyrie Mitford in January 1940 and her subsequent residence in Hill View Cottage in Wigginton, near Oxford. Used now as a private dwelling house, he passed by out of curiosity before parking outside the Horse and Groom Inn, the closest hostelry he could find, in the next-door village of Milcombe. He walked briskly from the car to mitigate the worst of the weather and pushed open the door. Inside, the low-ceilinged pub hosted but two elderly men each drinking alone while an equally elderly and disinterested barman, one elbow on the bar, one supporting his heavily jowled chin, read the Banbury Guardian.

Positioning himself directly in front of the newspaper, Morrison took his wallet from his pocket and attempted recognition.

"Hi."

The barman sleepily raised his puzzled gaze as if attempting to understand what possibly might be being asked of him.

"Sir?"

Morrison nodded towards the gantry. "A Glenmorangie, please. No ice."

Slowly the barman stood erect and took the bottle from behind him, removing its cork as he did so.

"What's the measure here?" asked Morrison conversationally.

"Twenty-five mils, same as everywhere." He studied Morrison with fresh eyes. "You not from 'round here?"

"Further north," responded Morrison.

"Thought that. You Scotch?"

Morrison poured a drop of water into his glass and ignored the demonymic inaccuracy.

"Place called Benbecula. It's an island off the coast of Scotland."

Some seconds elapsed as the barman considered this information before remembering his job.

"That'll be four quid, please." His interest was piqued. "You have different measures in Scotland?"

"Thirty-five, sometimes. But this is grand. I'm driving." He lifted the glass to his lips and sipped.

The barman pondered this intelligence, calculating the conversation he'd have later that evening as more regulars appeared.

"It's a lovely village you have, here. Quite small." He hesitated. "Don't suppose you know of the whereabouts of a Ms. Valerie Hann? I'd like to chat with her for a few minutes."

42

The barman's eyes narrowed and his lips thinned.

"Here we go. You one of them journalists, eh? Come to investigate Hitler's baby?"

Morrison unveiled the cover story he'd developed on the several steps he'd taken on the way into the pub.

"Actually I'm writing a book sponsored by the Automobile Association. It's about public houses in some of England's most beautiful villages and I just thought I'd add some colour to Milcombe. Make the place sound interesting. Maybe encourage more people to visit."

The change in demeanour was instant. The barman's eyes darted round the pub.

"It's normally much busier here," he insisted. Great atmosphere. If you were here tonight about nine, we've a Country and Western act on. Billy the Kid. He's great. You'd see a different side of the pub then."

"Sounds interesting. Maybe I could pop back in after I chat with Ms. Hann?"

"Leave your car. We've a couple of rooms upstairs. I'd do you a good deal and you could enjoy the night."

"Well, that sounds like a very generous offer." He allowed a pause. "Ms. Hann?"

The barman hesitated. "Val's getting on in life. It'd be better if I phoned her first and asked if she felt up to seeing you."

"That'd be much appreciated. Thank you."

The barman retreated to a side area where a white phone was affixed to the wall next to another which offered free communication with a local taxi firm. After a few moments he returned to Morrison. "She's happy to see you. I had to speak for you, mind. She'd probably have said no if I hadn't spoke for you."

"Can she see me now?"

"One, School Lane, Wigginton. Just up the road. She's putting the kettle on for you."

Morrison placed a five pound note on the bar.

"Keep the change."

He finished his whisky and left the bar, raising his arm in silent salute as the barman shouted after him about reserving one of his rooms.

* * *

A few minutes later, Morrison pulled up outside the address he'd been given. A woman stood in the doorway, a shawl around her shoulders. She waved him towards her as the rain continued to fall heavily.

Covering the short distance briskly, he entered the porched area and was bid welcome.

"Come in out of that rain. It's pouring," she said unnecessarily. "Alfred the barman says you're a good sort."

"That was kind of him," responded Morrison. "Allow me to introduce myself. My name is Donald John Morrison and I'm writing a book about the village and understand that you can tell me a wee bit about Unity Mitford and Hill View Cottage."

"I do love your accent," she smiled. "Alfred mentioned you were Scottish." She offered him a seat in front of which was a cup of black tea on a low table. A small jug of milk and a sugar bowl sat nearby. "You're not a journalist?" She sat opposite him in an armchair where she'd obviously been knitting prior to his arrival.

"Ah, no." Anticipating her reservation, he added. "I've no intention to sensationalise, Ms. Hann. I merely thought it wise to speak to someone who knew something of the facts. I know you've spoken to newspapers before and I've read much of what you've had to say but... well, straight from the horse's mouth, eh?"

"Call me Valerie. Or Val. That's what most people call me."

"Sure, Val."

She apologised. "I'm out of biscuits."

"Tea's fine, Val." He smiled his way into his first question. "So your Aunt used to run Hill View Cottage?"

"Yes she did. Betty Norton was her name. My mum's sister. She ran Hill View when it was a maternity hospital...a private maternity hospital. My Aunt Betty ran it for the gentry in Oxfordshire during the war; for them's with money, and that Unity Mitford was one of her patients. She had no doubt about that."

"She was a controversial woman, our Unity."

"Certainly was. They shut the docks when her boat arrived. At Folkestone, there was an armed guard at the harbour and Miss Mitford was brought ashore on a stretcher. All very hush, hush. Course you know why?" she teased.

Morrison shook his head.

"She was only the cousin of Winston Churchill! That's why!" She gathered pace. "Greatest Prime Minister we've ever had, ol' Winston. A great man."

"He certainly was," responded Morrison before trying to return her to Mitford. "Unity must have embarrassed him."

"You bet she did. And so did her sister, Diana. *She* married the British fascist Oswald Mosley. She and Unity both went to Germany in the Thirties to support the Nazis. Unity stayed and ended up back here with Hitler's child in her belly...'cording to my Aunt Betty."

"And the child was born?"

"'Cording to my Aunt Betty. A boy. Sent for adoption straight away."

Morrison pondered this information.

"Has no one from Government asked you about this?"

"No. Only a chap from the New Statesman came down a few years back and I told him what I knew. After he published I was besieged by another journalist. He were downright rude. He wrote some terrible stuff. Just made it all up and made out it was me that said it."

"They can be very intrusive," empathised Morrison. "But no one from Government? No police?"

Ms. Hann shook her head.

"I'd have thought they'd have been interested in the baby."

"Course they would. But no one ever asked."

"And if *I* asked?"

Ms. Hann hesitated. "My Aunt Betty had to live in the tiny village of Wigginton. Small place...as you can see." She gestured at the window. "She depended on discretion for her business and she told no-one except my mother that Unity had had a baby. 'Course it's all out in the open now."

"Except the whereabouts of the baby."

Ms. Hann fell silent. After a moment she rose, levered herself on to her walking frame, and slowly manoeuvred it unsteadily to a book case from which she took what appeared to be an encyclopaedia. She placed the heavy object upon a nearby table and opened it, removing a sheet of paper from within. She removed her spectacles and replaced them with a second pair she used for reading. Scanning the paper, she leaned one hand on the wing of a chair and limped her way back to Morrison.

"You won't find this in the records at the Oxfordshire Registry Office."

She passed it to Morrison who read it for only a few seconds before raising his gaze to meet that of Ms. Hann.

"He was adopted by a Mr. Earnest and a Mrs. Judith Warren?"

Ms. Hann nodded. "I knew them. I was friendly with their daughter Grace. We were the same age. They moved away shortly after getting the baby. Back to Northern Ireland, I'd suspect. That's where they came from. Grace was English, though."

"So the baby would be...let's see...he'd be eighty-one by now if he's still around." He smiled. "Well at least he doesn't appear to have led a Fascist revival during his lifetime. I dare say we'd have heard about it."

"I'm eighty seven now. Can't have long to go. To be honest, I'm glad you came here today, Mr Morrison. It's off my chest now and no longer a secret." She rubbed her jaw thoughtfully. "You'll use this information responsibly?"

"You have my word, Val."

Morrison stayed a further hour drinking tea before thanking Ms. Hann and returning to the Horse and Groom Inn where he took rooms.

Chapter Eight

Giles Grantham entered the small room on the third floor of Thames House wherein were gathered four men and one woman. Seated at the top of the table pouring water into a small paper cup was Sir Robert Cavendish, one of MI5's longest serving and most senior operatives.

"Ah, Mr. Grantham. You're welcome. Please take a seat."

He shuffled some papers, took a sip of his water and commenced the meeting.

"I've met you each individually but this is the first time we've met as a group. I've already advised you of the nature of our task but would like further to underscore the importance we place on the covert nature of this group. If its existence and purpose were to become known, merry hell would ensue. MI5 is a broad church and frequently its interests are best served by compartmentalising its activity."

He took another sip of water.

"Matters discussed within these four walls must remain so. They will *not* be discussed with colleagues and if anyone expresses interest or seeks information in regard to your tasks you must refer them directly to me but say nothing whatsoever to them. I have known each of you for some time and understand that you support totally the agenda I am pursuing, but we must also understand that we'd be given very short shrift if these matters were known, so this meeting is to be kept completely secret...and as you each know, I have prejudicial information on each of you that gives me confidence that these rigours will apply totally. Am I clear on this point?"

A murmur of assent prefaced his continued monologue.

"You are each aware that MI5 is entrusted by the state to ensure that Scottish Independence never takes place. Our politicians will continue to make the case but we must accept that north of the border they also have extremely able politicians and at present they make a case sufficiently compelling to see the polls drift in a direction not necessarily in favour of the status quo. Indeed, if we consider the matter over a period of some twenty years, the nationalists have made considerable gains. From a fringe party we could rather ignore, they've demonstrated a cohesion and popularity that could not have been foreseen. The ill-judged decision to legislate for a Scottish Parliament, rather than shooting the fox, has seen the body politic down here infected with a horde of nationalists, as well as them dominating their Edinburgh citadel. The Labour Party in Scotland is frankly no more, and the Conservatives are a mere whisper of their previous strength. *My* perception is that MI5 has been unduly inactive in these matters and that unless we find innovative, covert and effective methods of turning the tide, the Union is lost. As part of my Scottish remit in here, I've set in motion the assembling of a large group of Unionist supporters...some Conservative, some Liberals and Labour who will write to newspapers at length and frequently taking issue with Scottish separatism at every turn. Their existence will remain confidential and represents the kind of activity our seniors expect of us. But it is frankly, insufficient! You have each been allocated a mission. While discrete, they may also present opportunities for collaboration. Our meeting today is to establish progress and to consider future action. Unfortunately, I've been called to an urgent meeting so we'll have to be brief."

He looked round the room at those gathered.

"Ms. Fowldes, may we start with you? Just a summary if you will."

Wearing a grey suit and white blouse, her hair tied in a bun, Jenifer Fowldes epitomised the bland look of a civil servant whose duties that morning had consisted of writing a report on NHS procurement. In fact, she had four months previously returned from a six months tour of duty based in the British Embassy in Damascus where she had been wounded by shrapnel and had been returned to London for treatment and rehabilitation. She was now recovered.

"Sir Robert. Thank you. I have identified a woman employed as a senior official in the office of the Director-General for Education, Communities and Justice in Scotland. She has considerable contact with the Minister for Justice, Ms. Lorna Gillies MSP. Ms. Gillies is a lesbian. The woman I refer to has considerable financial problems and may soon lose her house. She has problems with alcohol although she functions well and these problems are not known to her colleagues. She too is a lesbian, but was married previously and has a son whom she is desperate to see secure a place in Cambridge. He has the necessary qualifications but having secured his Higher results in Edinburgh's Leith Academy, is most unlikely to secure that place. I've agreed that we could arrange admission and that we could see her mortgage cleared with financial support put in place to assist her son and to supplement her income for a period of five years at which point she intends to retire. The overall sum, which includes university fees, would amount to two hundred and forty-three thousand pounds. For this consideration she is prepared to testify that a date in the near future when alone with her in her office she was assaulted both physically and sexually on the basis that under Scots Law she can do so anonymously. Further she is prepared to state that the Justice Minister has no confidence in Scotland's First Minister due to their differing views on a strategy aimed at achieving independence."

She raised her hand slightly to halt Cavendish's intended intervention and to intimate a final flourish.

"If approved I would wish to take steps to establish supplementary evidence, whether a witness or circumstantial in nature, to support her allegations."

Cavendish nodded.

"The money isn't a problem. I can advise this morning that dark money has been flowing into an account over in Northern Ireland and that thanks to our Mr. Grantham here, we've been allocated a considerable sum which we can use specifically for the purposes to which we turn our efforts. This money will not be recorded anywhere, is at my personal disposal and so can be used imaginatively." He stroked his chin thoughtfully.

"My limited knowledge of Scots Law is that for conviction, corroboration is a necessary requirement up there, so before we spend money on your contact, make sure you have the secondary source to which you refer."

He scribbled the sum mentioned on a file cover before him and turned to another agent.

"Mr Caruthers. If you will?"

"Certainly Sir Robert. I have researched the prospect of utilising apparently neutral think-tanks in shaping Scottish public policy and attitudes towards independence. I've covertly established an infrastructure to refute any positive impacts of self-governance. This approach will be used to pour doubt on economic claims and will be used by friendly editors of both tabloids and broadsheets to launch attacks on independence in general and create a new narrative of risk, tested on focus groups and honed by both the print media and television. Essentially we intend to focus efforts upon presenting independence as a mortal threat to their very economic existence."

"Cost?"

"Somewhat north of a million for starters. It's likely to increase in line with our ambitions and will depend on its success."

"Agreed." He wrote the figure underneath the last.

"Benjamin?"

Benjamin Gold opened a green folder and consulted the notes it contained.

"Different approach, Sir Robert. I'm attempting to revisit the approach we took prior to the 2014 Scottish Referendum when the Government promised a massive carbon capture and storage facility in Peterhead then abandoned it as soon as the vote was secured. So, I've been in touch with the Department of Transport and have agreed with their Permanent Secretary that a feasibility study shall be undertaken to provide an additional runway at both Glasgow and Edinburgh Airports and that a bullet train be considered that will connect Glasgow Airport, Glasgow city with Edinburgh Airport and Edinburgh city centre, drastically reducing travel time and improving inter-connectivity in Scotland. The costs of this study will be something in the order of six hundred thousand in the first instance. Now this is an entirely...what shall we say... *aspirational* project and need never see the light of day after any poll, but prior to that it would dominate headlines and might sway, or at least hold fast, a proportion of voters who believe that their needs are better dealt with by the munificence of Mother Westminster. Transport is a devolved matter but we'd argue that this initiative involves hi-speed, or Maglev, short for Magnetic Levitation, technology and not being 'normal' rail transport, must require British governance. Most aviation responsibilities are also devolved but it would flush out the nationalists as we'd insist on it being a London-based initiative managed by our Secretary of State for Scotland in tandem with the Secretary of State for Transport. They'd have to deny these social benefits to their people or allow us to demonstrate that our deep pockets can achieve what they cannot."

"Six hundred thousand for feasibility studies of this scale seems rather a low estimate."

"The Department of Transport has itself rather a substantial budget, Sir Robert. The Permanent Secretary is completely on board and will set aside contingency budgets if necessary. Money shouldn't be a hindrance in this proposal. I'm also ready to push the button on targeted advertisements on social media. The database we'll use holds details of many thousands of soft 'Nos', floating voters, disillusioned nationalists and our mainstay of Unionist diehards. They will be each sent adverts designed to match and strengthen their attitude towards independence. It's expensive...half a million ... but the quality of return is exceptional. Nothing happens until you say go. Finally, I've recruited two individuals who will set ablaze second homes located in the Highlands of Scotland known to be owned by English nationals. They will plant Saltires and leave graffiti messages encouraging English nationals to go home. Very low cost. Perhaps a couple of thousand."

"Yes, to the transport idea Benjamin and the social media adverts. I'm okay on the arson proposal but must insist we keep an eye on public opinion in respect of this. Rich people from London swanning up to their second home in Scotland when locals can't buy somewhere to live and work isn't very popular across Scotland. We might find that there's a measure of sympathy for them being burned out."

He read a note he'd prepared earlier.

"One more thing. Intelligence is coming in that Seed of the Gael intend to close all twenty-five roads that cross the ninety-six miles of the border between Scotland and England. We've no information as to *when* they intend doing this but our source reckons they'll employ a variety of methods so I've alerted our people to be ready to act, apprehend the miscreants and keep the roads open. It'd be a real news headline if they succeeded."

Cavendish turned to a man on his right who had been busily capturing the discussion on a tablet. "You got all of that, Michael?"

His assistant, Michael Kowalski gave a brief nod.

"Sir."

"There's one more, Sir Robert. The Scottish Government have provided electronic ballot counting in support of their Scottish Local

Government elections for some years now and it has been highly successful. We've taken some steps using the 77th Brigade to ensure that if and when polling does take place on the matter of Scottish independence and if it appears from exit polling that the Union is compromised, the system will be caused to fail bringing any result into question and allowing for an argument for a re-run to be made. In addition, as you will be aware, though local government in Scotland is in charge of the electoral register, the Westminster Government has responsibility to contract an annual national canvas of people entitled to vote. This task has been outsourced to a number of private companies and in some of these let's say, we have a measure of influence. Their responsibilities include the scanning and verification of all postal ballot papers and accompanying Postal Vote Statements, to ensure that only authentic votes are put forward for the count. You can be assured that the ballots submitted from Scotland will be scrutinised in the interests of the Union."

Cavendish gestured his approval.

"Very well."

He turned to Grantham. "Mr. Grantham you have been off to a fast start, haven't you? Your intervention in Glasgow recently achieved everything you said it would. The headlines that followed the Nationalists' march were all about importing the Irish troubles to the mainland. Well done. Now...where are we today?"

"Thank you, Sir Robert. I must confess myself delighted at the outcome. Not only did we secure the headlines we sought but social media commentary supported, I must say, by our colleagues in the 77th Brigade, saw distinct dismay being evinced in normally upbeat nationalist comment. It appears to have affected morale and upset an important middle-class segment of the separatists' sympathisers."

He cleared his throat. "My next initiative is somewhat more delicate and I'm loath to share it beyond your own person, Sir Robert."

"We're all in this together, Grantham," growled Cavendish irritably.

"Nevertheless..." Grantham held his ground.

Cavendish conceded. "Very well." He placed both hands palm down on the table. This meeting is adjourned. Sorry it's been so brief but I'd like to thank you all. Each of your proposals are agreed subject to the few reservations I've expressed. We meet again in two weeks. Michael here will be in touch. In the meantime everything we have discussed is *top* secret. I must insist that these matters must be discussed with no one inside the agency. Absolutely no one. I seek not only discretion but absolute secrecy. I hope I'm being very clear on that. Thank you again."

He allowed the door to close as the room emptied of those leaving.

"What's so delicate then, Mr. Grantham?"

A long sigh preceded Grantham's comment.

"I'd like to shoot the Secretary of State for Scotland."

Russel sat back in his chair, momentarily silenced.

"Well, I can see why you wanted the room emptied."

"I have a good man, Sir Robert. A fellow traveller but not linked with us...name's Emil Rotermundt. A Unionist to his fingertips and engaged, once removed, with our efforts in Scotland for more than a decade. Presently he manages dark money operations out of Portrush in Northern Ireland. He and a small group of four others fund Unionist and Conservative interests. It was he personally who was behind the disruption of the recent nationalists' march. He can access two revolvers used by the IRA in a shooting in a Ballymena pub. Once used by us it'll be a simple task for the ballistic boyos to have the weapon identified and connected with the IRA. We'll take steps to link it with what we'll leak to the media is a nascent military arm of the SNP and further enhance the feeling that there is credible proof of both sectarian and nationalist paramilitary activity in Scotland. I'm certain that elements of the nationalist cause would take to the streets in protest at this foul calumny. If matters deteriorate, given the reaction of the adherents of the Orange order as I'd intend...we have a second revolver, equally tainted and should there be civil unrest, Westminster might find cause to take such steps as may be necessary to prepare a Special Powers Act, as was enacted in respect of Ireland. This would allow the troops to be deployed on the streets of Glasgow, Stirling, Edinburgh and across Scotland." He leaned forward in emphasis. "By militarising the situation, Westminster takes control."

"Shoot the fucking Secretary of State for *Scotland*?"

"Well, perhaps *wound*. A flesh wound in the leg. An outpatient injury."

Cavendish grimaced his uncertainty.

"I don't know, Giles. Shooting a fucking Minister! We'd be hung, drawn and quartered if it ever got out."

"I agree, Sir Robert. I fancy I'd have to do some personal cleaning up before the matter could be put to bed."

"How so?"

"Frankly, once the deed had been done, I'd have to eliminate those involved at levels below me. My man, Emil Rotermundt, is a Conservative Councillor. He is the very epitome of Loyalist, Unionist Conservatism. My suggestion is that the second gun would be used to end his life. He has no dependents. It would have the benefit of furthering the sense that a second attack was being made upon Conservative Scotland, but yet would block any suggestion that the security services were involved. It would escalate the act from a wounding to a murder. His role as one of our intermediaries is known to only a few trusted men. They'd take the obvious view that he was killed as a consequence of his role. That'd be an end to the matter."

"It's something of a high wire act. If anything went wrong..."

"Sir Robert, the objective is the retention of Scotland in the Union. As you yourself have argued, the economic impact of us losing North Sea gas and oil, wind-driven electricity, water for parched East Anglia, a border at Carlisle and no consequent control over immigrants flooding south after settling in Scotland is fearful. We'd almost certainly have to face up to a Celtic partnership between Ireland and Scotland and a hostile Europe bookending our great nation. If we have to surrender one man to accomplish this, then so be it."

Silence reigned for some moments before Cavendish came to a decision.

"Who knows of this plan of yours?"

"Myself and Rotermundt. Of course, Rotermundt, phase one only," he corrected himself.

"A flesh wound only then...but your man can subsequently be disposed of in the manner you suggest." Further reflection followed. "Costs?"

"Very little. I'd suggest a budget of three hundred thousand. Frankly cost isn't the issue here. It's careful planning, competent execution and clever exploitation of the results."

Cavendish pursed his lips as he reached a final decision.

"Agreed. Don't fuck this up! And don't mention a single syllable of this even in your prayers. We need absolute deniability on all of these actions within the organisation never mind the outside world."

"Indeed so, Sir Robert. You have my word."

Chapter Nine

Morrison opened the door to his small rented flat and bid enter his new boss, Jack Kemp, the Deputy Director General of MI5 who was accompanied by the diminutive figure of Professor Henry Joseph, Head of Far Right Politics. He showed them into his living room which had been tidied for the occasion.

"Nice flat, Donald John. Handy for work."

"It's somewhat removed from my home in Benbecula but it's sufficient for my needs right now."

"Well, thanks for agreeing to host this meeting. Henry and I are keen to hear of your investigations."

"Would you like a coffee? Tea?"

"I'm good, thanks." Joseph also demurred. They sat.

"Well, it appears that there may be some substance to the story," began Morrison. "I've been to visit the Oxford sites associated with Unity Mitford. I've interviewed the niece of the woman who ran the maternity home, Hill View and I've inspected the records in Oxfordshire Registry Office. Each of these revealed information but..."

He picked up a sheaf of papers he'd written earlier.

"I was also able, thanks to your rank, sir, to have access to our own files on the matter. They were quite revealing and tended to bear out the testimony of Ms. Hann, the niece."

"Go on."

"Well, the Mitfords were a wee bit controversial to say the least. They came from upper-class English stock. Lord and Lady Redesdale were parents of the six girls and one son. They were rich in land but not in cash and reports at the time suggest that when it comes to English aristocracy, you couldn't get more posh than they were. They had familial ties with Winston Churchill...Clementine Churchill, his wife, was Lord Redesdale's cousin...and they weren't in the slightest *distant* cousins. Unity was one of the Mitfords who visited Chartwell frequently. For over forty years it was the home of Winston Churchill.

While growing up, our files show that Winston's brother Randolph fell very much in love with Diana Mitford, Unity's sister and he also counted her brother, Tom Mitford, as his greatest friend at Oxford." He turned a page and continued. "I mention this relationship because our head of counter-espionage at the time was Guy Liddell. He was at that point Director of 'B' Division and his diaries show quite clearly that instructions had come down from the then Home Secretary, John Anderson which prevented Mitford even being *questioned* on her return from Germany - despite us knowing of her relationship with Hitler. She was returned to Britain on Hitler's instructions for her own safety only weeks after he'd invaded Poland but she was not even searched upon disembarkation. Our files also suggest that the shooting...her suicide attempt...may have been invented to permit her relative isolation following her return to these shores. Instead of interrogation, she was met by her father who had been waiting for her at Folkestone for three days. There was an armed guard at the harbour and a full hour was allowed to elapse after the other passengers had left before Miss Mitford was brought ashore on a stretcher. Despite reports that she had shot herself in the head, newsreel footage of the time shows quite clearly an attractive, engaging and apparently quite well young lady acknowledging the gathered press corps. She was sufficiently *compos mentis* to state to the press that...and I quote, "I'm glad to be in England, even if I'm not on your side". I might also say that she had something of a reputation of being, how should I put it, more a 'child of the sixties' rather than of the forties."

"Explain, please?"

"Well, she was rumoured to be rather loose morally, a bit of a hippy if you catch my drift. In Germany she was known to be an enthusiastic companion of many blond, leather-clad SS men, she had an affair with an RAF Pilot Officer called John Andrews, a test pilot, who was stationed nearby at Brize Norton. Churchill learned of this and had him posted to the very north of Scotland where he later died in an accident, the circumstances of which are as yet unknown to me but I'll follow it up lest it could have been at the hand of the state. Following his departure, she was reckoned to have had a reputation of picking up airmen by hitching lifts in the highways and byways of Oxfordshire before she was herself sent to rehabilitate on the otherwise uninhabited Isle of Inch Kenneth on the west coast of Scotland. Her family had bought a rather large manor house there...the only building on the island. So in the later years of her life she was conveniently isolated from society. Churchill must have been delighted."

"But she wasn't arrested immediately upon her arrival on these shores?"

"Folkestone harbour and its rail head was rendered a prohibited area. This prohibition was in operation only for the day and it was introduced by authority of the Security Control. Soldiers with armlets bearing the nomenclature of the Field Security Police were at the harbour gate." He turned another page. "MI5 were up to their oxters in this!"

"Oxters?" puzzled Kemp.

"Sorry, boss. 'Armpits'. That is to say, our organisation was heavily involved in ensuring that Unity Mitford was hidden from public sight using a cover story."

"Continue."

"Well, she was wheeched away..."

Kemp couldn't conceal his irk.

"Might we continue using only the Queen's English, Mr. Morrison?"

"Sorry, sir. She was taken to Hill View private maternity home near Oxford ostensibly to recover from the wound to her head but..." He produced the green form given him by Valerie Mann. "This document shows that she gave birth to a child. She intended naming the child Kurt apparently, but the baby was taken from her immediately, given over to and was subsequently adopted by a Mr. Earnest and a Mrs. Judith Warren who took the child to Northern Ireland."

Professor Joseph leaned forward and proffered his hand in a silent request for the document which he read for some moments.

"This is indeed new information. I can confirm much of the earlier testimony although I hadn't been given access to our own files on this matter, but everything stated by Mr. Morrison here seems completely in line with my own thinking." He read the adoption certificate. "This looks authentic, boss."

"There's more," interrupted Morrison. "The niece, a Miss Valerie Mann, whom I interviewed, was mildly confident that the family came from the city of Derry in Northern Ireland."

"Londonderry," insisted Kemp.

Morrison ignored the rebuke. "They also had a daughter named Grace, now aged around eighty-seven if she still walks the earth. I've not followed up on this as I figured you'd want to hear of progress and decide if any further steps should be taken." He laid his papers beside him on the small sofa.

"You've done well, Mr Morrison. Very well." Kemp shook his head. "D'you know, I find it bloody incredulous that MI5, the security organisation we view as the best in the world, could be so asinine as to allow the politicians and frankly the upper-class dimwits in the Establishment at that time to deny us the opportunity to track down possibly the greatest threat to the anti-fascist cause we'd ever have to face. Hitler's son? Alive and well and walking on England's green and pleasant land?"

He turned to Joseph.

"Henry, are you of the view that there is merit in Mr. Morrison's investigations and that they should continue?"

Professor Joseph scanned the document again. "We need to get to the bottom of this."

"We do," agreed Kemp. "But discretely."

"If he's still alive, he'd be eighty-one. So we've probably seen much of his potency ebb," suggested Morrison.

"Even so...even so..."

He decided. "Donald John, head off to Northern Ireland and track this bugger down. Keep things tight. We don't want to stir up a hornet's nest inadvertently. Report back to me personally when you have something concrete to tell us."

* * *

Following their departure, Morrison spent an hour organising his notes and reading more of the two books he'd obtained detailing the life and times of Unity Mitford. As dusk fell he looked at his watch. *Seven o'clock.* He looked at his phone for long seconds before picking it up. *She should be home by now unless she's on the late shift.* A long sigh preceded self-admonishment. *She'll not want to talk to me...and if she did, she's got a tongue on her, I'd just be shouted at.* He touched his smart phone and awakened it. Pressing it, his contacts list came up and he scrolled down to the letter 'F' whose only inhabitant was one Iona Forbes. At the Kelvingrove Art Gallery in Glasgow, he'd used his phone and had taken her photograph next to the painting of *Christ of St John of the Cross* by Salvador Dalí. Despite it being one of the most famous paintings on the planet, he'd later cropped it so that all that remained was the dimpled smile of Iona. He'd used it on her contacts page and she now smiled at him from behind the glass screen of his phone. His courage deserting him, he closed the screen before almost instantly reawakening the device and pushing the number. *Bugger it, no time like the present!*

The phone rang for some time, each ring reducing Morrison's confidence. Just as his finger moved towards the red symbol to end the call, a voice on the other end said, "Hello, Iona Forbes?"

Morrison gasped audibly before answering.

"Iona...it's Donald John."

The delight in her voice was palpable.

"Donald John! It's great to hear from you." He could hear the laughter in her voice. "How's your backside?"

Now rather more at ease, he responded light-heartedly. "Och, it's fine. Not that I can see much of the wound without standing on the toilet seat and looking at the mirror over my shoulder. As you said at the time, just a flesh wound."

"Glad to hear it." She changed the subject. "Is that you back on the island?"

"No. Still in manky old London town. I just felt the need to hear my own accent on the other end of a phone. It's like a foreign language down here. I'm being rebuked for using words like 'oxters' and 'wheeched'. All that 'apple and pears' stuff. I'm a pretty straightforward kind of guy and when someone goes on about the 'dog and bone' I just presume they're talking about their pet, not a telephone...and their beer's keech!"

Iona giggled. "Och, poor Donald John. D'y'know, I don't know why you put up with it. You obviously don't like London much. All those crowded streets..."

"Aye, there's many times I look at my wee suitcase and just imagine packing it and heading towards Euston Station."

"You're an island boy at heart, Donald John."

"I know I am, Iona. I go to sleep at night thinking of the island when it's still and dark clouds rest on the hills over South Uist. I love the island life; its people, its way of life...but I'm doing some pretty important work down here so I suppose that compensates."

"Well, you just pick up the phone anytime you want a blether." Again she changed the subject. "I was talking to your mum the other day. She was in good form but she misses you."

"God, Iona," he groaned. "Don't make me feel any worse."

Another giggle. "Sorry, Donald John. It sounds like I'm beckoning you homeward, but if you've important fisheries' problems to deal with, you just work right on."

Morrison frowned resignedly. "S'pose."

"Anyway, listen. I'm really sorry but I must away. I'm just in from the hospital and I'm away out for dinner with your best pal, Hamish Bain. My hair's a mess. Ever since we chatted a while back at the Dark Island he's been plaguing me for a dinner date and I've relented. He even sang a song for me last Saturday in the Dark Island; *Fhir a'Bhàta*. We're meeting at eight in the hotel bar."

Morrison surprised himself by his reaction.

"Hamish?"

"Aye. Your pal." She tugged at her hair. "I've had a busy day in the hospital and I could do with a few drinks. Torquil The Taxi's coming for me in..." She consulted her left wrist. "God, twenty minutes and I'm a mess."

"Well, say hello to Hamish for me...and say hi to Torquil."

"Will do. But I must dash. When I get back tonight I've to organise myself. I'm off to stay with my friend Emily Thorburn in Belfast for a week. We trained together and I'm going to enjoy a few G&Ts in what used to be Europe's murder capital."

Morrison's heart sang. "You're kidding me. When are you going? I'm off to Belfast...well, Northern Ireland *myself* for a wee while. Maybe we could meet up...unless of course you and Emily have plans."

Iona screeched! "God, that would be *wonderful*. Emily has a few shifts to do while I'm over and I was resigned to looking round the shops or catching a movie or something. Don't think you've met Emily either. You'd love her. She's a real looker. Unattached. Bright."

Morrison heard little of the attractions of Iona's friend.

"When are you leaving?"

I catch the Loganair flight on Saturday morning. Down to Glasgow then over to Belfast. How about you?"

"I'm pretty much my own boss so I could travel over the weekend, I guess."

Iona remembered her deadline. "Look, I must dash. I'm staying at Emily's flat in the city centre. When you get settled, phone me and we'll meet up." She reached for the zip at the back of her dress. "It'll be great to see you. Bye."

"Bye."

Morrison ended the call and leaned back thoughtfully in his chair. *What the hell am I doing? I'm meant to be hunting down the son of bloody Adolph Hitler and instead I'm making arrangements to see a woman.* His mood darkened. *Hamish?...Bloody Hamish?*

Chapter Ten

Now back home in Scotland, Rotermundt lifted his phone and recognised Grantham's call as his details appeared on the screen. He accepted and placed the phone at his ear.

"Yes?"

"The task we discussed has been agreed. You may now take steps to implement. Also, your suggestion about the lower region is preferred. Make contact with the individual I've specified and secure the items. Pay whatever you require. I need to take possession of one of the items prior to you initiating step two. Thereafter I seek only to hear from you once matters are concluded. Are you clear on all of this...particularly the matter of a lower limb only?"

"Perfectly."

"And you have sufficient resources?"

"I have if you supplement them. I've prepared a budget for the entirety of the funds at my disposal and new initiatives such as this have to be paid for."

"Then I will arrange to meet you once you've obtained the items and until then will bid you good day."

The connection ended.

Rotermundt placed his phone on his kitchen table and stroked his chin thoughtfully. He'd never taken to Grantham and most certainly didn't trust him. Having just agreed to shoot the Secretary of State for Scotland in the leg, he was aware of just how dangerous was the position in which he'd placed himself. *Get it wrong and the shot might sever the femoral artery...*he lifted a bottle of Macallan whisky and poured himself a large glass, almost emptying it in one visit before stepping into his study where he consulted a bookshelf. Finding the book on anatomy he sought, he laid it on his desk, sipping again at his glass, this time emptying it. He consulted the index and turned to the page on ' The Circulatory System' flicking over to the passages on the Femoral Artery, its importance and its location in the thigh. He ran his finger down the page as he read almost to ensure that he didn't miss a single syllable of description and explanation regarding this vessel. He murmured in a whisper to himself...*penetrating trauma...gunshot wounds... isolated blunt femoral vessel injury...blood loss and death... amputation*...Now he found his voice.

"Jesus Christ!"

He read on before closing the book slowly. What have I agreed to? He thought further, opened the book again and looked at the circulatory system in the *lower* limbs. *Perhaps his shin? Traumatic vascular injury triggering bleeding...ischemia...amputation rates as high as 48.9%...death...* He placed the book back on the shelf. *I need another drink.*

Settling on his armchair with a second Macallan in his hand, he mulled over possible outcomes. *I shoot him, I slip away, he receives prompt medical attention and it's mission accomplished.* He sipped his whisky. *I shoot him and miss, big scare, lots of media attention but Grantham tells me my life might be forfeit as a consequence.* Another sip. *I shoot him, the wound isn't treated quickly enough, he dies but I slip away undetected...regrettable but again, mission accomplished.* A further sip. *Any of the foregoing and I'm caught? I spend the next twenty years in prison and journalists start to ask why a prominent Conservative shoots another prominent Conservative. They investigate dark money flowing from Northern Ireland to the rest of the United Kingdom in general and Scotland in particular. Disaster!* He finished the glass. *And I've never shot a fucking gun before!*

* * *

Rotermundt knew Alan Colquhoun, the Conservative Secretary of State for Scotland very well. Fellow Conservatives, each members of Scotland's Freemasonry they occasionally met at social gatherings, Colquhoun's constituency down in the borders of Scotland necessitating a measure of geographical if not social distance. Although finding him something of a stuffed shirt, he acknowledged a decent man and someone who worked hard in pursuit of his beliefs. Why on earth those in command of the Unionist cause chose to shoot a man of his stature escaped him although he realised the political impact his assault would have in Scottish politics...*if it's successful,* he breathed. He reflected further. *That said, it'd do Colquhoun's political career no harm if he survived the wound!*

He consulted his computer screen seeking information on Colquhoun's itinerary. Westminster, Monday through Thursday. Back up to Edinburgh on Thursday afternoon if he could manage it. A drive down to the village of Eastriggs south of Annan, right on the Scotland/ England border and he was home. Constituency matters Friday and all weekend...*That'd be the easiest shot...but the most difficult to escape. Edinburgh's more certain as his flight times are predictable but there are armed cops around.* He closed the site and entered a maps' site where he considered the route from Edinburgh to Colquhoun's house in Eastriggs. He zoomed in on his house. *Jesus, if he stepped out of his back yard and waded to the centre of the River Esk when the tide's out he'd be in England! No wonder the Nationalists take the mick out of his Anglicised accent.*

He returned to the kitchen and poured another drink. *Okay,* he thought...*first order of business...I don't get shot and I don't get caught. How do I pull that off?*

* * *

Mobile technology having largely reduced the availability of phone boxes gave Rotermundt pause for thought. He decided it was foolish to call his contact using his own phone and had discovered using a search engine on his computer that one of the few places where coin-operated telephone kiosks were still available were in Scotland's railway stations. *Obviously not any local station,* he reckoned...*and they all have CCTV cameras.* He thought further. A hat, glasses, a turned-up collar and a limp would suffice. From his wardrobe, he took a coat and reaching up, found an old trilby he hadn't worn in years. Dusting it off, he placed a pair of sunglasses on his nose, turned up his collar, placed the trilby on his head and decided that no one would be able to identify him should ever the need arise. He could make the call thus.

* * *

Two hours later as dusk fell, Rotermundt arrived at Cathcart Railway Station. A transit destination usually quiet, he'd taken the precaution of arriving just after the departure of the Neilston train and twenty minutes before the train in the other direction to Glasgow Central. Railway staff, he knew, would have left their part-time positions at mid-day at which point passengers seeking tickets had to use automated devices placed at every station. Manufacturing a heavy limp, he climbed the stairs and approached the phone kiosk, reassured somewhat at the empty station. From his inside pocket he consulted Grantham's note. His contact was to be referred to as Mr. Morecambe and he was to be identified as Mr. Wise.

Licking his lips to return a measure of moisture to them, he dialled the number. After a few rings a voice said, "Yeah?"

"I'd like to speak to Mr. Morecambe."

A thick Irish accent responded, "And who'd be lookin' for him?"

"My name is Mr. Wise."

"Been expectin' your call, Mr Wise. What ye sayin' to it?"

Flummoxed at the question, Rotermundt ignored it.

"I'd like to meet you to discuss a proposition I have."

"And would it be the proposition I'm told to expect?"

"Well, I'm sure I don't know what you've been told to expect but I'm equally sure that if we met we could resolve matters in our mutual interest."

"I dare say." There was a silence before Morecambe continued. "Tell ye what. I've things on. S'pose we met next Sunday. How'd that suit ye?"

"Next Sunday would be fine. Where and when."

"Well I'm in Belfast. I'd meet ye in a pub here say, eight o'clock that night?"

"That works."

"Do you know your way around Belfast Mr. Wise? Know many pubs?"

Rotermundt looked around anxious to establish that he wasn't being overheard. The station remained empty of passengers.

"I know two...The Royal Bar in the Shankill Road and the Crown Liquor Saloon in the city centre."

Brighton laughed a laugh that quickly developed into a gurgling coughing fit.

"Well," he hawked, "we'll not be meetin' in the feckin' Royal Bar any time soon, Mr. Wise. That's not welcomin' territory if you have my meanin'. Let's agree the Crown at ten o'clock on Sunday night."

"And how will I recognise you?"

Just you come carryin' a Tesco shoppin' bag. Order a drink, stand at the bar and if I think it's safe I'll introduce myself. And don't worry. You'll be safe."

The phone went dead. Rotermundt again checked the empty platform. Satisfied, he wasn't being observed other than by cameras, he remembered he had a limp and exited, pulling his trilby further over his face.

Chapter Eleven

Three planes landed at the George Best Belfast City Airport on the Saturday afternoon. One from Glasgow carried Iona Forbes, one from Edinburgh conveyed Emil Rotermundt and one from London delivered Donald John Morrison.

Rotermundt hired a large Mercedes Benz CL Class at the terminal and drove immediately to Portrush where he checked in at the Adelphi Hotel, not the most salubrious hotel in the town but most convenient due to its location on the town's Main Street. The powerful V8 5.0 litre engine saw him register at the Adelphi one hour after leaving the airport, the benefits of the high performance car being lost somewhat on the slower and congested roads favoured by tractors and other agricultural vehicles.

Rotermundt checked his watch as he waited impatiently for a young French receptionist to complete his details. *They'll be here in an hour. Time for a shower.*

* * *

At seven-fifteen, Rotermundt entered the small windowless conference room made available by the hotel. Thanking the young receptionist with rather more grace than an hour earlier, he closed the door behind him and set his briefcase on the table. From within, he took a radio frequency detector and turning it on, carefully swept the room, stopping every so often gently to lever a painting from the wall the better to view its rear. Detecting no hidden cameras, hard-wired recorders or microphones, he laid the device upon the table and turned on its audio scrambler which generated white noise and obscured conversation. *That should fox any bug I've missed*, he mused. Returning to his briefcase he took from its depths four sheets of paper which he assembled in front of him. Then he sat quietly and awaited the opening of the door.

Punctually at seven-thirty, three men entered together. Rotermundt didn't rise, acknowledging them merely by a slight upwards movement of his head. He didn't smile.

One of the men, heavily set, red-faced and sweating, his appearance screaming hypertension, attempted light-heartedness.

"Our Scottish chairman seems as chirpy as ever, eh?"

Rotermundt ignored the jibe.

"Take your seats, gentlemen. I've checked the room. There's no evidence of surveillance."

He waited until all were seated and had poured themselves coffee.

"To business," he instructed. "This meeting will be short as usual. It will not be minuted. In a moment I will pass round a single page set of accounts. These will not leave this room." He removed a small manual shredder from his briefcase. "They will be shredded here and burned the moment I can do so without setting off an alarm."

"Is this all really necessary, Emil?" asked a second man, as thin and emaciated as his colleague was corpulent.

Rotermundt raised his eyes to the ceiling in obvious disdain before levelling his gaze.

"Henry J., we are dealing with many millions of pounds which are designed to bring about political change in complete defiance of all democratic principles. If our efforts were to become known we might escape prison...*might*," he emphasised. "But what I will share with you momentarily may not sit easily with the authorities and could see us incarcerated for many years. Our mission would be compromised and I dare say there are forces out there who might seek to exact revenge, so you'll forgive me if I take every precaution."

The third man, exhibiting an extravagant naval-styled beard that stopped just short of embracing within it a waxed moustache, agreed with Rotermundt.

"Gentlemen. Not only does our chairman organise our meetings, he looks after the finances and expedites all decisions we make. If anyone is to become a person of interest to the authorities, it is he so let's be careful and give him every support. Our job is to consider spending proposals and to advise. Let's constrain our advice to those ends."

He sat back as Rotermundt continued, licking the friction ridges of his thumb as a prelude to allowing it purchase on the paper.

"Here's an update on our finances." He passed the sheets round. "You will recall that we had a sum of four million, three hundred thousand in the year of our Lord, two thousand and thirteen prior to the Scottish Referendum on Independence. One point eight was used in that campaign. A further nine hundred thousand was used in support of the United Kingdom leaving Europe. This left us with one million, six hundred thousand to deal with the expected second Scottish Referendum. We win that, we win the Union forever...certainly for twenty, thirty years. In parenthesis you can see that our various initiatives...the wrap around adverts, the payment of 'volunteers' to skew social media, the hire of halls and buses, the commissioning of favourable polls and the use of consultancies and think tanks were all very successful. In consequence, our favourable legal position here in the north of not requiring to inform anyone of the sources of income is continuing, and we have been asked to increase our efforts. In addition to the one point six million available we have recently been allocated a further ten million pounds sterling."

A murmur of approval met this announcement as Rotermundt continued.

"Now before we get too excited, a proportion...half...of five million pounds has been excised from that amount and is to be made over to a separate account that will be made over to Her Majesty's Security Services for initiatives that needn't concern us. Suffice it to say that they have an ability to engage in ways denied us. We, for our part, are to continue the activities that have proved so successful in thwarting those Scots so foolish as to seek to depart the Union...the most successful political and economic union known to man."

"A question, Emil," interrupted the beard. "If, as you say, the security services use money we allocate them and if this involves skulduggery, would we be legally responsible if things went awry?"

"No written minute exists or will exist. Our fingerprints will not be seen on these deeds. The money is in the process of being diverted as we speak before it arrives here."

"Indeed, but if it is, in the first instance in our name, and should it come out might we be culpable just as would those who act at our bidding. Accessories before the fact as it were."

"You may be right, William but those are the risks we take. Thus far, we have had a charmed existence. It is in no one's interest, at least within the Establishment, to see our work interrogated. Much of what we have in the way of donations has come from the very people who would be judging whether or not to investigate. They're not stupid. If we go down, they'd be next against the wall."

"Still..."

"Look, William! One of our beneficiaries, the Scottish Unionist Association Trust, an unincorporated association based in Glasgow, failed to report two donations totalling two hundred and seven thousand pounds within the required timescale. A mistake. They were fined the princely sum of one thousand eight hundred pounds after a fourteen month long investigation. Not a bad return on investment, eh?"

Rotermundt sensed that some measure of discomfort remained.

"Somewhat foolishly," he continued, "a former Scottish Tory leader told the media in interview last year that almost all the party's candidates would have benefitted from our investments. An avoidable error. However, while there is a requirement for legal political entities in *Scotland* to keep proper accounts and to set out the sources of funding, there is no such requirement on us. It's a simple process. We fund the Scottish Unionist Trust and others, they fund party associations but the trust, for example, always operates independently of the Scottish Conservative Party and donations are given to local associations or the central party. That way, everyone can point the finger elsewhere. Accordingly, it is easy to see why the media refer to these contributions as 'dark money'. Right now we can operate effectively without oversight and if and when there are investigations, they take so long, the next election or referendum is upon the nation before a verdict is recorded."

Finally he relented and allowed a more sympathetic tone.

"Gentlemen. We are doing God's work. We are protected by the political class that benefits most from our activities. We are maintaining the Union whilst ensuring that we step back from the European adventure...and we are all committed to those ends are we not?"

Consent was given and the group turned their attention to the disbursement of several hundred thousand pounds to the Scottish Conservative Trust as well as smaller amounts to local initiatives. A further sum of two hundred thousand pounds was allocated to Conservatives in Wales and further monies to constituency parties in the north of England, former Labour bastions.

At eight-fifteen, only some forty-five minutes after the commencement of the meeting, significant amounts had been expended and dinner had been called. Now in more ebullient mood, Rotermundt gathered up the paperwork, ostentatiously shredding them individually before announcing, "Henry J., you're on the bell. You get a round in and I'll burn these shreddings. I'll have a bottle of foreign lager. I'll be back in ten minutes." He stuffed the ribboned tufts of paper strips into a pocket of his briefcase and left the room.

Chapter Twelve

Anxious to fulfil his duties early so as to have some time he could devote to seeing Iona Forbes, Morrison shouldered his small case onto the double bed in his hotel room. Resisting the inclination to call her just to say he'd arrived, he instead opened his wallet and removed the two identification cards he'd had made up prior to leaving London. The MI5 graphics department had done a good job and in his hand he held perfectly sound photographic credentials complete with holographic emblems to mark their authenticity, each presenting him variously as a member of the Salvation Army and as a journalist with the Guardian newspaper. He also held his legitimate warrant card, showing a photograph, name, rank as an intelligence officer with his signature and that of Sir Humphrey Ashton, announcing him as a *bona fide* officer of MI5. Each phone number, if used to check authenticity, would connect to MI5 for verification.

He placed two cards in the rear pocket of his wallet, inserted the one showing him as a member of the Salvation Army in the transparent Perspex window and lifted the phone to reception asking whether his hired car had arrived. Having been informed that the *concierge* had paperwork that, when signed, would permit him to drive away, he placed the phone on its receiver and went downstairs.

Half an hour later, Morrison gunned the accelerator and steered his rented Ford Mondeo onto the slip road of the M2 and thence the M22 trying to make best use of the seventeen miles of motorway before he'd have to compete with slower local and more agricultural traffic. He reached Londonderry mid-afternoon thankful that his on-line research with the Public Record Office of Northern Ireland had allowed him to avoid the inconvenience of having to wait until the Monday opening to make use of the Derry City Council research facilities. He pulled in to a lay-by and removed a piece of paper from his inside pocket. The London check on the voters' roll had shown a family of Mr. Earnest, Mrs. Judith Warren, daughter Grace and son Gerald living at 126

Academy Road. Earnest had removed himself from the roll first by the simple expedient of dying, followed some years later by Judith. The two children, now adults, had remained there for many years until Gerald disappeared in 1970 and finally Jane in 2010. No documents could be found showing that either of them had either married or died. The house now appeared to be owned by a Mr. and Mrs. Adams who, according to property records had purchased the three-bedroomed, mid-terraced house in 2011. They were to be his first lead.

Slowly he drove along Academy Road checking numbers until he arrived at his destination. He parked and from the passenger's seat lifted a clipboard especially designed to offer further solidity to his Salvation Army cover. A neat if small garden outside 126 was tidily planted with flowers amongst which the fragrance of the lavender plants fought for air superiority with the heavily scented lilacs. Four steps allowed access to the front door upon which he knocked. It opened immediately revealing an elderly woman whose hair was confined by rollers.

"You gave me a fright there, young man. I was cleaning the front door window when you knocked."

"I'm sorry. I didn't intend..."

"Oh, that's quite alright..." She gazed at his suited demeanour and clipboard and attempted to close the conversation. "I'm afraid me and my husband keep our politics to ourselves..."

"Oh...no...I'm not a pollster," he smiled. "I'm actually a caseworker from the Salvation Army." He proffered his wallet showing his ID. "I'm actually trying to find members of the family who owned this property before you. The people who sold it to you."

"Oh, my son...we've been here for about ten years." She appeared thoughtful as if determining whether or not to reveal her knowledge before relenting. "Lady named Mrs. Warren as I recall."

"Yes, that's her. Grace. And her brother, Gerald?"

"Don't know him, son. Never heard of him."

"Don't suppose you know if Grace is still around or where she might be?"

"Funny you should ask that. She was very friendly with Molly next door so I used to see her visit from time to time. She left here to go to a care home. I'm pretty sure it was Meadowbank up in Waterside." She pondered her recollection. "Yeah, Meadowbank up in Waterside. She got very frail then I think Molly said she got that forgetting disease."

"Alzheimer's?"

"Yeah. That one. She's still alive, though. Molly visited her a couple of weeks back."

"Mrs. Adams, you've been very helpful. I can't thank you enough." He tried one further question. "And you've no knowledge of Gerald?"

"So who's looking for them?"

"I'm afraid I can't say, Mrs. Adams. It's confidential, but I'll be able to tell them that you've been wonderfully helpful."

***

The Mondeo's satellite navigation took him accurately to the care home where he exited the vehicle before walking up a path and pushing open the door of the facility. Immediately he was met with a reception desk situated behind a sliding glass panel which was opened by a smiling, uniformed care assistant.

"Afternoon! Can I help you?"

Again Morrison extracted his wallet and proffered it, giving the same explanation for his visit.

"Hello. My name is Donald John Morrison and I'm a caseworker for the Salvation Army. We have a relative who'd dearly like to be reunited with one of your patients."

"Residents," she corrected him.

"Residents." He replaced his wallet. "I'm looking for a brother and sister...a Grace and Gerald Warren. I understand that Grace has been here for some time."

The care officer accepted his identification and reason for visiting.

"Grace has been here for maybe ten years but you won't get much from her I'm afraid. She's quite confused now. She has Alzheimer's and it's quite advanced. She can't feed or toilet herself. Can't speak much. She's very confused and frankly seeing a strange man would just confuse her more."

"Quite...I can quite understand that." He hesitated. "It's actually her brother we're keen to track down. Her brother Gerald. Don't suppose..."

"Sure...Gerry visits her regular. Once a month. He's over in Belfast but he drives down to see her regular." She laughed. "He's more of a pick-me-up for us staff actually. Great *craic*. He still sees her but to be honest, she's not aware of it."

"Any idea how I might find him?"

"Easy done. He's *Father* Gerry. A priest at St. Malachy's Parish Church next to the city hall in Belfast. A lovely man. I'll phone him for you."

Morrison demurred rather more forcefully than he'd intended.

"No! Please don't. I have to visit personally or I'll get into trouble." He smiled appealingly at the care worker. "Would that be okay?"

"Of course. Don't you fret."

"I'll make sure to mention to him how much you value his visits."

"You do that!"

Morrison turned and walked back to his car. *Adolph Hitler's kid might be a priest?*

* * *

He sat in his car punching the Belfast destination to his satnav and looking at his watch. It was now approaching Saturday evening. *What do priests do on a Saturday evening?* he pondered. He made up his mind. *No time like the present...and I'll be able to see Iona tomorrow all being well.* He rebuked himself silently for organising his duties around his desire to see Forbes. *It'll be better if I see him quickly in case that Derry woman phones him.* He settled on his excuse to himself and replaced the Salvation Army card in his wallet with that showing him as a journalist with the Guardian Newspaper.

* * *

It was dark when Morrison pulled up outside St. Malachy's Church. Lights burned in the Clergy House. He lifted a small backpack and secured the car before walking in darkness to a heavy, glazed door illuminated from within. A large old fashioned bronze bell-pull invited his attention and he obliged, causing a loud ringing from within the premises. Momentarily, an elderly lady opened the door and merely by dint of raising her eyebrows, solicited an explanation for the intrusion.

"Sorry to bother you on a Saturday evening but I was wondering if I could have a few minutes of Father Gerry's time." With no immediate response forthcoming, he offered his wallet ID. "I'm a journalist from The Guardian Newspaper in London. It'd only take a moment if he's free."

"Wait here, would ya?"

The large household door remained open allowing Morrison to view a hallway which led to a lounge in which two men stood warming themselves at an open fire. Both appeared elderly. One, he noticed stood well over six feet tall with a full head of white hair. The other was smaller, even dapper with darker hair. Both were dressed casually. After a moment the woman returned.

"Father will see you."

She escorted Morrison along the hall to the lounge where she announced him.

"Father, here's the man from the newspaper."

Instinctively Morrison held out his hand to the smaller of the two men.

"Donald John Morrison of the Guardian."

The man took his hand and shook it limply. "Henry J. Carson."

This occasioned a laugh from the taller man who offered his hand and shook Morrison's warmly.

"Henry J. Carson! He's a man inseparable from his middle initial. I'm pleased to meet you. I'm Father Gerry Warren. Neither a middle name not a middle initial. My parents had no imagination." He gestured towards a comfortable armchair inviting Morrison to sit. "We were just about to enjoy a small tonic. Might you care to join us?"

"Sure," replied Morrison still confused at the tall frame of Warren. He glanced at the more diminutive Carson. *He'd have been my bet as Hitler's progeny.*

"Whisky if you have it."

"Now, that's no English accent, Mr. Morrison."

"I'm from Benbecula in the Western Isles of Scotland."

"Are you now?" He continued pouring. "I know it well. I spent a summer there...or next door...at Lochboisdale in South Uist, your neighbouring island. In St Michael the Archangel's Catholic Church to be precise. We were blessed with beautiful weather for two full months and I returned to the streets of Belfast a much revived old priest." Finishing his ministrations, he continued. "You're blessed to live there."

"I'm afraid it's London for the minute."

"A hell hole!" He smiled broadly. "Get yourself back to the islands in short order. That's a Papal edict."

He handed Carson and Morrison each a glass and sat before continuing.

"When you return you must ensure that you give my very best to Father Scanlon. I'm sure he'll still be around. He was much younger than me. Now how might we help you?"

"Thanks. I'll do that. I suspect this might be something of a wild goose chase. But anyway, I'm over here on the instructions of my editor who wants to do a story about the importance of the church as the north comes out of the dark years of the Troubles. He reckons that not enough significance is given to the role played by the likes of yourself, Father. And in a pub in London a couple of weeks back I met one of your parishioners. Can't remember his name. He said you were someone I should speak to. I understand it's a bit of a weak connection but..."

Morrison allowed his introduction to ebb, sipped at his whisky, pleased at his subterfuge whilst chastising himself mildly for being so glib.

"Well now. That's interesting. So let me let you in on a secret, young Donald John Morrison. There are few things achieved in this world that don't involve collaboration." He raised his glass in a silent toast to his other guest. "This man here is Henry J. Carson. He's my friend. He's also Assistant Grand Master of Plumbridge Purple Heroes Loyal Orange Lodge 560. He's a Unionist, staunch Protestant, and he even supports the Queen's Eleven...Rangers Football Club, in Glasgow. I am everything he's not. He's everything I'm not. And some years ago we'd have been at daggers drawn, but progress is only made when people get together. The future belongs to those who see it first. And Henry and I saw many years ago that working together we might bring some solace and peace to those in our respective communities who would wish to harm the other."

"Fascinating. You were both brought up in different traditions?" Father Gerry equivocated.

"In a manner of speaking. Henry's roots go back a long way. Mine, less so. I was born in south-east England to a Catholic family and brought here as a kid. But there was no pressure on me to become a priest. Indeed my mother was shocked when I told her I wanted to go to the seminary. So there was nothing inevitable about me becoming a clergyman. I became a man during the thirty years of the Troubles and thought that God might offer more to the people of the north than the bullet. Henry here came to the same conclusion."

Satisfied that he'd unearthed the person he'd come to find, Morrison accepted one more whisky and discussed his invented question for an hour before drawing his interview to a close with many effusive thanks and promises to pay a visit to Father Scanlon in Lochboisdale. During the discussion, Carson spoke only in monosyllables to confirm Warren's assertions.

Father Gerry rose to walk Morrison to the front door. As he did so, Morrison slipped unnoticed the glass the priest had been using into his pocket.

"I hope I've been helpful."

"You certainly have Father Gerry." He allowed a beat. "D'y'know, I'm intrigued by your name. I've an Uncle Frederick Warren. He's dead now but he was an Oxford don. Warren was a common name down there in Oxfordshire but...."

The priest stepped back in some small measure of surprise. "That's my own background! Didn't my own folks come from there as well? A small village just outside Oxford." He laughed. "Maybe we're related, young Donald John."

Morrison smiled both at his confirmation of Warren's antecedents as well as reciprocating his infectious grin.

"I'll ask my mother when I get back to the island."

"And don't leave it too long! It's God's own country."

Morrison took two business cards from his pocket, dropping one on the floor.

"Sorry...in case you need to contact me."

The tall priest stooped and lifted the surplus card from the floor, returning it to Morrison.

"If I get stuck with one of your difficult crosswords."

Chapter Thirteen

Sir Humphrey Ashton looked out over the River Thames awaiting the arrival of his Deputy. Outside, mid-morning traffic on Lambeth Bridge moved ponderously in each direction, even on a Sunday morning. His reverie was interrupted as Jack Kemp admitted himself without knocking.

"Morning, boss."

"Good morning, Jack."

"It's lovely out there. Such a waste of good weather to be stuck in here all day."

"Tell that to the poor sods stuck in traffic on the bridge." He directed his deputy to a seat. "You wanted a chat."

"Hmmm." Kemp crossed his legs and placed his hands together over his knee, measuring his words. "I fear we may have a rogue agent, boss."

If Kemp's words were designed to evoke a reaction from Ashton he was unsuccessful.

"How so?"

"We've had a rather curious word from a senior civil servant who alleges that our very own newly appointed Secretary of State for International Trade, Liam Scott has accepted rather a substantial bribe from Crown Prince Dr. Mansour Almazroui in respect of their purchase from us of a desalination plant."

"How much?"

"Ten mill. But apparently it's not to line his own pockets. It's to add to the dark money washing around Northern Ireland politics...money that seems to end up shaping the political debate here on the mainland."

"Do we know why Almazroui is doing this?"

"Not yet. But if it's confirmed it'll be a clear attempt by a foreign power to influence British politics. But of course, of most immediate concern to the agency here is the additional suggestion that a proportion of the money has been disbursed to one of our own to finance activity beyond our ambit of control. If that is true we have a rogue agent who is well financed and using our intelligence to undertake God knows what in our name."

"What proportion?"

"Half."

"So some bugger is wandering around these offices with five million pounds sterling to act out their own agenda?"

"Looks that way, boss."

"Who's the civil servant?"

"Guy called Andrew Fletcher. He's quite senior in International Trade but while content to pass on the information, he doesn't want to go public or blow any whistles. He insists if he's put on the spot he'll deny everything as he's due to retire soon, suffers from high blood pressure and won't place either his health or his pension in jeopardy. 'Fraid he'll have to remain a faceless civil servant."

"That's fair enough. He's done the right thing speaking quietly to you although you might want to speak to him yourself in confidence to ensure that we have all the information he's able to give us."

Ashton tapped a pencil on the edge of a coffee cup as he pondered the situation before continuing.

"This has all the hallmarks of something that could end very badly for us. Our reputation would be reduced substantially if we don't deal with this internally. It is quite as bad both reputationally and operationally as having a bloody spy in the camp. And if the money is used to promote a political party and its policies...which is the entire bloody purpose of the dark money we've seen expended in the last two referendums...our goose is well and truly cooked. It'd be a scandal of the first water."

"It *would*, Sir Humphrey. And if we learned anything from Northern Ireland it was that public awareness of scurrilous activity by the security forces merely acts as a recruiting sergeant for those who would challenge the state."

"Indeed...And these facts are known by?"

"Well, the Minister in question, probably his PPS, Mr. Fletcher, you and me...and the recipient agent who may or may not have support in here for what he...or she...is trying to accomplish."

"And worryingly," interrupted Ashton, "if he or she is capable of this duplicity, what other treachery might they be disposed to carry out?" His demeanour took on a more serious disposition. "We must treat this exactly as if we have uncovered a spy in the camp."

He rose and walked to his sun-lit window.

"You need to speak directly with Liam Scott M.P., our Secretary of State for International Trade and threaten him with imprisonment if he doesn't tell us everything that took place in Saudi. I'll also haul in his Permanent Secretary...what's his name?"

"Lucas Bennett, boss."

"Lucas Bennett...well, suggest he brushes up on his knowledge of the Welsh language as he'll need it to count sheep in his new job in Anglesey or somewhere equally remote. You talk with Mr. Fletcher and invite further reflection on what he can tell us but allow the man some elbow room. He's trying to be helpful. I'm also going to give some thought into how we might unearth this agent of ours who thinks it's all right to play fast and loose with our resources and reputation. Let's meet again tomorrow to review progress."

"Certainly, boss."

* * *

Morrison rolled over in bed and consulted the hotel's alarm clock. Mid-morning. *Well, it's the Sabbath and I must have needed the sleep,* he reckoned. *I've been burning the candle at both ends down in London.* He rose and looked from the window of the Europa Hotel, whose reputation as the most bombed hotel in Europe, having suffered thirty-six bomb attacks during the Troubles, seemed other-worldly given its present four-star plushness. Outside, the sun shone on a peaceful city much removed from its gory and violent past. He sat on the edge of his bed mulling over the decisions he'd made the night before. *I phone my findings in to Kemp and he calls me home to London...hmmm. I buy some time and ask Iona to dinner tonight, then I phone Kemp and ask for instructions. Much more sensible,* he decided.

He lifted his phone from the dressing table and pressed Iona's contact number. It was answered almost immediately.

"Donald John! I was beginning to think you were stuck in London."

"Hi, Iona. No, I've been working since I arrived yesterday and I've just woken up. It's unlike me. Normally I'm an early riser but it must have done me good." He rubbed the sleep from his eyes. "I take it you travelled safely?"

"Absolutely. Got in yesterday afternoon. Emily picked me up and we had a good old blether and too many girly drinks. In Belfast too! I could have murdered a pint of the black stuff. I wanted to go to the Crown Bar but Emily wanted cocktails and it's her city so I relented."

"Well, I'm staying in the Europa Hotel directly across the road from the Crown. How d'you fancy a bite to eat followed by a few jars in the Crown tonight?" He checked himself. "I mean for you *and* Emily."

"No way! I'm keeping you for myself. Emily's *far* too good looking. I'd end up having to talk to the barman. Anyway she's working the back shift. If she's not too tired maybe she'll join us later on in the Crown."

Morrison's spirits lifted at the smile in Iona's voice.

"Okay, well that's settled. Is Emily's apartment near the city centre?"

"She's a flat on University Road. Perfect for her job in City Hospital and just a few minute's walk from your hotel."

"Well, why don't I meet you somewhere near you and we..."

"Don't be daft. I'll meet you in your hotel, we'll dine locally and sashay over to the Crown."

"If you're sure..."

"Seven o'clock?"

"See you then. Casual dress," said Morrison.

"Only kind I have. Denim breeks, denim shirt, denim jacket. The denim cocktail dress is at the cleaners."

"See you later."

Morrison ended the call and smiled at his own reflection in the phone screen. *I'm like the cat who got the cream. Look at me smiling like an idiot.* He considered his plan of action. *The hotel gym, a shower, bit of lunch, a walk, write up my notes on Father Gerry...then meet Iona. Perfect!*

Chapter Fourteen

A light afternoon shower curtailed Morrison's walk slightly, but had permitted more time to review and amplify his report on Father Gerry Warren. Comfortable that he'd be able to send it to Kemp using encrypted messaging in the morning, he inspected himself in the mirror behind the hotel bar as he awaited the arrival of Iona Forbes. He rebuked himself quietly as he found himself checking his watch for the third time. *Seven o'clock means seven o'clock to me but I suppose she'll be fashionably late.*

At seven minutes past the hour, a fourth check of his watch coincided with Iona's arrival. True to her earlier promise she'd worn an all-denim jacket and jeans with matching denim shirt. A bright yellow handbag so small it could only have contained credit cards was strapped across her body like a bandolier loop. A badge representing the Scottish Saltire which was pinned to her jacket completed the accoutrements.

"Am I late?" she asked, smiling.

"You look gorgeous," replied Morrison, ignoring her question, hugging her tentatively and receiving a slight peck on the cheek in return. "Love the country and western appearance. You look like a young Shania Twain."

"Iona raised a leg to present the left of a pair of cowboy boots she was wearing as part of the ensemble. I'll take that as a compliment. I'm a fan of hers."

Drinks were ordered with Iona again sticking to her earlier stated preference for a pint of stout. Morrison followed suit but asked for a half pint and a Glenlivet malt to which he added a small drop of water. They toasted light-heartedly and sat at a nearby table.

"So this is the most bombed hotel in Europe? Should I be concerned?"

"Some say the world... It's certainly unusual to find hotel blurb upon arrival that boasts of being blown up thirty-six times then tells you about room service and how to get an outside line. But it's fine now. And just across the road from your preferred pub."

Small talk continued along with an agreement that eating in the hotel was preferable to scouting the neighbourhood for two seats in a restaurant. Lots of chat continued about island life and Iona's work in the hospital. Morrison knew he'd be asked about his work duties in Northern Ireland and was ready when the question was broached by his dinner companion.

"I'm speaking to some people about the way some trawlers go about fishing up here." he lied. "There's evidence that some of them are bottom trawling. It's one of the most damaging methods of fishing because they use huge nets weighed down with ballast that get dragged down the sea bed, collecting and dragging everything that is in their way from fish to aquatic plants. They inadvertently catch a lot of different species and some are at a risk of extinction. The trawlers just return them to the sea and they're normally dead."

"That's horrible!"

"Yeah. We're trying to stop it."

"And have you many more people to see? Will you be here for a while or are you disappearing back to noisy old London town before the sweet course arrives?"

Morrison shrugged. "Don't know yet. I've a phone call back to London tomorrow morning and that'll guide my departure date." He smiled. "I'm going to try to find a way to stay on for a bit. Perhaps I'll tell them that I've discovered bottom trawling in swimming pools in Belfast."

His smile was rewarded by a reciprocal chuckle. "That'd be good. I've not seen you in yonks."

"You saw me a few weeks ago at the independence march. I seem to remember leaving it with a painful limp."

More giggles. "No wonder. You were lying in that wee lane with your bare backside flapping in the breeze. Fortunately you had prompt and expert medical care from a gifted anaesthetist."

"That I did...that I did..."

Morrison acknowledged both the humour and the truth in her statement. "Scottish Independence means a lot to you, doesn't it?"

"My work at the hospital, my health, family, friends and Scottish Independence are the complete focus of my life. I don't care for more money than I need to live, I don't care about life's fripperies but I am passionate about Scotland being able to make its own decisions."

"Is it a romantic thing, Iona? Like saluting the Saltire or singing *Scots Wha Hae* instead of the god-awful dirge they sing down south?"

"Nah...it's about creating a fairer society. In London the politicians are mostly spivs trying to make further millions on the backs of the poor. I'd like to think Scotland can do better. Presently there's every hope we can do so. Our Parliament in Edinburgh does us proud. Trust me, I'm absolutely committed to Scottish independence. I'll fight the Unionists until Hell freezes over and then I'll fight them on the ice."

"So it's not about *'Bruce and loyal Wallace'*?"

Iona responded by placing her right fist over her heart.

"But pith and power, till my last hour,
I'll mak this declaration;
We're bought and sold for English gold,
Such a parcel of rogues in a nation,'"

She finished the Burns' quote before continuing. "Sure it's about the past, although I cherish our history...a history we were denied at school...but it's about the future. I'm not a Scot who thinks we're better than anyone else. I'm just a proud Scot who refuses to accept that we're *inferior* to everyone else...that we're not the *equal* of everyone else. Too many of our 'House Jocks', our *'Parcel o' Rogues'*, want to cringe and bend the knee to what they view as a superior English culture. Surely, even with all your recent London experience you've not joined the Unionist cause?"

"Far from it, Iona. I believe in everything you've just said. It's just that as a civil servant, I'm not supposed to show partiality."

Forbes could hardly hide her disparagement.

"Partiality? *Hah*! In 2015, Sir Nicholas Macpherson, the civil servant in charge of the transport portfolio said something along the lines of 'when it comes to the referendum on Scottish Independence, the normal rules of civil service impartiality do not apply. We're all Unionists in the cause'."

Morrison nodded his assent. "That's certainly the attitude I've come across. Anyone who put their Scottish Independence head above the parapet would soon find it removed from their shoulders. They'd have kittens if they knew I was breaking bread with a swivel-eyed, committed *Independentista* like you!"

"Aye, I'll bet that's true. And David Cameron before he stepped down as Prime Minister, gave Queen's Honours to the senior civil servants who had led his campaign to keep Scotland chained to England. They were quoted as saying how delighted they were to be allowed to become involved in an overtly political activity, something normally denied them. The Establishment down there is viciously opposed to devolution never mind independence. Scotland's treated exactly as an English colony and it's not something I'm going to put up with."

Morrison raised his eyebrows. "Wow, I can see you're committed."

"You bet your *life* I am!"

Starter and main course along with another round of drinks advanced their conversation until, emboldened, Morrison asked the question that had troubled him since he'd phoned Iona from London.

"And did you have a nice time with Hamish the other night?"

Forbes eyes brightened at the thought.

"Oh, it was lovely. He's such a nice guy. We just had a few drinks in the Dark Island and he dedicated a song he sang to me, '*Eileen Beag Donn a 'chuain'*.' It was very sweet of him." She redirected the focus of the conversation. "D'you know, he should take up singing professionally. His voice is so beautiful. Although maybe his repertoire of Gaelic songs wouldn't be enough to propel him to the top of the charts. But maybe a ceilidh band might pick him up."

"Aye, he's a great singer," allowed Morrison. "And a good friend."

"And he's a good friend of mine as well, Donald John. As are you," she continued.

Morrison plucked up the courage to ask the question he'd manufactured as a consequence of his alcohol intake and attempted to present an indifference he didn't feel.

"So have we got a wee romance, going there then?"

Iona looked at him strangely. "No, we certainly do *not*!"

Relieved but surprised at her vehemence, Morrison stumbled over his words.

"I was just...I thought that maybe you..."

"Well, you thought wrong, Donald John Morrison." She stared hard at the half empty glass of Guinness before her and her tone changed.

"Look, I've been hurt by men before. Twice. I thought I was in love with them. One was a medical student when I was studying in Glasgow, the other was an older man, an epidemiologist in the Southern General when I did my training there. They both cheated on me. They both lied and I decided then that men were no good for me. That in the future, I'd only have men as friends due to them being lying, untrustworthy, heart-breaking deceivers."

Somewhat taken aback by the resolve of her conviction, Morrison attempted a defence.

"But *all* men aren't like that, Iona. It's like saying all *women* are meek or temptresses or nags or..."

"I'm aware of that logic, Donald John but I'm afraid it's how I feel. As friends, I'm delighted to have a good number of men whose company I really enjoy...like *you* here tonight...but as far as trusting men, well, I'm just being honest. I've been lied to too often and they hurt me deeply,"

Morrison allowed a silence mulling over her words. *A good number of men whose company I enjoy?* Uncertain whether to be pleased that he'd been admitted as a good friend or disappointed that all men were off the 'deeper relationship' menu he suggested they drink up and visit the Crown Bar across the road.

Iona's mood changed immediately.

"Excellent. I've heard so much about it. Let's go."

***

Entering the busy bar, Iona and Donald John peered over the carved wooden enclosures in an attempt to find an empty booth. All but one were occupied and the empty snug had a reserved sign on the door handle.

"We're out of luck, Iona. Why don't we order at the bar and keep an eye out for anyone leaving."

They each consumed a pint of Guinness in smart order and a further two were purchased.

"Your capacity to down the black stuff bewilders me, Iona. You have the body of an Olympian but throw amounts back that would fell a Highland shot-putter."

"I don't do it very often. And anyway, you're one to talk. You're in great shape by the look of you."

"Punishing hours in the gymnasium. I don't have your genes." He sipped his Guinness thoughtfully. "But you can hold your drink as well. I have pals who'd be on their back after what you've consumed."

A dimpled smile mitigated Iona's tease.

"Ah, well don't you be thinking about these drinks putting *me* on my back Mr. Morrison. I thought I'd made myself clear on that point."

Just in time, Morrison recognised the bait and merely smiled as Forbes continued.

"Although, of all my men friends..." She left the sentence unfinished.

"What?" invited Morrison.

"Och, I'm just flirting and being stupid." She paused then continued. "Well...let's just say, you'd be my *favourite* best male friend."

Taken aback, Morrison could only mumble, "I'm flattered." Taking his courage in both hands he pressed on. "And if it's any help..." He bit his lip as he approached words of no return. "You'd be my favourite best *female* friend."

Iona's face reddened as the significance of the conversation was appreciated by both. Suddenly she frowned.

"That man!"

Morrison turned to look in the direction of Iona's gaze.

"The man who just went in to that reserved booth. I know him from somewhere."

"Maybe someone from the hotel?"

"Don't think so." She thought further trying to place the face she'd seen.

"Never mind."

Before returning his attention to Iona, Morrison noticed a two further men bring drinks from the bar and enter the booth.

"Christ, that's...that's..."

"Who?"

Morrison immediately appreciated the prospect of his cover story unravelling.

"Nah...probably mistaken. Thought it was a guy who'd attended a meeting I had last night in Belfast."

"A fisherman's friend?" joked Iona"

"Aye...something like that," said Morrison distantly.

"You look serious, Donald John. Is he one of those horrible bottom trawler men?"

Trying to salvage his cover story, Morrison mumbled a guarded reply, turned again to Iona and attempted to offer a reassuring smile.

"I'm off duty. It can wait."

Two further rounds were taken and as words began to become slurred, Morrison proposed a night-cap back at the hotel across the road. Taking Iona by the arm, he began to guide her through the tight, remaining throng of people when the booth door opened and stepping in front of him was Henry J. Carson, Assistant Grand Master of Plumbridge Purple Heroes Loyal Orange Lodge 560.

Instinctively, Morrison greeted him.

"Henry J.!"

Quickly realising he couldn't allow Iona to hear anything of their conversation he turned to his drinking companion.

"Meet you outside?"

Thinking little of it, Iona walked towards the door and left Morrison to his conversation with the Ulsterman.

"So is this your local?"

A second man emerged from the booth and seeing Carson in discourse, eased past him. A third man followed, scowling.

Morrison eyed the doorway to ensure that Iona was outside and continued his drunken chat.

"Just in for a coupla beers," he explained. "Good chatting to you last night. Quite a man, our Father Gerry, eh?"

Carson was as curt and unforthcoming as he was earlier, making do with a series of 'Ayes' and half-smiles while his eyes darted anxiously towards the door where the two other men were exiting.

His senses dulled by drink, Morrison merely placed his hand on Carson's shoulder and bid him a good night, watching him as he left to join his fellow drinkers outside.

Funny wee guy, thought Morrison as he slowly pushed his way past fellow topers to return his glass to the counter and then, equally slowly, manoeuvre his way towards the pub doorway. Outside stood Iona with a frown on her face. She acknowledged Morrison with a question.

"The wee fellah who came out told the other two that you were a journalist from the Guardian and they started having a furious row. They threatened him and it was something about guns, shooting and wrecking their plans. Why would they think you were a journalist?"

Morrison thought quickly.

"Och, I was mistaken, Iona. The wee guy was drunk. *Really* drunk. I just apologised for mistaking him for someone I worked with and he thought he recognised my face as a sports journalist with the Belfast Telegraph. We both laughed it off."

Iona wasn't to be assuaged. "And that other man. The taller guy. I know him from somewhere. I just can't place him."

"Maybe another drink'll help your memory, eh?" He steered Iona across the road. She took his arm affectionately as he did.

The hotel bar was still busy as they approached. Morrison assessed the depth of customers prior to finding space to place an order when Iona intervened, mischievously.

"Don't you have a minibar in your room."

Flummoxed at the weight of her question, Morrison stammered a response.

"Well sure...I mean I've not looked but...I thought..."

"This bar is crowded, let's try your very own bar. If there's nothing decent to drink you can usually guarantee a Toblerone. Drink or chocolate...either work for me. C'mon! An early night is a night wasted".

She re-took Morrison's arm and guided him towards the lift.

Attempting to take command of the situation, Morrison stepped over to the concierge and asked him to send a bottle of champagne and two glasses to his room...

"As soon as you like!"

He re-joined Iona at the lift. "Let's not take chances. I've ordered a bottle."

Iona smiled a dimpled smile and placed her hand on the calling buttons.

"What floor"

"Seven."

Now woozy, the couple stepped from the lift and entered Morrison's room.

"Very nice."

"Make yourself comfortable."

"I'll just use the facilities first if I may," responded Iona as she disappeared into the bathroom.

Morrison took off his jacket and sat on the edge of his bed. *Didn't think the evening would end like this*, he thought. He squeezed his eyes and asked himself whether a coffee would not be a better idea than more alcohol. Removing his shoes, he walked round the bed and closed the curtains before sitting heavily on an armchair. *I'm drunk* he decided.

A shout from within the bathroom made him jump. Iona opened the door, her face flushed.

"I *knew* I recognised that man," she declared. "*Knew* it!" She sat on the edge of the bed and faced Morrison. "When you got shot in Glasgow...*he* was the man who was in the lane with that gang of yobs. I'd swear it!"

Morrison furrowed his brow in thought. "You might be right. I'd need to see him again."

The urgent demands of his bladder decided his next move.

"I need to go a place."

As he entered the toilet the door of the hotel room a knock was heard along with a call of, "Room service."

Precedence being given to his bladder, Morrison reached into his pocket and threw his wallet to Iona. "That'll be the Champagne. It'll be on my bill but there's some notes and a fiver in my wallet, Iona. Would you tip the guy?"

He locked the door and emptied his bladder, washed his hands and dried them before re-emerging into the hotel room. Before him stood a stern-looking Iona holding his wallet.

"These fell out!"

Morrison's heart sank as he recognised the three identification cards she held in her hands.

"So are you an MI5 Intelligence Officer, a member of the Salvation Army or a journalist?"

"Iona..."

Silent tears rolled down her cheeks. "Just when I thought I might be able to trust a man..."

"You *can* trust me, Iona. I'm just not allowed..."

"You lied to me from the very start. In the Dark Island Hotel, you *lied*. You told me you worked for Agriculture and Fisheries. You *lied*. You told me you were over here to discuss fishing. You *lied*. You told me I was your best female friend. You *lied*. You told me you wanted to drink in the Crown with me when all you wanted to do was keep watch on your murky spy friends."

"Iona! I didn't!"

"You're the same as all the rest."

She lifted the small yellow handbag she'd left on the bed and pulled the strap over her head in readiness for departure.

"And these men in the pub. They were no *fishermen*. One was involved in trying to shoot you a few weeks ago and the three of them argued about guns and plans...probably to shoot you *again*!"

"No, Iona."

Tears rolled down her face, glistening her cheeks. "You're just like all the others, Donald John Morrison."

The slamming of the door brought a measure of finality to the conversation.

Chapter Fifteen

The following morning, as the rush hour eased along with a light drizzle falling from an ash-grey sky, Rotermundt walked slowly along the length of Belfast's Duncairn Gardens, a 'peace line' which separated the city's Republican New Lodge area and the Ulster Loyalist enclave of Tiger Bay. Standing outside a converted church now recycled to bring culture to the denizens of Belfast, was the elderly man he knew as Morecambe who welcomed Rotermundt.

"You're feckin' late".

"New area to me. Didn't want to take a taxi. I'm here now!"

"And is that bag you're carrying full of readies?"

"It is, but it won't find its way into your possession unless the two guns we discussed are on your person."

Morecambe shook his head. "We don't do these things in the feckin' street, fellah. Follow me. It's not far."

Warily, Rotermundt followed a now silent Irish republican into a notoriously partisan loyalist area. A few minutes' walk along industrialised Edlingham Street and a right turn past a small allotment into Hogarth Street was punctuated by increasing numbers of flags denoting support for the Union, Rangers Football Club and the Democratic Unionist Party. Morecambe stopped outside number forty-two and cautiously checked his surroundings for anything suspicious. Deciding that all was well, he tilted his head to one side, directing Rotermundt into a red brick two up, two down nondescript dwelling house. The name on the door, noticed Rotermundt, was Spence.

Without knocking, Morecambe opened the door and entered. Rotermundt followed. In the living room, his head covered in a black balaclava sat a man pointing a gun at the doorway. He lowered it as Morecambe and Rotermundt entered and took charge of the meeting.

"Now, Mr. Morecambe here knows me well but you never will. And in case you think this address is important you should know that it's not. It's just somewhere we're using to conduct this exchange. The real owners know feck all about our meetin' here today...so I won't be offerin' you a cup of tea, largely on the basis that we don't know where the feckin' *tea* bags are."

"He says he brought the money," interrupted Morecambe.

"On the table," instructed the gunman.

Rotermundt unstrapped the briefcase he carried and emptied the contents on the table.

"Twenty thousand for each gun. There's forty grand there..." He turned to Morecambe who stood in the doorframe..."as we discussed and agreed."

"Do I need to count it?" asked Balaclava.

"It's forty grand on the nose," insisted Rotermundt.

"Still..."

The gunman stood and placing the handgun into his waistband behind him, walked stiffly to the window beneath which lay a black backpack.

"Mr. Morecambe, would you be a decent fellah and count those notes while I explain to your friend here exactly what he's buyin' if everything's okay, like?"

He took a pair of disposable gloves, put them on, unzipped the bag and produced two brown, oiled cloth wrappings which he laid on the settee beside him as he sat back on its floral cushions. He unwrapped the fabric on one of them until a pistol emerged.

"This here, my friend, is a nine millimetre Glock handgun. It's a first-generation pistol. You can tell by its smoother grip. It's a 1982 handgun and still in perfect workin' order. It's a short recoil semi-automatic pistol that uses a linkless, vertically tiltin' barrel with a rectangular breech that locks into the ejection port cut-out in the slide. It comes with twenty rounds."

He placed it gently on a cushion and unwrapped the second gun.

"Now this wee beauty is a Brownin'. It's a 'Hi-Power' which is one of the most widely used military pistols in history." He nodded appreciatively at the pedigree of the weapon. "It's been used by the armed forces of over fifty countries so it's got decent form. It incorporates a shortened, thirteen round magazine, a curved rear grip strap and a barrel bushing that is integral to the slide assembly. Now, one thing you'll need to watch out for is that this pistol has a tendency to bite your hand between your thumb and forefinger. This can be fixed by alterin' or replacing the hammer or by learnin' to hold the feckin' thing properly to avoid injury. And that is what *you'll* do. Take it somewhere quiet and try it out. It's a great gun but when you come to use it in anger, carry it with the hammer cocked, a round in the chamber and the safety catch on. Over in the States, they call this 'cocked and locked'. Over *here* it's called 'common feckin' sense'. Now, this gun was used to shoot a 31-year-old Protestant RUC reservist in Ballymena and its friend here, the Glock, killed a postman who was a part time member of the Loyalist Volunteer Force. I knew the postman bastard and he deserved it. Both guns were captured and both were used to convict our people so the Brits have all the ballistics on them but we managed to liberate them so if and when you use them they'll be traced back to these shootin's almost immediately. I understand that traceability is important to you."

Rotermundt was impressed. "You know your weapons, sir."

Morecambe interrupted for the second time as he finished counting the wads of money. "It's all here, Biro."

The balaclava sighed loudly. "Feckin' *names*, Morecambe...*names*! Now I'll need to shoot this fecker because he's heard my name."

Rotermundt's startled face brought a guffaw from behind the balaclava. "Don't sweat it, fellah. If anyone's gettin' shot it's this stupid fecker. Morecambe here. And by the intelligent way of you, I'm thinkin' that you're not stupid enough to remember anythin'...and I mean *anythin'*...of our transaction here this mornin'...because as sure as night follows day, you'd be found and then *lost,* if you have my meanin'."

Some colour had returned to Rotermundt's face.

"You need have no worries on my account."

Balaclava stood and placed his face only inches from Rotermundt's.

"I *don't*! Mr. Morecambe here will take you back to the civilised side of town. We won't meet again."

* * *

Morrison had showered, shaved and completed and reviewed his report on Father Gerry Warren. He pressed the button closing his tablet computer. Ruefully, as he sat in the edge of his hotel bed, he remonstrated with himself over the denouement of the previous evening's events. *I'm meant to be James fucking Bond and I've the track record of Inspector fucking Clouseau. The one person with whom I've found myself taken and I make a complete arse of it. She'll never talk to me again!* He consulted his watch. *Ten-thirty.* He'd arranged to telephone his superior, Jack Kemp at ten-forty. Stoically, he set aside his emotional problems and focused upon his operational ones.

Precisely at the time requested, he placed the call to Kemp. It was answered directly without any intermediaries.

"Kemp!"

"Morning, sir. Donald John Morrison here. You asked me to phone at ten-forty this morning."

"Ah, yes. How are things going? Have you tracked down the son of *Herr* Schicklgruber?"

"Think so, sir. I spent an evening in his company. His name is Gerald Warren and he's a priest here in Belfast. There's no doubt as to his lineage and it would also appear that he's not *Herr* Schicklgruber's son. He's about six feet three and sturdy. I fully suspect that he's the son of one of the blond SS Stormtroopers of whom Ms. Mitford was evidently so fond. He's now aged in his eighties and I have to say, perfectly convivial company. He's spent his life as a clergyman and appears to have no knowledge of his alleged antecedent. Because he's a priest, one would have to assume that he himself has no progeny, so the line stops with him. Certainly, he doesn't appear to be a man of any malice. I've also checked out newspaper reports on his activities during the Irish Troubles and he appears to be very much a man of peace. When I met with him in the Parish House, he was in the company of the Assistant Grand Master of Plumbridge Purple Heroes Loyal Orange Lodge. Guy called Henry J. Carson. He has friends across the religious divide and as far as I can tell would be absolutely no threat to the stability of Ulster or to the rise of Fascism in the UK. I also managed to obtain a drinking vessel and a card that should provide our forensic people with fingerprints and a DNA sample...but he's not our man. I'm sure of that. I've written it up and will provide this in report form once we conclude our conversation."

The line went silent for a moment before Kemp spoke.

"Excellent work, Mr. Morrison."

"Perhaps one strange thing, sir. I had cause to be in the Crown Liquor Saloon last night. It's a very famous bar in Belfast."

"I know it."

"Well, the friend of Father Gerry...the Loyalist Henry J. Carson I mentioned...he was there and acting suspiciously. He was with a couple of other people and they gathered outside the pub and discussed guns, shootings and...well, it just made me uneasy. I wondered if you might arrange to have any CCTV cameras interrogated so we might identify the people involved and possibly even overhear what they were discussing."

"You still in Belfast?"

"Yes, sir."

"Stay there for the time being. You've done a good job. I'll do as you suggest and contact you on this secure line once I've something to report. We might do some more follow up on Warren once we analyse the prints and DNA but in the meantime, take in the sights and have another Guinness in the Crown. I'll have that glass and card collected by one of our couriers today at noon."

"Sir."

Morrison ended the call and threw the phone lightly on the bed. *So I'm going to be around for a few more days by the look of it. Maybe there's hope for me and Iona yet!*

Chapter Sixteen

The Director-General of MI5 picked up his phone and pressed a button. Almost instantly it was answered by his Deputy, Jack Kemp. Sir Humphrey Ashton almost barked into the phone.

"Who've we got on Scotland?"

"Eh, Bob Cavendish."

"Fuck!" He paused. "So be it. Ask that bloody dandy of yours, Sir Robert Cavendish to join you and me in my office immediately. You free?"

"Certainly."

"Join me first while Cavendish's on his way up, eh?"

Another pressed button permitted him to ask his elderly personal secretary to delay Sir Robert Cavendish in the outer office until called.

A few moments later Kemp entered Ashton's office and sat across from him. Ashton rose and gestured towards a set of armchairs. They sat facing one another.

"We need to get to the bottom of this agent who's about to shaft us, Jack." He looked at him hopefully. "Made any progress?"

"I've some thoughts I was going to share with you. But not in front of Cavendish."

"You don't trust him?"

"It's not that really, boss. Just don't like the cut of his jib. I've always found him mannered and effete. He lives on Champagne, cigarettes and compliments. He's high maintenance and Cambridge. I'm relaxed and Loughborough. He's upper class and posh. I'm middle class and drink beer; my one imperfection being an occasional weakness for a fine wine. He's so bloody insincere in his dealings with anyone superior within the organisation. When he smiles it's like his teeth are on the outside of his face!"

"Can't disagree."

Having dealt with his mild personal disapproval of Cavendish, Kemp turned to the role he'd been allocated.

"Last year, you gave him the task of monitoring and steering the political situation in Scotland. I've met with him a few times and everything he seems to be doing is pretty much straight down the middle. He has the 77th Brigade interfering with the pro-independence social media, he has meetings with the BBC, the Telegraph, Mail and Express to beef up the Government Expenditure and Revenue for Scotland data to argue that Scotland's an economic basket case. He has links with a host of academics each of whom are eager to be interviewed on their views of the idiocy of independence, that sort of thing. Importantly, he has a number of agents embedded within ancillary organisations that surround the independence movement; organising marches, galvanising the woman's vote, that sort of thing and he'll shortly be orchestrating them to act as 'splitters' to divide the movement. As you're aware, we have very senior members of the SNP hierarchy on our books and at least one of them's little able to resist our requests for assistance due to his unfortunate enthusiasm for ladies with whips and chains. We're well practised in this as you know, our experience in colonies across the globe teaching us a thing or two about the worth of divisiveness." He paused to check that his examples were sufficient but hearing no discouragement, continued. "Our Embassies are now quietly being difficult in respect of any Scottish use of their services. He's hacked several phones of interest but assures me he has warrants for each of them and he's in touch with the Palace mandarins to keep the Queen on-side. Fairly anodyne and nothing illegal. He seems to get on well with the Home Secretary. Gets on well with the Shadow Home Secretary. Even gets on well with the Leader of the SNP at Westminster... largely because he has all the charm of a snake oil salesman," he said reverting to his personal dislike of the man.

Ashton held his counsel, merely harrumphing.

"Prime Minister's just been on. He's worried about his private polling that shows the 'Yes' movement in Scotland pulling away from the Unionist vote. I need a report from Cavendish that I can hand the PM to show that we're doing everything within our purview to protect the Union without crossing the line into illegality and without our efforts being noticed by the Nationalists or the media."

"I can get that. Why d'you want Cavendish here before you?"

"Just to put some fire in his belly. He's always struck me as all gong and no dinner!"

"Well, why don't you leave that to me? It's pretty straightforward stuff and anyway, I want to use this time to raise another matter with you."

His temper eased, Ashton conceded the point.

"Okay. Over to you. Now what's up?"

"Given the sensitivity of this dark money, I'm not sure we want to deal with matters in some grand, collaborative, inter-departmental fashion as might normally be the case. Our Scottish *teuchter* (he pronounced it *tyooktah)* appears to have come up trumps in regard to that Hitler baby thing. He's sent me a full report and it's pretty certain that the eighty-one year old man, the son of Unity Mitford who's been a six foot plus Roman Catholic priest his entire life, is actually the progeny of some lusty Stormtrooper and not the German Chancellor. I have it all here." He placed a printed copy of Morrison's report on the coffee table next to the Director General. "Morrison also got fingerprints and a DNA sample. They'll be in the lab shortly but he's done well."

Ashton nodded his approval.

"*So*, well, I wondered if he might not be of even *more* use to us."

"Go on!"

"Well, Morrison's shown that he's no fool. He's an outlier. Joined us from Agriculture And Fisheries..."

"And Food," reminded Ashton, smiling.

"Indeed. He's an islander as you know. Educated at Edinburgh, not Oxford or Cambridge. A recent recruit from an outlying department... and *most* unlikely to be involved in any way with this mole we appear to have spending dark money on our behalf. I guess my attitude is somewhat coloured by the fact of several of our agents in the past; Donald Maclean, Guy Burgess, John Cairncross, Kim Philby and Anthony Blunt were all recruited as Soviet spies while at Cambridge University in the 1930s. Sir Roger Hollis, the Director General who sat at your desk in the sixties, was also accused of being a double agent and his appointed 'Witch-finder-General', Peter Wright, were both members of MI5 educated at Oxford. Over the piece, we've not done too well when we've used Oxbridge toffs to investigate other Oxbridge toffs within the agency. You and I at least were spared the elite education of many of the patrician popinjays who still inhabit our organisation in senior roles."

Ashton indicated 'no contest' to Kemp's assertion by a low guttural murmur before continuing.

"And Morrison could help how?"

"Presently he's in Belfast. He spoke to me about a conversation that took place outside a pub he was in where money, guns and shooting was being discussed. As you know, this dark money we're concerned about is routed through Northern Ireland. Morrison has already done great work on the power-sharing situation out there and seems to have the nous and some decent enough contacts to get to the bottom of this. I spoke with him earlier today and have managed to have the CCTV footage he sought investigated. There's no audio but it shows four people of interest to us in concert."

"And who might they be?"

"The footage shows us pretty clearly that the first individual is a chap called Henry John Carson. He's the Assistant Grand Master of Plumbridge Purple Heroes Loyal Orange Lodge 560. A long-term Unionist. Previous convictions mostly for disorderly conduct, the kind of CV every self-respecting Ulster Unionist would aspire to. He was meeting a previous member of the IRA, chap called Daniel Sean Kelly who did two years for paramilitary activities in the seventies; interned in Long Kesh camp near Lisburn. The third person is Conservative Councillor Emil Rotermundt from Glasgow. He is second generation Dutch but has a British passport. He chairs a secretive organisation called the 'Council for the Union', a Unionist funding organisation based in Portrush that has used dark money over a period of several years to fund the anti-independence campaign during the 2014 Scottish Independence Referendum as well as the Brexit Campaign. It appears to be its sole function and because of the legal circumstances that apply in Northern Ireland, there are no requirements to publish accounts showing the beneficiaries of their largesse."

"And the fourth person?"

"Even more interesting. She's Iona McKenzie Forbes. Age thirty-one. Single. Works as a nurse anaesthetist serving the Western Isles NHS but her spare time is spent as an enthusiastic member of the secretive 'Seed of the Gael'...it has a Gaelic name that defeats me..."

"It's pronounced '*Siol nan Gaidheal*'."

"Ah, I'd forgotten you have the *Gaelic*, boss."

"A little. Enough to say 'hello' and buy rolls and milk up in Lewis."

"Well, as you'll know, it's a Scottish ultra-Nationalist organisation whose focus on the face of it is Scotland's historic national and cultural community. Very much on the left, it's, we *think*, likely to promote violence and civil disobedience, although in recent years they've only gone as far as exhibiting some fairly distasteful banners, let's say *distancing* Scotland from the ruling Conservative Party. The organisation has its roots in other paramilitary organisations like the Scottish National Liberation Army and used to have an offshoot called 'Army of the Gael', which was responsible for a number of petrol bomb attacks back in 1982 and 1983. The organisation was branded proto-fascists by Gordon Wilson, the Leader of the SNP back in 1979, and was proscribed by them. It hasn't really recovered since then but the embers still burn bright. It's a small, very tight-knit group so we've not been able to infiltrate it yet."

"And you think Morrison...?"

"Perhaps, but what on earth an Ulster Unionist, an old IRA soldier, a Scottish Conservative Councillor that manages dark money in support of the union and a member of an ultra-Scottish Nationalist organisation find to talk about outside a Belfast pub escapes me for the moment."

Ashton didn't need many moments before making up his mind.

"Brief Morrison. We might be dealing with a nexus of Scottish Independence, dark money and Unionist perfidy. He seems well placed to investigate. Don't reveal our concerns about a mole but invite him to investigate the dark money that appears to be pouring into Northern Ireland like a veritable Niagara." He pursed his lips in thought. "Has Morrison undertaken weapons training?"

"Pretty sure he has. I can check."

"Then if so, issue him with a light handgun. Wandering about the highways and byways of a province populated by Republican and Loyalist gunmen might require that he has an ability to defend himself."

"Will do. And I have dinner this evening with Liam Scott M.P., our newly appointed Secretary of State for International Trade, whom we understand to have been the intermediary who has facilitated the funds which are now in the hands of one of our agents."

"Good! Put the fear of God in him! Threats of prosecution and imprisonment usually ruins their digestion."

**

For a few seconds, Donald John Morrison found breathing difficult.

"Still there, Morrison?"

"Yes sir."

"Any questions?"

A further silence. "Let me think further, sir. I'll contact you with any requests although..."

"Yes?"

"Well, a first start might be to intercept the calls of Carson. That would be simple enough. I know from previous experience over here that a warrant would be granted without much trouble. It tends to depend upon which magistrate you approach. I can advise."

"What about Rotermundt and Forbes...even Kelly?"

Morrison's breathing became problematic once again. "Let me think through an approach, sir. Let's just start with Carson."

"As you wish. Keep me abreast of developments. Oh, and by the way, a handgun will be delivered to your hotel. Sign for it. It'll arrive this evening. Can't be too careful."

The line went quiet as Kemp ended the call.

As if placing the top card on a delicately balanced pyramid of others, Morrison gently set his phone on the bed beside him. For some moments he was immobilised in thought. Rising, he approached the window of his hotel room and gazed downward at the slated rooftop and chimney assemblies of the Crown Liquor Saloon. Below was the paved walkway that had witnessed the conversation he was now charged with explaining. After further considerations swam around in his head, he faced up to some uncomfortable truths and marshalled his thoughts. *I've missed the only feasible opportunity to explain to MI5 that Iona Forbes is someone I know well and is actually someone I'm sweet on. That'll come out sooner or later - certainly by Iona's hand as this progresses, so I can probably kiss my job goodbye. Once she appreciates I'm investigating her, she'll instantly assume it all dates back to me meeting her in the Dark Island Hotel bar. And what's that old saying? 'Hell hath no fury like a woman scorned'...Jesus!...so I can also kiss goodbye to any relationship with Iona. And what if this all leads to action against her passion of Scottish independence? Am I becoming the Unionist foot-soldier she accused me of being, where my behaviour runs counter to my own beliefs and values?* Almost robotically he opened the door of the mini-bar, removed a miniature of a blended whisky, unscrewed the top put it to his lips and dispensed in full its contents of fifty millilitres. *And this evening I'm taking delivery of a bloody gun? Jesus Christ...what have I let myself in for?* He reopened the fridge door, realised there were no more whisky miniatures and repeated his ministrations, this time with undiluted Bacardi. His face twisted in displeasure at the unfamiliar taste.

Chapter Seventeen

"I'll come down."

Morrison replaced the room phone on its receiver and tied the laces of his shoes. Deciding against his jacket, he left the room and after a brief wait for a slow elevator, descended to the ground floor where he approached the concierge as requested. Beside the uniformed hotel commissionaire stood a leather-clad figure still wearing a full crash helmet which completely obscured his face. He held a small case.

"Your man here wouldn't leave it with me, sir," said the elderly concierge irritably as if his integrity was being traduced. "Says he has to give it to you direct."

"I need to sign for it," replied Morrison affably.

He took a pen offered him by the motorcycling courier, signed a coded piece of paper confirming that he'd taken responsibility for a handgun and thirty rounds of ammunition and accepted a small metallic case.

"Thanks, everyone."

Morrison turned on his heel and caught the same lift he'd just exited, returned to his room and closed the door behind him. With mixed feelings of excitement and apprehension, he sat on the edge of his bed and opened the case with the six figure code he'd been sent earlier by secure electronic encryption. Inside the case in a perfectly configured mould was a German SIG Sauer P226 pistol, identical to the one he'd been trained with in the West Midlands. He removed it from its silver case and pulled on its slide to check that the magazine was empty. Satisfied, he counted the thirty bullets one by one and loaded nine-fold the parabellum cartridges to fill the chamber. Laying it beside him he checked the safety catch was on, removed the shoulder holster and strap from the case and adjusted it before lacing his arms through the leather straps and positioning it so the gun was positioned under his left arm. He walked to the door, lifted his jacket and put it on before a mirror, attempting to determine whether the weapon could be seen. Impressed by its evident concealment, he removed the gun once more, reminding himself of its light, thirteen-ounce weight, punchy ballistics and consistent accuracy and adopted a pose normally associated with the commencement of a James Bond movie.

Smiling at his childishness, he returned the gun to its holster and removed the apparatus, returning everything neatly to the metallic case.

The secure mobile phone issued him by MI5 rang. He took it from his pocket and glanced at the screen. *Shit, it's Iona.* Uncertain whether to take the call or let it ring out he found himself pressing the accept button whilst still debating the options with himself.

"Hi Iona...listen...."

"No! *You* listen, Donald John."

A silence suggested emotion on the other end of the phone call.

"I'm calling to apologise for my behaviour last night. I'm afraid your estimation of my ability to hold my drink was over-confident. I was drunk and should never have behaved as I did. To be honest, in the cold light of day I should never have been in your room alone with you at all. I was silly and drunk and I just don't know what got into me."

"I'd figure that what got into you would be about five pints of Guinness, Iona," interrupted Morrison. His mind fought for clarity while his mouth uttered words he hadn't thought through. "Look, we were both drunk. I was maybe a bit daft ordering more drink and I was stupid not telling you more about my work. It's just...well, it's just that I'm not allowed to say anything about..."

"Now *you* stop. That's why I'm phoning. I came to realise that unless you work for the Salvation Army, or are a journalist or are a civil servant with Agriculture and Fisheries..."

"And Food..."

"And Food... that you wouldn't be *allowed* to share your responsibilities with me or anyone. I just thought I'd ask one question then *never* ask another question about what you do for a living...and you don't need to answer if you think it contravenes whatever oath you've maybe been asked to take or any Official Secrets Act that you've had to sign."

"One question?"

"Just one. Tell me, does your mother or your best pal Hamish know more about what you do than I might know right at this minute?"

Morrison mulled over an answer.

"I think it's okay to answer that in the negative."

Iona was silent in confusion as she contemplated his response.

"Well..." Tears filled her eyes. "What do I feel about that?" she asked out loud. "I suppose I'm surprised, I'm worried about you, I'm annoyed that you're working for a corrupt government, I'm impressed that you're not exactly the boring civil servant you made yourself out to be... I'm.."

"Look, Iona. I am what I am. Whatever you think, I'm the same Donald John Morrison you've always known. I'm still your friend. You're still my *favourite* female friend. I wasn't drunk when I told you that last night."

A silence lasting many seconds allowed each of them to process the conversation.

It was broken by Iona. "Want to try again? Emily's on the same shift so I'm free for dinner tonight if you're not snooping around in someone's dustbin or meeting Russian agents."

Morrison looked at his watch. "It's nearly seven-thirty now. We could meet at eight here in the hotel if that suits?"

The smile he usually associated with Iona was evident in her reply.

"We have a date. I'll still be wearing denim."

Morrison ended the call. *What just happened there? Was I being invited out on a date with a young lady I'm keen on or was I being targeted as an agent whose responsibilities might be of interest to Siol nan Gaidheal?*

* * *

Jack Kemp stood as Liam Scott M.P. entered the restaurant. In doing so he assisted his identification by the Secretary of State for International Trade and Development as he made his way through occupied tables to greet him.

"Mr. Kemp?" He held his hand out. "I'm delighted to meet you."

"I recognise you from your appearance on Question a Time a couple of weeks back."

"Not my finest hour. I'm only a recent appointment and to be honest I'm a slow learner so I wasn't prepared for some of the questions about my own portfolio never mind those of my Cabinet colleagues."

They both sat and placed napkins over their laps. Kemp had ordered wine and had almost finished his first glass.

"A decent bottle of *Coche-Dury Corton-Charlemagne Grand Cru, 1980*. A good year I'm told, but if you'd prefer red?"

"The white sounds delicious, Mr. Kemp."

Small talk and ordering dishes took some time before Scott's curiosity bettered him.

"Delighted as I am to break bread with the Deputy Director General of MI5, I can only assume that you have something of import to discuss with me beyond my shortcomings as a panellist on Question Time."

"As you'd imagine, Mr. Scott..."

"Call me Liam."

"Let's keep it as Mr. Scott in the meantime."

Scott blanched at the rejection, calculating that the likelihood of the meal being a friendly briefing was ebbing before his eyes.

"We like to keep our eyes on politicians throughout the United Kingdom. Just to make sure that people who are serving the public as you do are working entirely in the interests of the electorate."

Scott's mind raced. *Jesus, he knows about my mistress...no...my family's money in the Cayman Islands.* He attempted to present as coolness personified.

"Well, I can assure you Mr. Kemp that my record as a member of the British Parliament is spotlessly clean."

"Perhaps so, Mr. Scott. And we would be delighted if you continued to serve in your post with such distinguished aplomb."

Scott recognised the implied conditionality of his statement but attempted a lightness of tone.

"Do you imagine there might be a threat to this continuation?"

"Perhaps. I'm dining with you tonight in one of London's finest restaurants. Other of my colleagues not, let's say, as *understanding* as I am, may have insisted on you being interviewed in a police station with the media tipped off beforehand to capture your image as you arrived in handcuffs."

He sipped his wine.

"I prevailed. Journalists can be such bastards, eh?"

Scott's attempted insouciance had evaporated and now immobilised, he held his wine glass precisely half way between the table and his newly dry lips.

Kemp continued. "Is there anything you'd like to share with me that would render you liable to being interviewed in a police station with the media tipped off beforehand?"

Scott's transfixion continued as his mind worked overtime. All he could muster was a shrug of his shoulders and a mild shake of his head. His mouth remained opened.

"The Chief Whip and the Prime Minister don't know we're meeting so there need be no troublesome outcome politically. The media know nothing of our meeting so there need be no troublesome outcome in tomorrow's papers. The police know nothing of our meeting so there need be no troublesome interviews at New Scotland Yard. It's entirely possible that we merely have a pleasant meal and a couple of drinks here tonight and leave as friends who refer to one another as Liam and Jack. It all depends."

Scott summoned up the ability to speak.

"On what?"

"Frankly, Minister upon whether you tell me everything there is to know about your meeting with Sheik Zayed bin Khalifa when you were in Saudi." He leaned across the table and refilled his wine glass, raising his eyebrows in invitation to Scott to accept the same. "But before you answer, might I suggest that you work on the basis that I already know every word that was exchanged between you, and that if your response tonight deviates even slightly from the testimony I already have, we'll just finish our drinks and head home. You'll be visited by uniforms just as you arrive back to see your lovely wife, Jenny and will be arrested in front of her and your children, Piers and Jeremy. We'll work out the charges later on."

He took a further sip. "So, what do you say?"

***

The Europa Hotel restaurant was busy but Morrison had been able to secure a table for two. As was the case on the previous evening, Iona was late by a few minutes but she arrived as promised wearing the same outfit she'd worn the night before.

Morrison stood and gave her a hug; this time the embrace being tighter and slightly more lengthy.

"Sorry about the get-up. I'd only packed for some boozy nights with Emily."

"You look great. Sorry it's the same venue. We might have wandered around Belfast city centre for hours trying to find somewhere suitable...and it *is* just across the road from the Crown if that's not a bridge too far."

Having taken their seats, ordered and eaten the starter course, Morrison leaned into the events of the previous evening.

"I can see now given your experience of mistrust of previous men, that I must have fitted the profile quite neatly. I don't blame you for what you said or did last night."

Contemplatively, Iona placed her gin and tonic on the table having earlier determined that Guinness consumption might have contributed to her previous behaviour.

"I'm a pretty rounded person I think, but there are times when my buttons are pushed and I turn into the Incredible Hulk. I've given this some thought and I don't think you're a deceitful person. I imagine you felt pretty conflicted given your *alleged*," she pulled down on two fingers on each hand mimicking inverted commas, "responsibilities." She went on, "I'm pretty conflicted too. I like truth and honesty over deceit and evasion but I understand that your *alleged* duties, if true, cannot be divulged to another living being and I want you to know that your *secret*," the fingers came out for a second time, "is safe with me". I just want you as a friend and I want you to be safe so it's easier for me to imagine that you're still a dull-as-ditch-water civil servant."

Morrison's had been listening and attempting to convey empathy but broke out in a wide smile.

"Dull as ditch-water?"

"You know what I mean," she grinned. "I don't want to think of you in danger. The idea of you running around shooting at people..." A thought occurred. "You don't have a gun, do you?"

Morrison had rehearsed his reply.

"Well, first if all you promised only *one* question about my work and secondly, if I choose not to answer it's only because it makes sense not to answer *any* questions about my job...in the Salvation Army," he added mischievously. "The Commissioner of the Sally-Ann would be most upset if he knew I was running around shooting people."

The main course arrived along with a change of topics, easing conversation.

Following a filling, well-done sirloin steak, Morrison now sated, leaned back in his chair and took stock.

"Hopefully we've ironed out last night's awkwardnesses and can continue as each other's best friends...whatever *that* means." He smiled. "Maybe we can work that out over the week ahead. It looks like I'll be around in Belfast for a bit yet."

"Chasing these terrible bottom trawlers you were telling me about, eh, Mister Agriculture and Fisheries?"

"The very same."

One more drink was taken before Morrison walked Iona back to her apartment and was rewarded with a restrained peck on the cheek and agreement to meet again once they were each clearer on their availability.

Chapter Eighteen

With minimum fuss, the personal secretary of the Director General of MI5 nodded in recognition of the right of his Deputy to access the office of his superior at any time. Kemp offered her a cheery 'good morning' but was met with reserve as he politely knocked the office door and entered.

"Morning, boss."

Ashton was seated in an armchair reading the morning papers. "How was dinner?"

"Well, I scared the bejesus out of our Secretary of State for International Trade and Development last night but to little avail. He admits agreeing to the sum of ten million pounds Sterling being deposited in a dark money account but knows no more than that. He doesn't seem to be a particularly bright man, but his father is a squash partner of the Prime Minister, hence, I suspect his recent rise through the ranks. I found him quite naive and gullible. He certainly bought all of my threats to arrest him as gospel so I'm inclined to believe him when he portrayed himself as someone who's ever so slightly out of his depth but who wants to be able to prove to the PM that he's terribly clever and politically astute. He insists he's not informed anyone of the dark money transfer but that it was his intention to advise the PM at the first opportunity. He has no idea how the transfer took place, or who was the intermediary but he did confess that the Sheik was pretty determined that it only be used to thwart Scottish Independence. According to Scott, the Arabs would apparently prefer to deal with the UK Government in matters to do with oil. They are concerned that all sorts of present understandings as well as arms manufacturing and sales could be affected if the Scots get their hands on the black stuff." He raised a finger in recollection of one more piece of information. "Ah, yes. And it would appear that the Sheik had no benefit or purpose in telling Mr. Scott about the transfer beyond attempting to further a potentially beneficial future relationship. There was no attempt to offer any inducement to the Minister beyond the consumption of a fine malt whisky. The entire transaction could have taken place without informing him of anything. Mr. Scott himself understands that his agreement wasn't necessary but his delight at being able to advise the PM of his successful adventure dwarfed his caution."

"Interesting. So ten million is washing around in support of British Unionism?" he asked rhetorically.

"Apparently so. It was the senior civil servant Andrew Fletcher who tipped us off. I've spoken quietly with him. He's terrified and doesn't want to become involved to protect his pension and will deny anything if put on the spot. He refuses to become a whistle-blower on the not unreasonable basis that everyone he's known who's done so has ended up in jail, in debt or in the papers. He won't identify the person he overheard discussing it, but he was the one who alerted us to the fact that it's being coordinated from within these walls, confirming what Scott told me last night, and that while normally these sums go directly to a Northern Ireland bank account, on this occasion half was retained by someone in this building."

Ashton was outraged. "I'll have the bastard's balls! Our covert interventions in respect of maintaining the Union must be calibrated very finely if we're not to end up in the mother and father of a political row. If whoever has this cash is cavalier and appears to be working in our name, we'd be crucified. It's simply essential we nail the fucker."

"Indeed. But it also may give further insight into the involvement of Iona McKenzie Forbes at that Belfast meeting. It just might be the case that she is herself some kind of Unionist plant within 'Seed of the Gael'."

Ashton ruminated on the welter of information with which he'd been provided.

"All rather confusing but perhaps we do two things. First, we might invite Morrison to accidentally bump into this woman while they're both in Belfast. They're both islanders and if I know anything about the personality of the Scottish Islander it's that the world over, they'll get together and before five minutes have elapsed, they'll know one another's cousins or uncles. It's a small world but in every nook and cranny in each of the seven continents, there's a Scottish islander enlivening the general discourse."

"And the second?"

"Have a word with your esteemed colleague, Sir Robert Cavendish and ask him if he has heard any whisper of any supplementary activities in respect of his work on thwarting Scottish Independence. Do not advise him of our knowledge of this tranche of dark money."

"I'll see to it boss."

* * *

Rotermundt punched in the eleven numbers on his phone that connected him to Henry J. Carson. After several rings it was answered. Rotermundt took the initiative.

"Thought you were dead!"

"I was in the bog."

"Are you alone?"

"Well, I'm not in the habit of going to the bathroom in company."

If the comment was intended humorously it wasn't taken so. Rotermundt's serious demeanour continued.

"I have now acquired the two items we bought."

"And are they exactly what you were looking for?"

"Exactly. Now we just have to get them to Scotland and execute the plan so to speak."

"Well, as we've discussed, there's no problem getting them over. I've a small fishing boat owned by one of my people who's a member of the Old Boyne Island Heroes Orange Lodge. He makes the journey regularly. It'll be easy to have them sent over."

"That's good. But it was the second of the tasks I wanted to discuss with you."

"How so?"

"You and I know that you have in the past seen fit to use the items such as I've obtained."

"So?"

"Well, you're experienced."

A new edge was evident in Carson's voice.

"Look, I've had cause to shoot at Taig heretics in the past but I won't be party to using violence against a fellow Unionist. And certainly not a politician as senior as your man."

"There would be a significant payment..."

"And that's my final word. I've done everything that's been asked of me. I'm more than happy to serve on The Council for the Union. Happy spending dark money to further the cause and protect the Union but my days as a violent man are over. Now it's over to you."

"Money would be no..."

"I said...that's my final *word*."

The phone line went dead.

Frustrated, Rotermundt cursed the phone and placed it back on the hotel room receiver. After a few minutes looking out of the window, lost in thought, he took his mobile phone and scrolled through recent calls. *Fuck it, Plan B is more expensive, but might just do more damage.* Selecting one, he pressed the number and waited to be connected.

"Who's this?" asked a deep Irish accented voice.

"This is Mr. Wise. I need to speak alone with Mr. Morecambe."

"Thought we was all good!"

"We are...we *are*...but I'd appreciate another discussion with you. It'd be to your own personal benefit."

"Would it now?"

"Substantially." Rotermundt sensed interest. "But I need to meet quickly. Like this evening. Same place, same time?"

"Nah, this'll be a home game. My usual gargle is in the Rock Bar in Falls Road. I'm safe in there. You come dressed in civvies. I wouldn't turn up wearin' red, white and blue if you have my meanin'. Eight o'clock's fine and don't be late like you was last time we met."

The call ended and almost immediately Rotermundt dialled a number connecting him to his stockbroker.

"Meridian Securities. Alex Alexander speaking."

"Still the stupidest name in stockbroking!" Rotermundt grunted, pleased at what passed for wit in his humourless world.

"Still Mister Cheery, eh? How may I assist, Mr. Rotermundt?" responded Alexander recognising his voice.

"I want to invest ten thousand pounds in Madden's Transportation. Irish business."

"You do, eh? You are aware that Madden's are under investigation for all sorts of tax fraud, they're reputedly... I say *reputedly*, mixed up in all sorts of Republican politics in both the north and the south of Ireland and they have the reputation in the past of making use of their vehicles to ferry arms, escaped Republicans and illegal substances on behalf of the IRA?"

"Well aware. Ten thousand pounds sterling. I may call you again later for a similar investment."

"Do you know something I don't know, Mr. Rotermundt? Are their legal problems going to go away? Are they opening up new routes to the continent?"

"Ten thousand pounds. And I'd like the shareholding to be made out temporarily to a Doctor Simon Doncaster"

Defeated, Alexander relented. "Okay. Simon Doncaster. I'll send you the paperwork electronically. Just complete it and I'll do the rest."

Rotermundt replaced the phone. *Once this shooting takes place, the media will doubtless be interested in why shares in an Irish Republican company known for their allegiance with the IRA is being held in the name of a prominent member of the SNP.*

Minutes after the three phone calls had been made, sitting outside the hotel in a Mercedes Sprinter van with blacked out windows, a man removed the earphones from his head and pressed a button which enabled any recorded phone conversation to be captured. He moved slightly to position himself before a large computer. Directing the mouse, he carefully established a secure folder which would forward any recordings electronically to the desktop computer of Jack Kemp, Britain's Deputy Director General of MI5. *Alright, anything that's said in that hotel room from now until I leave will be coming straight through my earphones.* He busied himself adjusting a unidirectional shotgun microphone aimed directly at Carson's front window.

Of the three missed conversations between Rotermundt, Carson and old Danny Kelly he knew nothing. It would have saved MI5 both considerable time and energy had he been but ten minutes earlier.

Chapter Nineteen

Morrison sat in an armchair in his hotel room, his feet resting on the edge of the large hotel bed, a laptop on his thighs. Having dealt with the encryption protocols, he opened up a communication from Thames House which provided a summarised account of his conversation with Kemp and included a brief dossier on the four individuals he was now meant to keep tabs on. As he read, he removed his feet from the bed and sat upright. A paragraph described the woman of his dreams; one Iona McKenzie Forbes, her age, address, occupation, antecedents, educational qualifications and an account of her connections with Nationalist politics, showing her to be a member of the SNP, SNP Socialists, Republic - a pressure group campaigning for the abolition of the monarchy - and CND, an organisation dedicated to the abolition of nuclear weapons. A separate paragraph set out MI5 assertions that she had attended four meetings of *'Siol nan Gaidheal'*. Photographs of her obviously taken from her NHS personnel file were included as were shots of her entering an unidentified building and one of her marching in support of Scottish Independence. Morrison scrutinised these to establish whether any had been taken during the last Glasgow march and whether he might be identified as accompanying her. Satisfied he had not been, he closed the lid and sat back in reflection.

Shit...Iona's quite the involved young lady. He re-opened the lid and read again. There's nothing illegal here. Siol nan Gaidheal is not a proscribed organisation even if they're not flavour of the month with the SNP. All of the other organisations are completely reputable. He considered the information before him. So far, she's as pure as the driven snow. But one misstep from me and I'm out of a job for not being open with my organisation...and if I don't handle this very carefully I make a mortal enemy out of someone I'm becoming very fond of.

He read a final note and sat upright. *Fucking hell! Kemp wants me to befriend her...islander to islander.* He laid the laptop open on the bed and stepped over to the window where he considered his next move. *Well...I suppose it legitimises my contact with her.* A darker thought intruded. *But what if she's some sort of terrorist who's broken the law and I'm involved in seeing her arrested?* His window rumination continued as he weighed matters.

***

The taxi pulled into the cul-de-sac of Rockmore Road, one of the smaller tributaries of the Falls Road, and stopped outside the Rock Bar whose blonde sandstone ornate facade was draped in a number of Irish tricolours. *No mistaking this for an Orange Hall,* thought Rotermundt. Paying the driver, he took the measure of the pub. It bustled brightly inside with the few smokers on the paved walkway outside paying him no attention. Hoping his bland attire would be acceptable to the man he still knew as Morecambe, he took a few steps back onto the Falls Road and entered.

Across the road, old Danny Kelly, 'Mr. Morecambe', as Rotermundt knew him, drew heavily on a cigarette.

"That's him arrived, Biro. I'll leave him to your tender mercies."

The bar was boisterous with drinkers. Mostly male, Rotermundt noticed, and completely Irish and Republican. A ceilidh band played a slip-jig unobtrusively in a corner. No obvious seat was available. Rotermundt approached the bar and uttered two words hoping to avoid any questions about his accent or particulars.

He nodded at one of several taps. "Guinness, please!"

He calculated approvingly that it took a full two minutes to pour and accepted the glass gratefully handing over a five pound note, waving away any change. A corner of the bar was unoccupied so he moved over and sipped his stout, his nerves resulting in half of the Guinness being consumed in a few sips. His eyes attempted subtly to scan the barroom for Kelly, his view blocked by another toper who, upon his receiving his pint and paying, turned to Rotermundt.

"Not from round here, eh?"

Rotermundt found himself looking at a man with a flourishing black beard, the walrus-styled moustache of which overflowed beyond his lower lip to create the impression of a black Mexican *bandana.*

"Nah," he mumbled monosyllabically hoping to dissuade any contact that might give Morecambe cause not to make contact.

"Then you must be Mr. Wise? Everyone else in here tonight lives only spittin' distance from the gantry."

Flustered, Rotermundt found himself nodding.

"I'm looking for a Mr. Morecambe."

"Ah, you won't be seeing him again. You're dealin' with me now."

Still disconcerted, Rotermundt looked round the bar hoping to see the now familiar face of his Irish contact but recognised no one.

"And you are?"

"You can call me Biro."

"Ah, Biro! You were wearing a Balaclava last time we spoke. You're the associate of Mr. Morecambe who sold me the items?"

"Well, you weren't supposed to know who I was but oul' Mr. Morecambe let it slip." He took a long pull at his pint. "I hear that you wanted to talk to Mr. Morecambe about a job. Now, what you have to understand is that our man there is a real soldier. One of our unsung heroes. He's been in more scraps than Barry McGuigan but as you'll know, he's gettin' on in years and he's asked me to fill in for him as it were."

Yet unable to comprehend the situation, Rotermundt dealt with it by saying nothing.

"But you're not being short-changed here, Mr. Wise. I've as much experience as your man but I'm that much younger, I'm far brighter if I say so myself and I've a lot of experience in the same fields of mischief as him. I've also got a contact list that beats most people's in the city."

Rotermundt found himself stammering.

"I...I...was looking for someone with Republican links. Someone senior...someone..."

"Ah well, you've found your man, Mr. Wise. Mind you, there's not many people drinkin' in here tonight that doesn't fit the same bill." He took a further long draught of his stout. "But I'm Mr. Morecambe's senior and he reports to me on matters that he thinks deserves my attention. I'm obviously aware that you've bought two of our guns and that you've got a few bob, according to my man, so he's asked me to have a chat with you tonight and see whether or not we're wastin' each other's time."

Rotermundt looked uncomfortable.

"Listen, would you like a seat? I'll get another round set up and we'll sit over there in the corner."

Rotermundt followed his glance to a nearby table with four men seated around it. Without waiting for agreement, Biro shouted over to its occupants.

"Boys, can yous move over and give us a seat?"

They did so with alacrity and both men took their seats. Leaning backwards to avoid a large pillar in his line of sight, he waved and caught the attention of the barman.

"Tony, two more over here when you've a minute?"

Having regained some of his composure, Rotermundt decided his interlocutor was very possibly better equipped for his proposal than Morecambe. He thought quickly.

"I have your two items safely under lock and key."

"And two good weapons they are. Sure they've served the cause well."

'*Weapons!*' The word stung sharply and Rotermundt found his gaze boring down on Biro's chest, now persuaded that he was talking to someone wearing a listening device. Biro caught his glance.

"Ah, you've no worries." He unbuttoned his shirt to a point below his rib cage. "I can say on the record that I'm not a peeler and that this is not an entrapment conversation." He thumbed a gesture at the crowded pub behind him. "Every man in here would vouch for me. You don't know me from Adam but I've a bit of a rep in Republican circles. You can speak freely. I'm not wearin' a wire and I'm not here to see you doing time in Maghaberry Prison. I've made that trip meself too many times to wish it on another man, bar one or two."

Rotermundt remained nervous. "You'll forgive my hesitancy. If I say what I want to say and it was overheard or recorded I'd be committing a very serious offence."

"So is it a strip search you'd be wantin'?"

"No...it's...it's..."

Biro stroked his beard with his left hand, wiping the remnants of the Guinness foam from his extravagant moustache.

"Look my friend. I've many things to be gettin' on with. If you have a proposal to make, go right ahead. If not, finish your pint and feck off out of my pub! I've some drinkin' to be doin'."

120

Rotermundt allowed his response to hang momentarily while the barman placed a further two pints of Guinness on the table. No money was asked for.

"Okay. Look. I need someone shot in the leg with one of your guns. In Scotland...he's in Scotland."

Biro pursed his lips in thought before answering.

"Shootin's cost money."

"You'd be recompensed and beyond that, I'd be prepared to make a sizeable donation to your cause."

"And how much would them two figures be?"

"I don't know...what's the going rate for a non-lethal shooting?"

Biro's face adopted the same puckered look as he gave the matter thought.

"It'd depend on how prominent the target was, how difficult the shot was and how easy it'd be for me or one of my men to feck off out of there without gettin' caught."

"Well, you could decide the where and the when but it needs to be in the next couple of weeks. The person in question is a senior Conservative politician and..."

"Mother of God...I shoot Tories for *free!*" he laughed before remembering he was in a negotiation. "Only kiddin' there Mr. Wise. And who might this Tory be?"

"You get the name after we agree details...so how much?"

"Well, you're looking at maybe, fifty grand for a big noise politician. He'll have protection."

"We don't think so."

"*We*, is it? So this isn't a personal request, eh? It's a political act?"

"I'd rather not say." He changed the subject. "But fifty thousand pounds in cash is about what I'd budgeted."

"Then I should have asked for more!" Another laugh.

Rotermundt continued his straight-laced dialogue. "One more inducement. If this operation goes well; the injury is as we discussed, we all get away undetected, the gun is left at the scene, I'm prepared to make an investment in a business which I understand is, let's say, not unconnected to Republicanism in the north. You could alert them in advance and make such arrangements as you deem appropriate to siphon the money back to yourselves. If there's a mistake, no investment is made."

"How much and which business?"

"We'd invest one hundred and ten thousand pounds in Madden's Transportation with no requirement made as to its purpose. We'd buy shares and they could come to an arrangement with you to transfer all or a proportion of this benefit as you saw fit."

Biro nodded appreciatively.

"And you don't want this fellah plugged? Just want him wounded?"

"Two things are very important. You *must* use one of the pistols you sold us and you must only shoot him in the leg."

Biro was silent for some long seconds before responding.

"If...and it's an *if*...we go ahead with this, we'll want to be assured up front that you're not a British agent of some stamp. And be assured that if we discover your credentials aren't up to scratch, you'll regret the day you ever booked to come over here on a cheap flight in one of Michael O'Leary's wonderful planes."

Holding Rotermundt's gaze he lifted his Guinness and consumed the entire pint in one final swallow.

"Have you a number I can reach you on? I'll take all this under advisement."

Chapter Twenty

Morrison opened the curtains of his hotel room and shielded his eyes against a blazing sun.

Lovely day, he thought as he absentmindedly pressed a button on the remote control device, turning on the UTV breakfast news.

A few general items of interest concerning the Northern Ireland economy were followed by some farming news and an item on a fire in a terraced property in the Castlereagh Road area of Belfast. Morrison busied himself in preparation for his ablutions as the newscaster continued with breaking news from Scotland that Minister for Justice, Ms. Lorna Gillies MSP had been detained by Edinburgh police and had been charged with a sexual offence against another woman. Sources suggested that he victim was a senior civil servant but this could not be confirmed.

Jesus, the Scottish Minister of Justice arrested? Scotland's top law officer? Iona will be all over this. It'll surely dent the cause. Anticipating further discussion when he met her, he turned over to the BBC News channel where the subject was being given significantly more attention. A potted history of Lorna Gillies had hurriedly been put together with overdubbed clips of her on film acknowledging a previous electoral victory, senior SNP politicians were interviewed urging deferred judgement until more information could be established and both Labour and Conservative politicians contested air space to emote sombrely their view that while no one should rush to judgement, it was clearly a very serious matter and one which might bring down Scotland's government if the allegations were both proved and found to have been known to the First Minister but concealed. Questions would be asked. This was serious!

Deciding he had obtained sufficient information, Morrison showered and dressed before picking up the phone and calling Iona Forbes who was in a state of some agitation.

"Donald John, Lorna Gillies is no sex pest. I've met her a few times and she comes across as a really nice person. She's a lawyer and holds the highest justice role in Scotland. I find this all very difficult to believe."

The conversation continued with Iona doing most of the talking until Morrison suggested lunch.

"I've a few phone calls to make to understand this better," responded Iona "but..." she consulted her watch... "How about one o'clock?"

"Meet here and I'll book somewhere nice to eat?"

"Yeah. Talk later."

* * *

Morrison spent the morning on his encrypted laptop seeking further classified information on each of the four people cited by Kemp. Iona's file was least voluminous; all of the information against her name being known to him other than her political memberships. Daniel Kelly had quite a record sheet, all quite in keeping with the activities of a now elderly member of the IRA back in the seventies and eighties. Rotermundt's file set out his political responsibilities in some detail but was rather deficient on his role as the financier of Conservative causes using dark money. Carson's details, like Danny Kelly's were not untypical of a Unionist involved in the sectarian politics of Northern Ireland; several findings of breach of the peace, some vandalism charges and an assault. His friendship with Father Gerry Warren was not recorded.

For some time he stared at the sun-lit Belfast city skyline from his room window attempting an understanding of why these four people would find common cause and how on earth Iona had apparently become involved with them. *Perhaps our luncheon conversation will reveal more*, he decided.

Checking his watch, he decided to leave his hotel early and walk to find a restaurant for lunch rather than booking a table on-line. *I need the exercise and I need to think.*

* * *

Iona arrived at the Europa Hotel almost punctually but with an earnest look on her face, hugging Morrison almost absent-mindedly before launching into a diatribe about Lorna Gillies.

"I've been talking to friends, Donald John," she gushed. "There's not one of them who knows Lorna and who thinks she'd have behaved improperly. If anything she's a very private and caring person and takes her job as Justice Minister very seriously. She's a lesbian and has been in a relationship with Oonagh O'Brian, an Irish lecturer in History at Edinburgh University for umpteen years. They're very close and it's inconceivable that one might betray the other. Everyone reckons it's a complete fraud. It's a set up."

Morrison had gently taken her by the elbow and had manoeuvred her onto the street during the onslaught, continually nodding in agreement as Iona's argument was outlined.

"Not far from here. Just round the corner," was all Morrison was able to interject as the flow continued.

"They live in Fountainbridge and do so quietly. She's never had a single accusation of any nature made against her in the papers. She's a close confident of the First Minister. She's kind and empathic." The information was spat out in staccato as they closed on luncheon.

Once seated, Morrison calmed her down and invited a menu choice.

"Can't concentrate, Donald John. This is all I can think about." A moment's hesitation then, "Soup of the day, a Greek Salad and a gin and tonic."

"Wow, that's decisive, Iona. Got it all off your chest?"

"Sorry, Donald John. I'm upset."

"Well there's not much you can do about it. Maybe we'll hear more about it on the news this evening."

"They'll have her convicted in the gutter press before the soup arrives," grumbled Iona.

The arrival of the waitress, ordering and the arrival of a couple of gins brought an easing of Iona's fretful disposition. The conversation, gently directed by Morrison, turned to Forbes' political involvement.

"I'm *so* pissed off with the status quo, Donald John. I could scream at the telly sometimes. It just seems that the Establishment are laughing at Scotland and we're half-full of gullible idiots who choose to believe their guff. We're administered by a colonial power but people are too lazy and uninformed to get up off their knees and demand our independence. It seems that Westminster and the Establishment is stuffed full of the wealthy and privileged who use their money and influence to persuade other wealthy people to cajole the middle classes into blaming the poor. Surely you must agree with that?"

"Well I'm a supporter of Scottish independence, I guess. It's certainly less of an issue now I'm down south taking the King's Shilling but any rational person in Scotland who is not in hock to a government contract, a British salary or who doesn't originally come from the Home Counties would be daft not to want more from the relationship."

"I don't want more," said Iona raising her voice, "I want *out!*"

Morrison decided to push a little.

"Maybe you should join one of the more militant wings of the SNP?"

"I'm already a member of the SNP Socialists, CND, Republic and I've gone along to a few meetings of *'Siol nan Gaidheal'* when I've been in Glasgow but I'm not going back there."

"Too militant?" asked Morrison almost hopefully.

Iona looked embarrassed.

"Not really...it's just that...well, I'm an island lass and they'd have me march behind a huge anti-Tory banner that used the 'C' word...you know, C-U-N-T?" She spelled it out rather than articulate the word. "The banner stretched from one side of the road to the other? Can you imagine the stooshie in church the following Sunday if I'd been photographed walking behind language like that?"

Morrison laughed despite himself. "So it's not that they're too militant or too reckless...just that they use sweary banners?"

"Aye. And I wasn't too fussed about some of them personally. The people I've met in the movement have been, to a man and a woman, all really lovely. The CND people are really agreeable and the SNP Socialists, while they're a wee bit more gruff, are also really nice. I don't really know about Republic. They're based in London so I joined because I want rid of the Monarchy but I just have an email relationship with them."

"But *Seed of The Gael* are too sweary," giggled Morrison, relieved at Iona's rendition of her political allegiances.

"And a wee bit too radical. When I first heard their leader, *Artair Muireachan* speak he was so charismatic I thought he'd set the *world* on fire but instead he set a *pub* on fire and was remanded. He's currently awaiting sentence. So I didn't go back. Too sweary and too undisciplined."

As Iona wrestled with her salad, Morrison took the opportunity to gaze upon her beauty. Large, blue eyes, a pert nose, dimpled cheeks, a taut jaw line and a delicate chin were each assembled in such a way as to have him feel weak at the knees. She was undeniably beautiful. Incontrovertibly pretty. Her body showed the benefits of her running routine, she had a mind like a steel trap and she was both passionate and kind. As he decided he was beginning to host unusually warm feelings towards a woman, she looked up and caught his regard.

"Have I got salad cream on my face?" she smiled, her even, white teeth gleaming.

"Embarrassed, Morrison could only shake his head. "I was just appreciating how deeply passionate you are about your politics," he lied. "I don't think I've ever met someone who was so out and out committed to a cause."

"Well, the trouble is, there are too many people equally committed to an opposite cause that I find repugnant and they have all the media wrapped up, all the money in the bank, all the political weight down south and all the mischief-makers of the 77th Brigade wreaking havoc on social media. We're right up against it. Those of us who refuse to bend the knee to Unionism are merely ignored or filed under 'M' for Malcontent."

"S'pose," agreed Morrison philosophically. He decided to attempt to lean into the task allocated him once more. "These guys last night...the ones you thought were arguing outside the pub. You only recognised the one who was with the demonstrators in the lane back in Glasgow?"

"Yeah. I'm sure that was him. The bald guy. Only one I recognised. He looks a nasty piece of work."

"None of the others?"

Iona placed her cutlery on the table next to her dish and folded her hands. She breathed deeply before answering and raised an angled eyebrow."

"Listen, Mr. Bond. Here's how it works if you're going to ask me spy questions. You ask me a question. I answer your question honestly to the best of my ability. I don't exaggerate or minimise my answers. You listen and we move on. You don't try to interrogate me like you would one of your criminal terrorist masterminds or whoever you're used to cross-examining. Agreed?"

Caught on the back foot again, Morrison could only mumble words designed to dismiss any notion that he was inviting a response other than in general conversation but found his face reddening.

"I was only...I'm afraid...I was..." He thought better of sculpting another contrived answer.

"Another gin?"

"No thanks."

Morrison attempted a recovery.

"Look, Iona. I need to know that you're not mixed up in anything. You know I can't say too much about what I'm doing over here in Belfast but..." he hesitated... "But let's say someone wanted to argue that you were involved in political activity that crossed the line...that may be illegal...subversive. With every fibre of my being I want to protect you but I'd find it problematic if you were somehow a target for the security services. I've given it thought and if you're up to some kind of political mischief, I think I'd inform my bosses that I'd have to resile my involvement in my activities over here. I couldn't in all consciousness have anything to do with anything that saw you harmed in any way."

Iona, frowning, considered his monologue and took a moment, looking into the middle distance as she formulated a response.

"Well, now. Am I some sort of terrorist?"

"I didn't..."

"No? An agent provocateur, perhaps?"

"That's not..."

"Well, let me make a few points. I am *absolutely* committed to Scottish Independence. If your people consider that worthy of investigation, handcuff me right now. Am I involved in anything I've not already told you? No I am not. Do I think anyone should be interested in me in the slightest? No I do not. What intrigues me is why you are asking these questions in the first place. I know all about your much-vaunted need to keep everything secret but can I ask you if I'm on the books of MI5 and if you are involved in spying on me...or surveilling me as I think you call it these days?"

"I'm just trying to protect you...it's complicated."

"Do you have a file on me, Donald John? Be honest!"

Morrison shifted uncomfortably in his seat.

"Not a *file* as such. It seems you may just have been unfortunate to have been photographed in the company of these people who were talking about guns, shooting and so on outside the Crown Liquor Saloon. At least that's my take on it and if I'm accurate...and from what you say I'm correct in my understanding, then you - and me, for that matter - have nothing to worry about. It was me who led you into contact with these three guys and it'll be me who'll protect you from them."

Iona grinned. "Sheesh...are those three bad *hombres?*"

"I know you're making light of it, Iona but they just might be."

Iona relented and smiled the smile that increasingly melted Morrison's heart.

"You're making a bit of an arse of your cover story about being a Salvation Army officer, Donald John." She thought further. "And if you thought I might have been involved with them, might these three be associated with Scottish Independence?"

Morrison shrugged his shoulders noncommittally. "Perhaps... possibly..."

Iona's mood brightened. Then I'm Robin to your Batman. Supergirl to your Superman. I'm here to assist. I'm..."

"Nope! Can't happen, Iona. You're *involved*, in that you're someone caught up in something that has nothing to do with you, and my job is to protect you. That's *it!*" He smiled. "It might mean placing you in my protective custody while I figure this thing out, though."

Iona returned his smile.

"Well, if it involves the odd glass of Guinness or gin in your company, you can lock me up and throw away the key!"

Chapter Twenty-one

Before Jack Kemp nodded his agreement to the sommelier pouring a small amount of his favourite *Coche-Dury Corton-Charlemagne Grand Cru*, he inspected the label on the bottle, checking its producer, style and vintage. Satisfied, he allowed him to pour a taste, whereupon he swirled the glass a few times to aerate the wine before bringing the glass to his nose, concentrating on the wine's fragrance. Only then did he sip.

"I can see you're something of a oenophile, Jack. I'm afraid it's all rather lost on me. I'm a thirty quid a bottle man. But if your choice of wine merits the care you've taken in choosing it I'm sure it'll be superb."

Kemp gestured his satisfaction to the waiter and was rewarded by a generously poured volume of wine.

"This is indecently good gargle, Hugh. All during my university years I enjoyed pint after pint in our rugby club but also found a friend in a decent bottle of *Claret*...and progressed to my *Corton-Charlemagne* after many enjoyable years of experimentation."

He held his glass at shoulder level awaiting the sommelier completing his duties in respect of his guest. He raised his goblet slightly higher.

"To the BBC and all who sail in her!"

"The Beeb!"

Some time was spent recounting past memories of events at White's Club, established in 1693, wherein they dined that evening; one of the oldest and most exclusive clubs in London. Eventually they ordered dinner and while waiting, Kemp found himself studying the ornate ceiling and expensive classical paintings that adorned the walls. The reminiscing continued.

"We joined this club at the same time. D'you remember, Hugh? I was a middling spy and you were a low level television producer who'd just been catapulted to fame following a Panorama broadcast on the stumbling leadership of the Labour Party by the donkey-jacketed

Michael Foot. Now look at us! I'm the Deputy Director General of MI5 and you're a knight of the realm and Director General of the BBC."

"Didn't happen overnight, Jack. A lot of sweat...and in your case *courage*, went into our upward mobility. We both worked hard, like Soviet *Stakhanovites* whereas many of our competitors as they advanced became hedonistic sybarites...too wrapped up in the accoutrements of power. They lost the stomach for the fight."

"S'pose."

He took another sip of his wine, appreciating its fine qualities.

"However, to business, eh?"

Sir Hugh Dalrymple leaned forward having anticipated some quiet concerns of Kemp's to be made known to him over dinner.

"Certainly, Jack. Anything I can do to assist."

"It's nothing really," countered Kemp. "Mostly a chance to catch up and enjoy a glass but I did wonder if you might offer me some background on attitudes within the BBC to this Scottish Independence tommyrot that's so exciting the natives north of Carlisle."

"Ah, our friends in Caledonia." He hesitated until the waiter gently laid starter courses in front of each of them and had retreated, before continuing. "I'm not unaware of your concerns, Jack. Your MI5 liaison man, I'm told, is busily engaged in ensuring that the political attitudes of Her Majesty's Government are threaded throughout all news bulletins in Scotland." He laughed. "I mean the nationalists really are on something of a sticky wicket and frankly, I can't see how they can succeed. They are opposed by three political parties all funded and controlled by London, they are spoken to each evening by the nation's broadcaster which holds dear to its mission of serving and upholding the Union, are funded by a government dedicated to these same ends and can read pretty much any newspaper they wish - each of which is owned either by an American, an Australian, or a Russian and of those publishers who *do* hold a British passport, two support the Tories and one supports UKIP. All of them back the Union. Even the few on the left, read exclusively by the lumpen proletariat, owe their allegiance to the United Kingdom."

"No rumblings in the ranks?"

"You have to remember that with the help of your liaison chap, we sift carefully before appointments so we don't have any real troublesome newscasters, producers or journalists. Now and again, someone will kick over the traces but we control all output. For example, Newsnight had a piece on the deep collaborative practices between Scottish Labour and Scottish Tories to galvanise the Union vote up there. From memory it was called 'Red Tory or Blue Tory?'. It wasn't broadcast. Panorama put together a piece on the unpopularity of the Royals in Scotland; on how once Charles takes the throne, it'll be game over for them up north. It wasn't broadcast. A BBC Scotland News investigation into why the then Tory Leader hadn't held more than a couple of surgeries in her constituency during a period when her SNP counterpart had held a couple of *hundred* was also not broadcast."

He paused awaiting a signal from his host that he'd offered a sufficiency of information. None came, so he continued.

"We don't tend to doorstep Tory or even the odd Labour politician, we often forget to mention the party affiliation of a Labour or Tory politician who has been sent to the naughty step while prolonging and boosting the misery of any nationalist caught similarly. And most importantly perhaps, all news up there is biased towards the Unionist position. Any impartial observer would sensibly arrive at the view that the nationalist cause is holed below the water line. Surely they worship at the feet not of St. Andrew but of St. Anthony of Padua; the patron saint of lost causes!"

"But yet, the polls tell a different story, dear friend. Despite everything, the Scots appear to be moving inexorably towards a 'Yes' vote."

Dalrymple chewed carefully on his *pâté de foie gras* before responding.

"Have you anything particular in mind that might reverse this?"

Kemp shook his head. "Not really. Just keep up the good work. Perhaps over-egg it a little here and there. There have to be a few story-lines that would have the nationalists frown over their porridge."

Dalrymple smiled. "I'll look into it."

* * *

The gentle breeze caused a tinkling symphony of clinks as small sailboats bobbed in the harbour at Warrenpoint, a small port town in County Down. Sitting at the head of Carlingford Lough, the harbour was quiet as darkness enveloped the town. Nearby, where the old harbour surrendered to more industrial purposes, bright lights illuminated the fishing vessel *Nimrod,* which issued blue diesel fumes as its captain tested her engines.

Parked beneath a tall sandstone wall observing the captain's preparations, Rotermundt's Mercedes Benz sat in shadow, unilluminated. Rotermundt and Carson watched the proceedings in silence until Carson assessed the need for action.

"Right. Give me the case. Billy's just about finished. I'll hand over these pistols and we'll get the hell out of here."

"Sure there's no one watching?"

"Just give me the case. If the security services are on to us, they're on to us. If we're lifted, we say nothing. I've lawyers set up but let's hope they won't be necessary." He took one further long look around the dock and, seeing nothing untoward, opened the door and made his way quickly to the rear of the Nimrod. He stepped over the low stern and hurried towards the cabin.

Nervously, Rotermundt watched him enter, observed the silhouette of two men in conversation through a frosted cabin window and after some mere seconds, saw Carson reappear and scurry towards the car.

Re-entering the vehicle, issuing instructions as he did so, Carson urged departure.

"Let's get the fuck out of here."

"Is your man okay about this?"

"He's been paid half, knows what he's to do and is about to leave on the tide."

"And he knows how to deliver them when he gets to Stranraer?"

"He'd better or he doesn't get the second half of his money."

Slowly, so as not to attract untoward attention, Rotermundt moved the car into gear and trundled over the cobbled dockside towards the exit. Less than a mile from the harbour, he eased the car to the kerb and parked in the industrial zone where he'd earlier collected Carson. He pulled at his seat belt to give himself manoeuvrability as he half-turned and spoke to his departing companion.

"I need to speak urgently to Ian Gibson but I don't want to use the phone. I'll be making my way back over to Scotland tomorrow afternoon. Can you ask him to meet me in the Crown at eleven o'clock when it opens? I've some business that I need to have him attend to."

Carson extracted himself with some small difficulty from his own seatbelt.

"I'll call in and speak to him on my way home. Eleven in the Crown." He opened the door. "See you at our next funding meeting."

Rotermundt bid farewell. "I'll be in touch."

Carson nodded and left the Merc. He walked towards his BMW and as he closed, pressed his electronic key, setting the lights flashing. In a few seconds he'd pulled out and had driven from sight.

Rotermundt smiled to himself. *Let's hope nothing happens to our little package. But then again, if it's intercepted, it's all good and useful information and merely confers another political advantage. We'll soon see who can be trusted.*

Chapter Twenty-two

Morrison drew a long blade down his cheek and parted thick white shaving foam as he attended to his ablutions. He pulled his jaw south, the better to expose his cheek to the razor. *What to make of Iona? A couple of nights ago she was in my hotel room at her own invitation but before any intimacy, we fell out. I've been over here for a few nights now and she's come close to assaulting me, she's kissed me on the cheek like I was her brother, we've laughed together and she's cried at my hand. She's the most beautiful woman I've ever seen but MI5 have her targeted as a possible Scottish terrorist - which she's not!* - he assured himself... *now she knows I'm an agent of the state but she wants to help me.* He looked in the mirror through the open door to his bed. *But still we haven't spent a romantic moment together.* He swept away the last remnants of shaving foam and wiped his face with a towel. *Is this woman exactly how I perceive her or is she taking me for a ride?...Is she the terrorist MI5 imagine she might be or is she merely a committed activist who works hard during the day to help those on Benbecula who are ill?*

He dressed slowly, weighing up the consequences of either contingency. Finally deciding...*I keep her close. I've given her an opportunity to come clean and explained honestly that I will do anything including stepping back from all this if it puts her in harms' way but she insists she's just a foot soldier in the independence army and has nothing to hide. So...I take her at face value and if she's being honest, all's well. If not...well, we'll cross that bridge when we come to it.*

He lifted his watch from the hotel's vanity table and glanced at it as he strapped it on. *Eight thirty! Breakfast downstairs, a note to Kemp that I've made successful contact with Forbes and asking for any more intelligence on my four targets then a short stroll along to meet Iona at Darcy's for a coffee at eleven, then...well? We'll see then.*

* * *

Rotermundt slid his Visa card along the reader on the credit card payment terminal and murmured a grunt of thanks as he stooped to collect his small suitcase. Accepting the receipt for his accommodation and meals, he turned and walked towards the door of his hotel before entering the taxi, ordered by telephone by the concierge moments previously.

"Crown Bar, please."

The taxi navigated the morning traffic with little difficulty and deposited Rotermundt at his destination. Arriving just as one of the bar staff was pinning the doors open, he stepped inside the empty pub.

"Don't suppose you'd do me a coffee, eh? It's a bit early for alcohol."

"Never too early or too late for alcohol, sir. Now what would you be lookin' for? We've got..."

"Black's fine." He gestured to the booth directly behind him. "I'll sit in there?"

"Aye, you go right ahead, sir. I'll bring it over. Anything else?"

"Eh, I'm expecting a friend shortly who might agree with your philosophy on strong drink. I'll order when..."

The tall figure of Ian Gibson appeared, silhouetted in the doorframe.

"Ah, he's arrived." He waved at Gibson, asking him his preference midst handshaking and placing his suitcase inside the booth.

"Guinness!" was the two syllable instruction as both men took a seat.

The twosome spent the first minutes in small talk until their drinks arrived.

"You wanted a chat that couldn't be overheard? If so, you've picked the right place and time. This place will be quiet for a wee bit yet."

Rotermundt's grimace signalled the endorsement of his wisdom.

"I need your help again but this time I need some adjustments."

"Sure! How?"

"Your last foray into Glasgow was a big success. It generated all of the right headlines. Exactly what we wanted. The connection between loyalist Belfast opposing the SNP was firmly planted and there was enough trouble caused by your boys to make sure the media ran the story in bold headlines the following morning. None of our guys was damaged badly and they all had a good time. So...a big success, I'd say."

"It was but look, Emil, this Scottish independence stuff has us all here in the north in a state of fear and trembling. If they were to *win* that vote, it'd be a racing certainty that the demand for a United Ireland would become irresistible. We're all on board here not just because we want to preserve the Union but because if we don't fight the good fight now, up here in the north we'll end up being ruled by Rome and it's surrogate, Dublin. Most of our people wouldn't stand for that and there'd be a lot more bloodshed. In addition, given the status quo, if things started to go against us, many of our people who are descendants of Scots/Irish settlers might have just decided to head back home to the old country but it looks like Scotland might just go its own way and deny people here the chance of living under the Union Flag unless they moved to England."

He lifted his pint glass but didn't drink. His demeanour changed.

"All that being said, it was a laugh alright. The boys still talk about it and they're up for more friendly exchanges if that's what you have in mind."

"Almost, Ian. This time I need you to make use of your contacts in Scotland. I want another appearance of our people opposed to Scottish independence but this time I need two different elements. First I want those in the square to be mostly from Scotland. You have your contacts with Rangers' supporters clubs and the loyalist community in the Lodge and the Order."

"I have that, Emil. Mostly what the Nats call our 'network of sectarian pubs' but you need to know that the supporters' clubs aren't as unified as once they were. We've been noticing that on some of the independence marches Rangers and Celtic supporters backing independence march together. It makes a big statement."

"Then I need you do two things. First, have some of your boys at the front of the march dressed in Scotland strips and carrying Saltires. The can wear fucking *kilts* if they have to but they blend in. Have them join in with the singing until they see an opportunity when there's lots of press around then attack some onlookers. Secondly, make a bigger statement by having your people attack the idiots who are wearing Rangers and Celtic strips and being all palsy-walsy on their march. Send one of your boys into their midst and have him phone when they approach a particular road end. Then get stuck into them...the lot of them. But this time I need more. I need people down, I need blood on the streets, I need ambulances but I also need some of the fallen to be those holding the office of constable. I want this march to be so violent it should be covered by *war* correspondents."

"You want cops injured?"

"Exactly that. I need this to be a march that can be condemned by the Prime Minister of the UK. I need there to be public outrage that this kind of violence on the streets of a Saturday morning is unacceptable. I need the large numbers turning out for these independence marches to reduce dramatically as grannies and families with kids think better of walking into a war zone in the future. This has to feature in the news headlines nationally, not just in Scotland."

Gibson looked into the middle distance as if trying to identify an eagle on the wing. Frustrated at the absence of a speedy agreement, Rotermundt growled.

"You have problems with this?"

"Well, some of the boys might not be happy taking a swing at fellow Loyalists."

"They're not fellow *anything*. They're fucking traitors to the cause, to the crown, to the United Kingdom we hold dear." He thought furiously. "Tell them that it's all a scam by the Nats. Tell them that those wearing the blue of Rangers are actually Celtic supporters masquerading as us in order to trick the public into thinking that we accept their views on peace and harmony leading to independence. Tell them that they're all fucking priests sent from Rome to screw their wives...I don't care...but I need a donnybrook." He held Gibson's gaze. "I have another seven thousand pounds here. Use it as you please. Feed them drink beforehand by all means and retain a fee for your services. But I need your assurance that you can deliver. So... can you?"

Gibson smiled broadly. "When that crowd of Nats passes our boys, the Old Firm marchers will have us around them as thick as flies round the wet shite of a Clydesdale horse. The cops will have to attend and I'll task one or two of the lads to see a few of them bruised."

Rotermundt opened his case and withdrew an envelope which he passed to Gibson.

"Here's your fee and expenses. They march in Glasgow on Saturday." He zipped and closed the case. "Now I'm off to meet this fellah you've picked to carry some contraband over to Scotland for me. He's reliable?"

"He's a doped up hippy. That was along the lines you asked for. Not too bright. In need of cash. No previous convictions. But let me ask you, Emil...we've known one another a long time. Why in the name of God are you now dabbling in cannabis smuggling?"

"Can't tell you that, Ian. Just trust me that it'll advance our cause. So...name and place?"

"He's called Malachy Fitzgerald. Comes from Newtownabbey. High school dropout. Indulges in weed. He insists there's nothing stronger. Not sure I believe him. He'll be inside the Kitchen Bar in Victoria Square from which the Cairnryan/Glasgow bus departs shortly. I've bought him and his girlfriend..."

"Girlfriend?"

"They're cut from the same cloth. Equally dopey."

Remembering his Guinness, he quaffed a substantial draught before continuing.

"Bought them both bus and ferry tickets to Glasgow. He's been told that for a fee of five hundred pounds he's to take a small consignment of cannabis across on the ferry and hand it to someone in Glasgow's George Square who'll identify themselves as 'Mr. Fitzgerald'...we figured he'd remember his own feckin' name... He'll also be wearing a red bobble hat."

He passed a red woollen hat over the table which still had the price tag on it.

"You meet him in the Kitchen bar, give him the parcel and this hat, hand over half of his fee and tell him Mr. Fitzgerald will give him the second half when the swap is made." He looked at his watch. "It's a fifteen minute walk along Howard Street to Victoria Square. I'd leave about now in case he gets cold feet."

Rotermundt managed a smile that didn't reach his eyes.

"Seems well organised!" He threw a twenty pounds note on the table and prepared to leave.

"Pay the chap, will you? I'm off."

* * *

Having spoken to Kemp and having received precious little information beyond the fact that Henry J. Carson had made no phone calls since the listening device had been set up outside his house, Morrison had met Iona and enjoyed a coffee as planned. Together they walked along Adelaide Street towards Belfast city centre where a shop specialising in knitted goods was to be visited on the basis that any trip to a large conurbation by a resident of Benbecula had to be used to purchase goods not normally available on the island. Crossing the road at May Street, Morrison took Iona by the elbow and stopped her before pulling her urgently into a shop doorway.

"There's that bald guy Rotermundt. The one you were photographed with outside the Crown."

"So it is...and he's in a hurry."

Morrison frowned, sighed deeply and made a decision.

"Look, I promised I'd protect you and I'll keep my word but I need to follow that fellah and in this instance four eyes are better than two. You up for some spying?"

"You bet your sweet bippy, Mr. Bond."

"Okay. Just do everything I ask without questioning me."

They started to walk quickly in order to catch up with the hurried stride of Rotermundt. Maintaining a distance of some twenty yards or so, it became evident that he was unaware of the likelihood of being followed other than offering a furtive glance around him as he entered the Kitchen Bar.

"I buy drinks for us at the bar and you find yourself a seat near him without inviting attention. Use your phone as if distracted by it but use it to make any notes of anything you overhear. Got it?"

Iona nodded and they entered. Rotermundt had ignored the bar and was seated talking to a man and a woman in a corner of the establishment. Warming to her part, Iona announced loudly to Morrison that a gin and tonic was her preference and sat but six feet from Rotermundt's table where she took out her phone and opened the 'Notes' application. Morrison fretted at the bar for some time while the drinks order was completed. As disinterestedly as it was possible to convey, he looked over to Iona's table whilst in reality checking on Rotermundt, mouthing the question, 'crisps?' to Iona as a cover. After what seemed an eternity, he brought the G&T and a whisky over to the table where Iona was busy entering details on her phone. As Morrison sat, Rotermundt stood and threw the red bobble hat on the table before growling a whispered directive to the couple, terminating the conversation.

"Don't fuck up!"

As Morrison thought quickly, Iona slid her phone towards him and spun it so he could read her notes. Digesting the information, he lifted his whisky and sipped it. Quietly he announced his decision.

"We stick with this pair."

Iona raised her eyebrows and whispered her surprise.

"But they're just about to get on a bus and a ferry to Glasgow."

"And so am I. You can return to your *pied à terre*."

"If you're on the bus, *I'm* on the bus. They've just taken a mysterious parcel from a bad guy who gave them an envelope obviously enclosing money. They're on a mission and there's two of them. Who knows what they could do on the ferry. If they split up, your goose is cooked. You need me to make sure we have eyes on them at all times."

As Morrison considered Iona's logic, the couple exploded in glee as the envelope was opened below their table height and a wad of banknotes was revealed to them. It was easy to overhear their joy.

"One for the pavement?" exclaimed Fitzgerald.

"A big wine," was the rejoinder.

"They don't seem to be very professional, do they, Donald John? Who knows what might happen on-board?" asked Iona in a low voice.

Morrison relented. "Okay." He pursed his lips and cursed. "Shit!"

"What's up?"

After a moment's silence, Morrison looked to make sure he couldn't be overheard by Rotermundt's couriers. Satisfied, he placed his hand on Iona's arm.

"Change of plan. *You* have to follow them on to the ferry by yourself. I have to return to the hotel first. There's a laptop computer and a...and other stuff...that I need to bring with me. I'll get a taxi and will probably be at the terminal before you." He squeezed her arm. "Oh, and one other thing...don't use your phone to call me. Given your assumed notoriety, someone might be monitoring everything you say or transmit. You okay with that?"

"Sounds straightforward. What's the 'other stuff'...a briefcase that explodes when you open it?"

A smile creased Morrison's face as he avoided the question.

"Maybe you'll be good at this secret agent malarkey."

"And so might you, if you stick with me, eh?" beamed Iona.

Chapter Twenty-three

Having dealt with news items assessed as having more significance to the main watching audience of England, the BBC newsreader turned her attention to a leaked government report which, she confidently asserted, was causing friction between London and Edinburgh.

"It appears that a secret government feasibility study has been undertaken to provide an additional runway at both Glasgow and Edinburgh Airports and that a bullet train is being considered that will connect Glasgow Airport and Glasgow city with Edinburgh Airport and Edinburgh city centre, drastically reducing travel time and improving inter-connectivity in Scotland. Where's the problem? Well, Downing Street sources inform the BBC that the Scots must see continued benefit accruing from the Union and the Prime Minister wants to deliver an ambitious project that's going to create thousands of jobs, improve Scotland's infrastructure and give a huge boost to its economy. However, there appear to be doubts as to Scotland's ability to deliver such a large scale project - particularly if Maglev technology is employed - and the Prime Minister is said to believe that it will require the expertise of the entire Union as well as the deep pockets of Westminster to deliver it. Perhaps unsurprisingly the Scottish Cabinet Secretary for Transport, Infrastructure and Connectivity, David McLean MSP, while welcoming the initiative, reportedly insisted that both transport and infrastructure were devolved matters under the devolution settlement and that Westminster had no role to play in the project beyond making the funds available."

An angry David McLean appeared on-screen pointing out that although the Scottish Government had had no sight of the feasibility study, it was about time that Scotland was favoured with funds to establish large transport projects and pointed to the UK government proposals to build a high speed rail link from London to Leeds and to construct the Jubilee Line in London...'both very expensive projects to which Scottish taxpayers contributed but where no benefit accrued to Scotland'. He went on to say that the Scottish Borders' Rail Link from Edinburgh was denied Westminster funding because it 'didn't *cross* the border' so it was about time that Scotland benefitted from funds derived from its own taxpayers."

The Downing Street source responded that the SNP merely wanted to play politics and that they ran the risk of alienating Scottish public opinion by putting constitutional politics before real benefit to the Scottish economy."

Sir Robert Cavendish sipped his coffee thoughtfully, placed the now half-empty cup on its saucer and turned off the television in the corner of his office. After further reflection, he lifted his phone and asked his assistant Michael Kowalski to join him.

"Bring the notes of our last Scotland meeting, would you?"

After a few minutes Kowalski appeared.

"What kept you?" asked Cavendish irritably.

"The file, sir. You asked me to keep it in the wall safe. It takes a few moments to open it."

"Ah! Yes, so I did."

Kowalski passed him the file and stood opposite the seated mandarin.

"That's all just now, Michael. I'll pass this back once I'm finished."

Kowalski regained his seat in the outer office and Cavendish opened the file to remind himself of the various initiatives he'd approved. He scanned the minute and thought for a while before picking up his phone and calling Benjamin Gold.

"Benjamin, old chap. Sir Robert here!" He continued to talk without any of the usual pleasantries associated with beginning a telephone call. "Your little idea of setting ablaze the homes of some of those English settlers in Scotland. Progress?"

"Funny you should call, Sir Robert. I've just fired the starting pistol on that. Two trustworthy young men are currently driving north with some jerry-cans full of petrol, Scottish Saltires and some spray-cans full of paint. I've given them some addresses I've researched where the occupants are English but are currently home down south. The fact of all of the charred ruins being owned by members of the English community and some graffiti encouraging them to stay south of the border should make the pages of the dailies...especially if we nudge them in that direction. Additionally, the two arsonists should be able to remain anonymous as they'll just make their way from one address to another. There's no obvious geographical pattern so the local constabulary shouldn't be able to get ahead of them."

"So it's underway?"

"And should be completed, I'd say, in three or four days. I'll pass the details on to your assistant, Michael for the file."

"Satisfactory!"

The phone was replaced on its cradle.

* * *

Rotermundt's mobile ring-tone suggested an old fashioned dial phone. He put it to his ear having first established that it didn't recognise the caller. He decided to remain anonymous until he knew who was calling him

"Yeah?"

"Biro here. I'm in. I'll be in Glasgow tomorrow. Make arrangements for your side of the bargain. I'll call you."

The call ended. Rotermundt stepped into an empty bus shelter he was passing and sat. Pensively he brought his phone before him and dialled Meridian Securities.

"Alex Alexander. How may I help you?"

"Rotermundt here. A further one hundred thousand pounds sterling shareholding in Madden's Transportation."

"Emil! It's good to hear from you." His tone changed. "Look, what do you know that I don't about Madden's? Your last investment resulted only in mild market interest but this'll have an impact on their share price. Without revealing anything you don't want to tell me, would you recommend these shares?"

"No comment! Listen, once you buy those shares, I need electronic confirmation that they're purchased. Make it clear that I own the shares but at the moment, put them temporarily in your company's name, not mine. I may have to transfer them shortly."

"You keep your cards close to your chest, Emil."

"You live longer that way, Mr. Alexander. Now get on and purchase these shares the way I've asked."

He pressed the 'off' button firmly. *Now I need to withdraw seventy-five grand in cash from my office safe in Portrush and transfer funds to*

Alexander electronically for these shares. He looked at his watch. *An hour and a bit to get there. Fifteen or twenty in my office. Another hour...and a half, given it'll be busier on the return leg...so...I catch an early evening plane to Glasgow and prepare to meet up with this Biro chap tomorrow. Better get moving...*

* * *

Morrison jumped from his taxi having earlier asked the driver to wait in order to take him to the Stena Terminal. Nimbly, he crossed the hotel entrance and headed for the lift where he drummed his fingers frustratedly at its slow elevation. Arriving at the seventh floor he moved quickly to his room where he removed his jacket and laced his arms through the leather straps which positioned the holster under his arm. He checked the pistol and placed it in the holster, securing it by means of a small leash. Deepening his trouser pocket, he removed his wallet and placed his MI5 credentials in its plastic window receptacle knowing he'd later be required to identify himself. *Fine show if I present as a member of the Salvation Army when asked to explain the Sauer P226. I'd get my head blown off!* Turning, he placed the laptop computer in his case and absently threw his clothes and toiletries on top. He closed the lid, secured it and made for the door.

Stepping from the lift he approached Reception.

"Sorry 'bout this but I've a family emergency. I need to check out and need you to deal with the hired car. I'm happy to pay any surcharges but I must return home immediately. You have my card details, just debit any outstanding amounts after I've gone."

The receptionist, from France according to her accent, understood Morrison's urgency.

"I hope you enjoyed your stay, sir. I'll deduct your hotel costs and the meals and drinks and will settle the car hire separately. Now, have you had anything from the mini-bar since this morning?"

Morrison's frustration reached boiling point.

"No...look...just bill me for anything you like. I must go. Give me my card please."

The receptionist hadn't achieved her career promotions without understanding all of the customer care imperatives necessary to satisfy hotel guests.

"Certainly sir. Would you like me to staple your receipt to the invoice?"

"Card!"

Almost pulling it from her hands, he turned and made his way hurriedly to the taxi where he seated himself.

"Stena ferry terminal. Let's go!"

* * *

Iona Forbes sat towards the stern of the huge Stena Superfast VII ferry to Scotland anxiously scanning the road network below for signs of a taxi carrying Donald John Morrison. As the last lorries were waved into the bowels of the ship, her concern rose and she surrendered to her disquiet, phoning Morrison even though at the next but one table sat the two couriers on whom she'd been asked to keep an eye. Turning her head from them she awaited her call being answered.

"Where are you?" she hissed.

"I told you not to call me, Iona! This is risky!" He relented. "Traffic. Sitting at roadworks at somewhere called Milewater Road. Hold on..."

He lowered his phone and shouted to the taxi driver.

"How long, d'you reckon?"

"We should get through these lights next time so maybe another ten minutes."

He returned the phone to his ear. "Guy says ten minutes."

"Then you won't make it. The ramp's being lifted and it looks like we're off in a few moments."

"Shit!" He raised his left hand to the phone, covering his mouth. "Listen. I'll catch the next plane to Glasgow. With luck we'll arrive around the same time. Your job becomes even more important now. Just maintain a watching brief. Do *not* make contact with them. Do *not* allow them to imagine you have an interest in them. Do *not* become involved with any security personnel when you dock at Cairnryan. The harbour doesn't look much but it has one of the most sophisticated port security systems in the UK given its role in managing the Ulster stuff. That said, people walking on to a bus carrying a backpack won't raise much in the way of suspicion. Nor will you. Remember, if you *are*...and I don't know this for sure...but if you *are* fingered for any reason you might find yourself a person of interest and detained if the photographs of you that I've seen have already been passed out to other agents or ports of entry." He shook his head, still annoyed. "Now don't phone me. Got that?"

"Okay. I'm a couple of tables from them. Everything seems fine. I'll keep an eye on them and you phone me when you get to Glasgow. I'll try to maintain contact when we arrive at the bus station." She thought further. "If I lose them, then what?"

"Try not to, but if that happens, I'll meet you back in the Steps Bar where we had a drink after the march a few weeks back."

"Okay, got it. See you. Safe flight, bye."

Iona continued her surveillance of the dockside as the ship pulled away slowly into the harbour. Before it had reached Carrickfergus, some eighteen nautical miles on its journey east, early boredom saw her decide to purchase something to read. The two couriers had ordered drinks from the bar and were happily chatting. *Can't see them getting up to any mischief on board. They've nowhere to go if I go to the shop to buy a magazine or newspaper or something.* With no carry-on luggage beyond her small yellow handbag, she surrendered her seat and walked steadily to the ship's shop as the vessel was still on the flat calm of Belfast Lough.

Buying a glossy magazine, she returned to her seat and began disinterestedly to flick through pages of minor royals, celebrities and wives of soccer stars. Her boredom unassuaged, she decided a drink from the bar was in order and leaving her magazine on the table as evidence of her rightful claim upon it, she walked the few steps to the bar where she ordered a gin and tonic, paying the barman who then poured the mixer with such carelessness that it overflowed the glass.

"Travellin' light, hen?"

Iona turned to see one of the objects of her attention leaning on the bar and addressing her with a wide smile on her face.

"Sorry?"

"Saw ye walkin' oan and now yer sittin' therr wi' nae luggage. See... *that's* the way tae travel. Footloose and fancy free."

The barman returned Forbes' change and turned his attention to her interlocutor.

"Eh, a big vodka'n coke an' a big white wine."

Do not make contact! The last instructions from Morrison replayed in her mind.

"Yeah. A last minute decision to travel."

"Saw ye lookin' oot the windae when the boat wis leavin'. Boyfriend trouble?"

Iona decided on the line of least resistance.

"S'pose. We argued and I decided to go back to Glasgow."

Her new friend lowered her voice as she looked conspiratorially at her partner who, catching her glance, gave her a big 'thumbs-up'. She smiled broadly in return before returning to her theme.

"See men? Therr a' bastirts so they ur."

Iona smiled. "You said it!"

The barman placed two drinks next to Iona's gin and was handed a twenty pound note. As she reached forward to pay, the girl's heavily tattooed right forearm revealed a long, swollen wound. Obviously untreated, it was red and infected. Iona's reaction was as authentic as it was concerned."

"Oh...*that* looks painful. What happened?"

The girl inspected the wound.

"Cut it oan gless last week. Lost a bit o' blood but ah think it'll be a'right."

Iona held her gaze.

"I'm a nurse. It looks far from all right." She placed her glass to one side. "D'you mind if I take a look?"

"Yer a'right, hen. Ah'd better take his voddy ower tae him or he'll get a' cranky."

Iona stood her ground. She placed her hand on the arm and turned it slightly to get a better look.

"From where I stand, this wound looks like it's infected the deeper layers and tissues of your skin. You can see yourself that it's swollen and red and I'd bet it hurts. If you don't have it treated, it could cause fever and dizziness. You might become nauseous, especially if the ferry journey is rough. If you're unlucky you could develop osteomyelitis which is a bacterial infection of the bone." She attempted another appeal, "It would only take a minute to treat it," but sensed continuing uncertainty. "Why don't you take your drinks over to your friend and we'll fix this in the ladies' toilet?"

Obviously unused to care and attention being lavished upon her, the girl took some moments before lifting the drinks.

"Only if it's quick!"

"Take the drinks over. I'll be back in a minute and we'll go and fix this."

Unsteadily due to her alcohol consumption, the girl returned to her seat while Forbes revisited the small shop and bought some first aid items, returning to find the couple arguing.

The man addressed Iona directly.

"You a peeler?"

"Pardon?"

"A cop. You a policeman?"

"Well, first off, I'm a woman so it'd be policewoman but no. Second, I'm a nurse. Your girlfriend needs her arm attended to."

The girl intervened.

"It's a wee bit sore, Fitz."

Fitzgerald drew his hand across his chin as if giving great consideration to his decision.

"Okay, but don't be long."

The two women made their way to the ladies' lavatory where introductions were made.

"I'm Iona by the way."

"Sandra Butler."

"That a Glasgow accent?"

"Govan. That Fitz therr is from Newtownabbey."

"I'm from the islands."

They entered and approached a sink which Iona cleaned with some antiseptic soap before inviting Sandra to offer her arm to the water tap. She tested the water temperature and played some on her own arm before positioning Sandra's arm under the tap, hearing a pained reaction as she did so.

Cleaning the wound in water into which she'd poured several bags of salt taken from the cafeteria, she carefully dried the wound and applied antiseptic cream on its length before placing some moisturised tissue she'd thickened with Epsom salts bought from the shop.

"That poultice will reduce the infection but you'll need to have it cleaned regularly. Now I'll bandage it up."

She dried the limb with paper towels, opened a roll of crepe bandage and expertly wrapped it around Sandra's forearm to protect the wound. Inspecting it, she decided all was as well as could be and looked up to see tears running down Sandra's face.

"What's wrong?"

"You're dead nice, Iona."

"I'm a nurse, Sandra, it's what we do." She decided to push a little. "Is your boyfriend nice to you? What did you say his name was? Fitz?"

"He's okay. When he's goat a drink in him he can be a bit o' a' bastirt." She decided more information was necessary. "It wis him that did *this*!" She proffered her arm. "We wis arguin' an' he smashed a boattle an' hit ma arm wi' it. Ah mean it wis a kinda *accident* so it wis."

Iona held Sandra's hand sympathetically.

"You don't need to put up with that, Sandra. You should just walk away from people like Fitz. He's no right to hurt you..." She smiled, attempting to unearth more information. "Anyway, what kind of name's Fitz? Is that his first name?"

"Name's Malachy Fitzgerald. But he hates Malachy so everyone calls him Fitz. But don't say ye know that. He hates it."

Iona squeezed her hand affectionately.

"You tell him you won't be treated poorly, Sandra. And find someone else who'll be nice to you if he doesn't change. There's places you can go in Glasgow if you need support." She collected the detritus around the sink and placed it in a receptacle, handing the antiseptic ointment to Sandra. "Keep this. Keep the wound clean and apply this every day before you go to bed. If you feel sick, get yourself to hospital. It might signify sepsis which can be life-threatening. I don't imagine it *will* be but it's better to be safe than sorry." She squeezed Sandra's arm reassuringly. "Now let's get back to our drinks."

The twosome returned to the seated area where Fitz had already finished his vodka and coke and had ordered a further round of drinks, including a gin and tonic for Iona.

"Decided ye were all right, misses!"

Iona and Sandra sat and Fitz lifted his drink ostentatiously.

"Thanks for sorting her arm..." he raised his eyebrows inviting a name. Sandra responded.

"Her name's Iona. She's fixed ma arm an' she's dead nice."

Iona decided that she might quit while she was ahead.

"Thanks. One drink, then I'll let you two get on. I've a magazine to get through and I wanted some sleep before we get to Scotland."

"Her boyfriend's just chucked her," offered Sandra sympathetically. "An' she's dead nice, tae!" A significant quantity of wine was swallowed as Sandra repeated her earlier assessment of the male species, moderating it in the company of Fitz but allowing the intended meaning.

"Some men kin be right bastirts!"

Chapter Twenty-four

The taxi driver, grateful for the increased fare, pulled into the drop-off bay at the George Best Belfast City Airport and rolled down his passenger-side window to permit Morrison to pay.

Stepping out, Morrison looked for a uniformed person in order to disclose his status as an officer of MI5. Seeing no one, he entered the concourse and asked directions to the office of Airport Police and within seconds was knocking at the door of an office that appeared un-manned. Frustrated, he turned to find two officers approach, each carrying a Heckler and Koch *Maschinenpistole 5* automatic weapon.

The taller of the two officers approached Morrison.

"Sir?"

"Afternoon officer. My name is Donald John Morrison. I am officer of MI5 and an authorised firearms officer. Under the National Aviation Security Programme I have to advise you that I am carrying a Sauer P226 pistol which is holstered under my left arm. My identification is in my wallet."

The smaller of the two officers stepped back and raised his weapon slightly in readiness for use should it be necessary. His colleague addressed Morrison.

"That'll be dead-on, sir. Would ye mind givin' us a wee look at your ID and we'll take it from there?"

Morrison dug in his trouser pocket and opened his wallet which revealed his photograph and particulars.

After inspecting it, the officer nodded his acceptance.

"Let's step into the office, eh Mr. Morrison? We'll deal with this out of sight of the great unwashed if that's okay."

Both officers removed their caps and while one kept his automatic pistol in readiness, the other continued his friendly approach.

"Willie here'll stick on the kettle for a wee coffee if you've time Mr. Morrison."

"Next plane to Glasgow?"

The policeman looked at the wall clock.

"Eh, there's one leaving at the back of six. You've time for a coffee unless you're wantin' to spend time in duty-free. Not that there's much point seein' as how you're just crossin' the Irish Sea."

"A coffee would be great. Black'll be fine."

"Well now, can I ask if the pistol is loaded and capable of discharge?"

"It is."

"Then would you mind carefully removing it and placing it before me on the desk, remembering that Willie here has a big gun pointed at your rear end?"

Morrison complied. The officer opened a drawer of his desk and took from it a clear plastic bag into which he placed the gun.

"No other weapons or sharp objects, sir?"

"None."

"And can I ask if you have need of this weapon while you are aboard the plane?"

"I do not."

"Then I'll hand this personally to the pilot when we walk you to the plane and a police officer will return it to you as you disembark at Glasgow." He took a form from another desk drawer. "I'll just make a note and maybe you'd sign this, Mr. Morrison?"

The kettle came to the boil as Morrison appended his signature to the paper.

* * *

After having imbibed both gin and tonics and engaged in some banal conversation, Iona excused herself and returned to her nearby seat saying she needed some shut-eye. Before leaving, she offered to buy a round for her fellow travellers but her suggestion was rejected by a now quite drunk couple flush with newly-found money.

Sitting alone while the couple made arrangements to buy yet another round, Iona took her phone and began making notes regarding her dealings with Sandra Butler and Malachy Fitzgerald. Satisfied she'd committed all of her gained knowledge to her phone, she felt the effects of the gin overcome her and closed her eyes, just as she'd presented to her new friends.

Forty minutes later, Iona found herself warm and reawakening from her brief nap. Aware of her gradual restoration to consciousness, she maintained her appearance of slumber as Sandra and Fitz argued, their poor attempts at whispering resembling low breathy shouts.

"Ye were telt no' tae open it. They might see ye tried and no' gie's the rest o' the money."

"I just opened the rucksack. The parcel inside is all sealed up. But it's not addressed to this guy Fitzgerald that we're meant to meet. It's..." he opened the flap of the backpack and re-read the address. "somebody called Doctor Simon Doncaster of eighty-five Ayr Road, Cumnock in Scotland."

Her eyes still closed, Iona started at hearing the name of the recipient. The SNP Member of the Scottish Parliament for Carrick, Cumnock and Doon Valley.

"Maybe we should just post it, Fitz."

"Then we don't get the other two hundred and fifty, dopey!" He closed the flap. "And I'll tell ye another thing. There's no way this is weed. It weighs too much and ye can tell from the parcel that it's got hard stuff inside it, no' soft like ye'd expect from weed."

"Then whit is it?"

"Maybe it's two half bricks, stupid. Maybe it's the Encyclopaedia Britannica."

"Naebidy pays five hunner quid to carry bricks or books ower tae Scotland, Fitz."

Fitzgerald was thoughtful.

"Naw...naw they wouldn't, would they?" He took a long drink of his vodka. "Maybe we should open it. It's got to be worth money whatever it is. I bet we could sell whatever's in here for more than we're makin' on this deal." He gave the matter more thought. "Naw...I've got a better idea. Let's see how much they're willin' to pay for this parcel once we get to Glasgow. I'm bettin' we could get another few hundred quid if we play our cards right."

"Fitz, Ah don't want nae trouble."

Due to the speed restrictions imposed during the tern breeding season, the ferry shuddered as it slowed to enter the length of Loch Ryan. Iona took this as an opportunity to open her eyes as if just reawakening. In front of her sat two unopened small tins of tonic and what she took to be two large glasses of gin. Her awakening was noticed by Sandra.

"Iona, we got ye a wee drink for the bus, hen. Drink up or jist hide wan an' take it oan the bus. They'll no' stoap ye ne'er they will. No' if they don't see it."

Iona smiled at Sandra's thoughtfulness.

"I'll attempt it here. I'd just spill it on the bus."

She mixed the drinks having no intention other than to enjoy a few sips before departure, and sat back to enjoy the luscious wooded scenery of rural Scotland along the loch side.

**

Morrison, now on first name terms with the two police officers, had purchased his ticket and was escorted to the plane where a package containing his pistol was handed to the captain along with an explanation of the line of work of the passenger now allocated complementary upgraded seat 1C. Some hand-shaking concluded the arrangement.

"They'll look after you now, Donald John. Have a safe trip."

"Thanks, Gordon." He nodded thanks to his partner. "Willie!"

The front three rows on each side had been reserved for passengers paying more for an early glass of Champagne. As the plane filled, Morrison accepted his flute glass and sipped at it absentmindedly. *Mostly businessmen*, he reflected as a line of travellers passed him by, each manoeuvring their carry-on luggage between those already seated. Suddenly his glass was stilled at his lips as, handing his ticket to the steward at the front door of the aircraft, was one Emil Rotermundt. He gestured his understanding to the steward who directed him to the rear while double checking his seat number as he made his way to the back of the plane, completely indifferent to the man now staring at him from seat 1C.

As the plane rose in the sky and levelled, Morrison unbuckled his seatbelt and approached a toilet located at the front door of the plane. Turning to check that the steward had drawn the curtain between the coach and business class passengers he stepped instead into an area used by the cabin crew and opened his wallet showing his identification.

"The police officers identified me upon boarding?" he asked rhetorically. "Can I have a look at the manifest?"

The young lady turned and produced a clip-board on which was a sheet of paper that listed all on board. Morrison thanked her and scanned the document. In seat 26B was listed one Emil Rotermundt.

"This man is of interest to me."

The steward took the manifest.

"26B? That suggests a late booking. Few people want to travel in the middle seat if they can avoid it. The passenger's name is Mr. Rotermundt. How might we help you."

"You have a weapon belonging to me in the pilot's cabin. I need to follow Mr. Rotermundt without his suspicions being arisen. If I have to wait for all protocols to be completed he'll have left the concourse before me. Either I am allowed off the plane first with my weapon or Mr. Rotermundt is detained somehow. Can you ask the pilot for his views?"

"Certainly, sir. Take your seat and I'll call you forward once I hear from the captain."

Twenty-five minutes later the green sward of the Heads of Ayr was the first part of Scotland recognised by Morrison as he peered over the shoulder of his fellow passenger sitting at the window seat. As the plane closed on Glasgow, the steward returned and closed the curtain fully, eliminating any likelihood of Morrison being observed from the rear of the cabin.

"You can enter the cockpit."

Morrison stepped into the cramped space occupied by the captain and co-pilot.

The uniformed man on the left claimed the title of captain.

"Ah, Mr. Morrison. I gather we have your artillery on board today."

"You have."

"I've called ahead. In order not to offend protocol...heaven forfend that we offend protocol...the first person on board when we dock will be a plain-clothes police officer trained to kill with a spoon. He will wear a hi-viz vest and represent himself as a regular member of the crew. The officer will remove this cannon you've left in our safekeeping and will return it to you upon your disembarkation. You will be first to leave the plane. The passenger in seat 26B will be one of the last to leave. You'll have four or five minutes advantage on him. How does that sound?"

"Perfect. I'm grateful captain."

He grinned. "No problem. Like to take the wheel and land this kite?"

Morrison returned the grin and re-took his seat.

Chapter Twenty-five

Ethan Collier and Ivan Chadwick were two recently recruited members of the English Defence League. Each had had numerous convictions for criminality and in Chadwick's case, a further charge of racially motivated hate crime had been presented, which required him to appear before Sheffield Crown Court some two weeks hence. Driving north to Scotland, they each sipped at a can of lager. Collier, who was driving, insisted on its inability to affect his blood alcohol level because of its relatively low alcohol content of only four percent.

"You just need to be careful when we cross into Scotland, Ethan," Chadwick warned. "Down 'ere, rozzers will nick you if you're at eighty per cent but once we cross the border they'll nick you if you're over fifty."

"Give over...y'can't be sober in England an' drunk in Scotland. We're one country. It's *United* Kingdom. *United.* Can't be havin' one law fa us and one fa Jocks. Anyway, I'm a good drunk driver. I actually fink I drive better when I've a few in me."

"Point taken m'friend...point taken."

Chadwick consulted the map he'd earlier removed from the glovebox and unfolded it, partially obstructing Collier's view.

"Fuckin' watch it, pal. It'll be *you* causin' me to crash, not t' lager! Careful now!"

"Just checkin' we're on right road, Ethan. Boys in pub told me that when we get to Scotland all road signs are in double Dutch. We'll know when we get there when we can't read t'fuckin' road signs."

"'Ow far to first 'ouse?"

Chadwick pulled a piece of paper from his denims' pocket.

"List 'ere says we've to go first to empty 'ouse just outside Lockerbie. 'Bout another forty miles, I'd say. Maybe an hour if you don't get us lost." He returned the paper to his pocket.

"I'm just t'drunk driver, mate. You're t'navigator."

They drove in silence for a while, Chadwick concentrating on the map. After a while he spoke up.

"I'm lookin' forward to this, Ethan. Torchin' homes of them fuckin' whingin' Jocks. They take our money and spend it on all the socialist shite of t'day. Free this and free that. Then they want *more*! It's a fuckin' liberty and it's you and me that pay for it. They actually want *more* immigrants! Muslim bastids who'll 'ate Scotland soon as they arrive, then they'll pour over t'border to England to start *Sharia* law and we'll be back where we started. Fellah that hired us told us that 'omes we're to burn down are all anti-English. They hate us. So now they'll pay the price. Rule Britannia, eh?"

"Fuckin' Rule Britannia, my friend!"

In the rear of the estate car, seven Saltire flags affixed to short poles lay neatly along the length of the seat. Two, six litre plastic jerry-cans designed to hold water but full of petroleum were strapped to the side of the boot. Two cans of spray paint ready for graffiti work were lying loosely beside them.

Chadwick asked a question of Collier that had been plaguing him for the past ten minutes.

"'Ow is it that they want us to burn t'Jocks' places down then leave t'Jock flag then spray paint stuff about English goin' home?"

Collier was silent as he too pondered the question. Some moments passed as he arrived at his answer.

"Double bluff, init! They want rozzers to fink it were Jocks what done it. It'll be to fool Rozzers, in my opinion. This bloke...'im what gave us cash, 'e looked sharp. It'll be double bluff alright."

Chadwick nodded sagely.

"Yeah, double bluff...though I still don' understand why they want rozzers to fink Jock homes are being torched by Jocks." His attention was distracted by a road sign. "Hey, Ethan...Scotland. Big sign there says '*Welcome to Scotland*' with that Jock language underneath. Bet they wouldn't welcome us if they knew what we were up to, eh?"

A jerry-can is a robust liquid container made from pressed steel. Designed in Germany in the nineteen-thirties for military use to hold just over four gallons of fuel, an important feature was an indentation on each side that strengthened the can while allowing the contents to expand. The interior is also lined with an impervious plastic, first developed for steel beer barrels that would allow the can to be used for either water or petrol. The can, when invented, was welded and had a gasket for a leak-proof mouth. Unfortunately, the water containers that Collier and Chadwick had used for their petrol had none of these features. The cap on one had not been screwed tightly and fumes had leaked from the moment they had set off from Sheffield. Some ten miles outside Lockerbie, Collier decided a cigarette was in order and offered one to his driving companion. As he ignited his cigarette lighter, it was the last communication he attempted on this earth.

As gas explodes, it produces a powerful shockwave that surges away from the ignition point, the blast and heat radiating from the combusting gas commonly being deadly in confined spaces. As Chadwick and Collier were consumed in a five hundred and thirty six degrees Fahrenheit blast, the impulse of the shock-wave caused abdominal organs and costal interspaces between the ribs of the two men to be devastated and resulted in the disintegration, evisceration and traumatic amputation of their body parts. Collier died instantly. Chadwick, minus a forearm, lay on the grass verge on the point of death.

***

Morrison walked ahead of the disembarking travellers and sat at an empty gate awaiting Rotermundt's arrival. Apparently indifferent, the plain-clothes police officer sat close by tasked with escorting Morrison through the airport. As the flow of passengers began to ebb, Rotermundt strode past prompting him to rise and follow. Through an abandoned passport control without challenge and down to luggage retrieval, Morrison remained behind and out of sight. Each lifted their case from the carousel and made for the exit, again without confrontation, this time by Revenue and Customs. As they lined up at the taxi rank Morrison stood behind Rotermundt as the taxi marshal asked him his destination in order to determine whether the taxi should be allocated a speedy return to the rank should the destination be local.

"City centre."

Morrison repeated the destination and took his seat.

"Follow my pal there, would you driver? It's a hotel in the city centre but the bugger's pissed and didn't tell me what hotel we're staying in."

"Too much bevy on the plane?"

"Too much bevy before he got *on* the plane, I'm afraid. He's an arse!"

The driver laughed in recognition of his passenger's not uncommon experience as Morrison sat back and awaited arrival at an unknown destination.

* * *

On the bus, Iona had positioned herself behind and to one side of Fitzgerald and Butler, both of whom were now fast asleep, their mouths open and emitting guttural noises almost capable of being heard over the noise of the bus engines. Seated towards the rear of the bus, no one sat behind them and Iona wrestled with her next step. Morrison's instructions echoed in her head. *Do not engage!* Deciding he'd both understand and would appreciate her actions, she fished the phone from her denims' pocket, activated her phone camera, moved forward and took a few unflattering photographs of the duo sleeping, mouths agape. Confident now that they were both completely asleep, she stepped gingerly into the seats behind them and, reaching up, removed the backpack from the overhead storage bin. Carefully, she removed the parcel and confirmed that the address, in bold lettering, was indeed that of the nationalist politician, Doctor Simon Doncaster. Quickly she took a photograph before manipulating the package to determine its contents. *It's not soft like it was cannabis plants or even a bit firmer like it was resin. It's hard...there's material in here protecting the contents...is that a gun butt? Could it be a bomb?* she asked herself. *I'm getting paranoid. It might be the Encyclopaedia Britannic just like Fitz suggested. No postage stamps,* she noticed. *This is to be hand delivered.* She took another photograph of it sitting partially inside the backpack then replaced it above the sleeping duo. Carefully, she sat again in her seat and compiled a report on her phone including photographs that she intended giving to Morrison when they met. *Who knows if Donald John's security services are now tracking my electronic messaging, she pondered. Face to face is safer...and I want to see his face when I show him all this information.*

* * *

In Stranraer Harbour, the fishing vessel, *Nimrod*, sat at anchor, its owner, Billy Wilson cleaning and tidying up after its journey from Carlingford sea-lough. As he screwed the mop into a bucket in order to relieve it of its bleached water, he noticed a dark-blue, leather-clad motorcyclist purr onto the decking enclosing the marina. Expecting him, he stepped down below the wheelhouse and brought up a silver case within which was a heavily taped, brown paper parcel addressed to Doctor Simon Doncaster of eighty-five Ayr Road, Cumnock. Checking to ensure that there were no suspicious eyes on his activities, he swung his leg over the side of the vessel and descended into a small rowing boat which, after positioning the oars in the rowlocks, he rowed to the deck of the marina.

The motorcyclist, without removing his headgear, had walked down a short flight of steps to avoid Wilson leaving the boat.

"You have a package for Doctor Doncaster. My name is Harley Davidson."

"Then why are you driving a Honda?"

"I prefer Hondas."

Satisfied the courier had navigated the coded welcome properly, Wilson handed over the case. With two bounds, the motorcyclist reached the top of the steps, taking them three at a time. Before Wilson had managed to organise the oars properly in order to return to his boat, he could hear the growl of the Honda as it navigated some lobster pots before its tone rose. It gathered speed, disappeared along Stranraer's King Street and into the town centre.

Chapter Twenty-six

"I tell you, Jack, I just don't *like* the man. He has more pernicious wickedness in him than an Al-Qaeda suggestion box. I've blocked his promotion twice and I'd do so again."

Kemp accepted the overall premise of his boss's argument.

"I wouldn't go for a pint with him, boss, but he's proven himself to be effective over the piece."

"Giles Grantham is a slimeball who diminishes our organisation, Jack. Remember his efforts in Bradford? Didn't cover himself in glory, did he? Remember Grimsby?"

"Fair points, boss but Grantham's delivered for us in a number of other circumstances where...where, well, where a more *creative* approach was called for."

"He should be drummed out of the Brownies, Jack. We either stand for ethics, values and honour or we're as bad as the baddest guy we're trying to lock up."

"You make a fair point, boss," said Kemp attempting to deflect the conversation.

"And now he's working with that other reprobate, your pal, Sir Robert Cavendish. Another who blights the organisation if in a different way. They're both involved in the Scotland initiative and they're both scoundrels." He raised his voice. "Tell me they're *not!*"

"Can't argue, boss." He took a beat. "What would you have me do?"

The Director General of MI5, tapped his pen on a glass of water, mulling over his response.

"You're happy that you have them under control...that they've nothing to do with this dark money?"

"I keep myself briefed as much as possible with all that's going on across the entire organisation, boss. You know that."

"But they've not shed any light on this dark money that's intended to influence Scottish opinion on independence?"

"You asked me earlier not to reveal our knowledge of this money washing around the system to Sir Robert. Nevertheless, I allowed a conversation to develop where it would have been raised by them had they any knowledge but neither he nor Grantham had heard anything, boss. And neither have I."

"I'm going to give this further thought, Jack. And I intend to act. We simply can't have a renegade operation within the confines of this great office of state. And I promise you that when we unearth this bastard, he'll swing. I'll have his guts for garters."

"Well, he, she or they will have it coming, boss."

***

Rotermundt's taxi pulled up outside Glasgow's Central Hotel in a sunny Gordon Street as did Morrison's. They each paid their driver and entered the hotel, Rotermundt clearly unaware he was being followed. At reception, Morrison delayed as he placed his case on the floor and feigned difficulty in finding his wallet while listening to Rotermundt's conversation.

"Two nights. Name's Emil Rotermundt. I have a reservation."

Morrison discovered his wallet and also asked a second receptionist for a room for two nights. As each had their details recorded, Rotermundt completed first and was allocated a room on the third floor.

As Rotermundt left to occupy room three-eleven, Morrison asked for a room on the third floor and after a cheery 'no problem, sir' was given an electronic card permitting him entry to room three-thirty.

Deciding that Rotermundt was probably safely ensconced in his hotel room for the evening, Morrison decided that meeting up with Iona was next on his list. He checked his watch. *Still early evening. A shower, meet Iona in the Steps Bar and I'll take care of Rotermundt in the morning when he checks out.*

***

Iona followed Fitzgerald and Butler as they exited Buchanan Bus Station and made their way downhill to George Square in the city centre. They stopped at the side of Queen Street Station where Sandra took possession of the backpack and walked to a nearby pub which looked out into the square. Fitzgerald walked onwards to George Square where he put the red bobble hat on his head and sat on a bench awaiting contact.

Iona stopped outside Queen Street station and held her position. After some time, a man approached the bench and sat on Fitzgerald's left hand side.

"My name's Fitzgerald," said the man. "I believe you have a package for me."

Malachy Fitzgerald, still drunk, remembered the name he'd been told to expect.

"Aye, well maybe I have and maybe I've not!"

Maintaining his poise, the man continued.

"Well, I have the second half of your fee in my pocket. It would be most advisable if we merely traded the package for this envelope. That was the agreement, was it not?"

"Ah, well y'see, I've been thinkin'. That package looks like it's worth a lot more than five hundred quid. I was thinkin' it was maybe more like a grand."

The man laughed. "A thousand pounds?"

"Well, as you can see, I don't have the bag with me so if ye want to see it again it'll cost you another five ton plus the two-fifty you owe me."

The man nodded in feigned understanding.

"Of course there is another way of dealing with this."

"And what's that?"

The man pulled his jacket open just sufficiently to reveal a holstered revolver.

"I could just take you into a nearby lane and shoot you in each leg until you told me how to get the bag and then put a bullet in your face so the mourners at your funeral...not that I imagine there would be many...wouldn't recognise the young man from Northern Ireland who left their soil only hours previously. Have you ever seen what a bullet in the face does to a man? I swear that even when it's tidied up for the wake it makes the old fizzog look like a half-chewed caramel and the pain of a kneecapping?...well it's just indescribable. Now, does *that* seem like it's worth five hundred quid?"

Fitzgerald still eyed the revolver concealed beneath the jacket and his alcohol-induced self-assurance dissolved.

"Will you still give us the two-fifty?"

"Where's the bag."

"My girlfriend has it."

"Well now, can she see us sitting here?"

Fitzgerald nodded.

"Then wave her over. Do it now."

Stiffly, Fitzgerald turned to face the window of the Counting House pub where Sandra sat in one of the window bays. He waved hopefully, all the time concerned that she might be at the bar, would miss his signal and he'd have to deal with a gunman intent upon killing him.

After a long silence had elapsed, Sandra emerged from the door of the pub and walked unsteadily towards them. The man stood as she arrived at the bench.

"Have you interfered in any way with this package?"

Both shook their head, mumbling denial.

"We just thought..."

The man leaned over each of them and theatrically pulled at his jacket in order to allow Sandra to see his holstered gun.

"You just *thought?*...I should shoot you both where you stand."

Holding their terrified gaze, he reached his right hand inside his suit jacket and removed an envelope.

"I keep my word. You two should learn to do the same. Here's your cash. Not a word to anyone or I'll find you and kill you both!"

Heaving the backpack over one shoulder, he strode away in the direction of the station without looking back.

Immediately, Fitzgerald and Butler retook the bench and opened the envelope, greatly cheered by a further wad of banknotes. Sandra asked no questions.

"'Mon back intae that pub, Fitz. The drink's dead cheap."

As the man entered the station looking for the taxi rank he knew must exist in every rail terminus, he passed a young lady obviously transfixed by her mobile phone. Unaware of her interest in him, he walked onward, completely oblivious to the artificial shutter click which captured his image.

* * *

Uncertain whether to follow the man or to join the couriers in the Counting House, Iona looked at her watch and decided both that while meeting Morrison was key, there was still sufficient time to purchase some female necessities. Returning her phone to her hip pocket, she took off in search of the last forty minutes of shopping opportunities in Fraser's apartment store just a short walk down Buchanan Street. *Just some essentials...knickers, socks, tampons, toothpaste and...well, it's Fraser's...some nice perfume.* She thought further. *Perhaps a blouse... or two.*

She set off.

Chapter Twenty-seven

Detective Sergeant Watson Baxter (known to everyone as *Tallman* on account of his six feet, six inch height) had been a police officer for fourteen years and a detective for four of these. Promoted only the year before, he'd enjoyed a solid grounding in generic police work albeit undertaking his duties solely in the Dumfries and Galloway Region of Police Scotland. A first responder when notified of the fatal car explosion, he'd surrendered responsibility for the scene of the event first to ambulance drivers and Fire and Rescue officers and then to his local detective pal, Stuart Cruikshank.

Three hours later, the road had been cleared, the car had been taken to the pound, Collier to the morgue and Chadwick to the Dumfries and Galloway Royal Infirmary at Cargenbridge, just outside Dumfries.

Disregarding his police radio in favour of his personal phone, he contacted Stuart Cruikshank.

"Stuart! Tallman here. Jean expects you, me and your lovely wife, Helen at eight. How are you placed?"

"I'm in hospital waiting to hear of the prognosis of the young fellah who lost an arm in that explosion."

"He going to make it?"

"Don't know, but if he does, I want to hear him explain the remnants of the Scottish flags, paint spray and why he had gallons of fuel in thin plastic canisters that would have been tested by distilled water."

"Well, I'm finished here. I'll join you at the hospital and we'll head off together. Okay with you?"

"Ward eleven. See you."

Watson drove his BMW police vehicle along the A709 towards Lochmaben and past two of the pretty town's five lochs. Driving the highways and byways of his locality had never lost its appeal; one of the reasons he'd refused earlier promotions to the Central Belt of Scotland with its 'urban squalor and Soviet architecture' as he'd explained to his wife, Jean at the time. The twenty minute drive was taken almost leisurely and he pulled in at the hospital, parked, and took the lift to the first floor where ward eleven was located.

Stuart Cruikshank was half-sitting on the edge of a desk at the nurses' station as the lift doors opened revealing Baxter.

"Hi Tallman, just talking to Wilma...Nurse Keane here. She reckons that our man will pull through but that he'll be under sedation until sometime tomorrow. He's lost a forearm and has first and second degree burns. Also broken his remaining wrist so he'll not be lifting a pint anytime soon."

"Shame." He nodded at the nurse. "Hi, Wilma." He looked at the closed ward door. "He been in theatre yet?"

"Yes. They've dealt with the arm, set his wrist and have done some work on his burns but there will be a further couple of visits to theatre, the surgeon reckons."

"So his clothes have been stripped from him and stored somewhere?"

"They're in a locker behind me."

"D'you think we could have a look at them?"

"Sure. What's left of them."

She opened a desk drawer and removed a set of keys, rose and opened a locker. Baxter took a plastic basket from the locker and lifted the shirt. Burned and blackened, it had no pocket. He laid it aside as he did the single trainer shoe, the other having been consumed by the fire. His denim trousers revealed a wallet.

"That's how we identified him, Sergeant. His name's Ivan Chadwick. He comes from a place called Burngreave in Sheffield."

Baxter let her information pass without comment. He opened the wallet and inspected its contents.

"So what have we here?" He counted slowly. "Four hundred quid. A driving licence in the name of Ivan Charles Chadwick. Date of birth, second July, nineteen ninety-two."

Baxter handed the license to Cruikshank for his own inspection.

"Some bank cards here...second class stamps; three of...a Tesco card, two credit cards; Lloyds and Halifax, an unused condom that looks like it's been in his wallet some considerable time and...let's see," he consulted a small white sheet of paper. A list of eight addresses."

Baxter made his way through the list. "All in Scotland."

He turned to Cruikshank.

"Have we identified the guy who was still in the drivers' seat?"

"Nah. It's a dental records' case. The fellah was charred."

Baxter returned the items to the wallet, to the trouser pocket and returned the basket to the small locker.

"We done here?"

"Aye."

"Nurse...Wilma...Many thanks. If you could just leave the belongings as they are we'll have them collected."

He squeezed Cruikshank's shoulder affectionately.

"Let's be off, Detective Cruikshank. Our wives await our presence."

As they walked towards the lift Cruikshank protested half-heartedly.

"You've done it again."

"What?"

"*I'm* meant to be the detective in the family, Tallman. I've been a detective for five years, you've only been one for four even if you did get a lucky promotion. *I'm* meant to go through his gear and make shrewd and intelligent assessments."

Baxter smiled. "Aye well, you were too busy interviewing wee nurse Wilma, weren't you?

Cruikshank returned his grin.

"Aye well, she was worth the interview, eh?"

***

With some difficulty due to the three bags of purchases she carried, Iona elbowed her way through the small double door that served as the entrance to the Steps Bar and laid her acquisitions on an empty table before stepping up to the quiet bar and asking for a pint of Guinness.

Taking in the somnolent atmosphere of the Art Deco bar and as she waited for the stout to settle, she nodded an acknowledgement to an elderly man and his wife who sat silently, having run out of conversation many years previously. The only other customer, another elderly man, had been conversing with the young barman but had paused his discourse while the lad attended to the Guinness.

Settling the bill, Iona retreated to the table and taking a first sip, replaced the glass on the table before inspecting the contents of her shopping bags without removing anything from them. Pleased at her purchases, she took her phone from her hip pocket and reviewed her notes, sighing in recognition of a battery that was now in low single figures. I'll just have to remember everything and tell Donald John how I should be promoted to 'special agent Forbes' when he arrives.

Not daring to reduce her battery life any further and with no other distractions to take her attention, she focussed upon her Guinness.

Raising her eyes to the television positioned above the doorway, the image of the Right Honourable Oliver Robson, the Westminster Secretary of State for Environment, Food and Rural Affairs appeared on the news programme.

Announcing that proposals to tackle water shortages in Britain's southern counties by building a vast 'super canal' between Scotland and England was being considered by the UK government, he went on to say, "The government believes that severe water shortages will be "inevitable" unless a solution can be found." He explained, "The Natural Grid is a proposed canal that would run from the Scottish Borders down to England's south-east. The ambition is to have a large-scale water supply, with a slight fall, so that no pumping will be needed."

Asked if the Scottish government had endorsed his department's proposals, Robson smiled oleaginously.

"We've yet to test these proposals but in the great union of these islands, we're all in it together. No one can deny that the rain it raineth on the just and the unjust, as it says in the Bible. But frankly it raineth a lot more in Scotland than it doth in England. So we feel sure our proposals will be met well. The Scots well know that there is more water in Loch Ness alone than in every river, lake and dam in the entirety of England and Wales. This is just sound, practical good sense where one part of our Union assists another part of our Union!"

Iona found herself slowly standing from her seat in indignation.

"Well, is it now? Yet another example of them stealing our resources without so much as a by-your-leave!"

* * *

Rotermundt's phone rang.

"Biro here. I'm in Glasgow. Where are you?"

"In bed. I'm an early-bedder."

"Yeah, but you're in Glasgow?"

"I said I'd be here and I am."

"You got the package?"

"Not yet but I've arranged to pick it up tomorrow morning. I can meet you at ten."

"Make it eleven. That's when the pubs open. I'm spending the evening in Kitty O'Shea's listening to some good Irish music. I intend to drink the place dry but I'll be fine for the morn."

"That's fine but we need to meet sharp. I've lots to do. Let's say, eh... the coffeehouse called Tinderbox. Nine-thirty. It's easy to find. Near Queen Street Station on Ingram Street. That suit you?"

"I'd prefer a pub at eleven."

"No pubs. I'm too busy to wait until they open."

"And you've my fee?"

"Half tomorrow, half on delivery as we agreed."

"Aye, I suppose that'll do." In the background, Rotermundt could hear him asking how much he owed the barman before he returned to the call. "Well, I'll see you the morn. Half nine."

The line went dead.

Rotermundt, far from being in bed, was fully dressed and consulting his laptop. He lifted the hotel phone and called reception.

"Has anything arrived for me yet?"

"As a matter of fact, sir there's a gentleman in motorcycle attire just arrived and insisting upon delivery of an item directly to yourself. He won't leave it with us at reception."

"I'll come down."

Deciding to walk down the broad staircase to reception, Rotermundt was in shirt-sleeve mode upon arrival. The motorcyclist who had retained his headgear despite being asked to remove it by a mildly nervous hotel staff member, recognised his customer as he stepped into reception.

Silently, he passed over the silver case. Rotermundt accepted it and laid it on a table otherwise festooned with tourist literature. He revolved two sets of three rotating discs until the two locks clicked open. As he did so, Morrison stepped from the hotel lift unnoticed by Rotermundt. Surprised, he continued his walk towards the hotel entrance observing the name *Doncaster* inscribed on a parcel within Rotermundt's case.

Without missing a beat he stepped outside and walked the short distance towards the Steps Bar as Rotermundt dismissed the motorcyclist without a word of thanks.

Chapter Twenty-eight

Iona had just ordered a third pint of stout as Morrison shouldered his way through the narrow twin doors of the Steps Bar. Noticing her, he tapped her lightly on the shoulder from behind, surprising her.

"A wee Glenmorangie and a half pint of Guinness, if you please," he whispered in her ear.

Iona recognised the voice. Without turning, she asked the barman to add a *large* Glenmorangie and a full pint of Guinness to her order.

"You've a bit of catching up to do, Donald John Morrison. I'm on my third pint!"

"As long as there's no singing."

He gave her a peck on the cheek in welcome. She responded with a distracted air kiss whilst paying the barman. They sat.

"Someone's been shopping."

"Just a few necessities. All my stuff is back in Belfast with Emily, remember."

"Three bags?"

"A few wee presents; some toys for my two young cousins; a wee gun and a doll just to imbed sexual stereotyping, knickers, bras, blouses, socks, a wee backpack to carry them and two phones. One for you and one for me. I've topped them up with twenty quid in each of them so we can talk without alerting anyone who might be trying to listen to me or follow my whereabouts. Most important were the knickers. A young lady can't have too many pairs of knickers."

"Apparently not," smiled Morrison. "Well, did you manage to keep our couriers in sight?"

"I did. And how did you get on with *your* chap?"

"He caught a flight back here and I managed to get on board as well. He's staying in the Central Hotel...as am I. I've a room there." He hesitated. "How about you? You're welcome to..."

Iona stopped him. "I'm booked in round the corner from here. I wasn't sure what arrangements...." She stumbled just as had Morrison. "Anyway, I've a room in Rab Ha's boutique hotel. It backs on to this pub."

"Good pub too," responded Morrison anxious to move on from sleeping arrangements. "I'm on the same floor as Rotermundt. As I was leaving he took delivery of a parcel that seemed to be headed for an address in Doncaster."

Iona started. "Doncaster?"

"Yeah. It was all I could make out on the parcel he was handling as I left."

Iona pursed her lips conveying her uncertainty.

"I suspect it might have been destined for Cumnock, not Doncaster." She took a long sip of her stout. "Maybe I should explain." She cleared her throat in anticipation of telling a story that would either incur the wrath or unalloyed approval of her friend. "I wasn't *entirely* able to follow your instructions *completely* to the last letter."

So saying, she told the story of meeting Sandra and Fitz, the wounded arm, overhearing the conversation regarding an attempt to extort more money from their contact in Glasgow and how she'd managed to inspect the parcel and had found it not to contain marijuana but possibly a gun or a bomb...certainly something hard. "I thought, maybe a gun butt?" Finishing, she began to explain the Doncaster address.

Morrison stopped her and spoke grimly.

"Iona..." he floundered. "I know you think you've done well...but I asked that you make no contact, to make sure they didn't see you, to stay out of the purview of security staff at the port...and from what you've told me you've managed to break all three rules."

Iona reddened. "I made the best of a bad job. It was Sandra who contacted *me*. I overheard their conversation, they were completely unconscious when I checked the parcel..."

Morrison interrupted. "I told you the port of Cairnryan was one of the most secure in the UK. So too is the Stena ferry. You'll have been captured on camera with these two couriers..."

"Sandra Butler and Malachy Fitzgerald. He's from Newtownabbey, she's from Govan."

Morrison sighed and continued.

"But the security services now have a pretty strong case against you, Iona. They have photographs of you outside the Crown with people of interest to them, they'll have you in the company of couriers commissioned by them to transport God alone knows what and now they'll have your fingerprints on what you think might be a wrapping concealing a bomb or a gun?"

Iona looked downwards into her pint tumbler.

"Didn't think of that. I was just trying to…"

"Aye!" Impelled to continue his denunciation, Morrison suddenly relented. "Look, you've done well, Iona. As you say, it was they who made contact with you."

Iona brightened. "And I have photographs." She removed her main phone from her pocket and manoeuvred it to show the photographs she'd taken, pulling them to the left until she came to the images showing both Butler and Fitzgerald sleeping. Morrison took it and having committed it to memory, flicked onwards to the parcel.

"Ah, the good *Doctor* Doncaster. It looks like the same black pen used on the parcel I saw." He paused in thought. "Now why would a prominent political member of the Scottish Parliament take delivery of two parcels of unknown contents from a rogue we know to be a Unionist up to no good?"

"It's a set-up, Donald John. I know Simon Doncaster and he's a solid citizen. Either the parcels are innocuous or he's being set up."

Morrison shrugged noncommittally and flicked at the phone's screen once more revealing the photograph of the man who received the backpack from Butler and Fitzgerald.

"Jesus!…" He took a moment to compose himself. "This guy. How come you photographed *him*?"

"He met Fitzgerald and they talked on a bench in George Square. Then Sandra joined them and they handed over the backpack. He gave Fitz something in exchange. He passed me in Queen Street Station and I took a shot of him as he passed. D'you know him?"

Morrison licked his lips uncertainly. *This shouldn't be revealed.* Abruptly, he changed his mind. He and Iona were now in this together, he decided.

"He works in MI5. His name's Giles Grantham. An Intelligence officer." He slumped back in his chair and looked at the ceiling. "Why would an MI5 field agent be handing over some form of recompense to a Belfast courier in return for a gun, a bomb or whatever that's been addressed to a major SNP figure?"

He downed his whisky in one visit and half emptied his Guinness, reflecting further on his conundrum. He asked himself a question.

"*Qui bono?*"

"Eh?"

"*Qui bono*... Who benefits?"

"*Qui* cares? It's obviously an attempt to blacken the name of those involved in Scottish independence."

Morrison pursed his lips in an attempt to suspend judgement and came to a decision.

"This can't be a session. I have to be up sharp to make sure I can follow this fellah Rotermundt. I want to know what he's got in that parcel and what's his connection with your political ally Doctor Doncaster."

"Well, I'm coming too. I didn't come all the way over from Belfast to sit in a hotel room. Anyway, it'd look less suspicious if we appeared to be a couple."

Morrison nodded his agreement.

"Only if you do what you're told."

"I'm not used to being bossed around."

"And I'm not used to *bossing* around but there are bad men out there who may or may not have guns and I'm afraid that there can be only one line of command even between you and me when there's danger to life and limb." He smiled. "I promise once this is over never to give you one further instruction!"

Iona reciprocated with a dimpled grin.

"Then we have a deal."

Morrison lifted his new phone.

"Phone me so I know your number."

Iona consulted a slip of paper and punched in the number which rang Morrison's phone. Immediately he pushed a respond button and triggered a ring in Iona's phone.

"Now we can talk. Sole use, okay?" He took his MI5 phone from his pocket. "Can I borrow your main phone?" He leaned over and took some time to manipulate both phones. "If you'd send me your notes and photographs that'd be very helpful. Also, I've set the phone-finding app to permit each phone to track the other. That way, each of us will always know within a few yards where the other's phone is...and therefore probably where we both are. It might or might not be helpful. You okay with that?"

"Seems sensible."

"Don't want you getting lost!"

* * *

In his hotel room, Rotermundt had earlier opened his parcel and had counted out on the bedspread the thick wads of banknotes contained within, checking that the sum he'd secreted within the case was equal to the sum he now had again in his possession. He'd satisfied himself that he now had four hundred thousand pounds sterling which would go towards funding a variety of local initiatives in Scotland all delivered by willing members of the Conservative and Unionist Party, all completely oblivious to the origins of his donations.

The transfer went well. If it had been discovered, that fine and innocent MSP from Cumnock and Doon Valley, Dr. Simon Doncaster would have had some explaining to do, but now it's here safely, I just need to parcel it up into the various sums promised to local branches and all's well.

He referred to a list he'd brought from his briefcase and started counting.

* * *

Parting from Iona with a chaste kiss on the cheek and an agreement to meet in the foyer of the Station Hotel at seven o'clock the following morning, Morrison walked back along a still bustling Gordon Street mulling over the evening. Despite troubling himself with the problem of why an agent like Giles Grantham appeared to have been dealing with people he believed to have been couriering suspect goods from Northern Ireland to Scotland, he found himself more distracted by what he decided was his ham-fisted handling of sleeping arrangements that night.

Perhaps I need to be more direct with Iona. He thought further. *But if I do and I'm rejected would I lose the friend of a lifetime?* More consideration. *But if I don't and she goes back to the island and is snatched away by Hamish...How could I cope with that? My two best friends and I can't reveal my feelings to either of them.*

* * *

Iona readied herself for bed having only had to walk fifty yards to her hotel. She'd carefully packed away her new belongings into the backpack she'd bought and had laid out her attire for the following day, having placed that day's garments into one of the plastic bags for future washing. Wearing only the hotel robe, she realised she'd not bought bed attire and smiled as she removed the last of the bags from the bed in preparation for sleeping.

Perhaps I figured I wouldn't be needing any tonight if the good Mr. Morrison had suggested we share a bed to save money. She sat on the edge of her bed looking at herself in the mirror. *I'm not bad looking but maybe I'm just not his type. He's probably into London society types now he's a big cheese in the spy business.* She pulled back the bedspread. *God, maybe I should just become a nun and wear only the roughest clothes! Or maybe I should settle for good old Hamish. A local boy who'd sing beautiful songs to me.* Her gaze fell upon a set of underwear she'd purchased. *So why on earth did I buy that particularly expensive and pretty set of nether garments, eh? I must be getting soft.* Her final thought before lights out contradicted her feelings. *But I could never live in London. I'd even swither about settling in Oban or Fort William!*

She removed the robe, *tonight, I sleep in the buff,* and turned out the light.

Chapter Twenty-nine

Having tasked his small police team on the early shift, Watson Baxter sat at his desk and proceeded to deal with the administrative duties he daily undertook diligently but unenthusiastically. Carefully he read citations, reports of crime committed the previous evening and a request from one of his constable for holidays. His personal phone rang.

"Morning Tallman. It's Stuart. That was a great meal last night. Your Jean is some cook. Helen wants the recipe for that lasagne."

"And we were both pretty sensible with the drink, I thought."

"First time I can remember us drinking less than our wives."

"Aye. Anyway, mind thon list of addresses we picked up from that fellah Chadwick in hospital yesterday?"

"Aye."

"Well, Special Branch are involved."

"In a *car* accident?"

"Apparently so."

Baxter placed the sheaf of papers to one side and lifted a pen.

"Did you get a note of the addresses?"

"I photographed it for interest along with his driving license."

"Send me a copy, eh? From memory I only saw one of the addresses in our jurisdiction. The rest were up north." He thought further. "Where are you?"

"Still in the house kidding on I'm out checking an assault in New Abbey Road last night. Early shifts after a night out test me more than they used to."

"I'll pick you up in twenty. Let's visit that address in Lockerbie."

"I'll still be in the shower."

The line went dead.

* * *

Morrison sat in the foyer of Central Hotel reading a Guardian newspaper, mildly cursing the day the newspaper barons had decided to halt production on true broadsheets. *You used to be able to hide a corporation bus behind one of them, not like one of these wee scanty things...almost tabloid size ...and most of them now read like they were tabloid as well,* he thought. He'd positioned himself so as to have a clear view of both the stair and the lift. There was an exit directly on to the station concourse and one onto Gordon Street but Rotermundt would have to pass through the reception area whichever egress he chose.

Iona appeared at four minutes past eight, an ever-closer approximation to punctuality.

"Sorry I'm late. Haven't had breakfast. Have you had breakfast?"

Morrison looked at her with feigned disdain.

"MI5 spies don't have time for breakfast, sweetheart," he replied in an American accent he immediately thought incongruous.

"Your Humphrey Bogart impersonation is as about as good as my impersonation of someone who isn't desperate for porridge or scrambled eggs."

"We eat later, I'm afraid, Iona." He folded the newspaper. "I'm glad you're here..." A thought flashed across his mind. "Sleep well?"

"Not really!" she yawned.

"Well, glad you're here 'cos I'm going to ask you to follow this guy Rotermundt on your own." He smiled. "You've had practice. Just don't take him for a drink or something."

"I learned my lesson, boss!" responded Iona sarcastically. "And what are you going to do while I'm wandering the highways and byways of Glasgow?"

"When he's clear of the hotel I'm going into his hotel room to see what I can find."

The twosome sat for a further hour, most of which was taken up with Iona making a case for her to be allowed to visit the Boots concession outlet on the station concourse wherein a sandwich might be purchased. Morrison eventually relented and was relieved that she returned in the promised two minutes and, having devoured the baguette, turned her attention to her need for coffee. Just as he feared he'd have to concede the request, the lift door opened and Rotermundt stepped out and, without leaving his electronic pass key at reception, stepped out into a busy Glasgow thoroughfare.

"Over to you, Iona. Stay with him and if you lose him, don't worry. Got your phone?"

Iona tapped her pocket in confirmation and rose to follow her quarry.

"Phone me if you need to. I'll head off upstairs while he's out. I'll text you before calling in case it's unwise to talk."

Iona headed outside as Morrison entered the lift to the third floor and headed for room three one one. As he did so, he opened his wallet and removed a twenty pound note which he placed in his jacket pocket. A long corridor was punctuated occasionally by trays of food left outside rooms. An elderly housekeeping assistant was busily replenishing supplies of shampoo from a trolley as Morrison walked towards her, bidding her a cheery, 'Good morning' as he passed. She responded with a smile as Morrison walked confidently to Rotermundt's room and ostentatiously presented his card to the door, exclaiming his *faux* irritation at its inability to open the door. A further three attempts increased the volume of his protests before he turned to the housekeeper.

"Excuse me. My name is Mr. Rotermundt. My door card is not working. Can you help me?"

The housekeeper, a lady originally from Poland, did not have a firm grasp of the English language.

Haltingly, she appealed to him. "Please Mister. Get open door at reception?"

Morrison pointed to the housekeeper's worksheet and directed her attention to his assumed name. He smiled reassuringly and pointed at his chest.

"That's me. Me, Mister Rotermundt," he repeated, sliding into pigeon English. His smile widened as she consulted the names against room numbers. "Can you open door?"

Satisfied that all was probably in order, the housekeeper produced her master key and slid it into the reader, opening the door. Morrison placed the twenty pound note on her trolley and thanked the cleaner who removed the money before it had lain for but a second.

Noting that Rotermundt had left the 'Do Not Disturb' sign on the door, Morrison stepped inside the room and took stock. Rotermundt had left it tidy. Morrison knew he'd have to leave it as he found it so care was to be taken. Standing completely still, he surveyed the room looking for any devices or mechanisms that Rotermundt might have used to detect and establish entry to his bedroom. Seeing none, he opened the en-suite bathroom and inspected it. Again he found no discernible ploy to detect his presence. Carefully, he opened Rotermundt's toiletries bag but found it contained nothing untoward. Some medications lay on a shelf. Morrison inspected them. *Ramipril and Ranolazine.* He read the dosage and purposes. *High blood pressure and angina?* He replaced the medicaments where he'd found them then checked the few cupboards in the bathroom but they were empty. Not satisfied, he withdrew them completely and checked both the base of the drawer and the interior of the shell. He returned them, satisfied that there was nothing to find and returned to the bedroom.

The bed had been made up in rudimentary fashion but Morrison ran his hands over the bedsheet and beneath the pillows looking for anything that may have been concealed. The base of the bed was solid and prohibited anything being secreted underneath the mattress so he turned his attention to Rotermundt's travel bag. Again it was full of expected contents, his laptop having been left open on a desk. Ignoring it for the moment, he turned his attention to a set of drawers opening them from bottom to top where he discovered the silver case delivered earlier by the motorcyclist.

Removing it, his eye caught the contents of the waste paper basket in which had been disposed the paper wrapping with Doncaster's address on it. *Looks like Iona was right and it wasn't destined for him after all!* He laid the case on top of the drawers and lifted the paper which he spread on the bed. Taking his phone from his pocket, he photographed it before crunching the paper as it was and returned it to the bin. The case was locked. Morrison turned it on its side manoeuvring it so the locks were uppermost. He turned on a table lamp and inspected the numerical combination lock closely just as he had been trained to do. Before touching the rotating discs, he noted the existing sets of numbers and recorded them on his phone's notepad. Carefully, he inspected the discs under the light in order to determine which of the numbers were slightly dirtier than others that gleamed due, he had been taught, to them having been protected by not having been exposed to the atmosphere. Gently, he turned the numbers so that those that were more soiled were facing him. He pulled back on the spring-loaded trigger but nothing moved.

"Shit!" he whispered. He was aware that the traditional way of working through the nine hundred and ninety-nine combinations would take less than six minutes on each side - and *that* on the basis that the numeric sequence was in the high nine hundreds. A lower numerical code would see him open it much more quickly. He checked the dials again and moved an eight to a nine. This time the trigger opened.

The second lock proved stubborn so he checked and adjusted the dials again for a third then a fourth time. This time the lock surrendered to his ministrations.

Taking a deep breath, he opened the case slowly, aware it might be booby-trapped and saw the bundles of money, each wrapped in hotel writing paper which was inscribed by an amount and a beneficiary organisation. He photographed the upper layer of the interior untouched so everything could be returned perfectly then spread the bundles out on the bed photographing each one. He then did the same with a further two layers. Before returning everything, he made a rough count of the money involved then removed the drawers as he had done in the bathroom finding nothing. Finally, he returned all of the contents in the order he'd removed them, closed the lid and, consulting his phone, turned the rotating discs to the original numbers.

He returned the case to its drawer and opened the laptop. Instantly he recognised that the model required an identified fingerprint to permit access and frustrated, he closed the lid. Stepping to the door, he turned and observed the room once more. Satisfied, he decided that he'd left no evidence of his having been there. He opened the door, exited and passing the housekeeper on the way back to the lift gave her another big smile as he pushed the button to call the lift.

* * *

Rotermundt had walked up Glasgow's Hope Street only a few yards before turning into the tight, cobbled Renfield Lane. Blocking any prospect of most vehicular traffic using the thoroughfare were numerous bin containers of all colours awaiting collection from the council's refuse lorries whose drivers were skilled at navigating these old, narrow alleys. Only yards behind him, Iona stopped at the entrance to the lane and watched as the man previously identified by Morrison as Giles Grantham, an Intelligence Agent of MI5, moved from behind a refuse bin and handed Rotermundt a backpack. *Hmm. That's the one brought here by Fitz and Sandra,* she determined. After a moment's conversation, the men parted, Rotermundt continuing on his way while Grantham walked back towards Iona who stepped back slightly and took an interest in a Highland dress shop at the corner of the lane until he'd passed.

So who do I follow now? she asked herself. Deciding that she'd better do as requested by Morrison for once, she walked sufficiently briskly down the lane to catch Rotermundt standing at nearby traffic lights awaiting the presence of the Green Man.

In the fifteen minutes that Morrison had been in Rotermundt's hotel room, he had met with Grantham and had walked to a coffee shop in the city's city centre and taken a seat. Irritably double-checking his watch, his temper had deteriorated further with every minute his guest was late. Nine-thirty became ten-thirty before Biro walked in to the coffeehouse. Waving his hand at Rotermundt in recognition he first stepped over to the counter and spoke to the barista who nodded at his suggestion that he bring the coffee over to the table once it was brewed.

Biro's opening remark wasn't designed to reduce his host's irritability.

"How's it hangin' then, my man?"

"We said nine-thirty! You're very late! I almost left."

"Jesus, Mary and Joseph, you're lucky you're seein' me at all! They serve a good pint in Kitty O'Shea's and I must have sunk ten of them."

As the two men growled at each other, Iona stood outside wondering whether it was her need for a coffee or the task of following Rotermundt that urged her to enter the cafe. Deciding to go in, she first turned her back on the long glazed windows and presented her phone before her as if taking a selfie but positioning the device so that it was directed over her shoulder and focussed on the two men inside. This task completed, she entered, approached the barista and ordered her much-needed coffee. Paying, she lingered at the end of the counter until served, whereupon she took a seat facing away from the men whose conversation merged with the general hubbub. Despite this she overheard a fragment of one sentence.

'So, what are you doing with the second gun?'

Chapter Thirty

Baxter's police car slowed to a halt outside a middle-sized family home just outside Lockerbie.

"No car in the driveway, Tallman!"

"Hmm, looks unoccupied right enough. Let's check."

They crunched up the generously loose-stoned driveway and pressed a bell which tinkled far in the depths of the house. Baxter peered through the small glass panel on the door. After no response they tried again and with no reply, walked round the perimeter of the house noting it was lock-fast and secure.

"No washing on the line, grass hasn't been cut, old circulars lying inside the doorway...looks like the place hasn't been occupied for some time. He turned and looked across the road. Two hundred yards away, another house with a short driveway had cars parked.

"Let's ask the neighbours."

Moments later they found themselves talking to Mr. and Mrs. Taylor who invited them in for a cup of tea. Thanking them but rejecting the offer, Baxter asked after the residents of 'Schiehallion' across the road.

Mr. Taylor sought to be helpful. "Och, they're a nice couple. Their name's Du Pont but they're not French. Keep themselves to themselves but we don't see much of them. They live down somewhere near Oxford. He's a big noise in their university down there."

"So's his wife," interjected Mrs. Taylor. "She's a professor of physics or something."

"They're big fans of Scotland and they told us they'd like to retire up here. I'd say they were in their sixties." He looked at his wife for confirmation but continued without it. "They're both English. In fact they were in the local paper last year because when they *do* come up, they fly the St. George's Cross and there was a bit of a stooshie because some people thought they needed planning permission but it turned out they didn't."

"When was that, sir?"

Taylor looked at his wife for guidance. "Maybe last summer?"

Mrs. Taylor seemed happy with his guess. "Aye, around then."

"Would that have been the Annandale Herald?"

"Aye, we take that paper."

Baxter seemed satisfied.

"Thank you both. Just checking on unoccupied houses. It's a community safety initiative."

They walked back to the police car.

"God, you lie so easily," remonstrated Cruikshank. "And I still didn't get a word in, and it's meant to be my case!"

"Aye, but I'm the *sergeant*!" They both laughed. "But your sleuthing skills could be useful here Stuart, because my bet is that all these addresses will feature on the pages of their local newspapers. Can you check that list against local rags and see if there's any connection?"

Cruikshank manufactured a comic salute.

"Will do, sir!"

* * *

Sir Humphrey Ashton lifted the phone and punched the button that connected him to his personal assistant.

"Get me Angela Marleigh in H.R., would you please?"

"Certainly Sir Humphrey.

Some thirty seconds later Ashton was connected.

"Ms. Marleigh. Might I trouble you to pop up to my office for a few moments? Can you bring me the file on Donald John Morrison? He's one of our Analysts and an Intelligence Officer in the Joint Terrorist Analysis Centre?"

Some twenty minutes elapsed before Ms. Marleigh was ushered in to Ashton's office, invited to take a seat and offered a coffee.

"I'm interested in young Mr. Morrison, Ms. Marleigh. I gather he came to us via Agriculture, Fisheries and Food."

"Indeed he did, Sir Humphrey. He is thirty-one years of age, is a native of Benbecula in the Western Isles, speaks, reads and writes Gaelic, has a first class degree in Economics from Edinburgh and simply aced our aptitude tests. Was Church of Scotland but now an atheist. A younger brother who is an accountant in Aberdeen. He lives with his mother when back on the island. His father is dead. He was our best performing candidate in his selection year and was closely aligned with our organisational values. His bank balance shows a rather frugal lifestyle. He contributes monthly to three charities, *Médecins Sans Frontières*, Water for Africa and Vision Aid Overseas, all African charities. He lives within his means, doesn't appear to have a relationship with a significant other and describes his sexual orientation as heterosexual. He scored extremely highly in interview and my notes show that he was assertive, witty and well-informed. His annual reports have been simply excellent. He was commended for work last year on the resumption of power-sharing in Northern Ireland as he was for another piece of work on a proscribed right-wing group. Regular and impressive weapons training. Physically he's in great shape, he's a member of a private gym and uses ours here extensively. His annual medical shows him to be in robust good health. On the face of it he's the perfect Intelligence Officer. The only two issues we noted was perhaps a tendency to be overly assertive. Our psychologist reckons he'd obey orders - but only if he felt they were commensurate with his own values. We decided that because his values were in such proximity to our own, we could overlook notions of him being unduly independent."

"And the other issue?"

"Probably not a biggie...but he was quite insistent that he self-describes as Scottish, not British. Indeed he was at pains to point out that he was an Islander first and foremost. He was also quite critical of Britain's colonial past."

Ashton smiled broadly.

"I have such respect for the Scottish Islanders. I'm almost one myself...or will be hopefully once I retire from this beleaguered organisation.

Marleigh ignored his frustration and continued to make her point.

"Indeed! The notes from the interview specifically addressed the issue of Scottish independence but he was reportedly neutral on the matter. We came to the view that if tasked with an issue to do with Scottish politics, he'd carry it out diligently."

"But he has no affiliation with Oxford, Cambridge, Eton, public schooling and all of that business?"

"None whatsoever, Sir Humphrey."

"And he's not a member of any London clubs?"

Ms. Marleigh consulted her notes.

"Eh, only his gymnasium in Brixton where he has a flat and...well, he lists his club as the Dark Island Bar in Benbecula."

Sir Humphrey roared with laughter. "Excellent! A fine establishment."

"What are his vices?"

"The most we could come up with was occasional binge drinking. He's a non-smoker, doesn't take drugs and the few friends he has are either up in Benbecula or a few down here with whom he drinks in a local pub called the Royal Oak. They've been checked out and are..." she consulted her notes again, "a maths teacher, a local lawyer and a dentist. Occasionally a local postman. All male. The dentist is of black Caribbean origin, the other three are white, they all hold British passports and they meet as a quiz team called 'The Brixton Brainiacs'. He even often wins at that!"

Ashton appeared contemplatively at his file.

"Perhaps you'd leave that with me for a short while, Ms. Marleigh. I'm looking for someone smart who is quite apart from those of us in the organisation who have had the privilege of an Eton and Oxbridge education. Someone who has no allegiance to toffs and who isn't interested in building a career via contacts in London's best gentlemen's clubs. I asked for Morrison's file because I thought he might fit the bill rather."

"In my opinion, Sir Humphrey, we have something of a diamond in Mr. Morrison. He's everything you've just described and will clearly go on to become a very important officer within MI5."

"Thank you, Ms. Marleigh. That'll be all for now."

Ashton sat back in his seat and grinned as a photograph of Morrison's club in Benbecula parted company from the folder and landed at his feet."

Ah, the islands!.. the island way of life. I must have another look at my pension arrangements. The sooner Doris and I can retire to the grassy machair of Lewis, the better.

* * *

A text message appeared on Iona's new phone. 'Where U?'

Lifting it, she responded in text, 'Tinderbox Coffee shop. Ingram Street. Wait outside.'

Still unable to make out only fragments of the conversation between Rotermundt and Biro, she nevertheless understood the tone of the discussion as somewhat fractious. She consulted her watch. *They've been chatting for twenty minutes.* As she pondered the wisdom of a second cup of coffee perhaps requiring a visit to the bathroom and temporarily aborting her surveillance of Rotermundt, Biro stood.

"I do it my way. If you want to tag along, so be it, but stay in the background or you'll get hurt."

He held out his hand and gestured a 'give it to me' signal with his fingers.

"You have something for me?"

Rotermundt leaned down and lifted his backpack from the floor beneath the table. He looked around to establish he wasn't being overheard, ignoring the young lady finishing the dregs of her coffee two tables away.

"It's all in here. Half your money, the gun and a suicide note you should sign if you try anything stupid. I represent very powerful people and it would be in your singular interest not to fuck up!"

Biro took the bag and sniggered.

"You English talk funny!"

Despite his devotion to the Unionist cause, Rotermundt, now a naturalised Scot, almost corrected him.

* * *

As the two men left, Iona only steps behind them, Morrison elbowed himself off the wall against which he'd been leaning and walked the few steps to his partner.

Biro and Rotermundt each headed in different directions.

Before Morrison could issue instructions or seek advice, Iona chipped in.

"That guy Rotermundt you followed has just handed a bag to his pal with what I think I overheard contains guns and money."

As Morrison was in the process of deciding to follow the weaponry, Rotermundt hailed a taxi. His instructions were clearly overheard.

"Take me to the Central Hotel, wait for me, then take me to the airport."

If Morrison had any lingering doubts as to his next moves, that decided him.

"Let's see where this fellah with the bag takes us."

Chapter Thirty-one

Detective Sergeant Watson Baxter sat at his desk when Stuart Cruikshank knocked and entered without being called; just the correct amount of deference yet signalling his personal friendship.

"You were right again, big man. These addresses...every one of them...all feature in the local papers of the area in which they're located. Look! The Buchan Observer, the Arbroath Herald, there's two articles in the Oban Times, the Caithness Courier and the Annandale Herald. Whatever event got them newsworthy...there's one here where the owner wanted to chair the local community council but was a non-resident, only visiting Montrose every few months, one where the guy was found guilty of fraud after a house fire when he was at home in Wilmslow...one where the house was burgled and the owner had left it unattended for more than sixty days nullifying his home insurance. I could go on. And every one of the articles makes two points. First the owner was English or at least was domiciled in that fair land and secondly that the house was a second home. These two guys had got hold of a list of houses which were known to be the second homes of English people. They had Saltires in their car - those that weren't cremated - spray paint and quantities of petrol that saw one of them end up in the morgue and one in hospital. Anyone would think they were intent on making a wee political statement."

"You told the Detective Inspector this yet?"

"He's not in until twelve."

"Then why don't you and me wander over to and see if this wee burned ned has anything to say for himself." As he stood, he thought further. "Special Branch been in touch?"

"Nah. They're good at communication when they need information. Not so good when they're meant to be on transmit."

"I suspect they've made the same deduction that we have. But they're up in Glasgow probably and we're only ten minutes away. Let's go before their big boots walk all over this."

* * *

As Morrison and Iona strode the breadth of George Square some twenty paces behind Biro, Morrison's phone rang. It showed no details of the caller. He answered it while continuing to walk.

"Aye?"

"Donald John? It's Joe Kingsley here. I'm on the surveillance job outside Henry J. Carson's house."

"Anything happening?"

"Well, it was slim pickings when I was only using an external microphone but it was enough to hear how desperate he was to watch a football match between his team, the famous Glasgow Rangers and Aberdeen last night. So when he was out yesterday, I buggered up his external sky box then tampered with his ISDN system, the circuit-switched telephone network box in his garden so that any phone call he made could either be ignored or dealt with by me. I waited until he told his wife he was going to phone a TV repair man, intercepted the call and said I'd be right round. I had half an hour in front of his television during which I planted a microphone inside, then had a second look at his box outside, sorted it so he has no idea that I wasn't who I said I was, and now have crystal clear recordings of not only his telephonic communications but everything he says conversationally to his wife and visitors." He hesitated. "One other thing, Donald John. I've not had time to've had a warrant put in place. I just saw an opportunity that was too good to miss so this information has currently been obtained illegally. I've asked admin to sort this out but in the meantime I'm passing it on in case it's useful to you as background info."

"Well done, Joe. Anything worth hearing?"

"You bet. If it had been legally obtained, I'd have had enough to see him charged under the 1968 Firearms Act with possessing firearms or ammunition without a firearm certificate, trading in firearms without being registered as a firearms dealer, selling firearms to a person without a certificate, possession of firearms with intent to endanger life or injure property and supporting Rangers without due care and attention."

Morrison smiled. Joe Kingsley, he knew, was an enthusiastic supporter of Celtic FC.

"Hear anything else worthwhile?"

"He talked with someone called Rotersomething and they spoke of two guns previously used by the IRA having arrived in Scotland. This guy, Rotersomething is to collect the weapons from someone called Grantham who's to keep one and then Carson and Rotersomething got into a big argument because apparently this guy was meant to carry out a hit on some Scottish politician but he's sub-contracted the job to an Irish guy called Biro." He checked his notes, "Yeah, that's right, his name's Biro, maybe a nickname unless he's Irish with Hungarian parentage."

"No idea who the target is?"

"Scottish politician. That's it!"

"Anything else?"

"Nah. But I'll call you if he says anything untoward. Anything you might be interested in."

"You're a pal, Joe."

"See you."

Biro was now making his way past the Gallery of Modern Art as Iona asked for details of the call.

Ambivalent about the amount of information he should impart to his informal assistant, Morrison stalled.

"Just had info to suggest that you were right about the item you felt in the bag being a gun. If everything we've unearthed is accurate it would appear that we're following someone called Biro who has at least one of the two guns in question inside that bag he's carrying on his back."

"So do we tell the police?"

"No. This is my domain. We follow and see what he's up to."

"But he might be armed!"

Morrison left Iona mouth agape.

"So might we!"

As she came to terms with his statement, Morrison's phone rang. Again there was no caller identity.

"Aye?"

"Mr. Morrison? Sir Humphrey here. Can you talk?"

Morrison slowed to a standstill, a frown on his face as he gestured Iona to continue her shadowing of Biro.

"Yes sir. I'm actually tracking someone. It flows from the task you set me in Northern Ireland."

"Should we speak later?"

"I'm fine sir. I have contingencies in place."

"Fine. I need you to come back to London forthwith. I want to speak with you regarding an important mission where you will report only to me. Do not mention to anyone...and I mean *anyone* that you and I are meeting. Can you be in London by this evening and might I be as presumptuous as to suggest that we meet at your flat in Brixton? I have the address."

"I'm unsure of flight times, Sir Humphrey. It might be late tonight. Might I call you once I know my estimated time of arrival?"

"I'll text you a number that will have you connected directly with me. Don't worry about how late it is. Just give me forty minutes to get round to your flat."

"Will do!"

Hurriedly he increased his stride until he caught up with Iona.

"Problems?"

"Perhaps. I need to think. Let's walk until he stops."

* * *

Baxter and Cruikshank entered the ward in which Chadwick was being treated. After some protocols at the nurses' station, they approached the bed to find the patient sentient, if subdued. Cruikshank took over.

"Mr. Chadwick. I am Detective Constable Stuart Cruikshank. This is Detective Sergeant Watson Baxter. You've been through a lot. How are you feeling?"

Chadwick's forehead corrugated in pain as he attempted an understanding of what was going on.

"Eh?"

"We're the police, Mr. Chadwick, and me...the man you're looking at...well, I'm the man who will decide whether you spend the next ten years of your life in a prison cell once you're discharged from hospital. The medics tell me you'll survive this. You won't die like your co-conspirator, Mr. Collier, but you're toast, I'm afraid...forgive the pun! You'll still be an ugly fucker and will never again win a young lady's heart, you'll never swim the length of the pool given you've only one arm, but you'll walk and talk again...just not in the open air unless you're smarter than you look."

He leaned over and poured some of the patient's orange juice into a small paper cup and sipped it.

"So...are you smarter than you look?"

"Eh?"

"Look, son. We have all of the evidence we need. We've the list of properties you intended to attack, the petrol containers, the Saltire flags, the spray cans...you're history my man. If I can prove you set the petrol alight, I'll do you for culpable homicide, maybe murder. In any event I've enough on you to see you in jail for maybe twenty years. You're a young man, Ivan. But even with good behaviour you get out when you're nearly old enough for a pension. That what you want from life?"

Chadwick, still confused mumbled his bafflement yet again as Cruikshank changed tone.

"Look, Ivan, we aren't your enemy. We can help! Your pal's dead... did you know that? You've lost an arm. You probably know that!" he said sarcastically. "Put all the blame on him. We'd understand that. But to be honest, we'd need to know some background information that'd help substantiate your claim that'd let you walk as free as a bird, or at least a free bird with some electronic tagging involved."

He took a further sip of the orange juice.

"Now, where did you get that list of properties from? Why did you have a few hundred quid on you when you don't look like you've so much as a paper round and how are you ever going to play bass guitar or the drums again when you don't have a left arm?"

Chadwick, now more alert, shrugged what remained of his shoulders while remaining otherwise uncommunicative.

"Dunno! Look, should I have a fuckin' lawyer here?"

Watson Baxter intervened.

"Look, son! He's the *good* cop. I'm the *bad* cop. I'm the guy who'll ask the nursing staff to leave us alone for a minute then stick what's left of your arm up your arse when no one's looking. And Detective Cruikshank here, although a *good* cop, won't be looking. It means fuck all to you now. We all know you're a felon. Soon you'll be a *convicted* felon once again. Your choice is simple. Help us, and taste freedom after twenty fucking hours community service for being a passenger in a car with a violent lunatic, or take it all on your shoulders and do a twenty stretch for being an arsehole. Your shout!"

Chadwick paid new attention.

"Now, son...we know more about this operation than you'd imagine. We know *everything*. If you *snow* us...one fucking word out of order, we walk out of here and you take it on the chin. I'll make it my fucking personal business to see you spent the rest of your adult life in jail trying not to drop the soap in the shower in front of some frustrated long-termer who hasn't seen a woman in years."

Chadwick cleared his throat nervously.

"Look, I've lost a fuckin' arm...an' a mate...an' a car..." he reminded himself. "I'm full of drugs an' can't think straight. I don' have a lawyer and you two fink you can come in 'ere an' fuckin' mess me about?"

Cruikshank nodded his agreement.

"That's *exactly* what we think, son. Now you tell us where you got that list of homes to burn and we don't bother you anymore. You're charged with a minor offence involving using the wrong petrol containers and you go home to mummy. You fuck us around and I bring a culpable homicide charge against you for killing your buddy and setting out to commit arson." He reached over and poured more of Chadwick's orange juice into his cup. "You take the hit. It's that simple. Just tell us where you got the orders to torch these addresses."

"I walk if I tell you where I got the addresses?"

"I've no interest in you once I know who sent you on this fool's errand. Now, you got paid, right?"

Chadwick accepted Cruikshank's assertion with the merest shake of his head and hesitantly relented.

"Me and Ethan are members of the English Defence League. The two of us joined after them fuckin' immigrant Muslims killed that soldier boy Lee Rigby in London a few years back. Them immigrant Muslims are takin' over the streets all over England so me an' the boys figured...well, we figured they needed fuckin' stoppin' so we joined up. We go to the football together, we have a few pints and a few fights... but it's just a bit of a laugh 'cept the immigrant Muslim bit."

"Yeah. But who gave you the money and the list?"

"We was in a pub in Sheffield. Fagan's in Broad Lane and this fuckin' geezer comes in and comes straight over to me and Ethan. It was like he knew us. We was drinkin' and 'e was a bit posh so we took the piss a bit but he told us he'd give us some big money if we did him a turn. He told us he was a big noise in the English Defence League. Well, we was *in* that so we listened and he told us that them Jocks, no offence mate, was fuckin' the English over and they needed to get taught a lesson. Then he brings out these two wads of notes and says he wants us to torch some 'ouses in Scotland. Says he'll give us four ton each and another four ton when we get back if we do all the 'ouses."

"His name?"

"He didn't give one, but when he opened his wallet to give us the fuckin' money I saw a name in one of them see-through bits and it had a card in it that said Benjamin Gold. I knew it was him because afterwards when he was on the cobbles, he took a call on his phone and although he tried not to let us hear what he was talking about, he called himself Ben on the phone. So I figured that was his name...Ben."

"And the list?"

"Well, *he* gave us the fuckin' list. He told me an' Ethan to blag a car. He knew a lot about us so I figured he must be genuine. Like from the League, you know wha' I mean?"

"And the flags and spray paint?"

"Well, that was all a double bluff. He told us they were all fuckin' *English* 'ouses but we had to torch them and spray paint 'English Go Home' on them. Me an' Ethan thought, well, why would that piss off the fuckin' Jocks? No offence. But Ethan reckoned it must be some kind of double bluff. We reckoned the League must know what they were fuckin' doin' so we figured we'd just torch the fuckin' places, take the money and go on 'oliday to Spain."

Cruikshank drank the remnants of the cup.

"Well, son. That's all very interesting. Now what's going to happen is that I'm going to write all you've said down on a bit of paper and you're going to read it and if it's just what you've said, you're going to sign it and as far as I'm concerned, the cops here want nothing more to do with you."

Chadwick managed a tight smile, still unsure of the conversation.

"Yeah. No probs."

"So, you lie back and think of England's Defence League. We'll be outside writing. We'll be back in fifteen."

"Yeah. No probs...but you guys don't fuckin' touch me?"

"Nope!"

As the two police officers left the ward seeking a room to prepare a statement, Baxter patted Cruikshank on the back.

"Why Detective Cruikshank, you are one *sleekit* son of a bastard. We get a statement, and you keep your word. We take no action because Special Branch comes along tomorrow, do all the footslogging and then *they* do him!"

"I'm a man of my word, Tallman. Not my fault if that wee shitebag doesn't understand the various and discrete responsibilities of Scottish law enforcement agencies. Now let's write up the wee ned's statement while he's still got one arm left to sign the bloody thing."

Chapter Thirty-two

Kitty O'Shea's was an ancient Irish pub in Glasgow fashioned from basement premises whose history went back at least ten years. A wooded interior had been constructed so as to hang items redolent of auld Ireland, many of which had been bought in second hand shops in the city and which owed more to the Irish migration to Glasgow during the famine than any authentic antiques from Eire. With a bar at one end, a performance space at the other and a series of booths in between, it was a popular drinking establishment for those who sought to imagine they were sinking Guinness in Dublin or Killarney.

At the far end, a bearded singer turned to his two accompanists.

"Play it in the general neighbourhood of '*E*', boys."

He strummed a chord and let it ring before the trio launched into a raucous version of '*The Rising of the Moon*' for the general delectation of the lunchtime crowd.

Biro had encamped at the bar, eyes shut, his Guinness raised, singing along.

"*And come tell me Sean O'Farrell, tell me why you hurry so,*
Hush a bhuachaill, hush and listen and his cheeks were all aglow..."

Sitting in a nearby booth, Iona watched the proceedings and offered an appraisal to Morrison.

"He has a fine singing voice."

Morrison sang softly the next two lines along with the band.

"*I bear orders from the captain, get you ready quick and soon*
For the pikes must be together at the rising of the moon."

He grinned. "It's not just Hamish who has a nice singing voice."

"No one sings like Hamish. He's still my favourite singer but your man over there might give him a run for his money."

Morrison adopted a serious tone and changed the topic.

"Looks like I may have to step back from this thing. I'm being recalled to London."

"Recalled?"

"Yeah. The organisation's priorities have shifted apparently. I'm flying back later."

"And what about our folk singer over there?"

"We take a back seat for now. I'm going to arrange for someone from Special Branch to pick him up once he leaves the bar here. There's only one way out. But he's unfinished business and I might be clearer on things tomorrow once I meet who I'm meeting in London."

"And what do *I* do?"

"I guess you go back to your hotel, sleep tight and make arrangements to fly back to Belfast or head back to Benbecula with the thanks of a grateful nation. Once I know what's what, I'll make contact. Promise." He placed his hand on Iona's arm and squeezed. "I've enjoyed our time together more than maybe I've been able to explain. I want to spend more time in your company but I must admit it's been a bit weird having you as a partner in crime so to speak."

"Have I earned my spurs as a super secret agent?"

"And then some. But I must fly...literally. I have to meet someone tonight. He'll be important in deciding where we go from here with our man over there. Will you be okay? I'd walk you back to your hotel but I need to catch a taxi back to the Central Hotel, get to the airport pronto and off to London. Can I phone you tomorrow?"

"Why d'you think I bought you a special phone if not to contact me any time you want? Now...you go on. I'll finish my drink, maybe some shopping and walk back to the hotel. It's not far. I'll probably go back to Belfast tonight or tomorrow to see Emily and get my gear. Depends on flight times."

"Not a word to her about our wee adventure, eh?"

"Not a cheep. I'll manufacture some story about a stormy love affair gone wrong." She squeezed the hand that was squeezing her arm. "Now go!"

Morrison slid along the bench seat in the booth and stood.

"Listen, stay here if you must and keep an eye on our friend Biro. Do *not* leave here when he does. Let him leave. He'll be followed by someone and I don't want to read a report in which he was seen leaving with someone from '*Siol nan Gaidheal*'. He looks like he's probably carrying a weapon so keep your distance. We'll pick him up."

He decided that faint heart never won fair lady and changed the subject once again.

"This last wee while..."

"Go, won't you!"

As he headed towards the stairs he reflected ruefully. *Jesus, this spying business is a hell of a lot more straightforward than courting a young lady from the islands!*

* * *

Iona lifted her pint of stout and took a long draught as she pondered Morrison's departure. *What am I to make of all this? From outward appearances, he seems smitten with me...and maybe I am with him. But can I have a relationship with someone who's a government agent? Flying off to London at the drop of a hat? Maybe to do something dangerous? Do I have what it takes to live with that?*

She glanced at the small television secured to the wall at the end of each booth. Normally used to show sports programmes, it nevertheless scrolled news items across the bottom of the screen.

'Minister for Justice, Ms. Lorna Gillies MSP to step down as allegations of sexual assault forces First Minister to act.'

Bloody disgrace. Someone makes an allegation against a decent woman and the media smell blood. She lifted her phone and searched for more information on the new headline spending some time reading the breaking news and comment. Lost in her thoughts, she barely noticed a man stooping to sit opposite her, then started somewhat when she realised it was Biro.

"Is this seat taken?"

"Eh, no. I was just leaving."

"I admire a woman that can handle a full pint of the black stuff. Not one of them cocktail concoctions they usually take."

"I enjoy Guinness."

Still in overtly chivalrous mode, Biro smiled as he continued the conversation.

"That's not an Irish accent."

Still uncertain how to deal with a situation she knew would upset Morrison, she decided to reply in a manner more curt than would have been normal in her social circle. Her eyes followed the backpack he laid beside himself on the cushioned bench, aware of her presumption of a gun being contained within.

"I'm from the Scottish islands."

"And why is a beautiful young woman from the Scottish islands drinking alone in an Irish pub at lunchtime?"

"Well, thank you for the compliment but I'm just out shopping and wanted a refreshment."

"And isn't that exactly what I'm doing meself?"

Iona found herself reciprocating Biro's smile and decided that she could have a harmless conversation with the man.

"My name's Iona."

"Now isn't that a lovely name? My name's Biro."

"Now that's an unusual name, Biro. I'm pleased to meet you."

Biro held out a hand and they shook, Biro lingering on Iona's hand just a second or two longer than necessary.

"I'm out of Guinness. Can I buy you a pint before you head for the shops?"

In for a penny, thought Iona.

"Perhaps just a glass for the pavement."

Biro lingered some minutes at the bar as the stout settled before bringing back both pints and laying them on the table.

Iona saw an opportunity.

"So what kind of name's Biro?"

"Ah, it's a long story. When I was a younger man I was involved with an Irish organisation that was involved in securing the removal of the British imperial forces from my nation of Ireland. I was too young to undertake duties carried out by the men but they trusted me because I was good at writing and so they allowed me to take the minutes...the *secret* minutes...of their meetings. My real name's Cathal Durning but they started to call me Biro and it's stuck."

Iona teased him.

"I'm almost persuaded you're talking about the IRA."

Biro laughed.

"Well, let's say I wasn't uninvolved with the Republican movement."

"I'm in the same boat, then!"

"Eh?"

"I'm a member of '*Siol nan Gaidheal*', Seed of the Gael. We're after Scottish independence and we're frustrated about the slow pace of progress towards our goal. We're sort of halfway between *Sinn Fein* and the Republican Army here in Scotland. We're not a proscribed organisation but we know the Brits keep files on us and monitor our meetings."

Biro's jaunty insouciance deserted him and a silence descended on the table. Slowly, he recovered a measure of his erstwhile confidence. He uttered his surprise in staccato.

"Well, I did not expect that!" Each word had its own weight and space. "I did not expect that." Suspicious now, his mind raced as he recounted the nature of the meeting and calculated the extent to which it might have been possible for Iona to have orchestrated it. Although he'd initiated contact, an attractive woman sitting unaccompanied in a bar might be an artful and sophisticated honey trap. He'd have to be careful. Then Iona smiled the smile that had so enchanted Morrison and Biro decided he was making a something out of nothing. Probably. He continued his attempted chivalry.

"In Glasgow long?"

"I'm heading to Belfast to meet a friend before flying back up to the islands. I'm a nurse there."

"I'm over here only for a short time meself. Bit of business then back to Belfast same as you."

Iona sensed another opportunity for information.

"When are you flying back?"

"Well that depends. I have in my grubby paws, a ticket for tomorrow night's Celtic match at Parkhead. Game against Aberdeen. No Irishman worth his salt comes to Glasgow without making an effort to support the bhoys." He pulled a wallet from his trouser pocket and with it, a second plastic holder.

"Got this from a friend. Season ticket." He peered at the ticket detail. "I'm in with the Ultras. Section 111 on the North Curve." He laughed. "That's where all the singing and dancing takes place."

"A match under the floodlights? Sounds great."

"Yeah. Then a few bevvies, a night's rest, a bit of business and back home to civilisation."

"Shame. I'm back over tonight or first thing in the morning. We could have shared a taxi to the airport."

"I'm staying with a friend in a house at Parkhead Cross. We could share a taxi back there before you head home."

"You're charming, Biro but I have other plans. Thanks for the offer."

She half-finished her Guinness and slid along to the end of the booth. Biro offered his hand and she took it but he held tight. Iona tried to tug her hand but his fingers tightened briefly, his eyes fixed on hers. She tugged again and he let her go, his hand slow to pull away.

"It's been a pleasure, Biro. Enjoy your match."

Biro toasted her departure and wrote off the conversation to experience, just has he had on countless occasions before.

Emerging from the gloomy downstairs entrance, Iona walked on a few paces then phoned Morrison who was negotiating his Sauer P226 pistol with Airport Security as he had done in Belfast.

"Hi! Just been speaking with your man, Biro. His full name is Cathal Durning. Seems to be resident in Belfast and he's not scheduled to leave Glasgow to do what he called a 'bit of business' until the morning after tomorrow's match at Celtic Park."

"How on earth...?"

"All will be revealed." She looked over her shoulder to establish that she wasn't being overheard. "If you don't want to involve Special Branch you can do so without losing him. He'll be in section 111 of the North Curve at Parkhead stadium until the match finishes. That's where the Ultras congregate. You can pick him up at that time."

Morrison was still nonplussed.

"How on earth...?"

"Enjoy your flight. We'll speak tomorrow."

The line went dead and Morrison found himself wordlessly staring at his phone as if by doing so, it would reveal how a young woman he was supposed to be protecting, continually provided him with such rich information.

Maybe I should become a nurse in Benbecula and she should become an agent with MI5!

Chapter Thirty-three

"I'm his brother."

The nurses' station was busy and Wilma Keane, the nurse on duty, was little concerned with a relative wanting to see one of her patients, even if it was slightly earlier than normal visiting hours.

Almost disinterestedly she asked, "What did you say his name was?"

"Eh, it's Ivan Chadwick, my brother. His name's Ivan Chadwick."

She turned and consulted a whiteboard on which was written the names of patients and the wards wherein they were being treated.

"He's in ward eleven. It's a single-bed room. I saw him half an hour ago. He was awake but feeling a bit sorry for himself. Are you aware he's lost an arm?"

Benjamin Gold could care less but managed to evince concern.

"That's awful...terrible. Ward eleven, you say?"

He picked up a clear plastic trophy shaped like a large diamond masquerading as crystal. It signified thanks from the parents of a young girl whose recovery had been due to the NHS staff on the ward.

"You've won a big award! Well done!"

He replaced it on the desk and walked unaccompanied to the ward. Inside, as accurately described by Nurse Keane, was Ivan Chadwick feeling sorry for himself. Seeing Gold enter the ward caused him to sit up anxiously.

"Fuck! What are you doing here? Everything's fucked up. Ethan's dead, I've lost my fuckin' arm an' my other one's broke."

"I'm here to look after you." He looked around the ward. "Have the police spoken with you?"

Chadwick was not by any stretch a clever individual but he was savvy.

"I've been unconscious. I've just woke up."

"Good! Where are your clothes?"

"Don't have none. They were burned in the fire that killed Ethan."

"Okay. We're going to get you out of here and treated in a private hospital where the police won't bother you."

"I'm burned to fuck as well as having no arm. What about all these drugs I'm on?"

Gold scooped up a few bottles and packets that lay on the table next to his bed.

"These come with us. I've a doctor on call. We go to him first and then to a quiet hospital where no one will know you. You'll be safe."

"There's no way I can walk, Ben."

Gold stiffened. "How do you know my name?"

"Heard you on the phone. Outside Fagan's! You said your name."

Gold's face revealed no emotion.

"Let's get you a wheelchair."

He rolled a wheelchair to the side of the bed, pulled the intravenous medications from his arm, uncoupled the monitors and positioned the chair so Chadwick could be slid from his bed with least effort.

"Now this'll hurt. Don't shout out. We can't have nurses coming in."

Every sinew in Chadwick's face strained in agony as he was removed from the bed and seated on the wheelchair.

Gold held his face close to that of Chadwick and spoke insistently.

"Look, I know it's painful but we need to leave here quietly."

He pulled the top cover from the bed and placed it across Chadwick's lap and legs. Tucking it in, he rolled the chair to the door of the ward and opened it. He checked to ensure there was no traffic and pushed the chair towards the lift in the opposite direction of the nurses' station.

"I've a car parked outside. We'll be there in no time."

Emerging into a drizzle of rain, Gold abandoned Chadwick at the edge of the walkway and ran quickly to his car which he brought round before somewhat unceremoniously heaving the patient moaning onto the back seat.

"Let's get out of here."

Chadwick was now screaming in pain, much to Gold's irritation. He dug into his jacket pocket and threw the assorted medicaments he'd taken from the beside cabinet onto the back seat.

"Here! Take some of these fucking tablets. Don't go to sleep. I need to find out exactly what happened."

"Go to fuckin' sleep? I'm fuckin' dying here. I've got one arm left and it's broke. How the fuck can I take a tablet?"

His exasperation now at boiling point, Gold steered the car onto the side of the road, stepped out and retrieved the tablets. He read the labels.

"Open wide!"

Three dihydrocodein tablets, each comprising sixty milligrams of the strong painkiller slid down Chadwick's throat.

"That'll sort you. Now answer my questions. Tell me from the very start. Whose car was used when you drove to Scotland?"

Still in agony, Chadwick tearfully started to tell his story, yet careful to avoid admitting he'd spoken with two police officers lest it interfered with the promise of recovery in a private hospital.

"It was knocked off. We stole it the morning we left. From outside Fagan's...that pub we met you in."

Somewhat relieved at the vehicle not being tied to either of his functionaries, Gold smiled and accelerated along the A75 towards Kirkcudbright, asking questions as he drove.

*** *

The Costa Coffee concession in Glasgow Airport, situated upon entry to the concourse, was busy with holidaymakers and staff taking a break. Empty cups and discarded wrappings testified to understaffing. Rotermundt sat tapping a coaster on the table, awaiting the arrival of Giles Grantham.

Yet another latecomer. My life is spent these days waiting on people who fail to understand the importance of punctuality.

From within a crowd of suitcase-pulling travellers, the burly, be-suited figure of Grantham, walking languidly, emerged into Rotermundt's view.

Would you look at that idiot? A man who clearly knows no sense of urgency.

Grantham navigated between chairs and sat before a clearly frustrated Rotermundt.

"I seem to be spending my morning waiting on people who can't seem to turn up at the time agreed."

"Pressing business matters. You're not the only individual I have to keep an eye on, Mr. Rotermundt."

"I'm due to catch a flight to Aberdeen. I'm making three drop-offs of cash to local party chairmen. Back tomorrow morning."

"And if I might ask, what, pray have you in mind for your responsibilities to do with the Secretary of State?"

Rotermundt bit his lower lip anxiously.

"There's been a change of plan. I'm no gunman."

"Really?...And?"

"I've commissioned someone more used to acts of violence to carry out the shooting."

"And you secured permission to make this change from whom?"

Irritated, Rotermundt couldn't conceal his disparagement of Grantham.

"I don't answer to you, Grantham. I am responsible for the dissemination of questionable funds to Unionist organisations and you need to keep your distance. Her Majesty's Government can't afford to be seen getting its hands dirty by handing out dirty money to support its mission of retaining the Union. You need me and I won't be told what to do by the likes of you."

Grantham retained his composure.

"My dear Mr. Rotermundt, I specifically remember passing you additional monies in a bar in Belfast for the purpose of buying weaponry but with the clear message that there must be no intermediary and that this was to be accomplished at your hand." He clasped his hands and leaned forwards on the table more clearly to emphasise his point. "You see my dear fellow, as you quite rightly say, my backers want absolute deniability. We seek the use of IRA guns in order to forge a link between Irish paramilitaries and what we will argue are *Scottish* paramilitaries. We cannot have this go wrong as it may have the unintended effect of bolstering the very thing we seek to do down. If the Scottish electorate came to the view that the British state was being underhand and denying them unfettered access to a democratic choice, well, the entire edifice might come tumbling down, so you can see why we require this to be kept on the very tightest of leashes."

Edgily, Rotermundt agreed the essence of his point.

"I'm not stupid. I am well aware of the points you raise and I acknowledge agreeing to do this myself but that's exactly why, on reflection I decided to employ another person. I'm a back room man...a committee man. I'm no terrorist." He hesitated. "I've already commissioned someone and paid him half his fee. He drives to Eastriggs the day after tomorrow. He tells me he has a public function he has to attend."

Grantham sat back and allowed a silence.

"I see." He thought some more. "And the weapon we went to such lengths to obtain? I have one, you still have the other?"

"*He* has it."

Grantham's anger surfaced.

"And you have checked the particulars of this man or have you perhaps access to reviews of capable assassins based in the United Kingdom?"

"He's ex-IRA. He's shot people before."

"Really?"

"He goes by the name of Biro. I've had him checked out by my Unionist colleagues over there and they insist that while he's an utter bastard, he'll do a good job."

"So let me see if I understand your strategy. Our goal was to persuade investigators that it was a *Scottish* terrorist who shot the Secretary of State for Scotland but the fingerprints on the gun will be that of a known IRA terrorist. That seems to me somewhat to undermine our attempts to deceive the authorities does it not?"

"I've already instructed him to wipe the gun clean before he discards it."

"So...this man can identify you, he already has secured funds from you, he is a known terrorist, has no stake in maintaining confidentiality after the fact and you know him only by a *sobriquet*. Half of Ireland might be informed of the action once it is completed and you have shared some details with other Unionist colleagues. Am I wrong on any of these points?"

"Look! It's too late. He's been given the job."

"Well, my dear Mr. Rotermundt, I must caution you once more in respect of our discussion in the Crown Bar. In addition to requiring your personal involvement in this act, I also distinctly alerted you to an understanding that this matter is so sensitive that it may cost you your life if things go wrong. You really must understand that you're playing with the big boys now. So...I must make myself perfectly clear. You will accompany your IRA friend to the home of the a Secretary of State at Eastriggs. You will offer him all assistance and will personally ensure that the gun is wiped clear of all detectable fingerprints. If Alan Colquhoun is shot and wounded as agreed and if you make your escape then all is well. However if any part of this fails, I fear it may be necessary for you and your friendly Irish terrorist to be dealt with. Now, you and I had what I thought previously was an understanding. That, it is now clear, has been found to be a *mis*understanding. However, on this occasion I fear there is no room for misinterpretation. Succeed and life goes on as now. Fail and you know the cost. Now!" He looked at his watch. "You have a flight to catch. I hope you have an uneventful journey. You have retained your room at the Central Hotel in the meantime?"

Rotermundt nodded. "I've booked two nights."

"Then I'll doubtless see you the day after tomorrow. Let's hope it's a pleasant occasion for both of us."

Rotermundt stood, collected his briefcase and headed for airport security, his normal scowl even deeper than was usual. Grantham sat back in his chair and lifted the same coaster used earlier by Rotermundt and tapped it thoughtfully just as he had done.

Well, this makes matters rather more complicated. I'll certainly need to shoot Rotermundt...no loss, just further evidence of Conservatives being shot at the hand of Scottish separatists... but I can't do similarly with this Irish chap. He'll need to be removed in a different way. A dead IRA man on Scottish soil would certainly muddy the waters. Perhaps once he's back in Ireland? That way it'll look like one of their usual Saturday night sectarian shootings. Yes, I can make that arrangement quite easily.

He looked round at the litter-strewn tables. *Disgusting!* He reflected upon his options. *No rush for the moment. I think a martini in the bar at the art-deco Rogano's I've read so much about would do nicely. Yes!* He stood and straightened his jacket, picking some fluff from his lapel. *Perhaps two.*

Chapter Thirty-four

Morrison had phoned and had alerted Ashton to his estimated time of arrival at his flat. Ten minutes earlier than anticipated he stepped from the taxi and paid before walking up to his apartment and taking a few minutes to tidy the living room.

In the midst of pouring himself a Glenmorangie whisky, the buzzer alerted him to the arrival of the Director General of MI5.

Admitting him from the street, Morrison waited at the door of his flat until he arrived, somewhat breathless after the climb.

He smiled apologetically. "Sorry 'bout the stairs. This is a young man's apartment."

Ashton entered and made straight for one of Morrison's armchairs, almost throwing himself into its comfort.

"Is that a whisky you're pouring yourself?"

"I'm just in and thought I'd indulge. Would you like one?"

"Which malt?"

Glenmorangie."

"It'll do. I prefer the island malts."

"Can't drink them, sir. And me an islander too."

He poured a generous measure, handed it to Ashton with one hand and toasted his glass with the other. As the glasses clinked, Ashton got down to business, first offering a toast.

"Confusion to the enemy!"

He raised the glass to his lips and gestured his satisfaction.

"I've decided to take a chance on you, young Mr. Morrison. I very much hope I'm not making a mistake."

"Anything I can do to assist, Sir Humphrey."

"We have a serious problem within the agency. Someone is freelancing and using our good name to finance God alone knows *what* mischief. I worry that it's to do with an element of our work that deals with this Scottish independence business. I can't use anyone with our traditional Etonian and Oxbridge background. I need an outsider but before I go on, I know you're a proud Scot and if you tell me that you'd rather step back from this, I'll enjoy this whisky and search for someone else."

Morrison thought instantly of Iona and of her reaction if he accepted a task that thwarted Scottish independence.

"Well...I'd find it difficult to undertake a task that saw Scotland reduced in some way."

"That's what our HR people told me you'd say." He sipped long at his whisky. "What I can say is that it would appear that there appear to be a rogue or rogues in MI5 who *would* go to greater lengths than we'd contemplate in, as you'd say, reducing Scotland and it's *them* I'd have you unearth and bring to my attention. I'll have their balls!"

"Then I'd be delighted to assist."

Ashton recounted information regarding dark money being made available from Saudi Arabia to Northern Ireland for underhand political purposes with a proportion - probably half - being provided to someone in MI5. He went on to explain how his Deputy, Jack Kemp had interviewed the minister involved who confirmed the donation, who was unaware of the name of the recipient in MI5 and how Kemp had believed him due to the threats he'd made quite obviously frightening him. He described Kemp's evident antipathy towards Sir Robert Cavendish who managed the organisation's dealings with Scotland but that he'd absolutely no evidence whatsoever that might suggest he was the target they sought.

"He doesn't like him because he's an old Etonian type. He's smooth, insincere, and drinks Pimms as opposed to pints. But you can't hang a man for that. Certainly not in MI5 or I'd lose most of my senior management team. He also has an assistant I don't fancy one little bit. Chap called Giles Grantham..."

"Grantham?" Morrison interrupted.

"Yes. Why?"

"Up in Scotland. I was following up on a lead that guns were being smuggled from Ireland to Scotland and our Mr. Grantham was photographed in Glasgow receiving the weapons from the Irish couriers and passing them on to someone we know to be a Scottish Unionist. I couldn't for the life of me understand the connection."

Both men sat in silence as they weighed this information.

"Might well be nothing," Morrison offered.

"Indeed. But he's a scoundrel in my book so I wouldn't be surprised if he was up to no good."

The conversation meandered and dealt with further concerns about rogue elements within MI5, the Scottish islands - with Ashton trying out some of the Gaelic he'd picked up - and after a second large Glenmorangie, a confession from Morrison.

"Sir Humphrey, there's something that's being preying on my mind."

"Out with it, laddie," said Sir Humphrey in friendly fashion, now fully occupying the role of the Highland Laird as played by James Robertson Justice.

"The young lady, Iona McKenzie Forbes...she of Seed of the Gael... she was photographed outside the Crown Bar in the company of a Irish Republican known to have a history as a terrorist, a Conservative Councillor from Glasgow known to have dealings in dark money and a Northern Irish Unionist member known to have links with Protestant paramilitaries..."

"I remember."

"Well, that night she was in *my* company...which is why she was where she was...she doesn't know these people...anyway, she's a fellow Benbeculan, I've known her since Primary School and...well, I'm sweet on her."

"Indeed! And would you characterise it as being in a *relationship* with her?"

Morrison's face reddened. "Heavens, no! I'm not even sure my feelings are reciprocated but I wanted to be completely honest with you." He took a deep sip of his whisky to bolster his nerve. "I can quite see that if she were involved with any aspect of this there'd be a conflict of interest but she's not. Actually, she's been of significant assistance. She identified the couriers who brought the guns from Ireland, she took a photograph of Giles Grantham receiving them, she obtained the name of the Irishman now known to be in possession of at least one of the guns..."

"All very neat, eh? Very helpful that she was always in the right place at the right time, don't you think?" He held out his glass inviting a refill. "I long ago learned to discount coincidences."

Morrison reached for the bottle as he spoke, replenishing both glasses.

"I *know* her, Sir Humphrey. She's completely supportive of Scottish Independence and totally incapable of being involved in anything untoward."

"And would she be aware of your place of employment?"

"I promise I haven't told her that...but she's guessed," he confessed. "I haven't confirmed anything but she found my ID card along with some cover ID cards and concluded that only one of them could be authentic."

Ashton laughed.

"Another Director General might have kicked you out of the service for such a concatenation of events but I confess that I met my wife Doris in very similar circumstances and she also guessed my job - when I was a lowly foot-soldier as you are today. So...I trust your estimation of her lack of involvement in this and can only wish you well in your pursuit of her affections."

He placed his glass on a nearby table to slow his consumption.

"I've given considerable thought as to how I might identify the person or persons involved in utilising dark money within the service. I considered merely allocating you to the Scotland team but they'd just carve you out of anything they didn't want you to see. Jack Kemp is a good man but he's overloaded with work and can't maintain oversight on everything. In consequence I propose to make a field promotion and give you responsibility for reviewing all aspects of the work to do with the Scotland situation. Certain aspects may not be to your taste as you will understand that Her Majesty's Government wishes to use all means at its disposal to ensure that Scotland remains within the United Kingdom. You've signed the Official Secrets Act and so must put all concerns over the merits and demerits of our approach out of your mind or you'll spend some Category 'A' time in Belmarsh. Your task is to unearth *unapproved* ancillary strategies which are funded out-with our normal budget lines, discover who's behind it and report directly to me, not to Kemp, not to Bob Cavendish, only to me. Do not involve other police supports. We may have to close this matter very quietly to avoid political embarrassment. You'll be able to trust Angela Marleigh who heads up Human Resources but no one else. She'll provide you with any background information you need and I can supply the minutes setting up the Scotland team. After that, it's up to you. You'll receive an email from Ms. Marleigh in the morning explaining your duties along with a note outlining a modest increase in your salary. A separate note from me will confirm your right to undertake this review without impediment. So don't take any snash from any of those colleagues I've just mentioned. They'll all be surprised and shocked at your role but merely refer them to me."

"Time frames?"

"Tight. I'd like this dealt with rapidly. The longer they're operational, the longer they're able to do real damage."

Morrison decide to assert himself.

"I have the sense that the activities I'm dealing with in Scotland...with Grantham...may be part of this. I'd propose to return there first thing tomorrow to try to put that to bed then come back to London immediately to focus upon those agents who are operational down here."

He awaited Ashton's verdict.

"And this has nothing to do with visiting your sweetheart?"

"I'd have been glad to see her but she told me she was heading back to Belfast and then back to her job as a nurse anaesthetist in the *Ospadal Uibhist agus Bharraigh.*"

"Then, Godspeed. Mr. Morrison. Just get these bastards for me. They pose a greater threat to Scotland than the famous midge."

Morrison smiled.

"One for the road, Sir Humphrey?"

"Perhaps just a top-up."

* * *

Ashton began his walk downstairs as Morrison shut the door.

Decent bloke, he decided. He looked at his watch. *Too late to phone Iona?* He decided not and pushed the re-call button on his new phone. It was answered almost immediately.

"Hi, Donald John. I was just heading off to bed. You caught me just in time."

"Where are you?"

"And it's nice to hear from you, too!" retorted Iona teasingly.

"Sorry. I've just been having a long chat with my boss so I'm still all business. How are you?"

"I'm fine and dandy. Had a nice afternoon shopping in Glasgow. They've some great shops. A nice meal in Rab Ha's Hotel where I'm staying, then a relaxing evening watching rubbish on television."

"Great. When last we spoke you managed to tell me the real name of that guy Biro and that he wouldn't be taking care of business until the day after tomorrow. You've been busy."

"Not really. I was minding my own business after you left. Just finishing my Guinness and he strolls up and sits where you were sitting and starts chatting me up. A real charmer. Hadn't been blethering for five minutes and he was inviting me back to his place for some sweaty rest and relaxation."

"Well, you *would* have been the most beautiful woman in the pub!"

"God, you're just as full of it as he was!"

Somewhat deflated at her dismissal of his attempt at flattery, Morrison decided to return to the business in hand.

"So what did he say?"

Iona trapped the phone between her shoulder and her left cheek and counted off the statements on her fingers.

"He's staying in a place at Parkhead Cross, he's going to watch Celtic playing Aberdeen tomorrow evening, he's got a place in the part of the stadium used by the Ultras, he's taking care of business the day after that and then he's going back to Ireland. In the process he told me his real name was Cathal Durning."

"You have a gift!"

"Yeah. You coming back up or are you allocated new duties?"

"Both actually. I'll be on a flight north in the morning. From what you say, I'll be able to pick him up after the match ends."

"Oh, you mean *we'll* pick him up. You're forgetting that we're partners now. I've a gift, so I've been told."

"Thought you were heading back to Belfast to get your things?"

"Phoned Emily. Gave her some stuff about a love affair gone wrong. 'Fraid I used you as a handy surrogate."

"Be my guest."

"Well I left it open. I decided if you were staying in London I may as well head over but if you were coming back up, you'd make a mess of things without me as your lovely assistant. I'll phone her in the morning and make my excuses."

Morrison admitted defeat.

"Okay. I'll be up mid-morning. I'll call you when I'm in the taxi."

"Night, sweetie-pie!"

Morrison ended the call. *What in God's name am I to make of this woman. One minute I think maybe she likes me and the next she's dismissive. One minute she's calling me sweetie-pie and the next it seems she's only interested in being James Bond! Looks like it'll be easier understanding what's going on in MI5 than what's going on in Iona's head.*

Chapter Thirty-five

Baxter had just coaxed his car into third gear as he headed towards his office in Dumfries when his mobile phone rang, setting off the vehicle's hands-free system. The name of his friend and colleague Detective Stuart Cruikshank appeared on his information screen.

"Morning, Stuart. This is early for you."

"Hi Tallman. Wouldn't have bothered you but our wee ned friend Ivan Chadwick saw fit to remove himself from his hospital bed and is nowhere to be found. I decided to let that lie and not bother you until you got in but I've just had a call to tell me that he's been found dead in a car that's been pulled from beneath fifteen feet of water at Kirkcudbright Harbour."

Baxter shouted over the noise of the engine.

"Last time I saw him he had one arm lying at the bottom of a surgical bin in the Royal Infirmary and the other in a pretty substantial stookie. It does tend to suggest that maybe he didn't drive himself to his watery grave."

"Yeah. I'm actually in the hospital now. Apparently he had a visitor just before he vanished and wee nurse Wilma who witnessed this is about to come on duty. I'm going to take a statement then I figured you and me could pop over to Kirkcudbright and identify what's left of his body."

"Sounds like a plan. I'll be at the Royal in twenty. See you then.

* * *

"Sorry it's so early chaps but I have to get back to Glasgow."

Three men sat opposite Rotermundt each either drinking or milking their coffee.

"My purpose here is straightforward. The organisation that I represent has deemed it appropriate to finance the activities we discussed earlier."

He opened his briefcase and withdrew a pile of banknotes approximately resembling the size of a small brick. Wrapped tightly in elastic bands, the wad had the words 'Aberdeen Conservative and Unionist Association' written on a piece of Central Hotel notepaper tucked beneath the bands.

"I'll need a signature on the back of that piece of paper. Don't worry. I'm the only person who'll have access to it but I have to demonstrate to others that the cash has been handed over. Now..." He consulted another piece of notepaper he had before him to check the name and organisation represented by one of his recipients.

"Eh, let's see...*Angus*, this is the sum of twenty-five thousand pounds. Every last penny is to be used as agreed in pamphlets and brochures which must be made use of before any election campaign starts at which time we'll have to start accounting for all monies spent. This should be used to soften the vote beforehand...That said, I'm also happy if you use, let's say four or five thousand, creatively. Perhaps a function or two to rouse the blood."

He withdrew a second similar brick of money and again consulted his notes.

"Malcolm?" He looked up to see who might respond to his name being called. A small man raised his hand.

"Malcolm. You asked for twenty thousand. It's all here. Same arrangement as Angus, okay?"

He slid the piece of identifying paper from the brick and passed it over to the beneficiary. Sign the back, there's a good chap."

A third pile was removed.

"Eric? You've won the lottery. You have thirty thousand here. Newspaper adverts in local papers in your constituency along with posters emphasising the merits of the Union? Good work."

He closed the briefcase and passed the third slip for signature.

"Short but very sweet. A total of seventy-five thousand pounds allocated in the service of Queen and Country. I believe my work here is done." He pressed the hinges that locked the briefcase. "Let me remind you that these monies, should they be challenged, have derived from tombolas, raffles, bingo nights, donations and the like. Under no circumstances can it be revealed even to your local members that this cash came from me. Many other of your constituency branches have received nothing because we cannot be assured that they will play by these rules. You have been chosen because you are each single-minded in respect of the cause of British Unionism and you understand that in times of great peril such as exist now, we have to be inventive and resourceful if we are to defeat the separatists."

He stood, promoting a similar response from the others round the table. He leaned across and shook each man's hand.

"I have a flight to catch."

* * *

Baxter approached the nurses' station where Cruikshank was seated on the edge of the desk chatting to the Nurse Keane.

"Detective Cruikshank!" hailed Baxter.

"Morning, Detective Sergeant Baxter. Nurse Keane, here...Wilma... was on duty yesterday and was the last person to see Chadwick other than his visitor."

"He had a visitor?"

Nurse Keane nodded her agreement. "Tall chap. Slim. I'd say late thirties, early forties. He was wearing a dark suit. Eh, English accent. Posh actually. He came about half an hour after I'd checked on Mr. Chadwick but when I next visited his ward, he wasn't there, his medications had been removed as had a wheelchair that was in the ward. It was found later outside."

"Aye, Tallman, but wait 'till you hear the best bit."

Baxter raised his eyebrows in the direction of Nurse Keane inviting information. She prodded a diamond-shaped item towards Baxter with the rubbered end of a pencil.

"The man lifted this and commented about how we had won an award. He was kind of smarmy...cheeky actually."

"So we'll have his prints!" Cruikshank smiled broadly.

"Got an evidence bag?"

Cruikshank removed a small plastic bag from his inside jacket pocket and opening it, lifted the trophy by the sharp corner edges of its base and dropped it inside.

"That's what he gets for being cheeky, eh Nurse Wilma?...Caught!... caught by one of Scotland's finest nurses!"

Baxter reached over and shook the hand of Nurse Keane in a farewell gesture.

"Thanks, Wilma. He's happily married by the way!" He turned to Cruikshank. "Got everything written down, Stuart?"

Cruikshank tapped his suit pocket while grinning embarrassedly at Nurse Keane who returned his smile.

"All in here."

"Then let's you and me go and visit Kirkcudbright Harbour."

* * *

As Morrison's plane flew north to Glasgow and Rotermundt's plane flew south to the same city, Iona sat on the edge of her hotel-room bed holding a hand mirror in front of her face as she applied lipstick.

Slowly she dropped her hands to her lap and looked wistfully at her image in the larger dressing table mirror opposite.

I'm not sure I know what I'm doing. I'm a nurse anaesthetist. That's my calling. I'm happily single. I'm an island girl who wants to see Scotland independent. In the space of a short time I find myself having feelings for a man who may or who may not share them. He's an Intelligence Officer for a Westminster government that I abhor...a man who takes a phone call and then disappears to who knows where...a man who carries a gun...who lives in London...

She lifted an angled eye-liner brush from a toiletries bag but made no effort to apply it as she continued her inspection of herself.

If I say so myself, I'm good looking, athletic, conversational and bright. If I lived in Glasgow or Edinburgh I could have an Olympian brain surgeon with the looks of Brad Pitt as a husband. But I'm an island girl. I get to choose between Hamish who'd talk fishing and sing to me in Gaelic or Donald John who'd want me to move to London and await the phone call that told me that Her Majesty's Government are grateful for the life he gave in defence of the capitalist and Unionist Establishment while defending the House of Lords or some bloody thing.

She looked at the clock on the wall.

Donald John will call soon. Do I tell him I'm off to Belfast or do I await his invitation to help him deal with Mr Cathal 'Biro' Durning?

* * *

Sir Humphrey Ashton folded his copy of the Daily Telegraph and placed it under his left arm in order to free it to collect the cup of coffee laid out for him every morning by his assistant, Miss Leyton-Willis.

"Thank you Elizabeth. Would you ask Mr. Kemp to join me if he has a moment?"

Some five minutes later Jack Kemp knocked and entered.

"Morning, Jack. Hope I didn't interrupt anything."

"A meeting of staff dealing with our problems in that mosque in Birmingham. No problems. They'll deal with matters in my absence. How can I help?"

"I've been thinking about this dark money business. I've decided to do two things and I need your assistance."

"Sure, boss."

"First, I've decided to introduce a free radical into the body politic of this organisation to attempt to get to the bottom of this dark money that seems to be floating around the organisation."

"Is that really necessary, boss? I'm trying to maintain a grip on things, keeping my ear close to the ground, that sort of thing. Last time I checked, a free radical was an unstable entity."

"No argument, Jack, it's a done deal. I've asked young Mr. Morrison of Northern Ireland fame to take oversight of the work of the Scotland team...to review progress...he's quite outside our organisational culture. There's no evidence that that's where the money has ended up but it's a pretty decent bet given the requirements laid down by our friends in Saudi Arabia."

"I guess that's my point, boss. That money could be being misused *anywhere* within MI5...our dealings with our new nationals previously resident in the Middle East, our Al-Qaeda people, our Irish contingent... the extreme left...they all might be recipients of this cash, although I'd agree that the Scotland people are prime suspects...and I'm working on that basis." He paused. "Also, I'm a big fan of our Mr. Morrison, but he's rather wet behind the ears is he not?

Ashton ignored the rhetorical question.

"Give Morrison every assistance. Our friend Sir Robert Cavendish will be apoplectic but I care little about that. When he protests at a young Scottish whippersnapper investigating his dealings, you deal with it. I haven't the patience."

"If that's your last word on the matter, Sir Humphrey."

"It is. Secondly, I want you to trigger your assets in the Scottish Parliament. I had a most interesting chat with Mr. Morrison last night and while ever more impressed by him, he has insights into the Scottish situation that makes me uneasy that we're not quite on top of things north of the border and there'll be political hell to pay if we don't use every lever at our disposal to shoot their fox. I'll have the Prime Minister all over me if we don't strain every sinew. Now remind me, what assets are in position in Edinburgh?"

"Well, the main ones are two nationalist MSPs, two retired but influential SNP Cabinet Secretaries, one Green MSP and three senior civil servants. They've all been in position for some years, we've never asked anything of them other than intelligence so they're sleepers awaiting orders. The civil servants are all on board due to their political bent while the others are all beholden to us in one way or another due to our uncovering their debt or little peccadillos. They jump when we say so or they end up in the divorce court, the debtors court, the Court of Session or the court of public opinion."

"Then I need them to become operational, Jack. Have them introduce controversial policies on anything you like. Something that'll split the ranks. They write newspaper columns supporting something that'll have half the separatists supporting their position and the other half insisting that it's nothing to do with independence. Once they achieve some sort of controversy, speak to Alan Bell over in Bell Polling and have him release contrived market research suggesting that as a consequence of this split in the ranks, the separatists have fallen back in the polls. Time it well but alert Bob Mathews and Jimmy Spence in the Herald and Scotsman respectively. Have them prepare a broadside. We need to cut the feet from the nationalists as this momentum they're building might easily become unstoppable...especially if the UK Government continue to make political *faux pas* after *faux pas!* They really have a tin ear and it just makes our job all the harder."

"Well, boss, we've already got green proposals developed involving cutting air flights that if approved, would deprive the great unwashed of Airdrie from visiting Torremolinos. We have a policy proposition that would nationalise the grouse moors which'll please many but piss off the business and conservative vote within the movement and we have a retired Minister whom we know will not unhappily propose barbed wire and machine guns turrets on the border. A civil servant will be asked to leak an earlier document that the separatists hate but still *discussed* to allow fox-hunting in rural areas where it's been deemed necessary to cull numbers. Any one of these will be front page and all will split and separate the movement."

"All agreed. Implement...but incrementally! If we trigger all at once it'll look contrived."

"And you're sure about our Mr. Morrison?"

"Implement!"

Chapter Thirty-six

Morrison phoned Iona once he'd cleared security and had retrieved his Sauer pistol.

"That's me back in Glasgow, Iona. Everything okay at your end?"

"S'pose."

"You had lunch yet?"

"Not hungry."

"You squared things with Emily?"

"Left a message."

Morrison's unease wouldn't contain itself.

"Sure you're okay?"

"Yeah."

"Should we meet up?"

"Well, to be honest, I was thinking maybe I should head over to Belfast, see Emily...I mean I've hardly been in her company because of all this...and then get back to Benbecula."

Morrison's mind raced. Was this a coded message from a woman who was somehow under threat? Or might it be merely be the not unreasonable presumption that he'd somehow pissed her off? Nothing was straightforward with Iona. He decided assertiveness was the best bet.

"Okay! Look! I need to debrief you."

Iona couldn't help herself.

"Ooh, don't be so forward, Mr. Morrison. We haven't even kissed."

Exasperated, Morrison pulled rank.

"Look, Iona. You were the one who described herself as my assistant."

"Your *lovely* assistant."

"Yeah. But before you head off to wherever..."

"Belfast."

"Yeah. I need to know all that you know. I've a job to do. Now if you want to bugger off, so be it. I'll deal with things on my own. In fact, that's my *preference*. You should have no part in these proceedings."

Iona sighed and gave way to her ambivalence.

"Look, I'm sorry. I'm just confused about a lot of stuff. That's all. Confused."

Christ, so am I, thought Morrison.

Morrison decided to bring his tone down a notch.

"Let's meet for lunch. You can bring me up to speed and then decide your next move. How's that?"

Unaccountably, Iona suddenly felt vulnerable and tearful. Her response was made in a quiet tone.

"Okay."

"Then Kitty O'Shea's. They'll have your Guinness, they have lunch-grub in quantities that would feed a family of seven and we both know where it is." He looked at his watch. "Meet at one-thirty?"

"Okay."

Iona returned to looking at her image in the large mirror.

God, I need to pull myself together. I've never felt this way about a man before but this one is just bad for me...I need to remember that. He's bad for me. I need to get back to my life at the hospital, simple pleasures and people I love, trust and can see every day in life if I choose.

* * *

Baxter and Cruikshank stepped from their vehicle yards from where a police cordon had been established. A uniformed officer lifted the tape as they ducked under it.

"Sir."

Baxter returned the acknowledgement with a more informal, "Hi!"

They walked towards a low-loader on which had been placed the car into which Gold had dragged Chadwick. Small rivulets of water still trickled from its undercarriage. The boot of the car was open.

An ambulance sat stationary nearby, its lights still blinking. Baxter decided that was the first order of business. He approached the paramedic, removing his police warrant card for identification purposes as he did so.

"Hi. Detective Sergeant Baxter. Is our one-armed bandit in your ambulance?"

"He is but he's not in a position to tell you much."

"Death by drowning?"

"We'll leave that to the Fiscal or Lord Advocate but unless someone can explain how a one-armed man and with a broken arm can drive a car whilst being tethered in a rear seat belt, you have to give short odds on him being introduced to the waters of Kirkcudbright Harbour by a third party. Your pals over there will tell you whether they've any idea who that might be."

"Aye, but was he drowned? Any other evidence of injury that might have preceded drowning?"

"Again, that's for others to decide but if you ask me?"

"I am..."

"Then he was drowned. I've not seen any other cause although a Procurator Fiscal-instructed post mortem examination might uncover things like poisoning, choking and the like but that literally seems like overkill when he's been subjected to immersion in several feet of cold water for an hour."

"Thanks. Can we have a quick keek?"

The ambulance man opened the rear door of his vehicle and both officers clambered aboard.

Cruikshank peeled back the sheet that covered the drowned man.

"Aye, well, it's him alright, Tallman. Not been a good day for the fellah, eh? Loses an arm, gets burnt to buggery, breaks his good arm, is wheeched out of hospital by someone and ends up drowned. Bet he wishes he'd stayed in Sheffield and spent the day shouting abuse at 'them illegal Muslims' he was going on about."

Baxter was thoughtful.

"Special Branch will be all over this. It clearly stinks and seems likely to involve some kind of underhand political activity. I guarantee they'll want to throw a blanket over the whole thing and hush it up. If they do, as far as I'm concerned it's a confession that this is state sponsored. If they don't then it's more probably a ned on the wrong end of a drug deal or something."

"So what do we do?"

Baxter looked round at the harbour scene, now in the process of being normalised.

"We await their next move."

* * *

Sir Robert Cavendish slammed the desk phone back on its cradle.

"Fucking incompetent!"

Having just been informed by Benjamin Gold that the efforts to blame the independence movement for anti-English sentiment had come to a watery end, he'd taken great pains to extract assurances from him that there were absolutely no...absolutely *no* loose ends that might lead to MI5 being accused of involvement. Gold had underscored the fact of both men being recruited from a low-life pub where they were known adherents of the English Defence League, that they had assumed he was also a member of the same organisation, that one had died at the scene, the other had been sedated and then done away with before being interviewed by the authorities and the car used to transport the two men to Scotland and the one he'd used to extract Chadwick had each been stolen. Fingerprints would have been eroded and DNA degraded by exposure to water and fire. There was nothing to worry about, he had confidently asserted.

Cavendish was less confident. He stroked his chin thoughtfully, his anger dissipating, if only marginally. He lifted his phone again.

"Michael. Would you bring through the file from the safe on our Scotland dealings?"

After a moment during which the wall safe surrendered the file sought by Cavendish, Michael Kowalski knocked quietly and placed the document before his boss before retiring.

Not bothering to acknowledge his departure, Cavendish merely turned to the minute which recorded the various covert actions he'd approved and ran his thumb down the list. Reading quietly, he slowly closed the buff folder and picked up his phone, punching in the four numbers that connected him to Jenifer Fowldes.

"Jenny. Sir Robert here. Give me a quick update on your progress in Edinburgh with the Scottish Cabinet member accused of sexual assault."

"Certainly, Sir Robert. Lorna Gillies MSP has stepped down following the allegations of sexual assault. The First Minister has had to act to see off media interest. The police have still to charge her but a statement from our complainant has been taken. Our legal advice is that it's sufficiently convincing to secure a conviction and even if we fail to impress a judge, the damage will decidedly have been done politically. We've not made any money over to the civil servant concerned nor will we until the matter is resolved in our interest. I've spoken only yesterday to her and she's determined to follow through on this as I've arranged for her son to be interviewed for Cambridge and she feels she can't disappoint him. I've guaranteed the money to pay his university fees but again no money has changed hands yet."

"So as far as you are aware there is nothing to connect us to this piece of work?"

"Nothing at all. The person interviewing her son is a close friend. A bridesmaid at my wedding."

"Thank you."

He continued to hold the phone and pressed the button ending the call before pushing another four digits and connecting himself with Ivan Caruthers who answered his call immediately.

"Caruthers!"

"Ivan, Sir Robert here. Just getting a bit anxious about our Scotland efforts. How are you progressing with the support we're giving to think tanks and the like?"

"It's all going very smoothly, Sir Robert. We've not had to set up any new organisations. The ones we've already sponsored are there in number and it's just a question of tasking them and paying them. I've also spoken to key editors and everyone's on-side. Once we have some positive polling data to shout about there will be wall-to-wall coverage in the print media and this, of course sets the agenda for the TV boys."

"Has money changed hands?"

"Not yet. We've had exploratory conversations and we're discussing the nature of the contracts which in turn will determine the costs involved. Is there a problem with the money?"

"No. None. I just wanted an update. Thanks."

Cavendish replaced the phone and took his mobile from his pocket. Scrolling through his contact names he stopped at Giles Grantham whom he knew to be in Scotland and therefore not contactable by landline. He pushed at the mobile number. In Glasgow, Sir Robert's name appeared on Grantham's device.

"Sir Robert. How good of you to call."

"I phoned because I'm on edge about our plans for Colquhoun. I want to make sure that whatever happens...*whatever* happens, there's no way of connecting MI5 to anything that might embarrass it. I need your reassurance that everything is going smoothly."

Grantham was himself not unconcerned about progress due to Rotermundt's decision to involve a third party but was unpersuaded of the need to trouble his senior officer. He'd been on many a delicate operation in his day and remained confident that there were few circumstances he could not resolve himself. His attitude coloured his response to Cavendish. He spoke in coded language.

"Everything is as we discussed, Sir Robert. The implements we required have been transported successfully from Northern Ireland. I remain in possession of one and will use it as we agreed once the first implement has been used in Eastriggs."

"The man you intend using...he is completely unaware of your intentions after the event?"

"Correct, Sir Robert. You have nothing to fear."

"Very well. But listen to me. I'm edgy. Do *not* take chances. I rescued you after that debacle in Bradford and again in Grimsby. I shall not do so again. This operation is very risky. If it works it could be decisive. It can be allowed to fail but it can never be placed at our door. I hope I make myself *crystal* clear."

"As ever, Sir Robert."

The conversation ended. Grantham consulted his watch. *Another visit to Rogano's would be entirely in order. Their martinis equal anything to be found in the best watering holes in London. Nothing to do until tomorrow so...* He looked out of his hotel window at glorious sunshine. *Looks like the weather will hold.* He put his jacket on, checked himself in the mirror and set off for one of Glasgow's most elegant restaurants.

Chapter Thirty-seven

Iona edged into the booth occupied by Morrison in Kitty O'Shea's.
She smiled, feeling a bit more at one with the world since he'd phoned earlier.

"Is that Guinness for me or are you having two?"

"I'm having two!"

"Maybe you'd share one?"

"Okay...but it's grudged," he laughed, pleased to see Iona more in her normal mood.

"Journey okay? She sipped her stout.

"Straightforward. How are you? You seemed troubled when we spoke earlier this morning."

"Aye, well women are allowed to be troubled whenever they feel like it."

"Sure you're okay?" He advanced the conversation quicker than he'd intended. "Heading back to Belfast today?"

"Well, the way I figure it, it's dangerous being around you. Since I bumped into you in the Dark Island, you've been shot in the arse, fought off three assailants, you've been chasing after people carrying guns, you've had me deputised as your beautiful assistant and had me traipsing after couriers carrying guns, I've outed you as a Salvation Army hit man of some vintage and you've allowed me to be hit upon by the very man you suspect of carrying the weapons you're trying so hard to uncover."

"Can't argue with any of that...although of course I can't confirm the part about me working for the Salvation Army."

"So this morning when you phoned...well...I'd decided that you were bad for me. I reckoned that one of us might get hurt...both physically and maybe even emotionally...like I said, you're my favourite male friend and the idea of me sitting somewhere waiting on you only to be told you were to be found in a hospital or on a slab, well, I don't know that I could handle that. I really don't."

Morrison weighed her words.

"If it's any help, I have no present intention of ending up in a hospital or on a slab."

Iona smiled. "Well, if it's any help to *you*, I have no intention of letting you." She took another sip of her Guinness before continuing. "I'm going to hang around for the short term while I work all of this out. I'm sure you can use me in some way. I know Biro better than you and will recognise him easier after the match tonight. A couple are always less suspicious than a man alone..."

"So you'll stay?"

"For the time being."

Morrison found himself grinning from ear to ear.

"Fancy some lunch?"

* * *

Baxter stepped backwards to his desk while still talking to one of his uniformed colleagues. Without looking, he passed his right hand behind him over the desk area on which he expected to find a phone. Brushing it, he lifted the phone and signalled to his colleague that he was now free to leave.

"Detective Sergeant Baxter."

"Oh, good afternoon, Sergeant. It's Inspector Alan Moore here from Special Branch up in Glasgow."

"Hi. How can I help?"

"Myself and a few colleagues are in Dumfries Royal Infirmary right now. We're following up the suspicious death of one Ivan Chadwick. I gather you're *au fait* with the case."

"I am."

"I'm actually with Nurse Keane here who tells me that you and another detective interviewed the deceased prior to him either being removed or removing himself from hospital."

"We did."

"Can I ask if you have had the time to commit any statement he made to paper?"

"I did."

"Was it signed by the deceased?"

"As far as he was able given the new writing style he'd had to adopt."

"Quite. Well, Special Branch is now taking over the case so I'll be over to collect the statement within the hour."

"And why is it now a case that interests Special Branch?"

"Can't discuss that just now. I'll be in your office within the hour. In the meantime, I'd be grateful if you'd hold all documentation personally and refrain from discussing any aspect of the case with anyone other than Special Branch."

"Absolutely. No problem. See you shortly, Inspector."

Baxter replaced the phone and left his office hurriedly, leaning into the doorway of his secretary and asking that when Inspector Alan Moore arrived, he be shown every courtesy if he hadn't returned.

"Just going to get myself a sandwich, Moira."

Leaving the police station by the rear door, he crossed the car parking area and walked along a footpath which took him to a row of shops, one of which sold bakery products. There being no queue, he was welcomed by a shop assistant used to his custom and a stranger to formalities.

"Oh, it's big Tallman. How are we today, big chap?"

"We're grand, Joan. And you?"

"Ach, fair tae middlin', Tallman."

Baxter scanned the plastic bowls of ingredients.

"Could you make me up something with tuna and some salad, Joan...and while you're doing that, can I use your phone? My battery's dead."

"Help yourself, big man. It's just round the back."

Baxter lifted the counter lid and was directed to a small room festooned with paperwork and cardboard boxes. He lifted the phone, consulted his contact details on his mobile phone and dialled the number of the Dumfries and Galloway Standard.

"Chris Beaton."

"Hi Chris. It's Tallman. Got a moment?"

"Always, Tallman. Sounds like you've sobered up after the golf dinner last week."

"Only just, Chris. Listen, I'm in a hurry. You print tomorrow, right?"

"Putting the finishing touches to the edition as we speak."

"I need a favour."

"It's as good as done."

"Look, I'll tell you a story off the record but your source when Special Branch asks you will be someone from the hospital. That okay with you?"

"Sure is."

"And also, when you mark it exclusive, and your print presses start, you phone a contact in STV and give them a copy of the story on the basis that they have to give you credit for it when it goes out."

"This sounds big, Tallman."

"It is, but I need your agreement to these conditions. My name is never mentioned."

"Agreed. Go on. I won't record this...I'll just write down the salient points."

Baxter provided a selective account of the basics of the story consistent with the information known to hospital staff and adding his own 'sources' which, with some 'allegedlies', permitted some scope for rumours and innuendo. Fictitious passers-by who heard uniformed talk about burned Saltires and plots to burn English second homes all allowed the editor of the Standard to run a story about a murder having been committed to hush up an attempt at blackening the name of the independence movement in Scotland.

"Got it, Tallman. This'll be fixed immediately and will hit the streets tomorrow hard on the heels on the TV news."

"Mind...not a word to anyone. This could come back to bite me."

"You have my word."

Tallman returned to his desk with his sandwich and had twenty minutes to prepare before his phone rang, alerting him to the arrival in the building of Inspector Alan Moore.

When introduced to each other, Baxter was most welcoming, handing him Chadwick's statement almost before he'd sat down. Moore took some moments to read it.

"So there were two officers involved."

"Aye, myself and Detective Cruikshank. It was actually him who persuaded Chadwick to cough."

"Is he around? It'd be better if you were both here."

Baxter used his phone to invite Cruikshank to join them. He entered and shook hands with Moore.

"Gentlemen, this case is now to be handled by the National Public Order Intelligence Unit. I'll be leading the investigation. There should be absolutely no comment from your side on any aspect of the case. All enquiries should be passed to me. As we speak, your Divisional Commander is being issued with the same instructions." He folded Chadwick's statement. "This is very helpful."

He stood and with a nod of his head, left the room.

Cruikshank spoke first.

"Looks like you were right about them wanting to cover it up, Tallman."

"Aye. And d'you know, in all the confusion, I forgot to tell him we'd picked up that award with the fellah's prints on them. Have you had any word back from forensics?"

"They've promised them by close of play today."

"Then I'll probably use that to jog my memory and let Inspector Moore know we have them."

"You just going to let them manage this story any way they want?

"I'm saying nothing to you, Stuart. You're a big Scottish Independence man, eh?"

"Ever since I watched Braveheart!"

"Well, I need to you to be able to look colleagues in the eye and tell them that you know the square root of fuck all about what may or may not transpire over the next wee while. As far as you're concerned, you attended a car fire, took a run up to Lockerbie to visit one of the addresses, interviewed a survivor in hospital, took a statement and visited a crime scene where the deceased was recovered from the depths of Kirkcudbright Harbour. And while you're at it, your boss, Sergeant Baxter did exactly the same and he hasn't been out of your sight since you got back here to the station."

"Aye, well that's all true, Tallman."

"I know. Just so *you* know!"

Cruikshank grinned. "I love it when you start your mischief!"

"Well continuing in that vein, I'd like you immediately to investigate an assault on a till operator in the Co-op in Lochside Road. Take nothing more to do with Chadwick. I'll explain later."

Chapter Thirty-eight

"We should have thought of this, Iona."

Morrison and Iona stood on the walkway above Section 111 on the North Curve at Celtic Park. The home team, Celtic were making heavy weather of a doughty Aberdeen team apparently determined to secure a nil-nil draw, thereby ensuring a tedious and dull chess-match of a game. Restless fans were making known their displeasure but below Morrison, the Green Brigade, reputedly Celtic's most energetic and enthusiastic fans, were all singing loudly and waving scarves in the air, oblivious to the absence of any real goalmouth action.

"We should have anticipated that every man jack of them in this corner would have dressed identically in green and white hooped jerseys."

"From where we stand, we can only see the back of their heads so I can't identify Biro from here. Everyone looks the same."

Morrison grimaced.

"I suppose I could ask the match commander if I could scan the crowd here from his control booth but I don't want to risk him leaving while I'm in another part of the ground." He looked at his watch. "There's only ten minutes to go." He glanced at the exits from the stadium and pointed at a vantage point. "If we stand over there and climb a few stairs we'd be able to see everyone head-on as they leave. This is more difficult than I'd anticipated." His temper got the better of him. "Shit! If we lose him tonight, who knows what he'll get up to tomorrow and we'll be none the wiser." He considered the crowd again. "Okay. Let's position ourselves."

With five minutes to go, some supporters began leaving the ground although the Ultras remained unmoved, still swaying and singing in the club's only standing area. Shortly, three blasts of the referee's whistle brought a dour match to an end and only then did the choreographic flow of supporters below them begin moving slowly towards their main egress.

"Aged maybe fifty, dark hair, full beard, five tenish..." repeated Iona for perhaps the sixth time.

Hundreds of fans, still singing, edged closer together as they approached the stairwell. Every so often a bearded fan would excite the interest of one of them only to be discounted. The numbers leaving now thinned and only a hardened few remained *in situ* still bellowing out their affection for their team. At once Iona grasped Morrison's sleeve.

"There he is!"

Recognising the man she'd identified as Biro, Morrison grasped Iona and hugging her, swept her round in celebration as if the home team had just scored on the way to the dressing room.

"Donald John!" cried Iona.

"You were facing him," replied Morrison speaking into the collar of her jacket. "If he recognised you he'd figure something was up."

Hiding her behind him, he turned his head to continue his observance of the man, still singing, as he walked unsteadily to the stairwell, holding the bannister with one hand and continuing to sing as he swayed slowly down towards the exit. He released Iona.

"He looks pissed but let's not take any chances."

The twosome followed their quarry from the stadium as he walked alone towards Parkhead Cross.

"I guarantee he'll head for a boozer," said Morrison, just as Biro turned off Springfield Road into Dechmont Street where the ubiquitous red sandstone tenements so particular to Glasgow, gave way to more modern homes with gardens back and front.

"Well done, Sherlock," teased Iona.

Biro stopped outside number forty and rummaged in his pocket from which he produced a set of keys. Pressing a button on a key flashed the lights on a red Nissan which Biro entered, searched for something in the glovebox and returned to the pavement.

"Think it's a bottle of something," said Iona.

"Half bottle, probably. Can't see a full bottle fitting in most glove compartments."

Biro stood on the pavement and unscrewing the top from the bottle, raised it to his lips and took a long draught. Sated, he returned the top and walked unsteadily up a short driveway to the house where he knocked the door and was given entry.

Morrison assessed the situation.

"Can't see him going anywhere tonight, Iona." He considered his options. "Tell you what, I'll walk you back to your hotel. You stay there and head for Belfast in the morning."

"But I thought..."

"Look, who knows what'll happen tomorrow. There may be gun-play and I can't have you mixed up in that. I'd be hung, drawn and quartered by London if I had a civvy in tow and something went wrong. But mostly, I just don't want you to get hurt."

Iona frowned. "In Kitty's at lunchtime we agreed that I was to retain my role as your beautiful assistant."

"Yeah but this is a stakeout. There is nothing...and I mean *nothing* more boring than sitting in a car waiting for something to happen. And tomorrow, things might get a bit heavy."

"Things could have gotten a bit heavy on the ferry. Your Mr. Biro was carrying a gun when he was chatting me up in Kitty's. They got heavy in George Square when you were shot in the backside. Seems to me that when things get heavy, I'm there to help you."

"Look, Iona, all of the car hire places will be closed so I'll have to visit police headquarters and try to persuade someone to allow me to commandeer a car. You have a good night's sleep and I'll return here and keep watch. I'll follow him tomorrow and let you know how I get on."

Iona shook her head defiantly, turned and started walking back towards the city centre. Morrison followed one step behind.

Somewhat vexed, Iona directed her comments over her shoulder.

"I'm catching a taxi. You do as you please."

* * *

Alan Colquhoun, the Conservative Secretary of State for Scotland, was seated in the back of his ministerial Jaguar XJ, the paperwork from his red box lying idly on his lap as he dozed. His plane from London had taken him to Newcastle leaving his chauffeur a drive of just over an hour to reach his home in Eastriggs on the Scottish border with England - almost identical to the time it would have taken from Edinburgh Airport but with extra flying time being required to land on the more northern airstrip. In the front passenger seat sat his Private Secretary,

Alison Lowrie; his Principal Private Secretary, Geoff Sterling remaining in London. Constantly checking the minister's phone, Lowrie would from time to time, pass on a bulletin that appeared on his screen which she thought might interest her political master.

"Good piece in the Border Telegraph on your visit to the new university spin-out in Kelso tomorrow, Minister. Helpful comments about the use of Westminster funds to assist its broadband capacity which is essential to its activity. Side article citing your ribbon-cutting at noon tomorrow. We might get a small crowd."

A silence followed as the powerful car navigated the rural roads, closing on Eastriggs. She read another news clip.

"The Kelso versus Melrose rugby match tomorrow of additional interest due to three players returning from injury. You're attending that at two-thirty for a meet and greet before the game starts at three."

Still Colquhoun dozed, his papers unattended.

Lowrie muttered as she read the next news item, her whispered utterances being issued to herself in a disbelieving tone.

"Jesus...Minister! Minister!" She turned slightly to signify heightened importance. "Scottish Television News is carrying a story alleging the death of two men following an alleged Westminster plot to condemn Scottish independence by employing members of the English Defence League to burn down second homes owned by English residents. One of the dead men was pulled from Kirkcudbright Harbour and police say his death was suspicious." She quietened as she read on before reading aloud again. "It comes from an exclusive story run by the Dumfries and Galloway Standard." She was silent again. "That hits the streets tomorrow morning. We'll need to get ahead of the curve on this."

Colquhoun was now fully alert.

"Better get Chief Super Brodie on the phone. I need to know what's behind all of this."

Some dialling took place, eventually tracking down Brodie to his home where he was enjoying a nightcap.

"The guts of the story is true, Minister. We're at a loss to establish how the Standard got hold of the story. My people insist they didn't leak it and I trust them. The Standard itself cites sources in the hospital. Two of my officers spoke to the man eventually found drowned and said he was a bit fevered and disorientated as he surfaced from his operation...he lost an arm in an explosion in a car filled with Saltire flags, paint and petrol. He had a list of addresses of residences owned by English people who used them as a second home and confessed to intended fire-raising and attempting to pin it on nationalists. My detectives said he could have said anything while he was under sedation or when he was coming to. We have a willingly signed confession, now in the possession of Special Branch, in which he confirmed that he and his mate who was killed by the explosion were paid to torch these premises. So far, the story doesn't cover the statement and hasn't got details of the list. The man Chadwick who was drowned was removed either with or against his will from Dumfries Royal Infirmary and wound up dead. At present there's a case to be made for a conspiracy to commit wilful fire-raising, possible culpable homicide, abduction, murder and there's an open question about the English Defence League being behind it all. It's a real can of worms, Minister."

"It is, rather," responded Colquhoun. "I take it you have no press comment."

"Nothing beyond our usual remarks about it being an on-going case."

"Well thank you for the briefing, Chief Superintendent. I'll mull over our own comments as I'm sure our political opponents will wish to make hay with this."

"I'm sure they will. But please be assured that the leak did not come from us."

"Thank you again."

Chapter Thirty-nine

For a couple of hours, Morrison had struggled to remain awake, having been watching Biro's car all night. A taxi pulling up round the corner from his borrowed, unmarked police car excited his interest. He looked at the clock on his dashboard; seven-fifteen. He pushed himself up in his seat in preparation for any action required and sat back again as the bedenimed figure of Iona appeared round a hedge clutching her bags, looking around to establish the presence of Morrison.

He pressed a small lever which lowered his side window and waved surreptitiously at Iona who approached the passenger side of the car, opened the rear doors, deposited her belongings and entered the car, sitting on the front seat.

"Morning, Donald John. Good night's sleep?"

Morrison sighed audibly.

"Shouldn't you be enjoying a morning coffee and a wee *croissant* in Glasgow Airport?"

"Until I fell asleep, that was my intention. When I awoke at six, I decided that if I found you still here and obviously in need of help, I'd join you. If you weren't here, I was quite prepared to redirect the taxi and head for the airport. But I found you here and obviously in need of help."

"And what particular help do you think I'm in need of?"

"Well, I had a good night's sleep and am fresh and able to drive. You've been sitting up like a mongoose on alert all night waiting to see if Biro appears."

As Iona spoke, Morrison stifled a yawn. Attempting to disguise it, he merely repeated the involuntary oscitation but pressed his lips together hoping to conceal his tiredness. Iona watched him carefully.

"You're out on your feet, Donald John! I don't want to be a nuisance but it'd make sense if I took the wheel and allowed you forty winks."

Morrison banged his head back against the head-rest admitting defeat.

"Look, there's a skill in following people unobtrusively."

"I'm not brain-dead, Donald John! I presume I try not to drive bumper to bumper, keep my distance and flash my lights at them. I'll follow all instructions you give me. Am I missing anything?"

"Usually we follow cars using perhaps half a dozen other vehicles. We're stuck with one so it'll be difficult. We don't know where this fellah's going; if it's mainly motorway, country roads or urban streets... but you have a point." Another yawn caused a pause. "I might just drive into a ditch if I try to do everything myself."

Iona took control.

"Then let's swap seats. I'll keep an eye out for Biro emerging and I'll awake you when he appears. You can assess how we deal with him and if it's a long journey, you can sleep until I nudge you."

It took only a moment for Morrison to agree.

"Okay. Let's do it."

* * *

As the clock showed eight-thirty, another taxi appeared and Rotermundt emerged. After being admitted to Biro's house, both men emerged and accessed Biro's car. Rotermundt took the passenger's seat. Iona nudged Morrison.

"Donald John! Wake up. They've both got into the car Biro was using last night. Rotermundt and Biro...they're getting ready to leave."

Morrison sat upright, rubbing his eyes. He took stock.

"Okay, we're heading in the same direction so just let them leave and watch which way they turn."

As they prepared themselves for pursuit, another car, a powerful BMW, slowly turned the corner and interposed itself between the two cars. As it passed, Iona observed the driver.

"That's the guy you know. The guy who passed the backpack on to Rotermundt. The MI5 guy."

Morrison's brow furrowed. *What's going on? Has Ashton put two of us on the case without telling me or is this guy Grantham mixed up in the dark money stuff?* He decided on caution.

"Follow on, Iona. There might be two cars involved in this or Grantham might be following Rotermundt just as we are. Just keep your distance."

Biro navigated his way through the streets of Parkhead and Shettleston before stopping at the lights at Carmyle Avenue, the last stop before the M74, the main arterial route south towards England. Grantham's BMW sat two cars behind; Morrison and Iona, a further two cars to the rear.

As the traffic lights gave permission to proceed, Morrison decided that Grantham was attempting to conceal his presence from Rotermundt.

"He's had plenty of opportunities to sit on his tail but he's always positioned his vehicle at least two cars back from him. Looks like he's following him just like us." Biro steered through the series of lights on to the motorway. "Well, the good news is that he's on the motorway. That'll make it easier to track...but now we follow Grantham. If he's following Biro as it appears, he'll have been trained in shadowing with vigilance and is unlikely to lose him but I'd be surprised if he's expecting surveillance himself. Keep back a good distance though, Iona."

* * *

In the car up ahead, Grantham was maintaining distance from Biro and following comfortably. On the seat beside him, the second IRA gun lay primed with no attempt to conceal it. The gun had come into his possession without a shoulder holster but as an officer of MI5, he'd decided he'd be able to explain its presence merely by showing his ID card in the unlikely event of police interest.

His mobile phone chirruped. Keeping his eyes on the road, he withdrew it from his inside jacket pocket and glanced at the screen which showed the identity of the caller; Sir Robert Cavendish. He returned it to his pocket unanswered, smiling as he anticipated accurately the apoplexy of the caller whom he presumed was now determined to call off the entire proceedings.

Too late now, me old chap!

* * *

Biro, who was behind the wheel, was in conversational mood.

"You're some man, Mr. Wise. All the money in the world and here's you, a committed Unionist givin' a whole lot of it to me, an unreconstructed Republican, to shoot another feckin' Unionist. No loyalty amongst friends in the Conservative Party, eh, Mr. Wise?" He turned his head to establish Rotermundt's reaction. "Now why on earth would you be wantin' to shoot another feckin' Tory? Not that I'd want to persuade you against it."

Rotermundt sighed deeply, disinclined to involve himself in discourse.

"The reason that I am *giving* you such a sum of money Mr. Biro, is precisely so I am not required to answer any of your questions. I merely wish you to carry out your task expeditiously. You shoot the Conservative Secretary of State in the leg, you wipe the gun of prints. As you disappear, I hand you an envelope containing the balance of your fee and we part as friends."

"Well now, I've decided on a wee change of plan there, Mr. Wise."

"Have you now?"

"Well in the aftermath of this shootin', I'm not happy about settlin' our account as the entire feckin' population of the south of Scotland is chasin' us. So here's the *new* deal. You hand over the cash now or I pull into the next lay-by and you can hitch a lift back to civilisation."

Rotermundt, never slow to anger, boiled inside.

"I am used to making agreements which are fulfilled by both parties."

"Aye, well you've never made a deal with Biro before. I make deals and renegotiate the ones that don't make sense." He attempted a more conciliatory tone. "Now look, Mr. Wise, it just doesn't make sense to stop and settle up in the heat of battle. Settle now and we can focus on the hit."

It took some thirty seconds as Rotermundt decided that Biro's argument had merit. Tightening his lips, he unzipped his attaché case and removed an envelope.

"Twenty-five thousand pounds. Full payment. As agreed!" he spluttered.

"And there was mention of a hundred thousand pounds worth of shares in Madden's Transportation?"

"That was dependent upon a completely successful outcome and will be dealt with electronically. You need to trust *me* on that one. I keep *my* word. Once you return to Belfast I'll phone you and make the documentation over to you or your nominated beneficiary."

Biro pursed his lips. "Okay." He slipped the bulky envelope inside his jerkin pocket. "Now, let's focus on this shootin'. You told me to head for Dumfries. I'll need more than that. I need a precise location, times, and how we identify the man you want shot."

Rotermundt had recovered some of his composure.

"We are shooting the Scottish Secretary of State when he prepares to open a university spin-out in Kelso at noon. My proposal is that we deal with him as he leaves his home in Eastriggs just south of Annan."

Biro spoke excitedly. "Eastriggs? I feckin' *know* Eastriggs. I was taken there on a school trip when I was young and returned on my own a couple of years back because I was so taken with the place." He shook his head. "I know you think I'm just a thick Mick with violent tendencies. Now, I'll *give* you the violent tendencies, but I've a double-first in chemistry and mathematics. I was involved in the struggle over-by from a young age and ended up as the main Armourer for the Republican movement. My job was to look after all our pistols and artillery. I had to know all the movement's weapons inside out and had to repair, maintain and adapt them. Every feckin' unit depended on me and a few others like me so don't worry about me being able to handle myself with a weapon. As a man interested in chemistry and explosives, I visited Eastriggs again a couple of years ago when I travelled from Cairnryan to Manchester for a bit of business that needn't concern you. During the First World War..." He hesitated. "D' you know about Eastriggs?"

Now more interested in his interlocutor, Rotermundt shook his head.

"No."

"Well..." Biro warmed to his story. "During World War One, the Brits began to run out of feckin' ammo. They had a chronic shortage of firepower on the Western Front. They needed cordite, the main propellant for ammo and they responded by the buildin' of a new munitions super-factory in Eastriggs. I visited the feckin' place because it was built in double-quick time on account of the fact that they used ten thousand Irish navigators...'navvies'. Ten *thousand* of our boys who refused to fight for the crown but who took the King's shillin' back to Ireland by buildin' the feckin' place in jig-time. It was the largest munitions factory in the world at the time. And then, when they built it, *another* contingent of Paddies, women this time, came over to mix the 'Devil's Porridge', a mixture of guncotton, nitro-glycerine, mineral jelly and acetone. It was *fantastically* unstable and would explode at the slightest feckin' provocation. Women couldn't wear anythin' with a button on it as if one of them, whether metal or bone, fell into the mixture, it was goodnight feckin' Vienna. Later on durin' the Troubles, our boys used Semtex. Much more stable and over the piece, we became quite good at usin' it, eh?"

"And all this helps us how?"

"Well I kinda know the place a bit. It's a huge parcel of land. And it's pretty quiet."

"He has a large house in its own grounds right on the Solway coast at Eastriggs."

"Well that sounds just like the thing." He increased his speed slightly. "Direct me to his house."

Rotermundt delved into his attaché case again and withdrew two Ordinance Survey maps; one of Kelso which he returned to the case, and one of the Solway Firth which after some gymnastics, he managed to fold in order to feature the area around Colquhoun's home on the River Esk.

Chapter Forty

"Tallman, it's the Assistant Chief Constable on the phone for you."

Baxter looked over his desk at his colleague Stuart Cruikshank.

"This is a first. Must be in line for a big promotion, eh?"

"More like I'll be asking my dad if he needs another mechanic..."

Baxter lifted the phone.

"Sir?"

"Sergeant Baxter. I've Special Branch all over me on this drowning. They're telling me you're withholding evidence on this Chadwick case. Tell me you're not."

"Well, I'm not sir. We managed to secure a signed statement from the drowned man while he was still in hospital. Special Branch appeared down here with no real notice and said they wanted the report I'd been preparing. They told us that they were now responsible for all matters to do with the case and left after a short conversation in what I'd describe as a rather peremptory manner. It was only later I realised the statement wasn't in the file. I contacted Inspector Alan Moore, apologised and faxed a copy over to him immediately. I'm sure Inspector Moore would confirm that I attempted to be helpful and was most polite during our exchange. Certainly, Detective Cruikshank who witnessed our exchange would confirm my attitude was one of overt cordiality."

"He thinks you were being disingenuous and sullenly disrespectful. Too clever for your own good."

"Not at all sir. Unless he can offer some examples."

"I asked him. He can't! He also reckons you were the person who leaked the story to STV."

"I can say hand on heart that I've never been in touch with STV and I explained to him that when Detective Cruikshank and I interviewed Mr. Chadwick in hospital he was a bit wandered, sir. He wasn't exactly delirious but he'd been through a lot and had been medicated. He could have said anything to nursing staff, to cleaners, to surgeons, anyone. The local newspaper down here also carried the story and they reported sources at the hospital as their informants."

"Quite. I've told them all that." His tone softened. "Look, Sergeant, I've a golf match in an hour, my back's killing me, my wife's just phoned to tell me how delighted she is to have purchased an expensive gold bracelet she doesn't need and I need inter-organisational disputes like I need a bad case of piles. The way this goes away is if you meet again with Moore and schmooze him. I've told him you'd be delighted to see him. He's on his way. Do what you can to ensure this doesn't cross my desk again, would you? There's a good chap."

The call ended. Baxter placed the phone on its receiver and addressed a curious Cruikshank.

"He didn't get round to mentioning the promotion but I'm sure he just overlooked it. He says that Special Branch think we...think *I* leaked the story."

"Fuck, Tallman, we *all* do!"

Baxter shook his head in mock disbelief.

"It's a cynical world we live in, eh? Anyway, Moore'll be back here shortly for another go at us. We've to be helpful."

"As ever," smiled Cruikshank.

* * *

Morrison's phone rang.

"Donald John. It's Joe Kingsley. I'm still on surveillance outside Carson's house."

"Hi, Joe. Did you get a warrant?"

"Yeah, we're all legal now and I've enough to hang him. I picked up a call last night from that Rotermundt fellah. The two of them discussed transporting two pistols across the Irish Sea to Scotland. So I've got them on handling weapons without a license. They discussed dark money that they hold which is being disbursed by Rotermundt's organisation to fund all sorts of mischief. Much of it was political and that's legal over here and some of it was being used to buy shares in a transportation company. Again, nothing that would get a man the jail unless the money has been stolen but your man Rotermundt is over in

Scotland just now and from what I could gather he's hired a Republican to carry out a shooting...he didn't mention a name but I'm assuming it's this guy Biro they discussed earlier when I didn't have a warrant. They discussed a target but the signal deteriorated just at the wrong moment and I didn't catch who they were talking about. Other than that, no dates, no locations. So depending on how this plays out I have the both of them as well as this fellah Biro for conspiracy to murder or something. They're also planning to fund a big contingent of Unionists to travel to Glasgow this weekend and provoke major disturbances when the Independence march takes place. I've already alerted the cops in Glasgow to that. They'll ask the Northern Ireland police to stop them even boarding the ferry."

"Joe, I'm following Rotermundt and the Irishman right now. All you've told me confirms what we already figured out. Keep your ear to the ground. We'll need these transcripts as evidence when we haul them into an interview room."

"Will do, Donald John. Keep between the hedges."

* * *

Alan Colquhoun's Private Secretary, Alison Lowrie stepped from a small room he'd had converted to an office in his large manor house.

"Lots of requests for a statement on the drowning, Minister. Seems even the Tory press are asking questions about whether it was a set up to accuse the Nationalists of targeting English second homes. One or two, the Express and Telegraph suggest that the English Defence League were at the back of it but are finding it difficult to explain why they'd attempt to burn down homes owned by English residents."

"Have the police been back on?"

"Their statement was as they advised you last night. Essentially no comment but they've not been back on to us."

"Have you drafted a statement?"

She handed a piece of paper to him which he took and read, summarising it to himself as he did so.

"So, we await police investigations to come to fruition, we regret the loss of life whatever the circumstances and we're encouraging the police to keep a closer eye on unoccupied second homes. They bring advantage to our economy and we support good neighbour schemes that monitor this kind of thing? Blah, blah, blah." He returned the press release. "Innocuous, I suppose but there's not much else we can say. I dare say there'll be a press presence at the twelve o'clock launch, perhaps at the rugby as well."

"There's no doubt, Minister. The local boys'll be there. I know that for sure and I'm advised that some Glasgow journalists will make their way south for a quote and a photograph. It's making headline news on the BBC in London so there's no escape I suspect, although it'll be Scottish parliamentarians who'll be in the firing line here."

"It may have escaped your notice, Alison, but *I'm* also a Scottish parliamentarian!"

"I refer, of course to MSPs, Minister."

"Quite," bristled Colquhoun.

Solway House had been in the Colquhoun's family for generations. A ten-bedroom manor house with mullioned windows, high ceilings and exposed beams, it sat in twenty-six acres of arable land immediately upon the River Esk where it emptied into the Solway Firth. A quarter of a mile-long tree-lined driveway connected the house, its annex and outhouses to the B721 and the nearby village of Eastriggs. At its rear, facing the firth, attractive landscaped gardens were surrounded by a walled, flagstoned sun-trap, a favourite place for Colquhoun to sit and think. Sitting and thinking was important to the Minister who often complained to his staff about their predilection for instant judgements on complex matters. In the lavender and lilac-scented garden at the rear of his house these pressures evaporated...but not entirely.

Colquhoun pulled his heavy Ministerial red box on to a sturdy wooden table and opened it. Top of the pile was a proposition put forward by his colleague Henry Goodwin, the Minister for Transport. *A high-speed rail connection between Glasgow Airport and its Edinburgh counterpart? This is brought to my attention via a Cabinet paper? No consultation with my department or indeed with the Scottish Government which will doubtless go ape-shit at a devolved matter being pursued by Westminster? No civil service input?* He turned the page. *This'll cost an arm and a leg. All very welcome but very strange.* A politician to his fingertips, he calculated the implications. *If this goes through I'm a hero although I'll have a devil of a time debating the point with the Scot Nats. If it dies a death, I'm a villain. It'll take a good while to percolate.* It may have short-term electoral benefits *while it's under consideration, maybe enough to improve our standing in the polls and our arguments for the Union. But if it's ditched after any referendum or election after short term gains, I could be hung out to dry.*

He set it aside and lifted a second paper; advance notification of a poll from Bell Polling, an organisation he knew to be well-disposed towards the Government. He raised his eyebrows at the loss of momentum shown by the SNP and the growth in popularity of the Conservative Party in Scotland. A smile creased his lips. *Bell Polling! Wonder what they charged for this nonsense?* he asked himself. A third and fourth paper was consigned to the pile he'd begun without reading them. He lifted the contents of his red box slightly allowing himself access to the bottom sheaf of stapled papers, a summarised account collated by officials of topical newspaper articles that affected his remit. Most articles were relatively innocuous although he spent some time reading the latest in the curious case of the Scottish Justice Minister facing a court appearance for sexual misconduct. *Met her a few times. She just doesn't seem the type.* He read another article on the same topic and thought philosophically, *Mind you, what type of person sexually assaults another?* Another page featured a slew of articles featuring condemnatory comments on proposals made by two retired SNP Ministers who argued for Scottish football clubs to lose points if the match commander reported that their fans had misbehaved and if the governing body agreed. *Crazy,* thought Colquhoun. *That's a big vote loser. What on earth would possess the SNP leadership, retired or not, to air these lunatic ideas in public? Suicidal!* He shook his head in disbelief. *They're way ahead in the polls and they shoot themselves in both feet?* Another couple of articles speculated on a leaked civil service report which would see the return of fox-hunting and another which quoted the Cabinet Secretary for Environment, Climate Change and Land Reform arguing for the nationalisation of grouse moors. *Well, there are two policies that'll both cheer and alienate the farming and business communities in one fell swoop. Internal divisions amongst the Nationalists are inevitable now...but why now?*

Wearily, he stood and closed his red box, heaving it from the table before walking back towards the house. As he entered, the eighteenth century, flame mahogany, long-case grandfather clock in the hallway struck ten times. *I'd better get a shift on. Kelso is an hour and a half from here. We'll need to be away in thirty minutes.* He turned the lock on the case ensuring its contents remained secure from prying eyes.

Chapter Forty-one

Biro had pulled into the car park of a hotel in Eastriggs and was inspecting the map provided by Rotermundt who was helpfully describing the lay-out.

"He'll have to drive along the single track driveway to the main road." His finger traced the route. "On the map you can see there are several wooded areas hugging the driveway. Some of them have farm tracks going through them which means there will be a widened part of the road to allow agricultural vehicles to turn in to them. If we pick one and position the car so it's facing away from the house, it should be a simple matter to step in front of the car as it leaves, shoot out the tyres and put a bullet in his leg."

Biro looked at Rotermundt with scorn.

"All of a sudden you're an expert assassin, eh?

The Irishman considered the map again before conceding the point.

"That said, it *is* the simplest way." He pointed to a part of the driveway where it formed an 'S' bend.

"There's a farm track right in the middle of those two bends. If we park there he won't see us until he's upon us but we'll hear his car from a distance." He looked at the contour lines on the map that indicated height and gradient. "The land around here's all pretty flat but those bends are a bit higher than the rest so we should be able to look down slightly on the house and see him leave. I'd say we'd have maybe thirty seconds or so to prepare ourselves before his car arrives."

"We have one problem, though."

"We have several Mr. Wise. What one would you be thinkin' of?"

"He can't be allowed to see me."

"Well I *know* that."

"But how will you recognise him?"

"That's easy. I *won't*. He won't have personal security. He's not important enough. If there is more than one male in the car I'll just shoot every one of the feckers in the feckin' leg. Problem solved."

"Violent tendencies, right enough!"

For the first time, both men laughed.

"Let's get on."

Biro took the wheel again and drove onwards towards the spot they'd selected.

* * *

Parked on the main street where they could see both Biro's car as well as Grantham's, Morrison was by now in a state of high alert.

"You've done brilliantly so far, Iona. I'm pretty certain that neither driver knows he's been followed. Let's concentrate. Perhaps we're approaching their destination."

Iona waited until both cars had travelled some distance down the road and a red post office van had interposed itself between her and Grantham before following. A short distance later Biro turned into a single track driveway whose signage informed observers that Solway House lay beyond. Grantham's car stopped at the turn-off and he emerged to peer over the rough hedge at the entrance to the estate. Iona had manoeuvred the car into a lay-by some two hundred yards behind and she and Morrison watched as Grantham opened the passenger's door, lifted a firearm and began to walk down the driveway.

"Looks like things might warm up a bit, Iona. Now look," he withdrew his Sauer P226 pistol and continued, "under no circumstances must you leave the safety of this vehicle. I couldn't have it on my conscience if you were hurt and I couldn't have it on my record that I put a civilian in harm's way. So please, stay put!"

So saying, he cocked his pistol, replaced it in his shoulder holster, left the car and walked briskly along the road towards the entrance to the estate.

* * *

Biro had undertaken a three point turn to manoeuvre the car into position so it would face directly towards the road-end, thereby facilitating an easy getaway.

Rotermundt spoke nervously. "So, I'll just take the wheel once you get out and prepare to drive away once you complete your task."

"Biro ignored his comment and looked at his watch.

"He'll have to leave any minute now."

He took the nine millimetre Glock handgun from his waistband and checked that the firing pin safety catch was on and that the drop safety catch on the gun housing was also engaged.

"Well you know Biro, Mr. Wise. He always has an alternative plan, eh?" he said, referring to himself in the third person. "I propose to make some changes to our arrangement, so...let's both get out."

"What?"

"Out, Mr. Wise. Get out!"

Both men emerged on to the driveway. Biro, still holding his pistol, looked over the hedge towards the manor house.

"Looks like he's leaving and we have to stop him. Now..." he continued manipulating the Glock. "Never let it be said that Cathal Durning here was not a polite man...a grateful man. You've very kindly given me forty thousand of your English pounds for two guns, one of which I hold in my hand right now. You've also paid me an additional fifty thousand pounds to shoot a Tory, something as I said at the time I'd willingly do for nothing. So the way I see it I'm ninety grand up and the only two problems I have is that you know who I am and that you're a very weak individual. So here's my solution...would you step out into the middle of the road, please?" Rotermundt appeared both confused and immobilised. "C'mon now, your man will be here in a moment. Stop acting the maggot. We need to stop his car." Uncertainly, Rotermundt took two steps to his left.

"I just want to thank you for the money and for the opportunity to shoot Tories. It's just like old times."

He lifted the Glock until his arm was level with his shoulder.

"Thanks again!"

He pulled the trigger and sent a nine millimetre bullet directly between Rotermundt's eyes, causing immediate, traumatic and fatal injury, buckling his legs and causing him to fall prone in the middle of the driveway. Hearing the approaching engine of Colquhoun's Jaguar, he stepped behind his car, stooped in part-concealment and lowered his arm.

Turning the corner, Colquhoun's driver slowed quickly and stopped when the way forward was blocked by the form of Rotermundt lying face downwards. His first reaction was to leave the vehicle and assist someone who had fallen or who may be ill until, emerging from the contour of the bend, he saw Grantham in a half-crouch holding a gun. Although not trained in security, he knew enough of self-preservation to slam the Jaguar into reverse and steer it heedlessly, wheels spinning, back towards whence it had come.

Surprised and confused at the abrupt retreat of the Jaguar, Biro stepped into the road as he watched it disappear from sight round another corner. A shouted command startled him.

"MI5 officer! Place the gun at your feet and raise your arms!"

Biro's thoughts raced. Hopelessly contumacious, it wasn't in his nature to surrender to instruction. Slowly he raised his arms while turning. He continued to hold his Glock tightly in his right hand.

Grantham repeated his instruction.

"MI5 officer. I *will* shoot. Place your gun at your feet."

Now facing Grantham, Biro took stock. A middle-aged man, somewhat out of shape, his gun held in the classic pose and pointed directly at him. He smiled.

"I'll do as you ask! Don't shoot! I'll do as you ask!"

"Lay your gun at your feet!"

The bonnet and front of his car somewhat protected his lower torso. Rapidly, Biro dropped and scuttled backwards, a shot from Grantham penetrating the windscreen and ricocheting harmlessly from the pillar of the driver's door. Still moving, he crouched and ran behind the vehicle before crashing wildly into the coniferous undergrowth. A second shot from Grantham took a deep wedge from a tree, again not troubling Biro who rolled and shot in the general direction of the MI5 officer more to remind him of his own armament rather than seeking a body shot. Keeping low, he scrambled from tree to tree. Hurriedly, he put distance between him and his pursuer. Now upright and less vulnerable, he held tight to a large Scots Pine and surveyed the wooded area behind him. Some fifty yards away, Grantham picked his way cautiously through the trees. Biro looked around. To his immediate right an indentation in the forest floor exposed some tree roots which offered both protection and concealment. He edged his head slightly to one side of the tree and observed Grantham walking slowly, carefully avoiding snapping a dry branch in order not to reveal his position, apparently unaware of the precise location of his quarry.

As silently as possible, Biro levered himself down into the depression and positioned himself so he had a worms' eye view of the woodland. Grantham continued to move carefully between the large pines as Biro raised his Glock. He waited until Grantham stepped forward from the cover of a Scots Pine and stood stationary in a clearing, listening for movement before attempting to reach the safety of a large Douglas Fir. As he moved forward, a single shot from Biro's pistol entered Grantham's skull at his left ear, instantly destroying brain tissue and vascular structures, passing upwards from the left frontal lobe tip toward the temporal lobe and brainstem. He died instantly. Maintaining his aim, Biro stood slowly, anxious to confirm the kill shot. As he reached his full height, he was propelled sideways as Morrison's full weight bundled him over. While lying on his back, a heavy blow from Morrison's fist snapped his head back. He recovered only to see Morrison stand above him, his Sauer pointed directly at his chest.

"MI5 officer. Your killing days are over."

Biro slumped back.

"Had to come one day, I suppose."

"It's come today."

"Is this where I'm meant to say, 'it's a fair cop, governor'?"

Morrison's hand remained steady on the grip of his Sauer. With the speed of a viper strike, Biro kicked his leg upwards, striking Morrison square on the groin. Yelping in pain, he dropped his gun involuntarily giving Biro the opportunity to repeat the blow, sending Morrison reeling. Furiously Biro groped for his Glock and having grasped it, fumbled wildly to position it within the palm of his hand so that it might be fired. Despite writhing in dull agony, Morrison used his fist to affect a glancing blow on the cheek of his adversary sending him backwards. Still, Biro fought. He brought his pistol round in front of him and found the trigger with his forefinger, managing to fire off a shot as Morrison clasped his wrist strongly, the bullet creasing his trousers at the rear and tearing a lump of flesh from him. A contest of strength ensued as both men struggled to gain advantage. Biro ended the competition by knocking Morrison to one side using his thigh to lever him from on top. As Morrison rolled, Biro lay back in the depression and levelled the gun at a now defenceless Morrison.

Breathing deeply, Biro yet managed a grin.

"Well Mr. MI5 officer. It looks like *your* killing days are over. But I'll give you this...you don't make it easy to shoot a Minister of the Crown! You pay well but you have to work hard to earn it"

A voice from over his shoulder saw his grin turn to a frown.

"Put your gun down, Cathal Durning. I've a gun pointed at your head and I do not miss."

Biro's frown deepened. He froze at hearing his name used and half turned to see Iona holding a black pistol, pointed as she had described, directly at his head. His own gun remained trained on Morrison whose own Sauer remained tantalisingly just out of his reach.

"Well, who'd have thought? It's Miss Beautiful from Kitty O'Shea's. There's me trying to persuade you back to my bedroom and you're a feckin' MI5 officer!"

He laughed loudly, still holding his gun at Morrison.

"Now, I know a fair amount about guns and the feckin' people who use them but I've never come across a trained arms officer who holds his weapon flat with the back of his hand facing skyward. That's how they do it in the feckin' movies. Well, unquestionably, you're beautiful enough to be a movie star. You're certainly too pretty to be an MI5 officer unlike this ugly bastard here and it'll be a shame to ruin your good looks but I'm going to take a punt and bet that you couldn't hit a barn door if you were standing on its handle."

As Iona was standing behind him and to his left, Biro had to bring his right arm across his body to fire at her. As he swung it across and took aim, a bullet smashed through his chest wall and buried itself in his left ventricle. He slumped as Morrison lowered his gun arm before falling back exhausted.

Iona ran to him.

"Donald John, are you all right?"

"I'm losing blood. He shot me and I can feel the blood running down the back of my leg."

"I'll look at it."

"Wait!" Morrison propped himself up on an elbow and pointed his pistol at a tree to one side of Biro. He fired a shot and lay back again.

"Wha...why did you do that?"

"Weapons training. Where there are no witnesses, a shot into the ground or a tree allows a defence of a warning shot being used to alert the deceased if it's necessary. There's no way anyone can tell which bullet was fired first, the one that ended his life or the one that warned him I was serious." He suddenly remembered the question he'd been wanting to ask for the past few minutes. "Where the hell did you get that gun?"

Iona smiled and caringly removed some dirt from Morrison's cheek .

"Remember the presents I bought in Glasgow for my wee cousins? Well, one of them was for young Angus who loves to play with his friends with toy guns. They all run around shooting each other. My sister doesn't approve but boys will be boys. When all his pals had guns, he just joined in with a wee stick. I decided that aunties were allowed to be indulgent so I bought him one and took it from my bag when I followed you down here."

Morrison groaned. "Jesus, you could have been killed!"

"Aye, but I wasn't. My knight in shining armour saved me. Now turn over 'till I see this wound."

Before he could twist his body, Iona reached for the buckle of his belt. "Here we go again. I need you to lower your trousers. Honestly, every time you're injured it involves me removing your breeks. It's almost as if you're doing it on purpose."

Too exhausted to argue, Morrison lay back and turned over to let Iona examine his wound.

She laughed. "Well, now you've a matching pair of lesions. One on each buttock. The bullet's caused a deep trench on your bum. It'll hurt, I'd dare say and you're losing some blood but again it'll just involve some antiseptic and some stitches. It hasn't gone anywhere near your femoral artery so you'll live."

"Patch me up, would you?" He reached for his phone and punched in nine, nine, nine. After a moment, "Police and ambulance please. There's been a shooting. Three men dead."

"And one wounded," volunteered Iona.

"...And one wounded. I'm an MI5 officer. Name, Donald John Morrison. Location, the wooded area on the right-hand side of the driveway of somewhere called Solway House, south of Eastriggs near Annan. Armed officers unnecessary."

He turned the phone off.

"Can you walk?"

His nod was imperceptible as he rose painfully to his feet.

"He kicked me in the balls as well," he said, explaining his grimace.

"Well, I'm not inspecting *them*. I mean we've hardly been introduced. You'll just have to suffer."

Chapter Forty-two

Special Branch's Inspector Moore strode into Baxter's office determined not to accept any nonsense from the police sergeant. He presented himself in front of the desk at which Baxter was writing. He looked up.

"Inspector Moore. Delighted to see you."

Moore started as he meant to continue.

"*Right*, Sergeant...!"

As Moore began the tirade he'd been rehearsing, Cruikshank opened the office door, ignoring the officer from Special Branch.

"Tallman, there's been a shooting in Eastriggs. Three dead. One wounded. Uniformed officers on the way. The nearest armed response unit is in Glasgow. Even with lights and sirens it'll be the best part of an hour before they get here. Ambulances in attendance."

Baxter stood.

"Inspector Moore. Duty calls."

He collected his jacket and left the room leaving his adversary open mouthed.

* * *

Alan Colquhoun had been loath to involve the police as his driver explained for the third time the reasons for reversing the car back to the manor house.

"Are you *very* sure, James? I'm going to look a proper plonker if it turns out to be nothing. I mean how can you be sure the chap was carrying a weapon? He must have been many yards away. Perhaps we should just walk up and check that the man who was on the driveway wasn't just taken ill?"

The sound of gunshots as Biro and Grantham shot at each other persuaded the Scottish Secretary that perhaps walking towards them wasn't his best idea.

"Alison, why don't you phone Chief Super Brodie and ask his advice. I'd rather avoid anything to do with nine, nine, nine. If the media get hold of it and it's something and nothing, I'd be made to look foolish. Then perhaps you'd phone Kelso and explain we might be half an hour late. I'm sure this is a storm in a teacup."

Because of Colquhoun's reluctance to act, Morrison's call to the emergency services was first taken. Until he heard the wailing of police sirens, Colquhoun continued in his belief that nothing particularly untoward was happening on his estate. His reticence was addressed by his private secretary.

"Minister, I think I should phone Kelso. I don't think you'll be opening anything today and the rugby match may have to take place in the absence of ministerial approbation." She awaited his agreement. "It'll also allow you to avoid the press boys and girls on that unfortunate drowning."

Colquhoun's agreement was then instant.

"Very well." His eyes fell on his drinks cabinet. "I think a small stiffener might be in order. Anyone care to join me?"

***

Cruikshank pulled tight on the steering wheel, sliding the car at speed into the driveway to Solway House.

"This is the fucking home of Alan Colquhoun, Tallman. If he's one of the deceased we've been told about we'll have the fucking SAS up our arse in no time!"

Two police vehicles blocked the road as did an ambulance. There appeared to be no obvious panic and an air of calm was evident if the demeanour of the two police officers standing before them while tying coloured tape across the road to seal the crime scene was anything to go by. Cruikshank pulled on the handbrake and both men exited.

"Hi Tallman. Hi Stuart." The elder of the two police officers greeted the detectives airily.

"Sandy! What's going on?"

"There's an MI5 spook down there in the ambulance. He's been shot but he's okay. Able to talk. He'll give you chapter and verse. He's armed, Tallman, but he emptied the clip so we didn't feel threatened."

The two detectives made their way to the ambulance. Inside, a paramedic was treating Morrison's backside as he lay on his front. She addressed Iona.

"Your quick thinking in stemming the blood flow using your brassiere was very effective."

Iona smiled. "Removing it without losing my decorum or removing my clothes was the most difficult part. It's an old party trick I used to employ at drunken parties when I was at university."

"Well, it was clean and staunched the blood flow."

"You MI5?" asked Baxter, directing his question to Morrison.

"Yeah. Donald John Morrison. My ID is in my wallet. Iona, would you pass it over to the officer."

Cruikshank interjected. "This man is a danger to society, Detective Sergeant Baxter. I'd be happier if we handcuffed the bastard and threw him in the nearest nick!"

Perplexed, Morrison half-turned and a slow smile spread across his face.

"Stuart, you old bugger. It never occurred to me that the next time I met you it'd be my arse you'd be looking at rather than my face."

Baxter's puzzled face invited an explanation from his fellow officer.

"This man here with the shot-up arse spent several days with me as part of a cohort learning how to shoot guns down in Merrie England. Most of the time we spent blethering in the bar. Him and me were the only Jocks."

The paramedic patted Morrison's right buttock.

"You're good to go. These stitches will see you okay. You've lost a bit of blood so just take it easy. Drink some tea and...here..." She offered the bloodied bra to Iona.

"Thanks."

Morrison stood uncertainly and awkwardly fastened his trousers.

Baxter helped steady him. "Can we speak outside?"

"I've learned when my backside gets shot up that it's better to stand than sit so outside would be preferable."

Iona offered to make herself scarce by suggesting she returned to the car to fetch one of the new bras she'd bought in Glasgow.

"Presently I feel a bit of a hippy, gentlemen." She waved the blood-stained garment. "I'll keep this one as a memento."

She walked on.

"Jesus, is every MI5 officer as good looking as her, Donald John?"
Tallman intervened and addressed Morrison.

"I keep having to explain to him that he's a married man."

"She's not MI5. She's...well, she's...a neighbour. A fellow islander." He watched her retreating figure and spoke as if to himself. "That said, she saved my life. She only saved my *life*!"

For the next ten minutes Morrison explained the events that had seen three men shot.

The relationship between Cruikshank and Morrison was evident, prompting the MI5 man to offer an investigative triumph to his friend.

"Listen, if you want to head up to Glasgow, to the Central Hotel and enter room three one one, you'll find a briefcase with hundreds of thousands of pounds in it. The room was booked in the name of our dead friend, the now deceased Emil Rotermundt and it will have this amount divided into various amounts and earmarked for a number of political recipients."

Baxter and Cruikshank exchanged glances.

"Who else knows about this?"

Morrison shook his head. "No one."

"Then we owe you."

Morrison was curious. "Listen, who lives in the big house at the bottom of the driveway?"

"Alan Colquhoun, the Secretary of State for Scotland. He's safe. Tell us again about the Irish boy."

"Well, the Irish guy, Cathal Durning, known as Biro, was in the process of trying to shoot this bloke Colquhoun. He was being assisted by the dead fellah in the road. That's Rotermundt. The other body's a guy called Giles Grantham. He's MI5. I'll put it all in a statement but this'll end up in some kind of enquiry. The IRA, MI5, a Conservative Minister being conspired against by another Conservative? It'll be twenty years before some judge decides to blame the Canadians or someone equally improbable."

As the debrief continued, Iona returned and insinuated herself into the conversation just as the armed response unit arrived screeching into the driveway. Carrying a new undergarment, she decided to visit the manor house to ask to make use of their facilities. Baxter excused himself.

"I'd better deal with these guys or they'll shoot the place up."

Cruikshank and Morrison fell into easy conversation sharing tales of past drunken nights until the chat turned to Cruikshank's work and his relationship with Baxter. Explaining his minor concern over the interest taken by Special Branch in the Chadwick case, Morrison found himself becoming more interested.

"So these two guys came up from England with the apparent objective of torching English second homes and blaming the *Independentistas*?"

"No 'apparent' about it. We've a written statement confirming it. We gave it to Special Branch but we kept a wee copy by accident."

"Wouldn't mind a wee look at it."

"No problem, Stuart." He continued. "These two were sent here by someone they thought was a senior figure in the English Defence League although that doesn't stack up. He said his name was Gold, Benjamin Gold. Anyway, one of them was killed in the explosion and the fella we interviewed lost an arm but before we could arraign him someone removed him from his hospital bed and he was found drowned in a car in Kirkcudbright Harbour. Now, it's beyond my pay grade, but a casual observer might conclude that there's dirty work at the crossroads and that the crossing patrol officers are senior politicians or their acolytes."

Morrison lapsed into silence until Cruikshank awoke him from his reverie.

"Donald John. This interests you?"

Morrison winced as his right buttock reminded him of his injury.

"Look, Stuart. I need a favour from you. I'll draft a statement for you while I'm in transit but I need your help."

"Sure!"

"Where's the nearest airport?"

"Depends. Where are you headed?"

"I need to get to London."

"Then Newcastle or Edinburgh. They're equidistant, pretty much, but there's more frequent flights from Newcastle."

"Can you give me a lift?"

"Certainly."

"And Iona..."

"Your neighbour?"

"Aye...well...She's also a friend. Look, you'll want a statement from her but once you have what you want, could you have someone take her to Glasgow Airport, she'll want to catch a plane either to Belfast or Benbecula. She'll be absolutely furious but I just need to...Eh, look, just tell her I'll phone her. Can you help?"

Cruikshank grinned. "Why can't Tallman take you to Newcastle and I'll take her to Glasgow?"

"Because she'd chew you up and spit you out in bubbles, Stuart. Now, how about you get your Sergeant to take her statement, make that call to fix her a lift and start driving me to Newcastle?"

Chapter Forty-three

Morrison's phone rang on four occasions; in each instance from a furious Iona just as he'd predicted. Each time he allowed it to ring out.

The plane he caught to London saw him arrive at Heathrow whereupon he caught the train to Paddington. A taxi took him home and the rest of the evening was spent with a notepad, writing down his thoughts. Arrows, circles and boxes gave heightened meaning to his scribbles. Twice his phone rang, this time from Sir Humphrey Ashton. This, too was allowed to ring out.

At midnight, having changed out of his bloodied trousers and dirtied suit jacket, Morrison stepped slowly downstairs and had to walk a few painful blocks before managing to hail a taxi to his office at Thames House. The streets were quiet as pensively, he neared his destination. Entering its portal, he greeted the security guard cheerily.

"Hi, Bert. I'm working late tonight."

He offered his ID card for visual verification before sliding it down an identity recognition slide which opened a barrier allowing him entry. Taking the lift to his floor, he approached a reception desk at which sat another security guard.

"Mr. Morrison, sir. Not like you to be in at this hour."

"Couldn't sleep, Simon. Going to pull a night shift."

He walked towards his desk.

"You're limping, sir. Blisters?"

"Aye, Simon. On my behind."

Both men laughed and Morrison walked on to his cubicle where he removed his jacket, gingerly sat down, edging his painful buttock off to one side of the seat and placing the notes he'd been making before him on the desk. After an hour, he returned to the reception area.

"Just putting this file on Sir Robert Cavendish's in-tray, Simon."

"Very good, sir."

Every so often a human presence was discernible as Morrison walked the relatively empty corridors of power and deceit. Lights had been dimmed to save energy, giving the place a look quite different from the usual hi-energy hubbub of activity. Occasionally a pencil-thin line of ochre light emerged from beneath a doorway suggesting another late night occupant. Stopping outside the outer office of Sir Robert, he checked to ensure he wasn't being observed and opened the door.

Inside, he moved quickly to Sir Robert's office. A desk lamp offered him sufficient illumination and he lifted and read the documents on his desk. Nothing untoward. He opened the desk drawers. Again nothing suspicious. He switched off the lamp, moved back out to the office of his executive assistant and checked his desk. A notebook aroused his interest; draft minutes of meetings, phone messages, 'to-do' lists. Some pages had been removed. Those he read were innocuous. On the back page, the numbers seven, two, eight, three, three, nine were written in faint pencil. He'd had to place it under the desk lamp to ensure that he was reading the numbers accurately so slight were the inscriptions. At a loss to understand their significance, he doused the second light and left, after returning the notebook to the desk drawer.

Two further floors up were situated the offices of Sir Humphrey Ashton. Again, Morrison checked the absence of any movements before trying the door handle of the Director General of MI5. The door opened and he entered the outer office occupied during office hours by Miss Elizabeth Leyton-Willis, his Secretary. Her desk was completely empty, the drawers of her desk all locked and Sir Humphrey's office locked tightly. Frustrated, he retreated to the corridor outside and returned to his own floor where the security guard, Simon stopped him.

"Mr. Morrison, sir?"

Morrison stopped, licking his lips to return some moisture to them. He manufactured a confidence he didn't feel and turned.

"Yes, Simon."

"These might help sir. The misses uses them for blisters." He smiled. "Though she's never had them on her behind. Least ways, she's never told me about *them* ones."

He handed Morrison a small plastic container of blister pads. Morrison thanked him.

"Simon. I'm exhausted. I'm seeing the boss in the morning and I'm knackered. I'm going to put my head down on my desk and I'm not going to move until tomorrow's cleaning staff prod me awake."

Simon took pity.

"Not that it's my place, sir. But sometimes in the wee small hours if there's nothing doing, some people...never me, you understand...just *some* people, well, they pop in to an empty cleaner's cupboard just behind my desk. There's nothing in it but a thick roll of carpet that's been there since the last refurbishment. There's even a cushion someone's brought in. You could have forty winks there no problem. It's very comfy."

Morrison was touched by the simple kindness of his colleague.

"Thanks, Simon. When do you go off home?"

"Finish my shift at eight, sir."

"Then would you be good enough to give me a nudge before you leave?"

"Be delighted, sir."

* * *

Groggy, Morrison awoke before being prompted by Simon, thanked him again as he passed, and headed to the men's room where he doused his face with cold water. Gingerly, he slipped his hand down the rear of his trousers and touched his wound, removing it to check for bleeding. There was a little which he ignored as it seemed unlikely to stain his dark trousers overmuch. Brushing his hair back and more convinced now of his plan of action, he caught the lift up to the offices of the Director General and sat outside awaiting the arrival, he presumed, first of Miss Elizabeth Leyton-Willis.

Promptly at nine o'clock Miss Leyton-Willis and Sir Humphrey Ashton arrived almost together. Stiffly, Morrison rose.

"Am I glad to see you! I've been briefed on the Solway House incident. We've lost a man and I was told you'd been shot."

"All accurate, Sir Humphrey."

As they entered his inner office, Ashton offered Morrison a seat.

"Rather not, sir. The bullet wound took a lump out of my backside."

"Have you had it seen to?"

"Paramedics fixed it."

"Then stand by all means." He pushed a button on his desk. "Elizabeth, two coffees please."

Spreading his hands flat on the desk before him, Ashton raised his eyebrows.

"Well? You'd better fill me in."

"I'm still working on it sir, but it seems clear to me that there exists some kind of organised plan to discredit the Scottish movement towards independence. Yesterday, I discovered the death of two English boys from the English Defence League who had been paid to burn down English second homes in Scotland and leave graffiti suggesting it was the independence movement that was responsible. One man was killed and another hospitalised. The survivor was then removed from hospital and drowned. Last night I was involved in the incident on which you've been briefed. On the face of it an IRA man attempted to shoot the Conservative Secretary of State for Scotland. However, the gun he used was brought over from Belfast. Why? Guns are in plentiful supply over here if you know the right people. He was being paid to carry out the task by a man called Rotermundt, again on the face of it a Conservative councillor but also the man who heads up a veiled organisation that disburses dark money to support the Unionist cause. So why would he attempt to finance an attempt on the life of another Unionist if not to involve the IRA on Scottish soil and allow commentators to suggest links between the independence movement and paramilitaries? Our colleague Giles Grantham was shot in action but he was in cahoots with Rotermundt. He helped bring the guns over from Ireland. So I ask myself, to what extent is our own organisation behind these actions?"

Ashton listened carefully.

"Believe me, Mr. Morrison, these questions have been plaguing me as well. I've never liked Grantham and believed him quite capable of this kind of adventurism. However, I need to know whether he was the main actor behind all of this or whether there are others involved." The coffees arrived. "Have you a plan to dig deeper."

"Starting this morning, Sir Humphrey."

"Then leave your coffee untouched. I need two this morning. Be on your way!"

Chapter Forty-four

Morrison walked back to his cubicle and sat again on the edge of his seat, protecting his wound.

Opening the top drawer of his desk, he reviewed the notes he'd made earlier before returning them and locking the drawer. He stood and limped towards the door and made his way to the office of Sir Robert Cavendish where he was faced by his Executive Assistant, Michael Kowalski who sat at his desk stirring a cup of coffee.

"Hi. Donald John Morrison from the third floor. I wonder if it would be possible to speak with Sir Robert. I'm here on the instructions of Sir Humphrey."

Kowalski picked up a mouse and opened his boss's diary.

"He's free just now but he's a meeting in one of the briefing rooms at ten and then he's lunching with the Shadow Home Secretary at noon."

Morrison stopped short as he listened to Kowalski.

"*De an t-ainm a tha' oirbh?* Kowalski? What's your name? Kowalski?"

Kowalski smiled. "I *wondered* about your accent. I thought I detected an island lilt."

Morrison returned the grin.

"I'm from Benbecula. Down here on missionary work."

"I'm from Barra. My father's sister is the postmistress in Balivanich on Benbecula."

"I know her *well. Beanie* Kowalski. So you're one of the famous Polish teuchters. You must be, what third, fourth generation now?"

"Aye. Beanie's talking about retiring now. She's getting on. We've been resident on the islands since after the Second World War. But I'm only down here for the work. I hate London and miss my family." He looked at Morrison conspiratorially. "Don't tell the boss."

The door of Cavendish's office opened.

"Michael, the file on the Birmingham mosque, please."

Kowalski was stirred.

"Sir Robert. This is Donald John Morrison from the third floor. He's asking for a few minutes of your time. I've explained you've a meeting at ten," he added helpfully.

Cavendish looked at Morrison with an expression bordering on extreme distaste. He turned on his heel.

"You'd better come in."

As Morrison accepted his invitation he turned to Kowalski.

"Coffee upstairs once he leaves for his meeting?"

Kowalski nodded enthusiastically.

Cavendish sat behind his desk. "I gather you were shot last night. You seem in rough good health, I must say."

"A flesh wound. I'll stand if that's all right. It's less painful." Morrison decided to move directly to business. "I understand that the Director General has explained my role."

"In so many words. Completely unnecessary, in my view. Smacks of mistrust. Everything that flows from this office meets the highest standards of probity. Always has!"

"Well, I'm sure that's the case but I'll want to look at the files you hold on all matters to do with Scottish independence. I'll need to requisition a desk in your outer office for the duration."

"Really! Is that completely necessary? I must have another word with Sir Humphrey. This materially affects my ability to get on with the job in hand."

"I've just left his office, Sir Robert. I know his mind. But you do as you please."

"I shall!" Cavendish's normal equilibrium deserted him.

"Now, last night one of your officers, Giles Grantham was shot and killed."

"A good man."

"I shot and killed the man who killed him."

"Just deserts! Well done."

"I have evidence that he was instrumental in bringing weapons across from Belfast that were used in the attempted murder of Alan Colquhoun, the Secretary of State for Scotland. Still think he was a good man?"

Cavendish's face reddened.

"I'd need to see your evidence."

"All in good time. But it's incontrovertible."

"Presently, my report to the boss will say you were running a rogue officer. I've yet to determine whether the adjective I'll use in respect of you is going to be 'incompetent' or 'criminal'."

Cavendish exploded. "Do you know to whom you're talking? I am one of the most senior and experienced officers in MI5. I will not be talked to as if I'm some corner boy."

"I have little regard for seniority. I have less regard for entitlement!"

As Cavendish sat with his mouth agape Morrison took his leave.

"I'll be outside. Mr. Kowalski will assist my administrative needs."

Morrison selected an apparently spare desk in a far corner of Cavendish's expansive outer office. Kowalski had brought him a sheaf of files to do with Scotland and Morrison had begun to read them when Cavendish's door opened and he left without any recognition of the two men sitting there. Both Morrison and Kowalski shared a laugh at his haughty demeanour.

"He normally closes the door of the front office a mite quieter than that, sir."

"It's Donald John." He closed the file he was reading. "Coffee?"

The two men walked to the lift discussing their shared experience of the Western Isles and took it to the nearest of several cafeterias strewn throughout the huge building. Morrison invited Kowalski to take a seat and brought two coffees and, in the absence of any breakfast, two fruit scones to the table.

"Think I upset your boss."

"It's not difficult. He always acts like he's Lord God Almighty. Doesn't like the Director General. Thinks it should be *him*."

"Thanks for helping me, Michael. It's appreciated."

"Happy to help, sir."

"Donald John, remember?"

"Okay. Donald John it is."

"Listen, the Director General has asked me to investigate the workings of your boss. I'd welcome any assistance you can offer."

Kowalski looked mildly distressed.

"Happy to help." Uncomfortable and ambivalent, his eyes remained focussed upon the table.

Morrison picked up his non-verbal communication but let it slide.

"Your man Giles Grantham seems to have been a bit of a rogue operator. Can you call Angela Marleigh in Human Resources...I'm told I can trust her...and ask for the file on Grantham?"

More comfortable territory for Kowalski, he agreed immediately and brought out a notebook, turned to a blank page and wrote an aide-memoir. Morrison recognised it as the book he'd interrogated the night before.

"Also perhaps you'd contact Intelligence and see if they have information on a man called Emil Rotermundt? He's a Conservative Councillor in Scotland and is involved in the transfer of dark money from Northern Ireland to Scotland."

"Sure."

"And also someone we think might have a background in the English Defence League. Guy called Benjamin Gold."

Kowalski stopped writing and held Morrison's gaze."

"Benjamin Gold? He's...well...there's one of Sir Robert's Intelligence Officers called that...called Benjamin Gold."

"Gold works for Cavendish?"

Kowalski nodded. He finished his coffee and picked at a remaining currant which had escaped from the scone.

"Donald John...I don't want to get into any trouble. I mean, I need this job here. My money goes home to support the croft and..."

"Look, Michael. You're in no danger. If we get to the bottom of this they'll raise a statue to you. I've been asked to find out what's going on here and Sir Robert looks to me as if he's been ploughing his own furrow."

Kowalski thought for a moment.

"These files I gave you?"

"Yes."

"They won't tell you anything."

He fingered his notebook uncertainly and opened it at the last page.

Morrison noticed he'd opened it at the series of numbers he couldn't decipher.

"Look, Michael. If it's any help, I was in your office last night and I had a look through your notebook. Some pages missing?"

Kowalski nodded. "Sir Robert has special meetings about Scotland. He doesn't want my notes to see the light of day so the pages are torn out and shredded after I type up a minute."

"A minute? You have minutes of these meetings?"

Kowalski bit his lower lip. "Donald John, you don't know how stupid I feel saying this but I was just following orders. I'm pretty new here…wet behind the ears and don't know what is usual and acceptable for MI5 to be doing and what is *illegal* for them to be doing. It's often so murky." He hesitated. "Perhaps…well, perhaps you could say you found my notebook last night and saw these numbers on the back page you…well you put two and two together and realised that this was this combination to the wall safe in the outer office. That way, I'm not really involved."

"There's a wall safe?"

"Aye. It contains the minutes of meetings and other items he has about Scottish Independence."

"Michael. Lead me to it. If it's as revealing as I anticipate, you're a hero."

Both men returned to the office and Kowalski read out the faint numbers as Morrison turned the dial. The safe opened with a click. After some minutes reading the contents of one file, Morrison reached in and lifted other loose documents which he skimmed. He turned to Kowalski.

"I'm taking these, Michael. Not a word to Cavendish. These documents finish him, but there are one or two matters I need to deal with before I confront him. Does Cavendish know the combination?"

"He depends on me for that."

"If for any reason he returns and asks you to open it, make sure there's something wrong with the mechanism and suggest someone from the company is called to open it. Don't let him near it, okay?"

"Sure thing."

Chapter Forty-five

Morrison left the building and caught a taxi to his local pub, the Royal Oak where his quiz team, the Brixton Brainiacs met most Thursdays.

He elbowed his way into the dark interior and approached the bar. The barman, Stevie was surprised to see him.

"Bit early, eh, Donald John?"

"Never too early, Stevie. Just need a wee snifter. Eh, a big Glenmorangie, please."

"A big malt before lunchtime? Everything alright?"

"Not really! Look I'm going to do a bit of work over there." He pointed at a table, while lifting the glass provided him and downed it in one visit. "Another big one. I've some thinking to do."

"I'll bring it across."

Morrison sat and opened the file once more.

"Jesus.H.Christ! This is dynamite." He read it a third time as Stevie brought him another large malt. "Stevie. You got a photocopier back there. Maybe a printer that copies?"

"Sure have. Help yourself. Back office."

Morrison copied the file and some supporting documents and folded them in half. He returned to his drink and phoned Maurice Malone his quiz team partner and local lawyer. After a few moments he was put through.

"Hi Maurice. You in the office?"

"Donald John. We've missed you recently. Haven't won since last you attended. Coming next week?"

"Dunno, Maurice. Look I need some help in your capacity as a lawyer."

"You in trouble, son? Remember I'm a conveyancing solicitor. I can't help you if you're up in court for some Agriculture and Fisheries offence."

"No. I need you to hold some documents in your safe for me."

"Easy peasy, Donald John. Can I read them?" He teased.

"Not if you value your life, Maurice. I'll be up in ten minutes."

He lifted a used envelope from a pile of discarded circulars and placed the copied papers inside along with his MI5 phone before fixing the seams with adhesive tape and returning to the bar area.

"Thanks, Stevie. I'm off. See you later."

After dropping off the envelope, Morrison caught another taxi and headed off towards Thames House. In the taxi, the phone given him by Iona rang. Again he disregarded the call. *Later*, he thought. As he returned it to his pocket, an idea occurred to him and he spent some moments looking at its few but various functions.

As he swiped his ID card and gained entry, it occurred to Morrison that depending on how he played his cards, this might be the last time he entered the hallowed portal of MI5 Headquarters. Still limping, he made his way to the office of the Deputy Director General of MI5, Jack Kemp where he introduced himself to his secretary and asked for an audience. Following a phone call, he was admitted to the inner sanctum. Kemp opened the door, hand outstretched, a wide smile on his face.

"Mr. Morrison! Our hero of the hour. How are you? I was told you'd been injured."

"Flesh wound. I'm fine."

"Come in, come in. Tea or coffee?"

"No thanks. I hope not to be long."

"You must tell me everything. You've become quite the celebrity here in Thames House. Shame about Grantham."

Morrison sat uncomfortably on one buttock.

"Well, as you know, Sir Humphrey has asked me to have a look at what's going on in respect of our approach to the independence debate north of the border."

Kemp's affability deserted him.

"And the agency's approach to this Scottish business is entirely appropriate, Mr. Morrison. As you know, under the Security Service Act 1989 we are required to be politically neutral and not act for the benefit of any political party. We only investigate matters that affect national security, within the remit set out in the Act. But anything, and I mean *anything* which threatens the safety or well-being of the state and which is intended to overthrow or undermine parliamentary democracy by political, industrial or violent means is fair game for MI5."

Morrison attempted unsuccessfully to interrupt as Kemp continued his diatribe.

"In the case of Scottish independence, that is a *direct* threat to the state. The state in question is the United Kingdom. I repeat, that anything that undermines parliamentary democracy, even by *political* means requires our intervention. We can't allow ourselves to be dictated to by the northern hordes! Now, I know you're a proud Scotsman but you've signed the Official Secrets Act and must act in the interests of the state...and *that* state is the *United* Kingdom."

Morrison maintained his self-possession and remained placid.

"I'm not a political person, Mr. Kemp. But what of democracy? What if the people of Scotland vote democratically to end the Union and regain their independence. Is *that* not entirely appropriate?"

"It's our job, Mr. Morrison to make sure that that eventuality does not come to fruition."

"You were responsible for supervising the work of Sir Robert Cavendish were you not? He in turn was responsible for Giles Grantham, now shown to have been involved in activities that go far beyond...*far* beyond the scope of anything that can be countenanced by MI5. He connived at the murder of a Secretary of State of this *United* Kingdom government. Now, I have proof that Sir Robert knew and indeed collaborated in this attempt at murder of a UK politician. That puts him on the same level as those extremists in *Al Qaeda, Hizbul Mujahideen* or *al-Shabaab* who would be thrown in jail were they caught in the act as he has." He cleared his throat, now slightly nervous at his intended comment. "In addition, Mr. Kemp, I now have proof that in addition to Sir Robert, you *too* have been instrumental in designing, approving and implementing acts which are clearly illegal and which also fall outside the scope of MI5. You've initialled actions, signed notes..."

Kemp flew into a spittle-flecked rage.

"So you have proof have you, you little pipsqueak? You haven't been in this organisation for half an hour and you're accusing two of the agency's finest and longest serving officers of illegality. Well, let me tell you, we will stop at nothing...*nothing* to protect the integrity of the United Kingdom. We once ruled the world...the *United* Kingdom. *United,* we once ruled the world. The greatest empire the world has ever seen. The sun never set on the empire precisely because we took no prisoners. We sacrificed everything, we endured any hardship and now, as our challenges derive more from internal pressures, we will continue our unremitting attack on *anything* that threatens the status quo and if that means we have to remove someone who stands in our way then so be it."

"And when you say, 'remove' Mr. Kemp, you allow that to mean 'murder'?"

"Of *course* it does. What does it matter if a junior Minister is shot; someone I wouldn't send for an errand, if it protects Parliament, the Queen and our armed services?"

"And you would blacken the name of another politician by inventing criminal allegations? You'd see an innocent person go to prison in the name of maintaining the United Kingdom?"

"I'd see a hundred innocent people go to the *gallows* were it necessary. You just don't appear to *get* it, Mr. Morrison. We don't organise cheese and wine parties here. We make tough decisions about delicate matters. Matters that our politicians pay us to deal with because they're too *awkward* for them. They'll turn a blind eye to our transgressions because they know that we do these things in *their* name, for *their* benefit and for *their* political agenda. Trust me! The worst-case scenario we face is a judge-led enquiry. That takes decades in most cases. Usually we investigate transgressions internally. You *are* aware that MI5 officers are permitted to commit criminal acts in pursuit of our objectives...and *we* decide if any transgression under the act merits action. *Not* you, *not* a judge, *not* the media...*us*! So you take Ashton's little investigation and shove it up your morally justified arse! He's a play-it-by-the-rules sweetie-wife who'd allow our country to be rent asunder without so much as a by-your-leave!"

Kemp's anger subsided and he slumped back in his chair, suddenly morose.

"I underestimated you, Morrison. To think I was foolish enough... *cocky* enough, to draw the dark money floating around here to the attention of our wimpish Director General. I couldn't take the chance of him finding out from another source and wondering why it had escaped my attention. And now this." He squeezed his reddened eyes, as tiredness overtook him. "I recommended your assignment to this case on the basis that without our usual supports, you'd flounder."

Morrison stood painfully, still feeling the effects of his wound. He removed his mobile phone from his shirt pocket.

"We'll have to see then, whether politicians, the media and judges take the view that Britain's security services are at liberty to end the life of an elected politician or deliberately imprison another elected politician on the basis of a tissue of lies manufactured in Thames House. They might *just* take the view that, well, 'there but for the grace of God, go I'."

He held his phone before him.

"Ah...stupidly I've accidentally left this phone on 'record'. Still, it probably didn't pick up anything important."

He limped towards the office door.

"I'll take my leave of you. There's a pain in the arse troubling me."

Morrison walked slowly to the lift and took it to the ground floor.

I need to think. Can't do it here. He spotted a taxi, hailed it and entered.

"Take me to a quiet pub, would you?"

Five minutes later he found himself ordering a large malt whisky in the Lamb and Flag in Covent Garden, one of London's oldest pubs.

"And a pint of Guinness as well."

"Expecting a friend, sir?"

"Just thirsty."

He made his way to a corner table in the darkened pub, brought out his notepad and added notes to his previous writings. His phone rang again and he almost answered it in order to confide in Iona but instead, allowed it to ring out.

Adding a small amount of water to his whisky, he decided to get drunk.

Chapter Forty-six

The following morning, with a sore head and a throbbing right buttock, Morrison wearily punched the button on the lift and set it to open at the floor occupied by the Director General. Levering himself off the wall of the elevator, he straightened his tie and knocked while simultaneously opening the door of Miss Leyton-Willis' office.

"Can I have a word with Sir Humphrey?"

"I'm afraid there's an emergency on. You'll have to speak with him later."

"Oh, perhaps..."

Ashton's door opened and his head appeared around the frame.

"Morrison! Come in. This concerns you, I fear."

Morrison closed the office door behind him and entered Ashton's room where the Director of Human Resources and a man he hadn't met sat in the informal conference area at the other end of Ashton's office from his desk. Ashton took the floor.

"You won't have heard yet. We've not broken the news, but Jack Kemp has committed suicide. He was found in his office this morning by cleaning staff. An empty bottle of whisky and equally empty bottles of paracetamol and dihydrocodein lay beside the body. Doctor Whelan here has inspected the body."

Dr. Whelan spoke up, repeating an earlier assessment given Ashton.

"Dihydrocodein is an opioid. It had been prescribed Mr. Kemp for a spinal injury from which he was recovering. Paracetamol was an over-the-counter medication. If we presume that all three bottles were full, his breathing would have become very shallow, he'd have become very sleepy, confused, his pulse would have slowed and he'd have drifted off. He's vomited but not sufficient to remove a substantial quantity of the toxins. I'd say he died about three or four in the morning."

Ashton took over.

"His secretary informs us that you were the last person to see him alive other than her. She says that after you'd left, he'd become very agitated and had told her to cancel all appointments; told her he needed time to think, closed the door and when she left, he was still in his office. She noticed through the opaque glass that he was still behind his desk and that is where we found him this morning. Phone records suggest he didn't make any calls during that period. So...might you enlighten us?"

Still standing, Morrison thought for a moment.

"I'll speak only with you, Sir Humphrey. I suspect I can explain his actions but in doing so I'll have to reveal information that's only for your ears."

Sighing, Ashton signalled agreement and ushered the twosome from his office.

"Very well, Morrison, explain yourself."

"Kemp was your dirty money man, Sir Humphrey. He was acting in collaboration with Sir Robert Russel, Giles Grantham, Benjamin Gold, and others of the officers in his team. I have all of their names."

"What! Jack Kemp was running a separate operation?"

"To protect the Union, as he saw it."

"But *I* wish to protect the Union."

"Not as fervently as Kemp, Sir Humphrey. He didn't have much regard for your initiatives. I now have proof that Kemp, Cavendish and Grantham set in motion a plan to shoot the Secretary of State for Scotland and blame it on paramilitaries with the intention of linking it to the Scottish Independence movement. They have conspired to blacken the name of the Scottish Minister of Justice who currently stands accused of sexual assault and is completely innocent. A senior civil servant has been paid to make these claims and her son has been interviewed for a place at Cambridge with his fees met using dark money. The proposal announced recently to improve transport links between Glasgow and Edinburgh is a sham which will be withdrawn as soon as electoral advantage has been secured."

"Dear God Almighty. And you have proof?"

"I have formal minutes, bank details from Coutts Private Banking showing the deposit of the sum of five million pounds sterling plus withdrawals, signed and initialled notes, photographs, police statements and recorded testimony that covers everything I've told you."

"Well, we truly find ourselves in the deeper waters of the River Cam without a punt pole, Mr Morrison."

"There's more, Sir Humphrey."

He groaned.

"Go on."

"Intelligence Officer Gold recruited two men to burn down second homes in Scotland belonging to English owners and spray graffiti suggesting it was people from the independence movement who had torched the buildings. They were operating from a list supplied by Gold; a list of targets which will be shown, I suspect, to have been written by him. A man was killed as they prepared the assaults and another lost an arm and was hospitalised. Fortunately, police officers managed to obtain a signed statement before the patient was abducted from hospital and drowned. We still have to check the results, Sir Humphrey, but the person left prints. We'll check them against Gold but his name was revealed by the now deceased man Chadwick prior to his death and I'm confident the prints and the handwritten note will be confirmed as Gold's. In essence, your officers stand accused of murder, conspiracy to murder; in Scotland, abduction and murder, handling weapons without a license, perverting the cause of justice in Scotland, making false allegations, conspiracy to commit fire-raising and malicious prosecution. In addition, the victims will have recourse to private prosecution. So, all in all, I suspect it's easy to see why Jack Kemp decided to end it all and not face the music. Beyond this illegality, he was also directly responsible for paying Unionist thugs to travel from Belfast to Glasgow to form a mob engaged in disorderly and criminal behaviour in order that the peaceful marches in the cause of Scottish independence be tarred with violence. I was myself shot in one of those riots."

Ashton was quiet. He rose from his armchair and moved to his desk where he sat. Morrison still stood.

"Well, I suppose the question is what do we do about all of this?" Ashton crossed his hands as he thought. After a moment, he made an offer.

"I can arrange for a good promotion for your excellent work here, Mr. Morrison. If you're so minded, I can arrange a transfer to MI6 and put you in charge of a station in say, Bermuda or Vietnam...somewhere exotic and warm. I'm sure we could also find a role there for the young lady you said you were sweet on. What d'you think?"

"I'm tendering my resignation, sir."

"You're *what?*"

"I'm westering home...going back to the islands, sir. Going home. But I have conditions. I've come to realise that while an organisation such as MI5 is a regrettable necessity in today's world, I'm not best suited to quite the levels of deception, violence and disruption to one's daily life that comes with the territory. On top of that, I've come to the view that London's a shit-hole," he said intemperately.

"I well understand the lure of the islands, Mr. Morrison but..."

"In addition, I'm aware that my departure might provide an opportunity for someone with fewer scruples than you, Sir Humphrey, to make allegations against me that I'd find hard to deal with given the expertise that abounds in here. In consequence, I've taken the trouble of making a copy of everything I'm about to leave on your desk. I'll also retain my MI5 phone which has photographs pertinent to my investigations. Finally, I'll make a transcript of the recorded conversation I had with Mr. Kemp yesterday and will also make a taped copy. These will all be made over to you as soon as practicable. In the meantime, my copies and devices will remain in a place unknown to you."

"I see. You have us somewhat over a barrel."

Morrison continued.

"My operational conditions are that immediate steps be taken to have the charges laid against Lorna Gillies MSP dropped along with an apology made by her accuser. Her son, who, as as far as I'm aware, has been an innocent in all of this, should be required to attend either Glasgow or Edinburgh University, and as higher education is free in Scotland, he won't need fees. I've come to understand that Cambridge may have the effect of turning a young man into something akin to many of the rogues I've met in here. A good Scottish education will do him the world of good."

"Mr. Morrison..."

"Scottish justice will follow Mr. Gold come what may and you will wish to handle that as you deem appropriate but the local police have his name, prints, motives, handwriting and description. They will also soon understand the connection between Grantham, Rotermundt and Cathal Durning's attempt on the life of Alan Colquhoun. I presently couldn't care less about that. However, the use of dark money concerns me so I expect you to establish rigorous investigations into the Unionist organisation that funnels money over here for Unionist causes. When money doesn't have to be accounted for, these are the kind of events that'll transpire. It manifestly encourages corruption. The police in Scotland will, by now, have secured the substantial sums that Rotermundt was intending to disburse in pursuit of the Unionist cause along with the names of the designated beneficiaries. There will be much more in other bank accounts in Northern Ireland I'd wager, and I'd expect you to clean up there. The use of this cash for murder and attempted murder surely gives you all the reason you need."

Ashton sat back in his seat as he gave consideration to Morrison's monologue. He paused before speaking.

"You appear to have covered all of the bases, Mr. Morrison." He lapsed into a silence. "Of course, all of this is predicated upon the truth of your assertions. Does this complete your conditions?"

"Not quite. I have need of the sum of seventy-eight thousand pounds. If I take gardening leave and you find it in your soul to award me a sum for injury, ongoing salary and maybe wee bonus for bringing this all to a conclusion, it'd help me resign without fuss."

"Blackmail?"

"Severance pay."

Ashton sat back in his chair. For some moments he held Morrison's gaze.

"Well, I suppose the organisation is five million pounds or so richer that it was ten minutes ago thanks to you."

Leaning forward, he pressed a button that connected him to Miss Leyton-Willis.

"Elizabeth, is Angela Marleigh still in the outer office?"

"Yes, sir."

"Have her join us please."

The Director of Human Resources joined the meeting.

"Angela, Mr. Morrison proposes to resign his commission. I am minded to make over the sum of one hundred thousand pounds in respect of severance incorporating a bonus as a consequence of his successful prosecution of a case in which he suffered wounding. Can you facilitate this please?"

"Certainly, Sir Humphrey. If you provide me with a request in writing, I shall make arrangements immediately."

Morrison interjected.

"I'll also need a 'To Whom It May Concern' reference that uses words like 'diligent, trustworthy, honest and hard-working.'"

"Goes without saying, Mr. Morrison. Angela?"

Morrison interrupted. "And within it, a wee commendation specifically referencing my work in bringing these matters to a conclusion would also be welcomed. I'd hate for my participation to be viewed in any other light later on in the proceedings. Mr. Kemp's assistant, Michael Kowalski was also most helpful in bringing these matters to a conclusion. I'll mention him in my report but perhaps Miss Marleigh would acknowledge his role and see him advanced within the organisation."

Angela Marleigh nodded. "I'll draft some words for you both to agree."

"One more thing in private, Sir Humphrey?"

He gestured at Marleigh who left the office.

"I intend returning to a simpler life. There will doubtless be a slew of enquiries, reviews and so on after this becomes public. In circumstances where it's within your gift, I'd expect to be interviewed in Benbecula not London."

Ashton smiled. "Good idea. It might educate others on the benefits of island life."

"Finally, I have all of these documents and recordings in a safe place. I do not hold them personally. If pressure is applied to me or if anything untoward happens, I have issued instructions that they be copied and forwarded to every broadsheet editor in Scotland, England, France and America with an explanation that I'll write over the next few days. Any attempt to deploy 'D' Notice 3 or 'D' Notice 5 will have no effect overseas. I'm sure these things will never come to pass but I'd be foolish not to imagine that lesser men in here might be tempted to act *ad hominem.*

"Very wise, if I may say so."

"Look, I'm going now. I'm very aware of the other methods being encouraged in here to manipulate polls, utilise social media, twist truth and generally corrupt honest political debate. It'll be for the people of Scotland to attempt to see through all of that."

Ashton rose from his seat. "I think it'd be good if tensions were lowered on both sides of the border, Mr. Morrison. These last few days will have far-reaching effects. We've been expecting '*Siol nan Gaidheal*' to block the twenty-five roads that cross the Anglo-Scottish Border. Nothing's happened. Quietly, we've had police on standby to ensure they stay open. Perhaps we'll have them stand down and work towards calming things a bit. I need to be open with you, I'm a huge supporter of the Union and intend to work towards its continued existence even while I'm planning a retirement with Doris up in Lewis. It's not without its faults. It's too incestuous, too many top people from the playing fields of Eton, too many Oxbridge types, too many minor Royals misbehaving, too many politicians on the make but it's the best system we've got. And I'm willing to bet now that rather than end up behind bars, Sir Robert Cavendish will be elevated to the House of Lords as his behaviour privately will be viewed by the Establishment as perhaps over-enthusiastic but he's one of them. Same clubs, same connections. He *should* be placed squarely in the latrine of infamy but they'll endorse his overall objectives and behaviour and will act quietly on his behalf."

"Which pretty much sums up why I want to get away from all this, Sir Humphrey. All of it...*all* of it, sticks in my throat."

Morrison offered his hand and Ashton shook it warmly.

"Perhaps despite all of this, when Doris and I move up to Lewis, perhaps I'll travel down to Benbecula and you can buy me a large *Lagavulin*?"

"I'd be delighted. And you'll remember my conditions?"

"Every one."

Chapter Forty-seven

Morrison knocked on the heavy door of the Clergy House at St. Malachy's Church in Belfast. The elderly lady who'd admitted him previously, opened the door and looked just as formidable as she had on his last visit.

"I was wondering if I might have a few words with Father Gerry. I wouldn't need more than five minutes."

"He's resting. He needs his rest, y'know. He's not a young man anymore."

"Five minutes?"

"Wait here, please."

She closed the door and left Morrison outside. After a minute, Father Gerry opened it. He peered at Morrison trying to identify him. Gradually he recognised his guest of some several days previously.

"Aren't you the young man from the newspapers? You were writing an article." He raised a shaky hand in a smiling apology. "I'm sorry, I don't think I've read it. I've been terribly busy when I've not been sleeping, slumbering, dosing or resting my eyes."

"Quite all right, Father Gerry. Have you a few moments?"

The priest looked skywards.

"It won't rain for at least ten minutes. Let's walk a little. I need a little exercise now and again or I'd fossilise."

They walked together slowly towards the chapel, the priest slowly, Morrison unevenly.

"You're limping. What did you do to yourself?"

"An old war wound," said Morrison evading the question before asking one of his own. "And how are *you* doing?"

"I'm still fighting the good fight. Praising the Lord and fighting the good fight."

Morrison cleared his throat.

"Your friend, Mr. Carson was arrested there, I see."

Father Gerry stopped, pursed his lips and spoke regretfully.

"Yeah, he's been charged and remanded. Some gun thing." He began walking again, still unsteadily.

"I was the man who brought him to justice, Father. I'm not a journalist."

The priest stopped again, having taken only a few steps.

"You're not a journalist? I seem to remember you giving me a card." He shook his head, a smile not far from his lips. "Can't trust anyone these days, eh?"

"I felt I had to return and let you know how much I appreciated your work."

"And what on earth did *I* do?"

"I've been looking into your life, Father. More than you might imagine. You've dedicated it to bringing peace to the warring communities over here. You're clearly a good man and you've spent your time working hard to help people see others' point of view. As I read more about you, I was ever more impressed and I didn't want to leave this short chapter of my life unfinished. I know you've had to sup using a long spoon with people who have hatred in their hearts; who would kill and maim without hesitation. Well, recently I've been dealing with those very kind of people and my esteem for you has risen with every day that has passed. You've been able to turn the other cheek, but your friend Mr. Carson was involved in an attempted murder of a senior politician. An innocent man was to die for Carson's beliefs."

Father Gerry rubbed his hand on his forehead.

"I was disappointed in Henry J. I knew of course that he still harboured views that I found abhorrent but always took the view that one more meeting, one more conversation might help him see the good in other people not of his religion or political persuasion. He could be helpful from time to time but it was usually minor stuff involving drug abuse amongst the young of the parish. He didn't like drugs, Henry J. Didn't like to see people enjoying themselves, in all honestly. Now, drugs are bad but young people need to be understood and helped, not beaten by self-appointed vigilantes."

He looked at Morrison again attempting a reappraisal.

"So, it wasn't me you were here to see, it was Henry J.?"

Morrison decided on some discretion.

"Something like that." They continued walking. "I just wanted you to know that me meeting you probably helped save a man from being murdered. Without you, Scotland could have become as troubled as Northern Ireland. I just thought you'd like to know."

Father Gerry stopped at the steps of the chapel and offered Morrison his hand.

"I'm going in to pray. You're welcome to join me. I'll pray for the soul of Henry. J. and for journalists who aren't journalists. They shook hands. "Now remember me to Father Scanlon next time you're in Lochboisdale. If I'm any judge, he'll be in St Michael the Archangel's Catholic Church praying for journalists who aren't journalists just as I am. There's good in everyone. God bless you my son."

Holding a brass handrail, he stepped up a few stairs and walked into the gloom of the church in an uneven shuffle before disappearing.

* * *

The Loganair Saab 340 plane banked to starboard as it positioned itself before landing at Benbecula Airport at Balivanich. Morrison placed a copy of the Scotsman he'd been reading on the seat next to him. The headline read, 'All charges dropped against Justice Minister Gillies'. A strapline announced, 'Civil Servant admits false claims'. He looked out of the window at his beloved island home. Mist obscured much of the view from aloft but ahead he could see the landing lights as the plane manoeuvred to line up with the runway.

Disembarking, he awaited the arrival in the terminal of two large suitcases which contained much of what he'd owned while in London. Heaving them from the small carousel, he placed them on a trolley and pushed it out the few steps on to the concourse where his friend Hamish awaited him.

"*Madainn mhath*, Mister Agriculture and Fisheries."

"And Food," reminded a smiling Donald John.

"It's great to see you back on the island, Donald John. I've the car outside and thought we could make a quick stop at the Dark Island bar before I dropped you off at your mum's."

"Aye, maybe later, Hamish. I could fair go a beer but my mother knows when the plane lands and she'll be up to high doh if I don't make my way there immediately upon landing."

"Och, one wee pint, eh?"

"Sorry. Up to mum's and then I'll have to face Iona."

"Oh, here! You're in the bad books, Donald John. I don't know what you two got up to when you were in Belfast. She's very tight-lipped but *boy*, are you in the bad books. I had a wee drink with her after she came off duty the other night and jeez, are you in the bad books! She was really upset, Donald John. In that mood, she'd frighten thon scrapyard Alsatian at the back of auld Pedro's garage down by in Creagorry."

Morrison eyed him.

"Sounds like I'm in the bad books then, eh?"

"Aye! And then some!"

Jessie Morrison greeted her son tearfully and hugged him tight for a long moment, rocking him when he stepped from Hamish's car. After he'd disengaged from her welcome, he shouted to Hamish that he'd call him and entered the small croft leaving his two suitcases outside.

"Oh it's great to have you home, son. And you weren't kidding about staying on the island? You're not going away again?"

"Home for good, mum. London's no place for an honest man."

"Oh, I'm so happy, Donald John. I've made your room up and just you bring those cases in and leave them. I'll empty them and do a big washing."

"Och, there's no need mum. I've actually become quite self-sufficient since I've been down south."

"I'll do them anyway. You'll be wanting to go down to the hospital to see Iona."

Morrison looked at her strangely.

"Whatever makes you think that, mother?"

"Well, I was talking to her in the post office the day before yesterday and well, not to put too fine a point on it, Donald John. I think you're in the bad books!"

"Aye, so I gather. There's not much happens in Benbecula that doesn't do the rounds."

Mother and son occupied the next half hour in small talk before Morrison decided he'd better face the music.

I'm going to phone Torquil the Taxi and get him to drop me off at the *Ospadal Uibhist agus Bharraigh,* mum. Hamish wants a beer later on and I don't know how long I'll be with Iona...probably two minutes by the sound of it. But don't wait up."

"Well, Iona's shift finishes in twenty minutes. She knows you're coming home and also when the plane was due to land. She told me that she was going straight to the Dark Island for a drink...she said, so she could forget all about you. She's got you in her bad books, Donald John. I don't know what you've said or done to that lassie but whatever it was, it's got you in her bad books!"

"It's just because I didn't phone her because I was busy getting out of London because I've not...because...I didn't..."

He lifted the phone and dialled the number for Torquil.

"Och, I'll explain it all later."

* * *

He stepped from the taxi and entered the bar of the Dark Island. It was quiet but one or two of the locals shouted their greetings as he limped towards the bar. Morrison acknowledged them and the barman.

"Hiya, Tam."

"*Madainn mhath*, Donald John. Good to see you back. I'm hearing you're home for good."

"Hope so, Tam. Em, I'll have a pint of Guinness..." He thought further. "Make that two pints, would you?"

An accomplished barman, Tam poured both pints according to the book and placed them before Morrison.

"These two are on the house, Donald John. A wee homecoming. I'm sure I'll make good profit from you in the years to come."

"Thanks, Tam."

Morrison took both pints over to a quiet table and sat them on beer mats before him. As he did, a voice from behind his shoulder had him sit upright.

"Is that Guinness for me or are you having two?"

Morrison smiled, grateful that Iona hadn't just stormed out as soon as she'd seen him.

He repeated his earlier banter from Kitty O'Shea's.

"I'm having two!"

"Maybe you'd share one?"

"Okay...but it's grudged."

They both laughed, but as Iona sat and lifted the glass in a light toast, silent tears glistened in her eyes.

Composing herself, she sipped at her Guinness. Morrison said nothing.

"I thought when I first saw you, I'd just slap your face and walk out."

"Well, I've been told I'm in your bad books so I suppose I was expecting that, but I'm glad you didn't. I owe you my life"

"And I owe you *mine*... but I phoned and phoned. With all the shooting that had gone on, I got more and more worried that you'd been injured or killed or something. Why didn't you answer? I was beside myself with worry. You could have texted."

"Well, some of the time I couldn't get a signal as I was on a plane..."

Iona raised her voice. "Some of the time...*some* of the time..."

"But I made a decision. I decided to pack it in and head home. To resign. But to do that I had to finish off the investigation into...well, I still can't say much. I'm still subject to the Official Secrets Act. But it involved taking out almost the entire higher echelon of MI5 that I was working for."

"On the Scottish Independence side?"

"Well, yeah, I suppose you already know that much already. They've been up to a lot of mischief directed against the good people of Scotland using dark money. I've been able to bring most of it to a halt. Some of it's just about the DNA of the British state. They pretty much think everything revolves around the London bubble, but I think I've managed to stop the most illegal efforts to subvert democracy in Scotland. To be fair to them, it seems that they're trying to lower tension levels. They're going to call off teams that were going to police the twenty-five Anglo-Scottish border crossings that they thought might be under threat from 'Seed of the Gael'."

"The dropped charges against Lorna Gillies...was that you?"

"I'm not allowed to comment." He smiled. "Let's just say I'm pleased at the outcome."

"Well, I'm still totally supportive of Scottish independence and hate the honours system but think you should get a knighthood for what you did."

"Wouldn't thank you for one, Iona. I've seen too many 'sir this' and 'sir thats' down there and I intend to cross the street next time I see another one."

"So you're finished with them?"

"I am." He lifted his Guinness but didn't put it to his lips. "Remember a few years ago I did the immortal memory at the island's Burns Supper?"

"I do. You were very funny...and informative. Who knew how popular he was in America?"

"Well, as you'd guess, I'm a devotee of Burns and one of his verses in 'Epistle to a young friend', states;

'Conceal yersel' as weel's ye can,
Frae critical dissection,
But keek through every other man,
Wi' sharpened sly inspection'.

Well, that might have been written for *me*. I've come to understand I don't like 'concealing myself', nor do I enjoy being in an environment where it's necessary to employ 'sharpened sly inspection'...so I'm out!

Iona smiled broadly. "Also with the Salvation Army and the Guardian?"

Morrison grinned. "Them too. No more secrets."

"Well, we all have secrets. As a medical professional I understand the need for confidentiality but, after tonight, no more secrets between us, eh?"

"Agreed."

"So what now?"

"Well, I've had a healthy financial settlement from my old job and while I was busy putting the world to rights, I discovered that old Beanie Kowalski is retiring as postmistress. I've been on the phone to her a few times..."

"Oh, so you can phone *Beanie*?"

"Aye, I phoned Beanie...and I'm in the process of buying her shop and the post office that goes with it. She's staying on for six months to show me the ropes and then I'll be Benbecula's new postmaster."

"Donald John, that's *great* news."

"I'm also going to fix up my dad's old boat. It's been upside down on the beach since he died three years ago but I want to see if I can recapture my legendary reputation as the best man on the island at catching lobster, langoustines and shrimps. That's either a dawn or dusk operation whenever I could be bothered, so I should be able to handle both that and the post office and I'd enjoy it."

"Fantastic!"

He averted her gaze as he contemplated the pint of dark liquid before him and spoke hesitantly.

"I've also decided that I need to settle down on the island and what with me as the new postmaster up here I think I'll be what the tabloids call a babe magnet. I shouldn't think I'll have a problem finding someone to share my life."

Iona met his gaze.

"Anyone in mind?"

"Well there's Morag down in Lochboisdale, she's pretty."

"She's an arse the size of Jupiter, Donald John."

"Well then, there's that new dentist. Helen, I think her name is."

"She only likes girls, I gather."

"Mhairi, the wee waitress through in the lounge?"

"Is she out of school yet?"

"Oh! Well, maybe Angela, the pharmacist in your hospital."

"Aye, she'd do. She's very nice." She took a long drink from her glass of stout. "Tell you what, you've still a lot to tell me about what went on. Suppose I head home, prepare a nice meal for both of us and we try to narrow down your choice of a partner here on the island? Seven-thirty?"

"Well, that would be lovely."

"I forgot to ask, how's your backside?"

"Still sore, still stitched. But my limp's improving."

"Well, I'll maybe need to have a look at it. I'm reminded every so often that old Mrs. McSween, the *seer*, told me that one day, I'd get together with one of my patients. If I'm to be in the running for the special person in the life of the new postmaster of Benbecula, I might need to care for the wounds inflicted on him in the line of duty once again."

"Well, that sounds fine to me. I'll bring a bottle."

Iona stood and grinned. She placed her hands on the table, leaned over and taking her time, kissed him full on the lips for the first time, the kiss lavish but tender. She stood back and lifted her handbag from the chair, her smile widening.

"Don't bother with a bottle...just bring a toothbrush!"

* * *

As Morrison sat back, happily contented, his Guinness hardly touched, he reflected on the events that had brought him home to Benbecula and considered his future. *Fridge magnets for the tourists, tins of beans for the locals, pensions for the elderly, fishing safely in shallow waters... and Iona...and Iona...*

Stepping outside the Dark Island, Iona decided to visit the local supermarket for some food and drink for her special guest. Before she opened the lock of her car, she fished her phone from her pocket, looked over her shoulder to confirm she wasn't being overheard, and dialled a number.

The phone rang for some seconds until answered.

"*Artair Muireachan* speaking. '*Siol nan Gaidheal*'."

"Arthur, it's Iona Forbes from Benbecula."

"*Iona!* Long time, no see."

"Yeah. Sorry 'bout that. Listen, I've only got a second. Two things. First I need to resign from '*Siol nan Gaidheal*. Personal reasons. Don't ask."

"But *Iona...*"

"Personal reasons," she repeated. "Not political. Second...and I have this from the *very* top but you didn't get this from me...The Anglo-Scottish border crossings are no longer going to be surveilled over the next wee while. You can seal the roads with impunity. Close the border! *Alba gu Bràth!*"

She put the phone back in her pocket. *No more secrets...after tonight!*